TRIBUTE

BOOKS IN THE PHOENIX FEATHER SERIES

Fledglings

Redbark

Firebolt

Dragon and Phoenix

TRIBUTE

SHERWOOD SMITH

BOOK VIEW CAFE

BOOK VIEW CAFE

Published by Book View Café
304 S. Jones Blvd., Suite 2906
Las Vegas, NV 89107
www.bookviewcafe.com

ISBN: 978-1-63632-213-1

Cover Design by Victoria Davies
Interior Design by Marissa Doyle

ONE

THE RAINS HAD COME at last, refreshing parched soil, plants, and animals. Even the demons who delight in the chaos of torrential downpours and rushing floods welcomed the season. Farmers, so close to earth, rejoiced as well, but the rest of humankind, with tangled affinities for air and fire and metal, might have hailed the first clouds with relief from the heat, but as the rain poured down, soon sighed and lamented.

It was certainly so with the people confined together at an inn as the deluge made mud-rivers of the road. At first the flock of scholars on their way to the spring examinations dominated the gathering in the main room. Eager to show off their studies of ancient wisdom, they began by daily debates, which by the third day had gradually become more acrimonious as the frequently repeated arguments signaled yet another round of the same time-worn sayings.

The rest of the company rejoiced in the appearance of a storyteller, even one rather unprepossessing in mud-splatter-ed, threadbare robes. Most listened eagerly to the latest pop-ular tales, but when those gave way to less popular tales as the rain poured without cease, the muttering began.

The storyteller bowed and smiled at ever more bold com-plaints. As the storytellers say among themselves, "If your teeth break, you must swallow them whole and smile." Or, put more bluntly, you must please your listeners if you expect to eat tomorrow.

"I have a new topic," cried a young scholar the following morning, as thunder rumbled and hail drummed on the roof tiles. "From the debate between the provincial governor and the monk in *The Five Elements and The Dialects of Enlightenment*: If great art becomes everyday to the perception of the enlightened, is it still great art?"

"Ay-yah, here we go again, jabber, jabber, jabber," muttered a carter—a big bruiser with a temper.

"I quite agree, friend," declared a young master, smiting his palm on the table hard enough to make the cups and plates rattle. "I don't want to hear debates about art. I get enough of that with my tutor." He swiveled around to glare at the storyteller. "I want to hear about great heroes, and if you have run out of hero tales, then great villains will do."

"He's right!" agreed the rich young master's sycophants.

"The hero has to be handsome," said the young master's languishing First Sister. "For preference, he must be a poet. None of your tree-necked military brutes whose only interest is in his sword and his horse."

"A calligrapher," put in Second Sister.

"No watering pot poets," muttered a servant, passing behind the storyteller with a tray of mugs, for the scholars began their drinking of beer earlier each day. "We've enough water leaking through the roof. At least we could have a laugh or two?"

"And perhaps a white head or two among them," sighed the elderly auntie accompanying the demure sisters.

The storyteller reflected that however much water fell outside, the throat of a storyteller remained lamentably dry when not as much as a copper tinket had dropped into the empty bowl after the first day, except from the kindly auntie accompanying the two sisters. And though those metaphorical teeth must be swallowed, even the most threadbare tale-teller has some pride. Here was this esteemed elder, no doubt of long and proud ancestry, whose forebears piled merit upon merit, judging by her generosity.

"I know an ancient tale with plenty of heroes," the storyteller began. "One so ancient you surely have not heard it." And when the room quieted a little, "It begins in one of the small islands far to the southeast, with the venerable Granny Zim."

"A granny?" the young master exclaimed with a roll of his

eyes.

"I've never heard of any grandmother being a hero," observed Second Sister.

"But so young and sheltered a personage has not lived long enough to hear a fragment of the world's heroic tales," the storyteller said with a low bow in Second Sister's direction.

We begin (said the storyteller) with white-haired Granny Zim, who often sat high on the wicker bridge over the waterfall tumbling through the midst of the island's single village, to play her qin as her mind ranged from past to present, and far through the world.

Now, you must understand that this Granny Zim was not merely an expert with the guqin, which at this time was considered a noble instrument in the imperial court. She had mastered the lute, that instrument of four strings of twisted silk, whose origins, it is said, go back to when gods often led martial forces. At night around the campfire, they plucked their arrow strings to make melodies to stir the heart and put courage in the warriors.

She had early mastered the bamboo flute, and the fishermen from her island when they were full of white wine claimed her festival songs were great enough to call a phoenix down from the heavens. She played the two-stringed fiddle, or uruh as it's called in the empire, bringing forth mourning wails heart-rending enough to draw the goddess whose tears filled the oceans. She played the gongs—oh, you get the general idea, and you are asking yourself, no doubt, (said the storyteller) how could simple islanders, even born with the most auspicious signifiers of talent in their Eight Pillars, have the time to achieve such mastery? What about the long hours of daily toil?

Here the servants moving about in the background exchanged looks and nods, noticed by the storyteller—who had learned that including the working folk in tales often translated out to an extra dumpling or two, warm rice, and maybe fresh straw in the byre that was inevitably the impecunious storyteller's resting place.

The storyteller assumed an air of confiding a secret.

The reason (so the story went) was because this particular cluster of islands had a tradition of music that pulled prospective candidates every ten years, when the chief musician commenced training a new crop of novices. Yes, novices they were, for those chosen no longer toiled in the fishing boats if they were boys, or at planting and weaving if they were girls. They studied music from morning until night. They had to learn all the musical forms, though they might choose one for their mastery examination, which began with the construction of their instrument. After ten years, some went away to various island villages, where they were greatly respected. Sometimes one or two remained to train longer, and these often were hired away to provincial capitals or even, it was said, by imperial relations—if they weren't poached by the empire's tribute ships.

Granny Zim had been quite popular in her younger days, but she was getting old and her tongue more tart with each passing year.

She had taken to retreating to Suanek's Way, the narrow wicker bridge leading to the ancestral temple, when she wished to be alone. There she often sat, where no islander dared disturb her, and this particular day she reflected on age. There were times, especially during the cold months, when she had to soak her hands in hot water before she could play. And there were days when her scrawny butt hurt if she sat too long.

The time had come, she decided, to teach her last cohort of novices, choose her successor and retire while she was at the height of her powers. Another ten years might see time, that great enemy that no human defeated, retire her by force.

There was not a lot of pride left. Her looks had faded long ago, and her walk was beginning to resemble the crab that the dockside youths sometimes called her when they thought she couldn't hear. By now most of the villagers had grown from birth to vigorous adulthood with her music, and all the remaining musicians called out for festivals, weddings, and the like, had been trained by her; it is sometimes said that even the most splendid art can become commonplace if experienced every day.

She summoned her daughter Linon, who was the village headwoman, and bade her put the word out before she could weaken and rescind it.

Having done so, she discovered that the sense of virtue lasted about two breaths before melancholy set in. She withdrew to the bridge again with her favorite seven-stringed guqin, and poured out a cascade of sound that rose above the rushing cataract from higher up the mountain as she let her mind wander to the past.

She had nothing to complain about, she told herself. It had

been a good life. Longer than many had. She still had most of her teeth. Her memory was as strong as those teeth. So many fond memories, outweighing the inevitable griefs. The sharpest of those was still for her husband Lu Teg, lost at sea some twenty years now, in one of the great storms that swept over the ocean. He had always been a little absent, apt to become entranced by the flicker of a butterfly, or by a pod of dolphins dancing in the sea; he probably ought to have been a scholar or a painter, but he had inherited a fishing junk, and that was that.

He had loved her playing. As her fingers evoked his favorite melodies, she remembered him muttering vaguely once that where chaos and order meet, music is made. He was very drunk that day. And he actually said art, not music, but Granny Zim, who could not draw a stick figure and who could barely read, shrugged off art as something for scholars and nobles over in the western islands, where grabby kings and emperors lived—and, she added with a pious bow toward the kitchen god, may they stay there.

The sun had begun to top Kanda's Peak when she became aware of an urgent need. She had to rock back and forth more than twice to haul her withered hindquarters up so she could visit the privy. But she had barely begun to get the rhythm going when she became aware that she had an audience.

"Who's there?" she asked sharply.

The shadow at the edge of her vision vanished. Immediately she doubted her own eyesight, for truth was, it had begun getting more difficult to see in the dark. She waited a moment or two, then recommenced the process of rising, and retired for the night.

She could not sleep. Perhaps it was the decision she had made. Maybe it was that shadow, which she had been very certain had moved. Only without a form to move it.

She tossed restlessly on the bed platform until First Daughter-in-law heaved a sigh, and muttered, "Are you unwell, Mother Zim?"

First Daughter-in-law worked hard, and managed well, but she did have a temper like a bite of fresh chili, especially if her sleep was interrupted. Granny Zim returned a negative and forced herself to lie still, staring up at the beams holding up the ceiling, carved with auspicious signs barely discernable in the weak light of one moon rising and the other sinking.

Eventually she slept, and the next day early she withdrew

once again to the bridge with her qin, though today was her usual day to practice the two-stringed uruh. She loved them all for their different qualities, but it was the qin that provided a conduit for the rapid waters of her emotions.

She settled down, removed the hand-warmer she had carried up to the bridge, then warmed her fingers from within as she tuned the strings. She closed her eyes, letting her fingers choose the melody they wished to play. She knew that instrument so well, made by her young hands so long ago, that she never had to look at the strings.

To all appearances she was lost in the entrancing melodia, but she was actually listening to the sounds around her: the rush of the cataract below, the buzzing of small insects, the rustle of wind in the trees that clung to the rocky bank.

Patience at last rewarded her when she heard a sound that she could not quite describe, except that it was not the wind or the water, the trees or the insects. She opened her eyes in its direction, and caught a shadow dissipating like vapor.

"I saw you," she said, and kept playing.

There was no recurrence. She was alone, then and for the following days as the news of Granny Zim's last audition flew from village to village, and over the water to the three tiny islands with whom there was much trade and intermarriage.

A few days before the gathering up at the temple, where the auditions were always held, she sensed that almost-sound again. No one on the entire island had dared to disturb her at the bridge for many years. But here was a small figure, round of face, black pits for eyes. Everything else looked like a child from poor folk, except for the hair that wisped to smoke at the ends.

This was a demon.

The island had charms against demon swarms and infestations, and there were ways to smite demons back to their realm. Most people hated and feared them. Granny Zim had, too. The fire demon that had manifested to her great-grandmother had been terrifying, an early memory that Granny Zim had never forgotten.

She did not know much about demons, though over the years she had heard a lot. She and her husband had talked about these things, when they were alone on the water, fishing for the family, or sitting up on the bridge while she practiced, during the months when the men were not at sea. She had come to the conclusion that talk about demons was similar to geomancy and augury, in that there was a lot of rumor taken as truth, but there was also some truth to be found, if more difficult to discern.

One truth she had accepted was that demons were not human. To her, that meant assuming they had human desires could be a dangerous thing.

Another truth? There were many kinds, drawn to this world to gain Essence, which to demons was life and blood and sustenance. Some—the most terrible—were drawn to the Essence spent in battles and war and fresh blood. Some, to fire Essence. Others, to the slow Essence breathed out through certain trees. There was even Essence available in foods, which everyone knew because of the offerings put out at funerals, and anniversaries of death days. *Someone* took the Essence of these offerings—one always hoped it was the departed relative, lingering until the new year, whence they would cross the bridge of two moons to be judged by the King of the Underworld, and reincarnated.

There was even a little Essence in simple ingredients that made up foods, though the demons drawn to kitchens most often were merely imps, easy to dispel with kitchen charms before they could spoil the produce.

Perhaps this demon was drawn to the Essence of music.

Did demons understand spoken language? "What do you want?" she asked.

The demon dissolved.

Granny Zim recommenced playing, alone for the remainder of the day.

Each day thereafter, she worked with a different instrument; when the demon returned, its form was more solid. It almost looked human.

Granny Zim looked at the expressionless round face, and it looked back. This time, deep in the black pits of those eyes, she discerned a red glow, like a smoldering cinder.

"You're a child, I see. Or, you've taken the form of a child? Girl or boy?"

A gruff, smoky little voice asked, "Which one are you?"

"I was a girl, long ago. Now…eh, hard to say." Granny Zim laughed.

"What's the difference?"

"Ayah, that is not always so easy to define. Let's start simple. Do you put out a fire or make a river when you pee?"

"Eh?"

Granny Zim accepted that, played a chord, and thought. Presently, the gruff little voice said, "I'll be one too."

"That does make things simpler. Next, do you have a name?" And, when there was no answer, Granny Zim said, clearly, "If you want music, you will have to have a name, and learn how to keep your hair from turning to smoke. Also?" She tapped her eyelids. "These give you away."

The demon dissolved into smoke and vanished.

TWO

THE STORYTELLER PAUSED, STILL holding people's attention, but barely. The young seldom want to hear about the old.

As for heroes (so said the storyteller, noting little signs of anticipation), they are coming. So are villains great and petty. But before we meet great villains or heroes, it's better to meet those of humble origin; between the worm in the soil and the dragon flying high above the thunder, we all know where the eye will go first, and stay. But without the worm in its soil, can there be a world over which the dragon flies?

This history's worm in the soil was called Bu, which — the clever scholar certainly knows — is old east-island dialect for "six" as well as a disparaging term for things too insignificant to count. "We have three golden tales, two silvers, and bu copper tinkets."

Thus Bu was not even a name but a designation, very common in those days among poor families, especially for girls. Bu's family was poor, and everyone deemed them luckless, themselves most of all. Her father — a distant figure to her, scarcely glimpsed before he died — had no sons, though he had two wives. Madam Lum the first wife had found the second one for him when she gave up trying for that longed-for son. Her four daughters were soon joined by a fifth girl from Second Mother — and then Bu, after which the father died (some said of a broken heart, though quantities of indifferent rice wine certainly helped him along). Madam Lum and Second Mother each had to turn to her relatives for succor. That put them at a great disadvantage, for their families were not much better off.

They dwelt on one of the tiny islands that survived by trading with the larger one, whose temple atop the mountain shone golden in the westering sunlight bright enough for even Bu to make out that gleam. Everyone was fond of calling Bu the most luckless of them all—and from there it was a few easy, heated words from Bu being the cause of all that bad luck. Father had certainly died after she was born. And, Bu was exceedingly short-sighted. Trees were blurs of green and brown to Bu. Dust in corners was invisible.

Bu was often scolded by her elder sisters for laziness, but Madam Lum and her Second Mother both saw her working slowly, always squinting. The neighbor children, whose chief entertainment was inventing ways to trip Bu into the mud and the midden, began calling her Squint except when Second Mother took a broom to them. She could not answer back to those superior uncles and aunties whose charity kept the family eternally grateful, but she could, and did, take out her frustrations on those brats.

Life was hard but predictable until Bu was nearly twelve, and word passed "down from the mountain," as the locals said, that there would be an audition for musicians—the last for Chief Musician Zim. The next audition period would come when Bu would be nearly twenty-two, and Madam Lum had no intention of letting that useless girl eat precious food that long before marrying her off. "Let us send Bu," declared Madam Lum.

Second Mother had long ago decided that life would be much easier if she agreed with everything Madam Lum said. However, at these words, a thorn pricked her heart. She had to shut her lips against crying out that Madam Lum had four daughters, but she had only the two. While she had long regretted the fact that Madam Lum was likely to marry Bu off as early as possible to the first man who would take her, at least that would have kept her daughter close by. But sending her to the great island was sending her away forever. If she lost quiet, uncomplaining Bu, that left her with Fifth Sister, who was the lazy one, though clever enough to get her younger sister to do most of her work.

But Madam Lum insisted. "The musicians take anyone,

man or woman, low birth to high. We must be practical. Too many mouths, and not enough to put in them. Bu!"

Here Bu was pushed forward by her sisters.

"Bu. Your eyes are so terrible that you're useless in the kitchen and at the loom or at stitchery. Your ears are good, at least. Maybe your luck went to them after skipping your eyes, so there is a chance they might earn you a new skill that would never occur here. And with a skill, even though you'll never have looks, with that squint, and those twig arms and legs, you'll have a better chance of securing your daily rice, and a mat to sleep on under a roof."

Second Mother could argue with none of that. She remained silent, and Bu saw her mother remain silent; she could not see the tears tracking her cheeks, but she could hear her mother's harsh breathing.

Having grown up being ordered about by five older sisters, Bu had learned that complaint was useless. Her only skill so far was silent endurance. She put her hands together and bowed her head in acceptance.

Madam Lum acted quickly. She arranged for Bu to sit in a trade boat, pressed two tinkets into her palm—one to be tendered to the trader, and one to get a yam when she reached the big island. Bu understood then that this sudden generosity was also a farewell. If she did not succeed at the audition, she was to make her way in the world somehow, for there was no tinket for returning.

"There's always the nuns," Second Mother whispered, giving Bu a last, trembling hug. It was then that Bu felt her mother's tears, and though the knowledge did not make the farewell any easier, Bu became aware of a certain comfort once the boat pushed off from the bamboo pier. It is not much to be missed, but that was all she had.

Bu sat squeezed between two laden baskets, her meager bundle of belongings on her lap. The shoreline was very soon a blur of brown, the stalk-shaped people already moving up toward the village to begin their day; she could not see if her mother looked back.

The heart of a girl nearly twelve, leaving her home forever, rends terribly, but it is also quick to mend. As Bu peered at the great mountain drawing closer, she began to wonder what life might bring. Until now, she'd known—for her sisters made it quite plain—that the best she could expect would be marriage as soon as she was of age to one of the laborers in the village's rice paddies. She knew most of the local boys by voice, if not by sight, and she'd heard their laughter after she flopped into noisome mud after stepping in a hole that she had not been able to see. Whatever life she might find on the big island would be preferable to that. And there were always the nuns.

As Bu's boat approached the busy inlet—which seemed enormous to Bu, who had rarely seen two boats off the village pier at the same time—excitement as well as apprehension grew in her. In so busy a world, anything might be possible!

The boat rocked horribly when it bumped up against a loading dock. The trader said, "Out you go."

Bu remembered to offer the tinket, for which she got a barely a grunt of thanks. As yet, she had no concept of value. A whole tinket seemed a great amount to a girl who had never possessed one, and she had no idea the trader despised her for so poor a gratuity. He was already busy with his baskets as she groped her way unsteadily in the direction she had been pointed. There was a ladder, slimy and crusted, which meant it was frequently under water. Bu slung her carryall—which was her threadbare winter cape, tied at the corners—over her shoulder and clambered from the boat to the dock, aware from experience that if she fell into the water, no one would give her so much as a second glance.

Once safely on the dock, she slowly dodged around the laborers, following the press of people into an ever louder hubbub of voices.

What to do now? Ask someone, of course.

Bu followed a cluster of young people talking and laughing, using them as a shield as she scanned as best she could to either side. Shop after shop with huge windows and beautiful upward curving rooflines, which meant tiles instead of fig-frond thatch, intimidated her. But in time, after she had stopped twice at fountains to drink away the dust from the street, she encountered booths of more humble vendors, including those whose goods were spread on blankets.

Bu walked slowly among these as the vendors expertly assessed her worn, faded garments and dismissed her from their notice. When Bu encountered one whose contours were female, she bowed and said politely, "I wish you luck in all things. Could the esteemed boss point the way to the music auditions?"

"Boss!" the vendor cackled derisively. "Do you see workers here? I only wish! But the way you squint, I imagine you don't see much beyond that mushroom nose of yours. Eh! Where else would it be, but up at the temple?" An arm waved toward the towering mountain.

Bu bowed, and began to seek pathways leading upward. Here and there were signs, but those were useless: when her eldest sister, tasked with teaching her to read and write, had noted how close to the page Bu had bent her head when she traced her finger over characters, she'd given up, claiming that Bu was too stupid and too short-sighted to learn to read. But anyone could learn to sweep. Madam Lum had agreed, deciding that First Sister had better uses for her time.

Bu ignored the signs with their blurred writings. She saw the complexity of wicker bridges over cascades and waterfalls as blurs against stone, many hidden by trees. As long as a path led upward, she would eventually find the temple.

In this, she was correct, though it took her a very long time to make the climb. Since this was the only "mountain" she had ever seen, bulking to the west of her island, she had no idea that what she'd climbed was a mere rocky hill to most of the rest of the world.

When she attained the top at last, a strong breeze off the glinting sea bathed her sweaty face. She found others more or less her size, and followed them toward the temple, which appeared to be made of a shiny light-colored stone, and not actual gold at all.

The crowd shuffled together into a line. It seemed one had to pass by someone ahead, seated at a little table. As Madam Lum had acknowledged, Bu's ears were quite sharp, having had to assume many of the tasks usually performed by eyes.

At length, as the sun began dropping toward the distant horizon, Bu neared the table. And when there was only one person ahead of her, someone quite short, the top of whose night-black head barely reached Bu's chin, she heard the nun say in a tired voice that betrayed the question having been repeated numerous times, "Are you a boy or a girl?"

"Yes?" said the short person.

Snickers and high, shrill giggles rose from those still in line. Used to derision from village children who had never tired of fooling her over things she couldn't see, Bu acted on impulse, laying a hand on the child's shoulder. "She can be with me," Bu said—having spent her life in a family entirely comprised of women, she always assumed female unless the person before her loomed the way men did, or spoke in a man's chesty voice. And that *Yes?* had sounded more a kitten's mew. Of course this was a girl.

The nun turned her way. "Names?"

"YinYin," mewed the child.

"Bu," said Bu.

"Which Bu," the nun said tiredly. "We have three already."

Bu understood then that this nun wanted Father's name, though at home it had been understood that only the elder sisters, daughters of Madam Lum, had any right to the dignity of Father's name.

But they were not here.

"Lum Bu," Bu stated.

"Lum Bu. YinYin. Girls go that way," said the nun, pointing. Ah, that explained the question, thought Bu. Of course boys would be housed in one place, and girls in another. YinYin followed Bu, who had never before been the elder and the guide. Though Bu had very little materially, she had possessed riches beyond material things in her mother's mostly-unspoken love. It had been conveyed mostly through touch, filling Bu's heart. Bu decided right then that she would help YinYin, who seemed very young, including sharing her yam tinket.

She explained this as they trod to where they had been pointed. Half a yam for an entire day was very little, but Bu was used to eating whatever was left once the elders and sisters had helped themselves. A low state of hunger was a constant in her life. Imagine her delight when her sensitive nose detected the aromas of cooking food, and the two discovered that the nuns were feeding the candidates! Bu was so used to scanty meals that the frugal, vegetarian fare seemed sumptuous to her eyes.

The two sat together on a mat, and Bu could not help noticing how carefully YinYin examined each bit of cabbage and carrot before slowly taking it into her mouth. While Bu ate, she sorrowed over YinYin's dusty bare feet. It had never occurred to her that someone might be poorer than Bu's family. YinYin didn't even have frond sandals like her own. Also, YinYin wore a single shapeless garment that came down to her knees, whereas Bu felt wealthy by comparison in her much-patched but sturdy robe over saggy-kneed trousers. By the end of the meal, she had determined that if YinYin needed anything, she would share what she had.

When they had emptied their bowls, and drunk the little

cups of tea everyone was offered, they were directed toward a huge fountain, where candidates were expected to wash their bowls and eating sticks before stacking them on the waiting table. Here, too, Bu discovered she had to demonstrate for YinYin how to wash a bowl. She spoke slowly and kindly, certain by now that YinYin, like Bu, came from a poor family who deemed her not worth much.

The brassy bong of temple bells startled both. For a moment YinYin seemed to blur, but Bu blinked, and the impression vanished. Bu was used to blurs, and merely peered around to see what everyone else was doing.

It turned out to be the call for the sunset sutras and prayers. Some candidates scouted away, leaving such things to the nuns. Others crowded to the front mats, hoping that their piety would be noticed and earn them favorable scores at the audition. The rest followed because this was a part of regular life. That included Bu, and YinYin followed her.

Once that ended, they were free. Those, like Bu, used to early hours, gathered to sleep. YinYin followed Bu, who chose a mat in sight of the privy, but not too close. Once she stretched out, she was asleep within a single breath, and only woke when others began stirring in the weak light of a new day.

Auditions!

At the far end of the temple, Granny Zim rose, bathed, carefully performed the sunrise rituals before the kitchen god, lit a stick of incense for Teg at the ancestral altar, and dressed in her best robe.

When she reached the temple, she trod up the steps and bowed to the nun there, who signed a blessing then rang her bell.

Granny turned to look out over the candidates, who sat cross-legged on the clean-swept tiles, faces uplifted. So many expressions: hope, fear, determination. A scowl here, pleading there. And over at the right, near the back, a small figure that Granny Zim knew immediately for her demon. It looked very much like a child of ten or so, but now had manifested narrow eyes instead of shadowy pits. A long soot-black braid hung down the square back in the style of unmarried girls. The little demon sat close by a skinny urchin of some ten or twelve years, utterly unremarkable except for an anxious squint.

Granny Zim lost sight of them as her chosen experts divided the candidates into ten groups, one for each of the ten primary instruments. Granny Zim tested for guqin herself, not because it was her chosen instrument so much as because those candidates who came knowing how to play were almost always fourth and fifth and tenth sons and daughters, or side sons and daughters, high-born but who would never inherit. Too often the rejected candidates would attempt to use rank against the instructors; Granny Zim, as Chief, could summarily dismiss such.

Also, there were always fewer of these than those who attempted most of the other instruments. This time she had only six, quickly tested, which gave her plenty of time to wander through the temple's side courts and observe the other groups.

She began at the door—and discovered that her intention to watch for that demon was a lucky sign, for they were being turned away before they even attempted an instrument.

Granny Zim cried, "Hold!"

Candidates and instructors alike froze into place, the instructors with heads bowed and hands together, poses quickly mimicked by the quicker of the candidates.

"Why are these candidates being turned away?" Granny Zim asked the nearest instructor, after gesturing her aside.

This instructor, one of the youngest of the previous cohort, said with lowered eyes, her tone sweet and soft, "This insignificant person was ordered by Instructor Higar to dismiss all candidates who cannot read or write."

Granny Zim pinched the skin between her brows. The humble tone used by the young instructor did not deceive her in the least. Higar, a superlative musician, was also a very difficult personality. One of the reasons Granny Zim saw to the guqin auditions herself was because this was also Higar's instrument, and she invariably favored better born candidates, without considering more important measures of potential.

She took a deep breath, then said, "Perhaps my rules were misunderstood. No candidates are to be dismissed for such a reason. They never have been, and we will not begin now." Then, seeing the curled lip of triumph in that downcast face, she stated crisply, "I want you to find and bring back any candidates dismissed for that reason." Thus making it clear that no, Higar was not going to be scolded or dismissed. And that smirk had been witnessed.

The instructor bowed and ran down the path to collect the rejects, and Granny Zim conducted the demon and the squinter to the nearest courtyard, where the twenty-one-string zither, grandchild of the guqin, was the instrument being tested.

Granny lingered in the background.

Bu, having no idea who she was, had forgotten her. She strained to follow what was going on, hoping to avoid blunders. She knew the sound of a zither. This one sounded different than the one she heard played at festivals and weddings. Better, like the difference between fresh tea, and much-used leaves left to steep a long time to wring the last of the flavor. Except…was that right?

Two candidates in a row knew how to play. The first performed a popular rice-planting air, and that candidate got pointed on to the next courtyard. He left with a hop and a skip.

The next player, a silk-clad girl a little older than the boy who had just played, flexed her hands, knit her brow, and stormed through a piece Bu had never heard before. It was quite loud.

At the end, the instructor said, "No. It would take too long for you to unlearn terrible habits. Everything is amiss, from your fingering to your breathing."

The girl's jaw dropped. She scowled, looked up — encountered Granny Zim's steady gaze — and stalked back toward the temple entrance and out of their lives.

Then it was YinYin's turn. Bu could not hear the preliminary questions over the screeling noise of a gourd pipe from the next courtyard. She could not see what exactly was going on with YinYin's hands, but presently two, then three strings reverberated, each note true. Ah, then the sense that something was not right merely came from that one string? Was it the player or the string?

The instructor looked up, saw Granny Zim's tiny nod, and sent YinYin toward the next courtyard.

Then it was Bu's turn.

She sat down. The instructor, a short woman whose blurred form reminded Bu a little of Second Mother, named the parts of the instrument quickly, then asked Bu how many she could repeat. She had to bend over to see the strings, and in so doing, changed her angle enough that most of the names went right out of her head.

The instructor then demonstrated the proper way to hold her fingers for plucking and for strumming. Bu strained to see, made an attempt to mimic, without knowing if she was correct or not. She sensed that this instructor had already decided against her.

Rejection was nothing new. Then it must be the nuns. Since she had already failed anyway, she said, "Honored Master, would you be kind enough to honor this ignorant one with an answer to a very small question before I am to go away?"

"You may," the instructor said, shifting in a way that suggested she was already turning to summon the next candidate.

Bu looked helplessly at the strings again—now *all* those names had fled. She said, "Is there a reason one of these strings sounds wrong? That is, this ignorant wretch does not know if the string or the finger was amiss…" She stopped there, afraid of her temerity.

"Oh?" the instructor asked, and a shadow fell across the instrument as Granny Zim stepped up.

"Which string?" she asked.

"This ignorant wretch has already forgotten those names the Master honored me with," Bu said, as formally as if she were speaking to Madam Lum back home. "But it's the one that goes…" And she hummed the sound of the string that had begun to go out of tune.

Granny Zim had already mentally dismissed the young squinter, just as had the test instructor, and had been about to follow on to see what her demon did with the next test, but hearing this, she changed her mind. She said, "Name?"

"Bu. Lum Bu," Bu amended quickly.

"Lum Bu, that is a practice instrument, with a repaired string. We might not see the flaw, but a repaired string is a weak string. You heard it just as it was beginning to go out of tune. You appear to have natural pitch." Granny Zim hesitated, aware that sight was not strictly necessary for musicians, but weak sight would compound the difficulties in teaching and learning. Yet it could be done—her own guqin instructor, whose hands could evoke sounds that broke crowds into helpless weeping, had been entirely blind. Very well, then, two challenges for her last cohort. "Lum Bu, join the candidates over there." She indicated the next court.

Granny Zim moved on to the remainder of the instructors, indicating that those two were to be passed as successful candidates, and as a result, by the time Bu and YinYin retired to their mats that night, Bu tried to contemplate the astounding fact that she was now a novice of the musicians. She had a place, a future! More importantly, their meals and their clothing would now be provided!

Oh, what riches!

THREE

"MUSIC," CHIEF MUSICIAN ZIM said sternly to the twenty faces before her, "moves humanity into harmony and order from the interior life." She touched heart, head, and life meridians. "Our rituals move us into order from the outside. What does that really mean?"

Before anyone could speak, the well-born who had had tutors chanted more or less in unison, as they had hundreds of times since they were five or six, "Music brings about harmony. Rites ensure obedience."

Oh, the complacence! And the puzzlement in the faces of those whose early lives had been dictated by survival, or by the rough labors expected at the lowest part of the social order.

"You say that," Granny Zim stated, "with all the meaning of a puppy who has been told to turn in a circle and sit, then expects a treat."

Ah, that startled them!

"Now, let us begin by forgetting everything you have been told about music. *Everything.*"

Bu let out a slow breath. Knowing herself the most ignorant person there, this first command was the easiest.

For the new music novices, life swiftly fell into a pattern.

The temple had sponsored the music school for generations, which meant that the days were organized around the temple's hours. The nuns cared for the students as part of their tasks, so the novices could concentrate on their work. To Bu, sensitive to the subtleties of hierarchy from an early age, that meant they had been catapulted to the rank of apprentices and novices of a respected calling.

Of course there were hierarchies within hierarchies. Lessons were one novice to one instructor, ending with assignments to be demonstrated the following day. With ten instruments to be learned, that meant a lot to be remembered and practiced. Bu, YinYin, and the remaining eighteen new novices — including those who had come with previous training — were not permitted to touch any instrument until passed by their instructor.

First there was proper breathing. Then correct fingering. With the guqin especially, there was not just plucking. This note required the hooked thumb of that hand, and *this* note the pluck of the middle finger of the other hand. Bu's quick ears caught the difference if the instructor demonstrated with the incorrect finger, or pluck.

When at last each was adept enough to be permitted to handle an instrument, they could not play if their clothing was not orderly, their seating position correct — for the guqin, with the stomach meridian opposite the fifth fret. Two novices were sent back to begin the fundamentals again when they began playing while incorrectly seated, both with warnings that another such error would see them sent back down the mountain. Sloppy habits were *never* overlooked.

The same occurred with the side flute, the notch-flute, and of course the high-pitched gourd flute, which was the most difficult of the three winds. The novices spent hours sitting up straight, legs neatly folded, holding a forefinger against their bottom lip as they practiced blowing across the hole drilled into the bamboo, their lips shaped to the size of a grain of rice.

Bu heard the proper hiss of breath across the hole, and struggled to emulate it. She had to rely on all her other senses to make up for her weak vision; there was no use in the instructor demonstrating how the lips were puckered, because all Bu saw was a round, brown blur that meant 'face'. She practiced assiduously by herself so that she would not fall behind.

In those early weeks, several novices got sent home. Three times, the girls returned to their dormitory to discover spaces where mats had been.

There was little chance of Bu or YinYin being dismissed. Ignored by the rest of the students, they turned to each other for practice partners, withdrawing to an isolated spot among the rocks and great intertwined fig trees back of the kitchen garden. Bu gradually discovered after making the full-lung breathing part of her daily habit that this breathing aided her in other ways. She ran more easily up and down the trails and over the wicker bridges, if sent on an errand like fetching new strings, or carrying messages.

She also discovered that she could sing far better than before. With true pitch, her singing had always been pleasing to the ear, though very soft, lest it disturb anyone. They did have lessons in reading and writing, but as she could not make out her characters without her nose almost dragging in the ink, the instructor decided that musical notations were useless for her. However if she sang a difficult combination of notes until she had committed it to memory, she could guide her clumsy fingers in learning to play it.

And they were clumsy. Each instrument required different movements, some quite subtle. Her hands had hitherto held a broom, or a bucket. She frequently went to sleep at night with her fingers flexing and twitching as she mentally tapped out patterns on the wind instruments, or plucked imaginary strings of the silk instruments.

Singing was *not* part of musician training. One of the older, silk-clad girls, overheard Bu humming her combination while bathing one morning and scolded, "You'd better not warble in future, or you'll end up in a pleasure house for the rest of your life, entertaining dung drivers and basket-weavers."

Bu kept to herself her observation that someone had to drive dung to the fields and weave the baskets everyone depended on. Honest work was honorable work, so said the nuns every day in the sutras, but that girl was seldom in the temple to hear them. Bu took the advice, and thenceforward made certain that her hum was too soft for anyone else to hear.

At last she was permitted to play a battered old instrument, used for generations for training beginners. She fumbled badly at first in her attempts to fit her imaginary practice to the actuality, but there were plenty of these old instruments kept for students, and she used them as often as she could find them, her eyes entirely closed so that her fingers would learn each type of wood, how it vibrated, the position of the frets, and the way the strings felt when correctly tuned. Her fingers explored the sharp edges of the holes in the winds, and sensed the brush of wind over it when she blew.

The only instruments she did not learn with her hands were the great dual-pitched chime bells, each reminding her of a helmet with an almond-shaped cross section.

"It's mainly boys who play these," one of the kinder older novices told the new girls. "You do have to learn them. As you've no doubt seen, it's a nun who strikes them for the hours and festivals. I can tell you, when she plays, the sound carries clear out to the harbor."

Bu could not only hear but feel through her feet and bones how correctly struck bells sounded, so when the nun came to the school side of the temple's warren of courts and explained that she swung the mallet from her heels, Bu watched carefully. The only way she'd ever been able to tell one person from another, besides height and general build, was how they moved. She was able to discern how the nun's feet were as firmly planted as fig roots, and how the mallet-strike came from her hips. *Bon-n-n-g!*

There was only one practice set to work on with their muffled mallets, so it was difficult to find time to practice when boys weren't already there, jostling impatiently to get a turn. Another senior novice said in a self-important tone, "If you aren't good on the chime bells, it won't truly matter. *You* will not be playing those anyway. In noble courts, it's only qin and zither and the two bamboo flutes. Everything else is played by paid musicians."

That dismissive tone of voice taught Bu a lot: that nobles played, that they regarded paid musicians as below them.

She, YinYin, and a boy who had been sold by a wharf laborer to pay his gambling debts, were at the bottom of the hierarchy. The boy was called Cricket because he chattered to anyone who would listen; some of the other boys liked him, especially since he cheerfully fetched and carried for them. Though Bu was wary of boys, after her village experiences, she sensed no threat in Cricket, and so she readily shared either instruments or extra rice cakes.

Her impulse to share stemmed from Second Mother having from Bu's earliest days repeated Suanek's saying that kindness cost nothing, and poured forth infinite spiritual waters. Bu had even discovered the gigantic statue of Suanek inside the temple, her feet upon the back of a fish made of real gold, in either hand the vase of celestial waters, and the fig twigs.

Yes, fig! (Exclaimed the storyteller.) In that part of the world, the ancient fig trees were believed to hold up the islands, and every part of them was used for so many purposes: the pods as cork for fishing, the great fronds for making roofs and other coverings, the thin tendrils harvested to make sandals, and so on. Who is to say that the people of those islands were wrong? For that matter, who is to say that Suanek is not capable of holding out leaves that are willow to one pilgrim, and fig to another?

And why am I speaking of Suanek, known to everyone here? We will be getting to the mighty heroes and villains by and by, but it's important to understand the worm in the soil, as you shall soon see.

Spring had passed and summer had ripened when Bu discovered that she was actually making music. Very little, and very laborious, for now she could hear her many, many errors of breathing and fingering, of loose string or emerging cracks in an instrument. YinYin, so much younger (or so Bu assumed) was always ahead. Bu practiced indefatigably, with all the verve of one who had had to work hard at tasks everyone else considered simple, all her life.

Because there were no classes, as yet—only individual lessons so that the instructor could pay close attention lest a bad habit creep in—there was no sense of how well one did in reference to others. Bu could hear practice up and down the many trails, and even in the higher reaches of some of the trees, but the new novices had learned that intruding on another's practice uninvited was considered rude.

From a remove, Granny Zim observed her demon. She saw that YinYin's main companion was still Bu, who was oblivious to the occasional startle reflex when YinYin's braid would flicker into wisps of smoke. But as the early days turned into weeks, those moments diminished to nothing. YinYin, Granny Zim was glad to see, seemed to be settling into being a human. The little demon even demonstrated the beginnings of personality, such as the discovery of the delights of candied haws, whereas before, YinYin had eaten with the flat affect of one who performed a necessary but tedious task.

As far as Granny Zim could tell, the two spoke very little— she was convinced that YinYin was still assimilating language, and it had become clear that Bu had been raised with the notion that as nobody cared what she thought or felt, it was far better to stay silent. YinYin seemed to be observing and absorbing Bu's little habits of daily life as well as those of the novices, the instructors, and the nuns.

At first, the demon had vanished at night altogether.

Granny Zim had gone herself to check the female novices' dormitory, and saw what she had expected: Bu curled in the utterly unconscious sleep of the young, the mat next to hers empty. But right after the Ghost Festival, Granny Zim came one night to discover YinYin lying on the mat, limbs straight, eyes open, a hint of glowing red in them. It seemed to Granny Zim that YinYin practiced humanity and music equally assiduously. That did not argue evil intent, did it?

Of course there was no answer.

FOUR

BU HAD NEVER TAKEN much interest in the night sky, as she could only make out three or four of the brightest stars. They looked to her like blurry snowflakes, and the moons like glowing blobs. But everyone on the islands knew that the men who were not traders or merchants left every spring, then returned from far-off places when the arrow of the First Archer of the Four Archers touched the rising Phoenix Moon.

The men usually returned well before New Year's, as everyone in all the islands scoured and renewed their homes and shops to ready for the year. Up at the temple school, the novices scarcely noticed these preparations. The daunting prospect of their first competition absorbed all their attention. Frantic practice could be discerned all over the mountaintop. The morning and evening rituals were now better attended, and those who could afford it consulted augurs. Others slipped out to hang red scraps of silk from the branches of the wish trees, in hopes of drawing luck Essence.

The novices knew that they would be ranked for the first time, which would initiate change in lessons and instructors. The real worry was the persistent rumor that those deemed to be last in ranking would be dismissed. *Not* those at the bottom of birth rank. That much was stressed by all the instructors, even Instructor Higar, though with a hint of reservation in her tone. The number of novices was already down to fourteen, and whispers spread at mealtimes or at the baths or along secluded bridges under the sheltering fronds that by the anniversary of the first year, there would only be ten novices henceforth.

"Do you think that's true?" Bu asked YinYin one day, as they raced along a huge limb of a mighty banyan on a shortcut between two narrow footpaths, as rain pattered overhead.

You have to remember (said the storyteller, after glancing obviously at the still-empty bowl put out for coins) that at first Bu only put questions to the instructors, because that was one of the rules: it was considered arrogant to never ask for enlightenment. She obeyed, with the most inoffensively humble manner she could contrive. YinYin was even quieter. But as the days had turned into weeks, the quite natural desire to check one's observations against another's, had prompted Bu to dare initiating a conversation when she and YinYin were alone.

At first YinYin's answers were monosyllabic, but never angry or scolding. YinYin was always calm, and Bu strove to emulate that calm. Gradually YinYin's answers evolved into a phrase or two, and finally simple sentences.

"What is true?" YinYin still spoke in a kitten squeak.

"That they will send away four of us, to make a proper ten."

"I wait for Chief Musician Zim to say," YinYin answered.

Bu exclaimed, "That's wise. I will, too."

Understood: they would work even harder not to be numbered among those four.

The weather had turned chilly, with intermittent rain, when the day of the competition dawned. The novices gathered in the Music Room, maintaining silence, and one by one each was called up to perform the assigned piece.

The competition began with the chime bells, located at the back of the room. As expected, the male novices fared far better with these, with the exception of a weedy girl who truly loved the deep-toned bells—and YinYin, who, though among the smallest, proved to be quite strong. Granny Zim looked consideringly after her demon as YinYin returned to sit down, apparently oblivious to the whispers that rustled through the room until hushed by a frowning instructor.

Bu's performance was like most of the rest of the girls' work, tentative, careful, and so muted that the overall effect was dull.

Bu did no better with the gourd pipe, but again, that was considered a male instrument. Though the history of many instruments reached back to weapons in some way or another, the gourd pipe had the most direct connection. It was still used today, not only on the field of war, where it could be heard over the roar and clash of battle, but it was a required instrument in official parades of generals and nobles, as well as in wedding and funeral processions of the great.

Bu took a first, hasty breath, which resulted in a squawk like an angry goose. She managed to right herself—barely. In contrast, YinYin again played the simple progression with methodical perfection, but with all the expression of a rock.

Both were about the same with the drums. Unexpectedly, it was Cricket who was very clearly the best here. Many had assumed he was just a merry jokester, good for sending on tiresome errands. But somewhere, sometime, he had found his way to practice.

Again, with the two-stringed eruh, YinYin excelled in precision, but Bu was not far behind, with the beginnings of a respectable variation in tone.

The two did even better with the lute and the bamboo winds, which the better-born novices considered their prerogative. When it came to the 21-stringed zither, currently the instrument of choice in royal courts, the two surprised the other novices with their nimble fingering. It had seemed impossible that those low-born oafs would possess fingers clever enough for noble instruments!

YinYin was the fastest and most methodical, but flat in expression. Bu was more hesitant, demonstrating a respectable attempt at expression.

The qin was last.

Everyone knew that the qin was Chief Musician Zim's instrument. And as chief, she was entitled to break the silence and put a question to the novices, "Why play the qin?"

She did not do this to everyone, and her expression never altered from answer to answer, so the novices did not know if the questions arose out of failure or excellence, or some other criteria.

Inevitably, most responded with what they thought she wanted to hear. Some cursed inwardly, wondering why they had not been warned about questions at this first test, which everyone had insisted was conducted in complete silence. The second best defense was flattery, "Your inspiration, Esteemed

Chief, causes me to aspire…"

Granny Zim did not listen past these initial words. She did not hold the emptiness of flattery against the anxious novices. Flattery was a part of life. It was even an art, in its way. But it was not an answer. It did not matter anyway. The only answer she was interested in was her demon's. "Why play the qin?" she asked YinYin.

YinYin said, in that tiny, expressionless voice, "Pure." A pause, then, "True…" Another pause, round, expressionless face bent downward, but Granny Zim saw a hint of smoke blurring the demon's head. Then it vanished, and all anyone saw was that neat braid that Bu helped make each morning.

Granny Zim said, "That is an excellent beginning. It is a question you ought to ponder over time."

Bu was called up after YinYin. By now Bu knew every one of the practice instruments with the briefest touch of a questing finger. Without hesitation, she selected the qin with the freshly peeled dragon-well sound hole, and the newly replaced goose-foot tuning pegs. Though the zither was the most popular of the silk-string instruments, it was the older qin, with its mere seven strings, that had at first reduced her to hot eyes and heavy throat with its absolute discipline in correct plucking and hooks and stops. She could not articulate why its sound affected her the most when she got it right, except that this showed that the required discipline had a reason. She could hear it when the qin sang true, as YinYin had said.

Bu faltered at first, tentative because she was so aware of that audience out there, but when she shut her eyes and sank into the simple song that they all played, a contemplative mood emerged from the shimmering chords. Every stop was clean, every pluck crisp.

Granny Zim had not intended to address Bu. She had begun the questions as a round-the-mountain way of interrogating her demon. But Bu's performance almost demanded it. There was hard work evident in those rudimentary skills, and even more elusive, the beginnings of passion.

Granny Zim said, "Why play the qin?"

Bu squinted up at her, face pruned out of alignment in the unself-conscious way of a child who has never in life seen a mirror, and said, "It…makes this ignorant one think. Ah, not only about fingering. Though it does that. But if the fingering is correct, there is music. Not only notes." As Bu's soft voice stuttered out each word, her fingers brushed along her Life meridian, and tapped absently near the Heart meridian. "That is, I understand that every note is 'a vital component of music,' for so we hear each day. And it's very true! It's…" Then, aware that she'd been talking far longer than she had since her arrival, she shut her mouth so quickly that her teeth clacked.

Granny Zim nodded, signaling acceptance of this hopeless morass. Clearly the child was struggling to express vocabulary that she had never been taught. No one had read to her from Kanda's *Conversations*, in which he'd instructed scholars on the discipline of restraint, which was the truest path to spiritual expression.

"Consider the question as you further your studies, Lum Bu," Granny Zim said, and added, as she only did to those whom she deemed had reached the top one or two of the given assignment, "Well done."

After that, they were released to celebrate New Year's Two Moons.

Before they were given their holiday, Granny Zim had explained that on their return, their new schedule would be presented to them, along with their new novice robes. Their lessons from now on would, for the first time, be shared. The time had come for learning to blend one's music with others'.

Then they were set free to enjoy the last days of the Year of the Rooster.

It would be overstating to say that no one had expected either of the two to play so well, because there had been no expectation at all. They had effectively not existed to those who had been born in silken beds, except as part of the background clutter.

But the signs of expertise always draw the eye. And inevitably, there are those who regard that expertise as a personal challenge. The three richest (and the single novice sent home) had vanished, but everyone else remained. Not all the comments muttered and murmured in line for rice bowls, or on the way to and from the temple, were sincere congratulations. There were the inevitable sneers: "Oh, anyone can finger if they're diligent, but composing? Hah! Like expecting a pig to write poetry." And, "Even a stray cur can catch a rat, but that doesn't mean it will get the cat's cushion."

Bu could ignore those. Harder to ignore were the "accidents" such as elbows jabbing the bowl in her hands so that food flew onto the floor, which she simply scraped up

with her fingers and put back in the bowl, as she had when
Fifth Sister had been annoyed with her and did the same.

The more competitive novices watching from the sides of
their eyes exchanged scandalized glances, finding this
evidence of uncouth behavior hilarious, but Bu didn't see
those looks. To her, the elbow digs and hip shoves was just
more of what happened if one wasn't careful around a crowd.
She became more reclusive, whisking in another direction if
she saw people-shaped stalks approaching her. She made sure
there was space before and after her in lines, even if she had to
stand out, her stomach growling, until everyone had gone
before her. As long as it didn't get any worse, she shrugged it
off. And the "accidents" did not get worse, because there was
a very strict rule: any physical altercation, for whatever reason,
and the perpetrator would be sent down the mountain. It had
happened once already, to the sixth side-son of a duke—it was
he, a furtive bully preying on the unwary, who had been sent
away in disgrace. Bu had never been troubled by him because
she was always wary, and his angry breathing had given him
away every time he was near.

The bells broke out suddenly at midday when there were
two days left of the Rooster year. It was a joyful sound, one Bu
had never heard. She was mending the elbows of her shabby,
worn second tunic entirely by feel, and looked up. "What is
that?"

She sat in the girls' dormitory, which was nearly empty. A
girl her age, who had uttered sincere compliments, turned her
way. "It is the ships! The men are back. Don't you want to see?
It's a grand sight!"

Ships at a distance were mere blobs, a fact that Bu saw no
reason to point out. "I will when I finish here," Bu said.

The girl flitted off, leaving Bu alone. No, she was not alone.
Here was YinYin, dropping down beside her. "There's a way
for you to see."

Bu slewed around to face YinYin, who of course was a blur,
her tiny voice not much more expressive. "I can? Is there some
Essence...ritual, or a charm, that you know about?" Bu
squinted to see if YinYin was holding an Essence paper, which
looked like long white fingers as they were cut into strips, with
charms written on them. But there was none.

YinYin was silent for a breath or two. "Yes."

"Does it cost? All I have is that tinket, and I was saving it
for the festival."

"No cost. I can give it to you."

"Give it?"

Another silence for a breath or two. "Inside you," and when Bu's face wrinkled up, YinYin said, "Not for very long."

Bu's face cleared. "Oh! Yes—I'm sorry, here you are offering me a gift, and here's me with my eyes growing above my head."

There was scarcely anyone in the entire temple who was less picky or snobbish, but YinYin did not point that out. "Come."

They flitted out, and YinYin took the lead. Bu had never gone exploring. What would be the use? She couldn't see much, and anyway there was never enough time for all the practice she felt she needed to do just to keep up.

They pounded over several wicker bridges, and once hopped up to follow a broad limb trained as a path over a crevasse in the rocky hillside before diving down to birth a new cluster of fig trunks. They emerged on a cliff where several others had gathered, exclaiming and pointing. YinYin took Bu to the far end, with a clear view of the curved arms of the harbor, and the ocean beyond, then touched Bu's hand.

Bu jumped at the coldness of YinYin's fingers. The cold seemed to sink into Bu's arm. She shivered and blinked as the chill bloomed behind her eyes. Then she forgot cold, hot, and everything else as the vista sharpened into clarity.

At first she did not know what she was seeing, and vertigo made her unsteady as her mind coped with the elements of depth and perspective for the first time. She clutched at a waist-high shrub as a rush of wonder flooded her. The ocean was not all one color after all! It was greenish, and greenish-blue, and dark blue beyond the harbor, with glitters as if pieces of the sun had rained down to float on the water. It was not only moving at the shoreline—all of it moved. Yes, she had felt that in the boat, but she could *see* the swells and whitecaps tossing foam skyward, and it made the inside of her chest ache the more with every breath.

On it, slanting at an angle, the ships cleaved the water with white running down the side, and rippling out in widening Vs that intersected, then sank into the restless billows. The sails were not brown blobs, they were slatted! And all around them streamers and flags danced in the wind.

Above them the sky was its familiar blue, though the clouds scudding northward were not vague blobs, but rounded in astonishing shapes, in so many shades of white-blue, and blue-white, and gray, and out there, big, heavy ones smeared with green.

On the decks of the ships, figures crowded, but they began to blur. The clouds blurred—was it tears? No, with heartrending rapidity, the sharpness loosened, just as a taut string flops when loosened.

"Thank you, YinYin," Bu whispered.

YinYin did not respond for another breath or two, then said, "I think…I know I can put some inside you." Her voice rose slightly, not quite a question, but tentative.

Bu wanted to shout, "Yes!" But she bit her bottom lip as she considered. Wasn't there some lesson, overheard long ago, about such things? She was not certain. She considered that coldness. *Put some inside her*, YinYin said.

Bu knew that there were a lot of things people put in themselves besides food. Like beer or rice wine. And she was fairly certain that there were other things. She thought about that cold, then said, "You are very kind to offer." Her voice rang with sincere gratitude. "But I am not sure I ought to have things in me that are not myself, other than food or water or tea."

"Oh."

Bu knew that *Oh*. It was the one that YinYin uttered when a thing was new to her. Bu had noticed that before, finding it interesting that oftentimes, YinYin found something new that Bu had always known. But of course not everybody knew the same things. Bu was very ignorant of so much, that was self-evident.

"Thank you," she said again. "That was a wonderful gift, and I shall always remember it. But the wind is turning cold, and I smell a storm coming. We ought to go back."

They scampered up to the temple. As she followed YinYin, Bu experienced echoing flashes of that wondrous sight. There were the clouds, so soft they had seemed! In contrast to the lines of the sail slats, and the rail and hull. She hugged the memory to herself when the storm broke, hurling down cold rain.

It wasn't until late that night that Bu began to wonder who had taught YinYin what must be a very complicated charm. She was so very, very ignorant about matters of Essence, and the unseen world.

FIVE

NEW YEAR'S TWO-MOONS arrived, clear and cold as the storm had blown off overnight.

Bu's heart knotted less each passing week whenever she thought about her birth mother, except on festival days. Though the only gifts had been given by Madam Lum to her daughters, and those were nothing more than a shared rouge pot or a carved wooden hairpin, Second Mother had always managed to save out a bit of a nut cake, or some fragrant cooked mushrooms, for Bu.

Now there would be no gift, but at least she had her tinket, which she had promised to share with YinYin. She went to the temple alone before dawn, and lit incense, praying to Suanek to send Second Mother good luck. She dutifully added in Father, bowing three times and hoping piously he was not a wandering ghost, but that was duty. So was adding in the names of Fifth Sister, Madam Lum, and all the rest, then she went out to enjoy herself with the other novices who had no home to go to, or no wherewithal to get there.

That included Cricket, who had passed his fourteenth year, unknown to anyone. Everyone assumed he was eleven or twelve. He was self-conscious about his short, scrawny body, having not yet become aware that regular meals had caused him to begin sprouting. During free time Cricket joined Bu and YinYin more often than not, the price of joining a group of better-born boys inevitably being to fetch and carry. If he wasn't eating, he was drumming. On himself, on anything to hand. Bu knew Cricket was near whenever she heard the soft plappity-plap of palms, or fists striking his thighs.

He popped up out of nowhere when YinYin and Bu headed toward the Suanek's Way path down to the village. No one said anything. It would never occur to Bu to say no, and YinYin accepted solitude and crowds with exactly the same blank face.

The three ran over the wicker bridges, Bu delighting in the smooth feel of the massive roots trained to form railings. When they got to the village above the harbor, Bu was at first anxious at the change in the sound of chatter around them. Then a chance remark from Cricket—"The men are back! That means there'll be more on offering than ear dangles and lip rouge"— reminded her that this change in sound was nothing more than the deeper men's voices mixed with the higher tones of mostly women, which she had been hearing ever since her arrival.

They walked about, Cricket pointing out the rooster decorations that had been replaced by fat and smiling pigs. "Pig years are always considered auspicious," he informed Bu and YinYin. "I learned this, if nothing else, from my da—if there's a lot of pig decorations, there's sure to be something offered for free, for that's considered to be good luck. The more you give, the more the gods will grant in the next year."

"Is it true?" Bu asked. She'd never heard that; but then, she was beginning to realize since she'd begun spending months with other adults besides Madam Lum, the latter had scarcely had anything to say that wasn't a scold or a complaint. What kind of a pig year was it for the five sisters left behind? It would be more complaints about how the Lums and the Fus always cheated poor Madam and her fatherless girls.

"See! There! Steamed yams, for the asking. Let's!"

Bu was very ready for a free yam. She patted her pocket where her coin resided, and gloated contentedly at being able to preserve it a bit longer.

By the time they reached the smaller eastern dock at the other end of the main road where Bu had arrived what felt like another lifetime ago, they'd eaten so much that Bu's stomach began to feel uncomfortable. Yet she determinedly took advantage of every offering, always thinking that surely this would be the last.

The only one more gluttonous was Cricket, who agreed

with Bu that refusing an offering of fresh milk cakes or candied haws just because you were so stuffed your previous meal was pushing the backs of your eyeballs was a deliberate invitation to bad luck. As they whiffed the brine-and-fish smell that meant they were nearly at the dock, Bu wondered if the teasing at meals from some of the younger boys about Cricket having a hollow leg was actually true.

Then she forgot that as large, looming figures faced their way, and harsh, laughing voices called out, "Well if it isn't Little Maggot!"

"Got yourself a couple of wives already, Maggot?"

"You've nearly doubled in size, Maggot! Come, drink to the new year, or are you too high and mighty for your old uncles?"

"Wait here, I'll be back," Cricket said. "They won't bother you—it's only when my da has cheated them, or they're drunk, that they get surly."

At that he ran down to where the laborers were gathered. From the sounds, they were already well on their way on the rice wine tide toward the sea, as there was little business at this time of year. Bu was willing to wait, as she always preferred following a known figure when in a crowd, but YinYin began wandering back up the street. Bu scurried after.

Cricket rejoined them presently, smelling of sour beer. "Never turn your back on old tigers, just because the wolves have taken you in," he said airily. "And I learned something! Come on—Old Dour told me of a place where they're handing out braised meat on skewers!"

"Maggot?" YinYin said.

Cricket shrugged, his face red from sharing toasts with the wharfers. "They called me Maggot, Bird Turd, Dog Vomit, Tadpole, depending on their moods. The worse the name, the worse their moods. It was all kicks and swats and no meals, but I worked just as hard. Why do you think I begged where the headwoman's nosers would see me? It was they who got my father to sell me."

He forced a laugh, as if aware that he'd disclosed too much, though YinYin remained utterly impassive. Bu's gaze had dropped, so she could hide a wince at the sharp note of anger beneath the laughter.

"Let's go before it's all gone," he said.

Meat was too seldom tasted for Bu to find it as wonderful as others seemed to. Her experience was confined to fish, and until she joined the music school, the boniest and rankest. Tender fish had seldom made its way past Fourth Sister.

As the ruddy sun sank into the western seas, they reached the row of fine shops and pleasure houses at the top of the street. This small row of stores—which looked very grand to Bu—were lit with Moon Lanterns. Bu couldn't see what was painted on them, but she loved the cheery glow, especially when people launched them toward the sky.

Cricket grabbed their hands and eeled his way through the crowd to the splendid store in whose front court tender, tasty chicken that had been spoiled and cosseted for a year provided the feast, and the raucous voices around them hailed the news that at the end of next year it would be pork. Indeed, there was a sizable pig with garlands around its neck, busy gobbling tidbits thrown by the crowd, at the start of a year in which the animal would be treated like a king.

Bu nibbled her skewer and found it tasty, but she was beginning to long for a place to sit down when Cricket said, "Fireworks soon, I think. Let's find a good spot!"

Soon the three of them sat on a railing with a perfect view as fireworks were let off over the harbor. Bu loved fireworks. She had seen snow once or twice in her life. When she'd held a flake right up to her nose, she had seen its crystalline structure before it began to melt. That structure was akin to what fireworks looked like, and lamps and lanterns. They were just blurrier. All the bridges had been strung with lanterns, a grand sight.

They were finishing up a second helping of candied haws when Cricket leaned out, looking from one to the other. "How do you do that?" he addressed YinYin, on the other side of Bu.

"What?"

"The fireworks. I see them reflected in Bu's eyes. But not yours."

"Do fireworks reflect in people's eyes? Does everything do that?" Bu asked. "Do you see people in others' eyes?"

"You only see lights, after dark," Cricket said. "You mean, you've never noticed that? Oh. Of course. You're short-sighted."

The three of them had been sitting arm to arm. Bu felt YinYin tighten all over, then lean out toward Cricket. "Mine reflect."

Cricket leaned out again, and Bu had to lean back so Cricket could peer into YinYin's face. "You're right! Clear as a mirror. Even clearer. Must have been the angle, somehow." He shrugged the matter off. "Are you going to finish that stick of haws?"

YinYin handed half a stick over. Bu groaned, replete to the point of discomfort, and added hers. Cricket began champing enthusiastically as if he hadn't eaten all day, and when the fireworks ended, they trudged back up to the temple and separated to sleep.

Before she lay down, Bu tucked her tinket back into the corner of the sack she had made of that threadbare winter cloak of Fifth Sister's, to keep her scant belongings tidy. She wished she could send the coin to Second Mother, then remembered what she'd learned that day, as Cricket carelessly read out prices of all the things he'd like to have. For the first time, Bu understood that her tinket was barely worth anything. She wished she could send Second Mother a…a silver tael, all for her own. But one day, if she passed her mastery competition, she would earn her own money, and then she could send it all to Second Mother!

When the weather turned chilly, the nuns had issued quilts. As Bu snuggled under hers, she remembered someone saying that once they reached their fifth year, they would be given trunks, as by then they would not only have a robe for each season, but they would also be making their own strings and instruments. That sparked a worry: were they expected to buy the makings on their own?

At least that was four years off yet. Anything could happen in four years, she thought contentedly, and fell into the world of dreams, with fireworks springing from her hands as she played a golden guqin.

SIX

THE STORYTELLER PAUSED TO drink, and after a moment, the young master finally put a very small coin into the waiting bowl—hoping that the storyteller would get to the heroes and battles soon.

The storyteller continued.

After the festival, life settled into its usual rhythm. Or rather, the new rhythm. The novices were given clothes, which caused the expected complaints in those used to silk next to their skin, and gloating contentment in those who had arrived wearing all they owned, with perhaps a castoff rag to change to while the one was laundered. These were actual robes, with a very modest belled sleeve, tied at the right hip with a thin sash of the same linen fabric. These robes were, the instructor in charge explained, to be shared. Not owned. One took a fresh one from the stack on emerging from the baths, and left the soiled one in the basket.

Bu felt very grown up in her first robe. And a sash! It pleased her to see herself the same blue-gray color as everyone else. It made her feel she was safely invisible.

She seemed to be alone in being pleased. YinYin kept forgetting the sash, and when reminded, tied it with a speed that hinted at impatience. Cricket yanked constantly at his, so used as he was to that ragged, shapeless tunic open in front to the stomach, displaying his scrawny ribs. Tensi Yi Nis and the other silk-born novices minced about for a day or two with solemn, martyred expressions, aware that the future would establish them back in silk again.

Learning to play with others at first cost Bu a storm of nerves, as she still was afraid of lagging, or disappointing others in some way. But she soon heard that most of the others found it difficult to maintain a shared rhythm. This new addition to their regular studies—which did not abate—began at first with using the same instrument in practice duets, but soon word went around that the next competition would be duets with different instruments.

At least that was half a year off! Now was winter, with cold days that made finding a practice area a matter of some concern. Many days were too rainy outside, and one especially cold day rumors went around that the previous rain had covered Kanda's Peak with the snow that fell very rarely so far in the south. While Bu could have forced herself to endure practicing outside—she had early learned to sweep in all weathers—it was very bad for instruments. This forced the novices into proximity, and so those with the same instruments often clumped together to practice.

This in turn caused them to exercise the new skill: playing in duo, and rarely three, or even more. There was one afternoon when all five practice zithers were in use. Bu, always the first to rise and to commence her work, was surprised when the slightly older, and far better born girls did not immediately claim hers by insisting she was taking too long. Instead, they seemed quite willing to play with her, showering her with compliments that made her wonder if their tongues were oiled.

This happened twice more.

It wasn't until Cricket made a remark over their morning porridge the day of Fire Wishes Festival halfway through the second month that she began to understand the why of it. "Got any bribes yet?" he asked.

"Bribes!" Bu repeated.

Cricket snickered. "You make it sound like murder! I guess you haven't. But you wait. It'll happen, sure as brine is salt. It's happened to me already," he added proudly with a fist against his chest. "All the boys want me as their duet partner so they'll sound as good as me." He mimed drumming.

Bu hated the thought of having to choose as much as having to ask someone. Maybe she wouldn't have to. "Aren't we assigned partners?"

"That's for the method part of the test. For the song, you can choose your instrument and your partner, that's what Lek says, and his brother was hired by a duke to lead the musicians in his personal army."

Bu accepted this; 'method' was the most common word for the escalating difficulties in correct fingering, breath control for the winds, and complicated patterns in the oldest ritual music, which formed the fundament of all music.

"I'll have YinYin," Bu said, relieved.

Cricket wasn't surprised. He'd framed the question to test that friendship, aware by now that Bu, who was slow to move as she squinted at the ground she couldn't see, was equally slow in the daily give-and-take that he had been negotiating since he formed his first words. A friend like Bu, who willingly shared, and who was among the top of the ranks, would be useful to have. But only if he could pry her from YinYin, who spent time with no one but Bu.

He scampered away, leaving Bu puzzled. As she spooned up the rest of her porridge, she considered Cricket's question. There had been a reason he asked about bribes, surely. He was comfortable to be in company with because he liked to laugh, and also, he never confronted people, as others were apt to do, especially those who expected deference.

But she could sense his restless watching of everyone and everything around. His hands were always in motion. His mouth was, too, always joking, or making funny comments about people and things, and surmising what might happen.

Maybe even making those things happen? She was fairly certain, for instance, that it was Cricket who had contrived to get that duke's son exposed for his bullying. There had been no fight, which would get them both expelled. She'd heard whispers in the night, after the candles were blown out, that made it fairly clear that Cricket had teased that boy, who'd grabbed Cricket's topknot and began kicking him just as Instructor Ding came to inspect the boys' dormitory.

In short, she liked Cricket. But he reminded her of fire, which was warm and welcome at a distance, but you couldn't trust it not to burn. That led her to ponder the matter of friends, and how difficult it was to define it. Was YinYin truly a friend, or were they more like companions because of circumstance and habit, as she'd been with Fifth Sister?

Her reverie broke when men's voices startled her.

She had finished her porridge, and was about to retreat to the girls' dormitory when Granny Zim swept through, smiling in a way that no one had seen before — and when she spoke, Bu was startled by the note of joy in her voice. "Exactly what I hoped. You there, Bu. YinYin. Rareg. Yi Nis. And Cricket, you, too. Since today is a festival day and you have no schedule, please choose an instrument, come to the hall, and demonstrate your lessons." Behind her walked Instructor Ding, escorting a man and a woman no one knew.

The named novices were soon assembled in their hall, sitting straight and proper, hands on knees, each with an instrument before them, and Cricket with his mallets.

It was not Granny Zim's habit to discuss her private life. All the novices had seen Chief Musician Zim's First Daughter-in-Law speaking to the nuns each day, to organize matters of food, clothing, and supplies. She also stepped in to instruct now and then, if instructors were ill or had other demands. It was further known that Chief Zim's daughter was the village headwoman — but no one ever saw her.

No one knew who these newcomers were. A servant appeared, carrying a basket of refreshments different from the usual frugal temple fare. Instructor Ding chatted with the newcomers as these were set out, then Granny Zim said to the students, "Perform whatever pleases you most. This is merely an opportunity for you to experience being summoned to perform, which will surely occur often in your futures."

When Bu heard this, for the very first time, she gave a thought to the future. It still seemed impossibly far away.

When it was her turn, she ran her hands over her favorite among the qins. This one had only joyful songs in it, just as the one with the tiny shells atop the goose-neck tuning pegs was a melancholy instrument. She decided on "The Birds Among the Lotus" prelude, which was short and full of bright harmony. Cricket gave them "Thunder in the West" on a pair of drums, and YinYin, "Kanda's Rest," their latest assignment, on the notch flute.

Each returned to a cushion to wait until they were all dismissed, which happened after Rareg's stirring rendition of "Emperor Ban's Wedding" on the gourd flute. Then, to everyone's relief, they were dismissed to finish making their lanterns to release that night.

"Your thoughts?" Granny Zim addressed her second son.

He was the most like his father. That had been evident

from his birth, which had prompted them to combine Teg's name with another family name that evoked Suanek, Teg's favorite of the gods, into Huitaik, or TaikTaik. Granny Zim still sometimes used that fond childhood name, though Huitaik had graying hair, and two children approaching adulthood.

"Mother, as always your training is superlative. Even I can hear it, ignorant as I am."

Here, she sighed. They both knew he had inherited talent, which he employed with his homemade notch flute aboard the ship to while away long evenings when the sailors were confined belowdecks. He had wanted badly to audition at the temple school, if it hadn't been obvious from the time Third Brother could walk that he was going to be what people carelessly called demon-touched. Leading the fleet was First Brother's responsibility, and leading the family ship fell to Second Brother, though he would have stayed on the island if he could have.

Third Brother, born the year after Huitaik, had from birth been incapable of settling to any one thing. He was always the center of any group, leading the laughter and fun, usually at the expense of work. And he had refused to marry, preferring his freedom, until he was well into his forties. But he could get stubborn, usually at the wrong times. Such as when he insisted on marrying that almond-eyed, willow-browed wife of his, in spite of warnings from Mother, Father, both elder brothers, and even *her* brother. She was the same age as First Brother's eldest son, not suitable even if she had been a different sort of person. But she was the prettiest in the village, and he would have no one else. He could not see, though everyone else could as she teased and flattered, that her languishing eye was not on him but on the handsome Zim house, highest on the hill overlooking the harbor.

"And?" Granny Zim said to her son, after his cautious compliment.

At this, his thoughtful, silent wife rose to her feet, murmuring that she would bring fresh tea. This way mother and son could speak freely, which was impossible at home, with Third Daughter-in-Law always with her ear to any door with conversation behind it.

"Mother, that small one is a demon. Did you know that?"

"Of course I did. How could you tell?"

"I was not completely sure at first. When I passed it, I thought I caught a whiff of … ayah, it reminds me of snow on the wind. Though it is truly less of a scent than a sense. So I looked more closely. That soot-colored hair with no shine, those eyes. I was watching it play, and at a difficult passage, I detected the briefest red glow deep in those eyes." Huitaik sighed. "You have been thinking of Father, and his questions about demons?"

"Yes."

"But you know his philosophical questions were just that. Never suggestions."

"Who would know better?" Granny Zim said, which was unanswerable, especially from as filial a son as Huitaik.

"Have you spoken with it? That is, does it know you recognize it for demon-kind?"

"Of course I did! It was I who gave YinYin hints about appearing human."

"Did it give a reason for doing so? Surely you've interrogated it!"

"No. Not yet. My good son, I am truly honored at your caring, but you must remember I've been chief for decades, and teaching twice as long. I know when those below me strive to say what I want to hear. It isn't until they begin to trust me — when the distance between us lessens — that I might hear the truth. I believe it's even harder for a demon, because there is human language to be learned first."

At Huitaik's skeptical look, she patted his hand. "Let me tell you how it came about." And at the end of her story, "Do you see? That is the purest proof that demons truly are drawn to our world by different things. Good things as well as bad. What possible evil could be done with music?"

Huitaik put his work-roughened hands on his thighs. "The ancients are full of warning stories about music that maddens as well as gladdens, that harrows the soul."

"Anyone can do that," Granny Zim scoffed. "Doesn't take a demon. Only talent and intent. And human hearts, as you are aware, can be full of evil."

"I agree that your demon does not appear to be any threat, but have you considered that it chose the most unassuming form deliberately?"

"To what end? I believe if YinYin had evil intent, *she* — I like to grant her human status, she has worked so hard at it — she ought to have befriended that white-eyed wolf of a son the Duke Sinodai sent us, probably because he was too much trouble in the ducal mansion, clever fingers or no."

"That does seem a good sign," Huitaik said cautiously.

"I can see it, you're about to lecture me," Granny Zim said. "You're about to warn me of the dangers of deliberately taking in a demon, as if this white hair of mine covers an empty head."

"Esteemed and honored mother, no one could hear you speak a word and assume your wits had gone wandering. You are as needle-sharp as you ever were. It's just that there is one truth among the rumors about demons that I do believe," Huitaik retorted. "I have traveled this part of the world for forty years, now, and I have seen some strange things. I believe that demons can, and will, invade humans to scour out all their Essence, leaving the empty husk to die. It is also attested by the augurs, who ought to know if anyone does, that they eat souls as well, so that even after death, the dead cannot travel with the others to the King of Hell to be judged and sent to the next life. I respect and esteem you above all others, but are you certain you know what you are doing, Mother?"

"Augurs," Granny Zim said, making a warding motion.

"I know their reputation. But not all of them are anything like Ban Erno the Traitor," Huitaik said. "You know as well as I do that our own Tai Han is the most amiable and good-hearted of men."

Granny Zim acknowledged this with an impatient wave of a gnarled hand. It was true enough; she long suspected that Augur Tai made his comfortable fortune telling people what they wanted to hear, but there was no doubt that his very occasional general predictions usually proved true.

Huitaik went on, "Father always said to be wary of those who let themselves be drawn into imperial politics, which we know Ban Erno did."

They both considered the gruesome history of that augur's end in the imperial Execution Square, but that was after he had brought down the former dynasty. Which, if the stories could be believed, had been corrupt.

Granny Zim waved off far-distant imperial politics. Like the Northern Wars of the past twenty-five years, those belonged to those imperial islanders in the west. "We have strayed from the subject of demons. Those that eat souls are surely the evil demons drawn to blood and lust and so forth. My YinYin was drawn to music. When Kandabin Rareg slipped with the knife while he was repairing a fret, YinYin was in the next courtyard. She never stirred, and did not even spare him a glance when he turned up with a bandage over the fresh wound. That was at harvest moon time. She has been accumulating more human characteristics as day follows day."

"I pray you will be right," Huitaik said, and she knew this was no idle promise. "It—she—certainly played with facility, if not with what I would call expression."

"I believe that will come, as she settles into her human life. She has tastes, now. She avoids mung beans, unless it's soup, and seems to relish milk cakes."

"It does have to be interesting, watching a demon learn."

"The thing I find most interesting is that YinYin seems to be progressing at the same rate as the better students. Is that purposeful, a way to conceal the demon within that little girl's shape, or is this merely a limitation of a non-human learning to be human?"

Huitaik listened as his mother aired her surmises. He had lost his father to pirates, a battle that had nearly lost them First Brother as well, and Mother looked older every year. Every wrinkle on her face, every new white hair he came home to, knotted his heart.

When she had finished, he said, "Tell me at least you've seen to Essence protections."

"Indeed. Trust the nuns for that! The place is stuffed with Essence paper and mighty charms. We have all the protections we need," Granny Zim declared. "And I notice that they do not affect her, as each charm is dedicated to warding evil intent."

"Mother, I will say one more thing. The word 'demon' still conjures up deeds of evil."

"I still believe that there are demons who do no harm, who abide between worlds without disturbing us. So we never hear about them."

"Do we ever hear about demon deeds of merit?" he countered.

She laughed. "Your father asked that once, and do you know what he said? He said, *Is it possible that when demons contribute good, they have another name altogether? After all, they do not call themselves demons. That's our term.* But I know what you will caution. And I promise. At the first sign of trouble, off she goes. I just want to see what a music demon is capable of."

SEVEN

WINTER GAVE WAY TO spring and the first anniversary of the novices' arrival. Focus narrowed to the duet competition. As Granny Zim wandered about, listening and evaluating, her ears caught, more than once, the words "Bu the Ruh."

Her first reaction was amusement, but subsequently, when she detected scorn below the caressing surface tone, she had to bite back an exclamation. She knew her mood was sour. It always was through spring season, after the men sailed southward for the enormous pearls they traded to the west for silk and linen and other commodities the islanders could not grow or make themselves. She always missed her eldest two sons quite sharply, even if she was sometimes relieved to see her third take his restlessness out to sea.

She waited a few days, considering what she'd heard, before approaching First Daughter-in-Law, a sober, hardworking woman who looked older than her fifty years.

"Daughter," she said—causing a blush at the implied compliment, which was sincerely meant. "I'm hearing one of my younger novices called Bu the Ruh, and not necessarily before her face. Are you aware of this matter? Does it require my attention?"

First Daughter-in-Law was *aware* of everything. She did not consider herself qualified to understand everything, and so she seldom interfered directly, a vigilant and perfect guardian whom the novices scarcely perceived.

Her long face lengthened, thick brows drawing together as she said, "It appears that some of the older novices are jealous of Instructor Higar's attention to Lum Bu, though no one argues that she has not earned it."

Granny Zim had placed Bu in Higar's eruh class, attending to qin lessons herself. "Bu is excellent on the eruh," Granny Zim observed.

"That she is. As well as the side flute." First Daughter-in-Law's hands flashed up, miming the horizontally held flute.

"Ah," Granny Zim said, beginning to perceive the whole.

"Instructor Higar is teaching Bu to make silk strings. There are only three who have earned these lessons so far, which, as you yourself decreed, ought to be taught more toward the third year. Bu is often praised for her excellence on the instrument." This was said with an air of question, as both knew it was true.

Granny Zim nodded once, and decided it was time to point out what might not be as obvious to her straightforward daughter-in-law. "Bu is praised loudly for her excellence on the eruh. Not on the flute, which, like the qin and the zither, are the toys of courtiers. Though she plays all three equally well." Especially the qin, Granny Zim was thinking — at least, the signs were there, though Bu was still too tentative to risk the deeper sounds.

First Daughter-in-Law said contritely, "Ought I to chide them? Or leave that to you?"

Granny Zim considered. "I think…I will do nothing. That child is past her thirteenth year, on the way to fourteen, which in some islands is two years from marriageable. Has she had her moon blood yet?"

"That happened before the New Year. She has many older sisters, and knew what to expect and to do."

Granny Zim gave a nod, and then asked casually, "YinYin?"

"No sign of it, but she has not grown, either. We think she was probably younger than we assumed when Sister Suli brought her over, and of course she did not know how old she was. Orphans seldom do."

Granny Zim shook that off, turning her mind back to Bu the Ruh. "Thirteen, almost fourteen. There will be many temptations ahead of her. And many discoveries as the training continues. She might choose any instrument. If she takes to the eruh, what is the harm?"

"Wisely said, Mother Li." As a sign of her profound respect, First Daughter-in-Law used the most formal term for mother, and bowed; she was one of the very few permitted to use Granny Zim's personal name.

"Let's even make it easier," Granny Zim said. "Let it be known that the novices may select their instrument for both aspects of the duet test. They may also select their partner. Let us see if Bu heeds the flatterers and obliges them by permitting herself to be gently jostled into choosing the eruh."

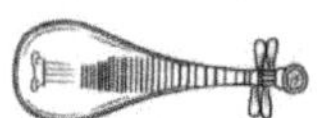

When the weather permitted, Bu loved sitting in a tree to practice. The slight sway, the whispering wind, were perfect accompaniment for the side flute, which was so easily played while perched in a tree. Somewhat less easy but still possible was the notch flute, held vertically. The gourd flute could be played from a tree, but she so disliked its strident, high-pitched cry that she confined its practice to the thick-walled room next to the cellar, and then only until she had mastered her assignment. She did not play it for pleasure.

The lute and eruh were awkward, but the guqin and zither were impossible in trees. She would never disrespect even the oldest, most battered qin by hauling it up on the mighty branches. This ancient instrument required a flat surface, with the left end resting on its legs, and the neck end at the edge of the table. It also required solitude as well as correct posture from its player.

The flute had begun to speak to her. It was like a bird in that way. Birds all looked alike, quick-moving blurs through the air, but she could tell them apart by their songs as they sang and chattered from tree to tree. The flute spoke like a bird, and like a laughing child. It was the eruh that crooned like a mother to a fretful babe, or wailed like grief, its heartfelt emotions sliding one from another with a stroke and a change of key.

The notch flute sometimes spoke, but it was distant, still. Beautiful, but not bird-like.

The drums were just drums to her, a method to sharpen her sense of rhythm. When she played the drums, it felt like someone plodding uphill, and she could sense from Instructor Ding's dry manner that his evaluation was the same as hers.

No. Lower. Whereas Cricket's drumming reminded her of people dancing, or marching, and Cricket's lessons tended to be longer than anyone else's, though two other boys strove to compete with him.

The bells were too solemn. Important. Harbingers of the unseen world when played right, their metallic bongs shivering on the air long after they were struck, as if the mysterious door between the underworld and this world remained open in the poised moment.

The zither…it was full of lovely sound, but it was the qin that spoke in the cadences of poetry, the kind that could nick the heart when you weren't looking, and make it bleed then heal over again with fragrant osmanthus or lotus.

The more she played the instruments, the more she began to comprehend that she did not yet understand them. Their wisdom was still hidden, just as words from adults could be comprehended individually, but their gathered meaning often exceeded her grasp. She consoled herself with the reminder that this was only the end of her first year. She had nine to go. Wisdom would sure be hers in ten years.

As the duet examination approached, there were more immediate concerns. Such as the vital question of partners. Bu had assumed that YinYin would be her partner in both method and meaning, which had become the shorthand used by the students. "Meaning" being expression.

She said after the auspicious day of the examination had been announced, "What instruments should we choose?"

YinYin turned to her. "I want to play bells. Cricket said bells and drums can compete for meaning. I want to try that."

"Oh?" It startled her, the fact that Cricket and YinYin had been talking, apparently a lot, if they were already partners for one of the duets.

"Will you play with me for the method test?" she asked tentatively, comprehending that she could no longer expect YinYin to be convenient when wanted.

"I will play with you."

The bell rang Horse first hour, and they had separate lessons, one to strings, the other to winds.

Bu hid a sigh as she walked to where Instructor Higar held lessons. This instructor had been saying many complimentary things about Bu playing the eruh, especially with Tensi Yi Nis, who was of so exalted a birth that she had three names: the family name, Tensi, and a generation name, Yi, as well as her personal name, Nis, which she only permitted the other silk-born friends to use. Even Granny Zim had only two names: Zim and Li.

Outside of eruh class, they had nothing to say to one another, but when Instructor Higar was there, Yi Nis said sweetly and softly, "I would be so honored if Lum Bu would condescend to play with me for the examination," and similar flattering things.

Instructor Higar and Yi Nis had even chosen the piece, one of Kanda's most beloved melodies, "The Cry of the Osprey." Bu liked it very much. But she preferred to play it on qin. And alone.

Alone was not possible. And Instructor Higar said one morning, when she bade the two girls demonstrate the piece for her, "Lum Bu, this is an especial honor, for here you are, barely your first year, and you are already learning a court piece."

Bu sensed herself being swept into a decision, the way the tide could carry a boat, even if you tried to paddle in the other direction.

In the days leading up to the examination, Chief Musician Zim sometimes introduced questions. Three days before the examination, she addressed the novices by reading from *The Dialects of Enlightenment*, emphasizing Kanda's declaration that music was the harmonization of Heaven and earth, as ritual reflected the order of Heaven and earth.

She said, "I want you all to meditate, before your duets, on the ancient saying that a single voice cannot produce harmony. Harmony is by necessity the alliance of two or more."

Everyone bowed and thanked her for sharing her wisdom, but later that day, Instructor Ding, with whom Bu had scarcely exchanged a hundred words since her arrival, called them all into the hall and said abruptly, "Mana Ta teaches in the *Ancient Annals* that to understand rhythm, the musician must first truly hear the sound generated by the wind, which proves that the world itself is a musical instrument."

He looked around. Cricket shifted from side to side. Instructor Ding's voice lightened in tone as he said, "You have an observation to make, Cricket?"

Cricket struggled to find words that would sound scholarly, for otherwise the silk-born boys would be scoffing for days. He fell back on quotation, as they all did. "Our tutor gave us a lesson to copy from the *Ancient Annals*, where it said that from nature's perspective, this earthly music is emotion-less."

"That is correct. It seems you are gaining a modicum of knowledge from your calligraphy lessons. What does that suggest to you?"

"That emotion is what humans add," Cricket said.

"Correct. In addition, I require you to contemplate Mana Ta's second exhortation, that the wellspring of human music and the arts of carving of wood, or the making of porcelain vases, are alike in that when the carving is finished, and the vase is shaped and painted, these have been created at the expense of all the wood that has been carved away, the clay that was cast aside, the paint left on the board unused. Only the music of nature is complete and undiminished."

Here, Instructor Ding scowled, having caught one of the silk-born boys rolling his eyes. "You were no doubt about to interrupt your fellow novices' listening to me in order to complain about how many times you've written that passage?"

"No, Instructor Ding."

"No? Good. Then you may merely copy it out fifty times, instead of a hundred. Perhaps tomorrow you will reflect on the wisdom of interrupting others' learning, even if you choose to remain pig-ignorant yourself. Dismissed!"

The boys moved out in a clump, and Cricket had almost made his escape before a heavy hand landed on his shoulder. Cricket looked up into the taller boy's face, two silk-born friends at either shoulder, and forced out some breezy words, "Ayah, why don't I copy those for you? I need the practice."

His reward was a broad smile, and a loosening of that grip to a friendly pat. "Good boy, good boy." It was said in the mode of addressing a pet dog.

Cricket accepted that with an internal shrug, the way he'd learned to accept the kicks and curses of the wharf uncles when he was small. That was the world. And besides, when he did such chores, his writing did get faster and better. That was something, for a wharf-bred brat.

For the remainder of the day's lessons, each instructor had a piece of wisdom to add, after which the novices went away to practice, those determined to excel frantically striving to express whatever it was they had been taught in their rehearsals.

Instructor Higar waited until two days before the

examination before imparting her bit of wisdom.

She faced the expectant novices and said composedly, her hands folded in front showing the width of her sleeves, "Kanda of the Path teaches that there are two types of music, pure and vulgar. Pure is elegant. It is written and performed with taste. It is the ritual music of the court and the temple. On the other hand, most other types of music, especially that of the common folk, is vulgar. Pure music inspires orderly and harmonious emotions, while vulgar music excites lower lusts and causes disorder. Tensi Yi Nis and Lum Ru, come forward and demonstrate for us the purity of 'The Cry of the Osprey.'" As she spoke, she pointed Bu toward the eruh, and Yi Nis toward the zither.

Bu complied, striving to infuse her eruh's sound with purity and elegance, though its part had been written to serve as support to the zither. Support was necessary to complete the whole.

When they had finished, Instructor Higar gave a definitive nod, saying, "Elegantly done, the both of you."

That meant Bu as well!

Bu sat down, aware of whispers, "Yi Nis, you are so clever," and "Ah, we know which two will rank highest in expression!"

Bu heard that with misgivings, for she had not played with expression. Her concentration had been on her posture, her hands, and drawing true notes, exactly as written, from the backs of those strings that she had made herself: method.

When they were released to their own practice, Bu went to YinYin. "I did so want to make eruh my method examination, but I don't think I can, or that's two people I would disappoint, and one an instructor! I do like the eruh. But its strength is a single melodic line, and how much expression can I get with that? I did so want to do expression with you, playing qin."

YinYin said, "We can both do method. In counterpoint."

"Oh?" Bu tipped her head. "In counterpoint. Yes! I see! Oh, that's so clever. We'll be sticking strictly to what is written, but the counterpoint makes it…" She wound her hands in a circle. "Interesting. Which instruments?"

"You will want qin," YinYin said, to Bu's agreement. "I will take a wind." She said abruptly, in the same tone, "I have a gift for you."

"A gift!" Bu repeated, delighted, followed by instant remorse. "I've nothing for you."

"Something I found on the ground. There is no money exchange in this gift. That means you may find a thing for me. There will be no money exchange. If you find milk cakes, I'll like that gift very much."

"But we get those every time Phoenix Moon is full," Bu protested scrupulously.

"My gift is very common, too. I found it at the top of the mountain."

"The top of the mountain," Bu repeated. "When did you go there?"

"I go often," YinYin said.

Bu accepted that. It seemed YinYin had fun while Instructor Higar required Bu to come for silk string making. Ayah!

YinYin placed an object on Bu's palms. It felt like…"A rock?"

"Its name is *crystal*." YinYin sketched the characters for "brilliant water" in the air, though that meant nothing to Bu. "You have to look through it."

Confused, Bu brought the rock closer to her face. It was colorless, except for sun glints. She pressed it against the bridge of her nose. "It is…*clear*. And I see other shapes."

"Turn it very slowly," YinYin said. "Very. It should…"

Bu gasped. The broken shapes altered, then sharpened. Bu moved the crystal with incremental slowness—and there! Suddenly there was YinYin's face, looking at her out of two very black eyes. Was that what people's eyes looked like, seen clearly? Bu shifted her attention from those to YinYin's robe. She could see every detail—she could see the fabric, the *weave!*

She gasped again—and everything broke into distortions, with lances of sunlight making her blink. "Oh. I moved," she said.

"Practice with it," YinYin said. "There is another thing. We will see it tomorrow, but we have to go before the sun comes up."

"Oh? What is it we will see?"

"The toss," YinYin said carefully. "I have learned that it is a very important part of spring planting."

Bu's curiosity withered. "I know what the toss is. It's when the rice seedlings are pulled apart, and planted in the paddy once the water is let in. I had to help with that."

YinYin said, "Did you sing, too?"

"Sing? No. We could not even talk, because Madam Lum—

that is, First Mother — thought we worked more slowly if we chattered, and Fifth Sister always complained…" She dropped the subject. "Singing?"

"I was told," YinYin said with painstaking care, "that it will only be two or three days, until the seedlings are planted. I heard it this morning. Come hear it tomorrow with me. What you said about the eruh. I think you should hear it, too."

Planting rice had been an arduous chore, working in the heat of late spring, and inevitably being scolded for being too slow. However, she reminded herself, being a friend meant sharing, and if YinYin wanted to share this big-island spring planting, then Bu would share. "I hope it's not too far," she said doubtfully.

"On the other side of the mountain."

The temple, being quite high up, lay on the southwest slope of the mountain. The northwest slope was beyond a certain crevasse, or canyon, that wasn't far from where she sat in her tree to practice the side flute.

They went on to their regular tasks, Bu intermittently pulling the crystal out whenever she had a moment, and twisting it and turning it as she peered through it. It startled her unpleasantly when she brought faces into clarity — and caught staring eyes, and twisted mouths, or questioning faces. People looked so very different from how she had imagined them, her impression based mainly on voice and how they moved. Yi Nis's open contempt stung as she said, "What are you playing with, Bu?"

"It is a rock called crystal," Bu said, and tucked it back into her sleeve.

"Might we go over our piece now, unless you are too busy with your rock?" Yi Nis said in that sweet voice that had a barb beneath it.

Yi Nis reminded Bu of First Sister, who it was always best not to answer. She went to fetch her eruh, promising herself that after this duet she was going to avoid playing with Yi Nis forever more, unless paired with her in an assignment.

The next morning, the east had barely begun to blue with weak light when YinYin shook Bu awake.

Bu scrambled into her clothes and rinsed her mouth with a waiting cup of cold tea, wondering irritably if YinYin had stayed up half the night, to be so awake and ready now. In silence the two moved up the familiar path and over two bridges. At least there was her crystal to experiment with, and no one there to make comments about playing with rocks.

When they crossed the last bridge and rounded a shouldered slope, Bu found that they had left the tangled fig forest among the rocks for an entirely different world of uneven shades of green.

YinYin paused, and said, "It's still dark. Only a few of the spring planting people are here. Look."

Bu reached into her sleeve pocket, and pulled out the crystal. By now she'd found the best place to place her fingers as she raised it to her eyes. A little turning and twisting—

She gasped. What she'd taken as uneven stripes of different greens was in fact a long slope beautifully terraced in rows and scallops, water filled in each paddy.

She turned back, spying the tangled great fronds of the oldest, highest fig trees sticking up on the other side of the shoulder. Some of those thick, shiny fronds were almost as long as she was. "How could it be so different?"

"This is a fire mountain," YinYin said. "In…years and years and years before, a dragon came forth, that way." She pointed toward Kanda's Peak at an angle. "The dragon flew away, leaving fire rock to spill all down this way." YinYin's hands smoothed down parallel to the terraced paddies. "All the rocks tumbled to that side, and the fig trees liked the rocks to climb over. This other side took a very long time to cool off for things to grow."

Bu was going to ask how YinYin knew all that, then remembered that YinYin had had a year of writing and reading. Feeling more ignorant than she ever had, Bu said, "Do you think I can learn to write? And read?"

YinYin, seen through the crystal, blinked. For less than a heartbeat Bu thought she saw pinpoints of red glow in her eyes, but that was gone, and YinYin said, "Maybe? I can show you my lesson book, and you can try?" Then she held out her hand. "Here they come."

A snake-train of rice farmers worked their way up a pathway from a cluster of frond-roofed domiciles far below, on the hitherto unseen northern shore of the island.

The people divided off to begin the back-breaking work of peeling off the tightly bound clumps of seedlings that had been tossed in the middle of each paddy, and planting them one by one a hand's distance apart. About the time most of the people had dispersed, a lone voice rang out in the quiet morning air. He had a rich, beautiful voice as he sang a planting song.

At first one by one, then in twos and fours, others began singing it, joining him—then breaking off to sing in round. Two, then three, then four parts, so the single melodic line wove itself into something altogether different.

Bu hummed under her breath, and then picked up the song, singing softly in a descant counterpoint—the notes she might play on the eruh. Could she take what she had learned here, to the Osprey song?

"This music is sung by farmers," YinYin asked. "Is it vulgar?"

"Not to my ears." Bu lowered the crystal and clasped her hands around it. "But then I'm vulgar. That is, vulgar born, which to those who understand ranks means I remain vulgar. Madam Lum would scold terribly if she knew I had given the nuns the family name as if I had a right to it."

YinYin said, "I don't understand."

Bu remembered that YinYin, like Cricket, had a single name, Yin. Strictly speaking, she ought to claim the same, for Madam Lum had said countless times when she was angry with Bu for missing dust in a corner, or tripping and dropping a bucket of offal, that Bu was luckless and worthless, and despite all Madam's care and patience, Bu would never be good enough to be written into the Lum ancestry.

Rather than explain all that, she said, "It's just that I gave the family name before the audition because I thought it was required. I was afraid they'd send me away if I didn't." She lifted the crystal again, and brought the workers on their terraced paddies into focus. "How could so clear and so beautiful a melody be vulgar? For the singing brings me pure feelings of harmony, and patience, and awareness of growing things."

Bu remembered one of the sutras often repeated. Now the much-heard words glowed to meaning like a lantern lit up. "I see," she said, and laughed a little, sweeping the crystal back and forth over the slope. "I see! This singing is what that Mana Ta meant in saying that music inspires the kind of pleasure that humans cannot do without."

YinYin stirred at the word *humans*, but when Bu turned in question, YinYin peered off toward the singing farmers at their work.

EIGHT

YOU MIGHT THINK (SAID the storyteller) that I'm going to give you nine more years of lessons. But if that had happened, do you think I would have a story? Those waiting for heroes and villains, dragons and tigers, fire and clouds, I thank you for your patience as we finish establishing our ground.

Lum Bu, as you have no doubt seen, would regard herself as a worm in that ground, feeling safest buried in the good soil. Granny Zim would not claim to be hero or villain. Cricket would insist that he was a hero. And you know that YinYin is a demon.

Though nobles could play for pleasure, performance was the musician's purpose. Every novice knew that.

It was the *intent* that varied. For Tensi Yi Nis, performance meant appearing in court, beautifully groomed from jeweled hairpins to embroidered slippers, artfully and skillfully playing to catch the idle eye of whatever powerful noble her parents directed her toward. Courtly music was a trapping, like those hairpins and embroidered shoes. Kandabin Rareg's intent was to use music to mask the fact that he would never be a scholar. Music gave access to places of power, if you were well born, handsome in dress and demeanor, diverting, and talented. And besides scholarly debate, poetry, calligraphy, and painting on silk, what is more diverting than music?

Even emperors, as you know, crave the distraction of

entertainment.

Then there were those who looked forward to a safe, comfortable life as a hireling, preferably by some very wealthy patron who would provide luxury as well as generous pay. The narrow path between these two mountains was trod by those for whom music was an end in itself.

"The interesting thing," Granny Zim observed over tea to Second Daughter-in-Law, who had walked up Suanek Way to listen to the duets, "is that those who come up here as children sometimes leave as adults with a very different aim. It's my experience that between the second and sixth years, the best will respond to the call of music. If not by then, even the most talented will end up some day in some tea house, or duke's house, playing to the cat."

She grunted and winced to her feet, then swept into the hall.

The novices sat in orderly rows, hands neatly posed, their breathing proper. The performance instruments had been brought in and set at one side, adjacent the bells and the big drums. There was one of each type, as duets in this assignment could not be on the same instrument.

Method was the first half of the testing. Six pairs played before Bu was at last called. She and YinYin performed upon qin and notch flute, each note precise, but they varied from the expected by playing in strict counterpoint. After quick looks gauging the instructors, who displayed no signs of disapproval, several novices exchanged uneasy glances from the sides of their eyes, and one or two lifted their chins in challenge. The wiser of these two was not merely fulminating about the competition; this performance had set a standard that must be matched. A challenge.

Counterpoint appeared again, most often with drums. Instructor Ding's austere face did not exactly smile—he never smiled at novices—but the lines in his face eased with approval.

The second half of the examination was meaning, or expression, which permitted embellishment as well as variation in tone and tempo. The young often assume that big emotions and thunderous playing impress the most, and it was no different today. They were as yet too inexperienced to comprehend the emptiness in assuming theatrical emotions that have in reality never been felt.

The silk-born all chose court songs, again nothing

unexpected.

The first surprise was again offered by Bu.

Instructor Higar gestured toward Bu and Yi Nis. The pair settled down, and Bu drew the bow in the long note that set tone and tempo for Yi Nis to demonstrate her expertise. Bu was supposed to play the melody through once, in strict method, providing support as Yi Nis played the "Osprey" melody three times, shifting key half a step upward and adding carefully rehearsed embellishments.

But this duet was to test expression of both players.

Halfway through that first melody, the eruh echoed the melody in a higher key, the string version of a descant. Yi Nis glanced, startled as the eruh responded to Bu's touch, playing the melody simply, in round, adding no embellishments. But the overall effect was sprightly, lovely, the two instruments not quite talking to each other, but speaking past one another, like a pair of dancers performing the same dance, one a few steps ahead of the other, facing opposite directions.

In other words, they played not only as equals, but it was Bu's skill that bound the two melodic lines into partnership.

They finished, Yi Nis's mouth in a straight line that did not relax even when the instructors all praised the piece. Bu could hear in Yi Nis's breathing how irritated she was. However Bu had stayed within the assignment. As for not telling Yi Nis what she was going to do, that was for partners. Yi Nis had not once regarded her as a partner — further, Yi Nis knew it, and sent a questioning glance toward Instructor Higar, whose direction she had followed. The instructor did not look her way, but two spots of color glowed in her cheeks.

For the first time a very small rebellion stirred deep within Bu. They were here to make music, and every lesson had some mention of being true to music. She could feel in the susurration of whispers that she had stayed true to the music.

"Rareg?" Granny Zim asked, severely suppressing her smile of triumph.

Rareg and one of his followers played a martial piece on gourd flute and drum. It was rousing, gaining general approbation, and so it went, until Cricket and YinYin got up, one moving to the drums, the other to the bells. Now, that was an interesting combination, the instructors thought, though the boys shrugged off Cricket as a jokester errand boy, and the girls dismissed silent, unexpressive YinYin as a nonentity.

Cricket had already played method to one of the other boys

on the side flute. Everyone knew he was excellent on the drums. But what could he get from flat-faced YinYin, who was the personification of method?

It began as competition.

Ayah, it's important to state that Cricket and Bu were too young for the duet—or duel—of attraction. Cricket's interest in Bu was not even remotely for her beanpole person, or her squinting face. He had come to the temple school because of the promise of food every day, and no beatings, but he was the first to discover the power of music through rhythm. He was also ambitious, and his nascent plan was to draw the best novices around him, with him as leader. He knew Bu was a follower.

He was not at all certain about YinYin.

The piece they had agreed on was an adaptation of one of the many poems about the famous General Liad Il, who had gone to war with his wife at his side, herself a famous archer. But though the general won his greatest battle, he lost his beloved wife, and so laid aside the trappings of war to become a monk dedicated to the Snow Crane.

This was a martial piece, yet melancholy, foreshadowing the bitter victory. Cricket began with a whisper of wind over the drumheads. YinYin's bells echoed softly, steadily, peaceful temple bells.

The thunderous storm of battle broke, Cricket pounding away until the listeners' teeth rattled in their heads. He did not have quite the command that he needed for that piece—he had not yet mastered the complicated rhythms over all five drums, but he never missed a beat.

YinYin's bell reiterated the temple rhythms—the eternity of the heavens—gradually gaining in tone and power until the crashing rumble that signified the fall of Silver Commander of Virtuous Bravery Ranek, surrounded by a mountain of corpses. The bells resounded, each note so true the metal reverberated with the purity of crystal.

And there, despite Cricket's thunderous display of the General's wild grief, the bells in their mourning tolling, tang bong tolling commandeered the listeners, reminding them that death comes to all humans. Only the unseen world remains, the heavens above, the underworld below. The novices sat, rapt, and Granny Zim heard, for the first time, what her demon might be capable of.

Cricket tried to win back the focus; General Liad could

rage against the heavens, he could carry battle to every island, but there was no bringing General Liad's beloved archer back in this life. YinYin darted back and forth, braid swinging, mallet striking precise and true, subduing the drums until both players brought the grieving general at last to the mountain, and peace.

Then YinYin sat down beside Bu, impassive as always.

Absolute silence seized the listeners, past the time the last ringing echo died away.

"Well done," Granny Zim said. "Dismissed to your next class."

Granny Zim retired that night laughing to herself. She had not expected that level of expression until at least the third or fourth year. Was it due to the demon, or was the demon influenced by what was already there?

She could not discuss this conundrum with anyone until Second Son returned at the new year. Instead, she changed the schedule once again. Lessons were longer. Stricter. Further, she broke her own rule, and began choosing this or that novice to play with her, something she ordinarily did not do until the fifth year.

The air of challenge spread to them all.

The Year of the Pig raced by, and when the men returned again, Granny Zim brought Huitaik over to listen.

He was startled. "Your students have always been excellent," he said later, when they had returned to the Zim house. "I ask not to slight anyone in the past, or to hint that things were sloppy in the past, but are these novices advancing more rapidly?"

"They *are*," Granny Zim gloated. "They are, they are, they are. Oh, some days I feel young again—except when I'm hauling this old carcass to the privy for the third time during the night. I'm already permitting certain of them to join selected local musicians, who won't encourage bad habits. That gets them used to the chaos of crowds, and to playing with others trained elsewhere. I'm thinking of giving these novices the fundamentals of composing, something that ordinarily waits for the fifth or sixth year. I've heard some experimenting that officially I can't notice, and I *long* to hear what they can come up with."

Huitaik had been on the watch, as Granny Zim had been, as they entered the house, but he slid the door back and took a quick look out, then shut it again before saying, "I will be very interested to hear what your demon comes up with. You know it's said that only humans create art."

"I know," she said. "I know. And I never believed it. Neither did Teg. He always said that humans made art that humans recognized. Who is to say that eagles don't make art that is only visible from the sky?"

"All I ask is that demon art—if such exists—be not destructive to our kind."

"Oh, I think we can trust our fellow humans for providing plenty of destruction," Granny Zim said, leaning over to gently caress a new white scar on his arm. "Are the pirates getting bolder while all the northwest fights one another?"

Huitaik shook his head. "That I cannot rightly answer. Harbor rumors are always conflicting. What I can tell you is that this was not from pirates."

"Don't try to tell me it was a shipboard accident. I know a sword slice when I see it. I tended Teg's too often, especially in those early, wild days after the fall of the empire."

"Yes, it was from a sword, but that fleet claimed to be imperials."

Granny Zim scowled. "The Kun empire is finished! That's what the Northern Wars are about! Is that not right?"

"It is, but the capital island has never relinquished its claims. Which is one reason for their wars. The other being the usual greed, everyone claiming everyone else over there."

Granny Zim remembered Teg telling her that the problem was, those huge islands in the northwest were all too close together. The year he had taken her with him, she'd even seen the truth of that. In those waters there were always bumps on the horizon, unlike their own small set of islands, surrounded by nothing but sea.

"We were attacked off White Jade, which has remained open for trade all along. We'll have to send scouts in future next year, to discover whether or not they are still trading. If we have to go one of the farther islands to trade off our pearls, you know the risks."

None better. Teg had made it plain: either they cut short their harvesting of the great pearls, which in itself was arduous, for they went to a different island each year, in a far-off cluster. Some were more difficult to get to than the others. It was therefore either fetch half their cargo, or else get a full cargo, but trade at such a distance that they might have to winter over.

Granny Zim had learned on her single voyage that Lu Teg had to navigate by the stars until they reached the pearl grounds far, far to the south, which only they knew about—the knowledge passed down from Lu father to Lu son, written nowhere. Their scouts were vigilant the last weeks before landing, making sure no one had followed them. Then came the difficult crossing to the western clusters of islands, always with an eye to the stars, for once First Archer's Arrow touched Phoenix Moon, it meant they must depart to cross east again, before the last of the easy winds gave way before the terrible winter storms out of the north.

The door opened a crack, and there was Third Daughter-in-Law, carrying a tray herself, when usually she dispatched a servant. "Do I intrude?" her honey-sweet voice intruded. "I beg forgiveness—this daughter is so absent and stupid, but this humble empty-head assumed honored mother and esteemed elder brother-in-law might welcome fresh tea, as Cook just brought out some of the leaves my dear husband brought back especially for you..."

She shouldered her way in, dropping hints for compliments, which both politely gave. After she withdrew, mother and son looked at one another. "Do you think she heard?" he whispered so softly that Granny Zim could barely hear him.

"You did check the door. But..." She stared thoughtfully at the rice-paper covered windows, which usually showed shadows against them—if the light came from outside. But, she realized now, the light came from the lamp beside her cushion. "I don't know."

Third Daughter-in-Law said nothing the following day, nor the next. If anything, she became even sweeter in her flattery, and her occasional offers to help with the making of new robes, or arranging for winter shoes for growing feet. Granny Zim was the more assiduous in thanking her, and complimenting her for her contributions, because she did not trust this almond-eyed simperer whose single daughter was showing signs of being in every way exactly like her mother.

Weeks slid by, then months, a year, then two years, and she began to doubt her judgment, wondering if old age had made her intolerant. Of course her own children would never admit it even if she asked. They were too filial. She forced herself to include Third Daughter-in-Law more often, even though the sound of her voice clanged like a much-repaired string below the sweetness. Old age is cruel, she'd say with a sigh to Teg, when she played alone on her bridge. What was she missing?

The novices' skills refined as fast as the instructors could teach. Granny Zim discovered that in playing with the better of the novices, her own skills, too-long resting on old excellence — also sharpened. She felt it in shoulders and hands, but those small pangs were worth the heady exhilaration that she'd thought forever gone, along with her black hair.

The exhilaration was not confined to her. The novices, in advancing toward adulthood, became aware of one another in the usual ways, which both heightened the competition and shortened the personal distances in the ways of nature for centuries untold.

Not all the novices discovered romance. YinYin, whose growth now matched the rest, maintained the same impassivity whenever anyone tried to get close to her. Bu, on the other hand, was so entranced by the world of letters and books that she spent all her free moments hunched over scrolls.

Once Granny Zim understood that the crystal Bu was constantly playing with actually enabled her to see, she passed the word to the instructors to permit her to use it if she chose to. Bu was also included in the reading and writing classes, though she was always at the very bottom. It took much effort, and many tears, to manage holding the crystal with one hand while tracing characters with a finger. Then, even more difficult, attempting to write without getting vertigo; if the crystal shifted the slightest, the letters danced on the paper.

She was at, or near, the top in every other class. Including drums, for Cricket wouldn't let her off. He still had dreams of himself, Bu, and YinYin leading the school, based on an inchoate idea that those who had been born at the bottom of the ranks ought to rule in *some* way.

It would be wrong to say that Bu did not care for rank. She did. She cried bitterly as soon as soon as she was alone if she did not perform at the top in tests and competitions. Though it wasn't the rank in itself that gnawed at her, it was her obvious failure to achieve the sound she heard in her head. Then she would short her reading to intensify her practice.

Though she was well respected by the other novices within the context of learning, for she was always willing to share, when purely social occasions were suggested she was never there. One could say that in her heart she was still Squint, the luckless unwanted sixth daughter, which kept her from making the attempt, but that would not explain how vital her music had become.

She had slowly made the discovery that the instruments not only spoke to her, but she could also speak back. No, she could speak *through* them. Self-expression through words was impossible for all the reasons we have seen. But music could serve where words could not. Every assignment, no matter how technical, became a vessel through which she could pour the emotions she had constrained within her since she was small.

All that young passion on the wondering cusp of adult life flowed through music. When she wasn't practicing, she slowly discovered reading, which opened the door to the unseen world.

By the time she passed her fifteenth year, she had begun to read everything she could find.

Everything. Including old, dusty scrolls left behind by YinYin when the latter was summoned away. It seemed to Bu that YinYin was very interested in the unseen world, too, which included the subject of demons.

NINE

IT WAS TWO WEEKS after Grave-Sweeping Day, traditionally observed by the women of the islands, when they woke to change.

The men had departed with good, strong spring winds the week previous to Grave-Sweeping Day. This was three months into the Year of the Tiger. Dawn had barely lifted the darkness in the east when a small granddaughter tore into the bedroom where Granny Zim habitually slept on the platform next to her daughter Linon and First Daughter-in-Law, during the last cold weeks before spring, once the men were gone.

"Grandmother! First Aunt!" the child cried. "Come, come! Everybody says they're going to kill us all!" And she began to wail as she ran out again.

There was no time to pin braids up, or change out of nightclothes. Zim Linon, frowning ferociously as she pulled a robe over her night gear, stalked out ahead of the others. First Daughter-in-Law schooled her temper and helped her mother-in-law rise and pull a cloak around her. "It can't be…the imperials? Can it? Aren't they still at war with themselves?"

"Pirates," Granny Zim said bitterly, "would be worse."

"We haven't…" First Daughter-in-Law pressed her fingertips to her forehead.

"Haven't practiced to hide the children for decades," Granny Zim muttered as they hurried down the hall to the nearest window facing the harbor. The Zim house, the primary house in the village, had been built into the side of the mountain high above all the others, its wings connected by ancient wicker bridges. At the top, the family bedrooms, below that, the family chambers, and below that, mostly hidden by the tangle of mighty trunks, the servants and service rooms. The kitchen was off to one side, opening to a cliff turned into a terrace, for summer cooking.

All the windows had been pushed wide along that upper floor. Sticks propped them open, letting in chilly air, as the Zim women and Lu wives gazed out at the gray-green ocean, on which a line of ships stretched from beyond both harbor promontories. For once even Third Daughter-in-Law seemed stunned, Granny Zim thought grimly as she turned away, shivering.

"I've tea ordered," Second Daughter-in-Law said, joining them. "And hot food. Come away, honored Mother-in-Law Zim. You'll take cold standing here. Sister Linon is raising the harbor roamers. I heard her issuing orders."

"And the children?" Granny Zim asked sharply.

"Being gathered as well."

"What are those ships?" asked Third Daughter-in-Law, abandoning her customary honeyed lisp. "Why are they here? And why are the children being gathered?"

Granny Zim considered before answering. Third Daughter-in-Law, as yet, only had the one daughter, whom she tended to forget about unless she could use the child in some way, to gain attention. And when she paid attention to that child, it was invariably to exhort her about her looks. But even that showed love, though it was a form of love Granny Zim thoroughly disliked.

Granny Zim said, "You are much too young to remember, but the imperials used to come for tribute every five years. They stopped when the dynasty fell. It seems they, or someone claiming the old dragon standard, is back again."

They peered westward once more. The light, already brighter, picked out the golden dragon on the long banners, waving in the rising wind.

"I don't understand when you say tribute. Does that mean they will take away my sapphire hairpins, and the silk shoes my dear husband brought me from the Silk Isles?"

"No," Granny Zim said, childhood memories welling up, fears and questions she had thought forgotten. Her own mother, putting her hands either side of her face, and saying, "You children are our greatest treasure. To them, you'd merely be slaves. You must endure down in the caves where the rats and snakes live, until we call for you."

"They have those things. Better things. They would take our pearls if they could—but they get their share from the Silk Islands traders I was told long ago. What they want," Granny Zim drew a breath, "is *people*. They pick and choose the handsomest and the strongest and most skilled among the young, and take them away to slavery."

Third Daughter-in-Law dashed away, muttering, "My daughter is the prettiest girl on the island. *No one* is going to…"

"What can we do?" Second Daughter-in-Law asked, more quietly. "We can't fight them. We have no defenses."

Granny Zim sighed. "What defenses we used to have are so long unused, we might as well say there are none. The island itself has been our defense since the Kun Dynasty fell. You have to understand that the rare pirate who comes by doesn't see anything but our trees on this side, and while they might try to navigate the rocks on the north side, they would see at a glance that it's all rice farming. If pirates wanted rice, they would be traders, eh?"

She got the expected smile, but it was perfunctory.

"From the sea, we're a merely a rocky cluster among uncounted clusters of small islands. We're not worth robbing, which is an impression we want to keep, which is why the only fine building visible is the temple, and it has no visible gold. It looks austere from the west side, and it's all the way at the top, so pirates sail on by. As for these out there now… My daughter will soon tell us what they want."

They peered down at where a series of boats approached the primary pier in an orderly line. Three tiny figures advanced along the pier, Granny Zim's daughter Linon, the headwoman, and her two huskiest assistants, both women taller than she was, and both adept with bow and spear.

Granny Zim said, "I'd better get up to the temple and warn the novices."

"I will help you dress," First Daughter-in-Law offered.

By the time they'd climbed the short distance to the temple, the nuns—specifically the dauntingly tall, strong one who handled the bells—had gathered the novices in the hall.

The prioress, a tiny, very elderly woman with snow-white hair, had emerged from the inner chambers of the temple.

Granny Zim heard her quavering voice as she entered from the back. "…days, the music novices would dress as novices, or join the children as directed. Once your chief… ayah, she has come."

Granny Zim bowed low to the venerable prioress, who was reverently helped to a cushion by her two attendants.

Rareg rose, bowed to the prioress and to Granny Zim, then said, "Is it true that those ships are flying the dragon banner? We were not permitted to look before there was enough light."

"It is true," Granny Zim said. "Until we hear otherwise, we'll assume they are here to demand tribute."

"Tribute?"

"What's that?"

"Is it slave-hunting?"

"You might as well call it that—"

Granny Zim nodded at Instructor Ding, who rapped sharply with his strong hand upon the big drum, causing everyone to jump.

"Do we need to review first-month lessons in deportment?" Granny Zim asked into the sudden silence. And when they bowed and apologized in unison, she said, "We don't yet know for certain. From what I recall from a long time ago…" She closed her eyes, the image of Teg so close in all senses it cost her a sharp pang. Briefly, so briefly, there was his arm slung around her waist, his scent, a mixture of sweat and his favorite tea and salt-laden hair, as they looked across an unfamiliar island belonging to some western clan or kingdom, Teg's voice murmuring in her ear, *These are war ships, yes. But not all. And that is not an attack formation, just as this is not an invasion — unless the locals are mad enough to give them trouble. It's a tribute gathering. And that's a defensive line, to keep someone from slipping past in the night. See those big ships in the middle, with the big bellies? Those are troop ships. They'll carry the tribute in those: horses, cows, pigs, people, whatever is fairest and strongest. Trunks and trunks and trunks of valuables, but not from our islands. All we grow are people and figs, and just enough rice to feed us.* And he'd laughed before giving the command to sail.

Granny Zim suppressed the memory and said, "I saw troop ships midway along what they call a defensive line, which will keep even a single boat from slipping by. In the past, because we make or delve or grow nothing the emperors want, they claimed people as tribute."

A little susurrus, quickly stifled.

She nodded slightly, then went on. "They searched among our young people, and took away the comeliest, the strongest, and those who had whatever skill they were searching for. They always claimed it was for ten years' service, but you must understand, no one *ever* came back."

A quick hissing, as quickly stifled.

"Therefore, I want a few of you to dress as novices. Enough to equal the number of beds and places at a glance. The rest of you are going to descend into the caverns we used in the past to hide our young people."

With that, the division was made, and those chosen to remain (scrawny, squint-faced Bu among them) were put to work turning the music school into temple space, for the treaty the imperials had first imposed on the islands excluded temples from tribute. "We don't know if these will heed the treaty, but we will prepare as if they will," Granny Zim said.

"Are they going to shave our heads?" Yi Nis asked the other girls chosen to remain in the temple—she being horse-faced, with rabbit teeth.

"If it keeps us from getting taken away, I'll go first," the daughter of a tea merchant responded shortly. "Hair grows back."

"But the nuns—"

Granny Zim entered, interrupting, "Have you not seen in all these years up here that only three of the nuns shave their heads? Everyone else wears the head covering."

Bu remained silent, as she could not discern whether or not there was a dark line of hair bisecting the dull gray-blue head covering from the blur of faces, but the others muttered shame-facedly. It was the silk-born who scarcely noticed the nuns, except to regard them as servants.

Granny Zim could see from huge pupils in wide eyes and shallow breathing that they were all very near panic. She decided that details might keep them from combusting. "The nuns following Suanek and the Snow Crane don't shave their heads unless they wish to be hermits or recluses within the temple. Now. I see you have done what I asked, and all the music books have been tidied away, except those pertaining to temple rituals. Go get your breakfast, and when you are told to, you will come in here and begin copying out sutras. Do nothing to gain their attention. If they speak to you, remain silent."

Bu fingered her crystal, more for its reassuring shape, well-known to her fingers now, than for prospective use. In the early days, she had only taken it out to examine trees, and birds (they were different colors and sizes, and oh, the beaks! How could there be so many different beaks?), and of course the characters as YinYin began to teach her to read and write.

Gradually she dared to use it to see what people looked like to one another, but she hated being caught at it. It was like a slap, eyes meeting eyes. It made her feel unclothed. She'd abandoned the practice of looking at people—voices were more reliable than faces anyway.

But now there was a different instinct, to use it to look for danger. Foolish, she scolded herself as she followed the others to the refectory. Would she know danger if she saw it? How would it help her if she saw whether or not they grew mustaches, or what sort of embroidery they had on their clothes? Or even what weapons they carried? One thing for certain, if one of them caught her looking, it would bring unwanted attention. No, no, no.

That meant, she discovered some time later, that she must sit over a text without actually seeing what it said. She resisted the impulse to put her nose down close, and stilled every muscle, the way she did before she began to play.

And while Bu sat woodenly through the entire day, terrified nearly witless, not far away, at the top of the Zim house, Third Daughter-in-law stood equally motionless, watching the search parties land. She watched them separate into groups going methodically through all the houses along the street, and then through the jumble of small huts and cottages off little alleyways and over bridges beyond the street.

She watched as the sun began its descent toward those ships at their post along the horizon, their banners slack in the afternoon warmth. Then, as the warm air began moving over the cooler ocean air, bringing up the afternoon breeze, one party, then another, reappeared on the street, with at least one, sometimes two, and finally about ten, huddled figures, surrounded by armed guards. These had swords bared. She could see the metal glinting, though the points were down, the disconsolate prisoners making no trouble.

The search parties withdrew with their gleanings, and rowed back to their ships. She looked up and down the street, where people stepped out tentatively, cautiously, clustering to exclaim.

She didn't need to hear it. She had seen what she needed

to see: these imperial pirates were indeed taking mostly people, along with the occasional trunk, but they had as yet only covered maybe half of the street. There was still the other half to be done, before they spread to the more remote tiny clan villages, and to the northside rice farmers, and the wretched little islands that she always thought of as pigs and dogs begging for scraps from the big island.

She turned away, and smiled, and said to one of the servants, "Tell Honored Mother-in-Law, and Sister Zim Linon, that I wish to speak to them."

TEN

As soon as Granny Zim heard the words from the servant's mouth, grim certainty gripped her by the neck and made her hands tremble. That girl had never done a truly kind thing in her life, if kindness included disinterested generosity. Granny Zim knew she was about to hear the real reason Third Daughter-in-Law had been so helpful around the temple this past couple of years, and she was going to hear it at the worst possible time.

Granny Zim turned authority over to one of the older instructors, who was finishing up getting hot food sent to the caverns, and made her way home.

She found her daughter and daughters-in-law there, a rare gathering of the five of them.

Third Daughter-in-Law began in that honey-sweet tone that rang as false as a flawed string, "Thank you for taking the time from what I know is an arduous day, Esteemed Mother Zim." That honorific implying the closeness of blood.

Granny Zim closed her lips against correcting her, knowing it was a foolish gesture to insist on *Mother-in-Law Zim* from someone she thoroughly disliked.

Then Third Daughter-in-Law said, "I will get right to the matter between us. Which is this. You have a choice before you. Either Zim Linon makes me her heir, so that I become headwoman after her, or else I will tell these imperial pirates—

and whoever else wants to listen — that you, Mother Zim, have been cultivating a demon."

Linon gasped. First Daughter-in-Law, whose temper could get spicy, shifted on her chair, and with all the strength in her arm, slapped Third Daughter-in-Law across the face.

It was a good, ringing slap, nearly knocking her from the chair. She gasped, then her face twisted into contempt as she checked to see that her dangling golden earrings had not fallen out. "You think that was a slap? My mother could strike your head off your shoulders, but I took it smiling. However, it will *never* happen again. I think I had better add a full apology, on your knees, before all the children, to my offer."

First Daughter-in-Law flushed, but said as she slipped from her chair to her knees, "I apologize. It was not well done. But that is all you will get from me. First, no one saw it but the five of us, and second, to address Mother-in-Law Zim in so insolent a manner was rude as well as unfilial."

Third Daughter-in-Law eyed her, then said, "You remain on your knees until we finish, and I'll consider the matter done." She turned to Granny Zim. "Well?"

Linon leaned toward her mother. "Is what she says true? A demon? An actual demon?"

"Yes," Third Daughter-in-Law stated. "And if you will not believe me, *you*." Here she addressed Second Daughter-in-Law. "Can ask your husband. He knows. And he did nothing about it. I've spent two years investigating, and I believe I have sufficient proof, though in truth, that demon can fool anyone. But it isn't human. I am reasonably certain I saw red eyes once. But the real truth," she added matter-of-factly, "is this. I followed her — it — to the privy once, and after it came out, there was no smell. YinYin goes only to be seen going, but I have a scroll my husband brought back this very winter that says demons who take human shape burn the food within because they are made of fire, or of ice, or something, but they don't have human parts. And that's why, when they invade and devour a human from the inside, they leave only a burned-out husk when they leave."

The first and third of Granny Zim's daughters-in-law turned to Granny Zim, one face shocked, the other horrified.

Granny Zim sighed. "YinYin is a demon."

First Daughter-in-Law's bottom hit her heels, all pretense of kneeling gone. No one noticed; Third Daughter-in-Law abandoned that petty conflict as she waited for resolution in the great one.

Granny Zim began, "I accepted that child—"

"*Demon*. Yin is a *demon*." Third Daughter-in-Law crossed her arms.

"I accepted YinYin to prove something your own father believed, Linon. Which is that what we call demons can vary as much as humans can. We humans can be the most tender and exalted of beings, equal to Suanek in merit, if not in power, and we can be the cruelest and most petty." Here, she turned her gaze to Third Daughter-in-Law, who gazed back insolently.

"Mother." The word was a mere whisper, but Granny Zim knew, as a parent knows, that Linon's faith in her had been badly shaken. Not her love. But trust.

She shut her eyes, breathing against the trembling in her belly, and when she had control again, she opened her eyes, and said to Third Daughter-in-Law, "No one will accept you. Headwoman on this island has always been a Zim. Tradition is important."

"I am a Zim by marriage."

"No," Linon stated. "Demons aside, you are a Lu by marriage. The Lus and the Zims maintain clear lines—"

"They cross every five or six generations," Third Daughter-in-Law stated. "A Lu, heir to the fleet, marries a Zim. Usually the future headwoman, but your mother refused that honor in favor of her school. As was her right. Her sister had no daughter. Linon, your daughter is a tea merchant. She's too old to change, and too timid."

"She might have a daughter."

"*I* have a daughter, and her training can begin now, with me, as soon as you make me your chief assistant and heir. If you need to adopt us both into the Zim family, then let's go to the ancestors and do the ritual. In ten years, everyone will regard us as Zims. It's happened before. I've read the Zim ancestry, the first time we went up there to clean and sweep the memorial tablets. I also copied it out. The Zims have adopted girls from outside who weren't even married."

Linon drew in a breath, but Granny Zim, who had been thinking rapidly, raised her hand. "Give me until morning. I promise you an answer before dawn."

"At dawn, or I will begin spreading the word myself," Third Daughter-in-Law said, rising. "Just think how pleased those noble families will be that their precious children lived with a demon among them. I'll leave first, and you can all revile against me as you like. But I am going to be headwoman one day."

On that, she whisked herself out the door.

They all looked at that door, behind which she probably was pressed, listening, for she was an indefatigable eavesdropper.

With a shrug, Second Daughter-in-Law said, "She would be a wretched headwoman."

First Daughter-in-law picked herself up from the floor, and sat again with a plump. "A demon…"

"Mother, I do not know what to say," Linon murmured, tears spilling over at last.

"No, I am not descending into madness," Granny Zim said, taking her daughter's hand. "I can explain everything, including what your father always said and believed, but I need time to myself. As you no doubt hear, I'm a little breathless." She used a trembling hand to fan her face. She hated using the weakness of her age, but right now it was all she had.

The other two withdrew, and fairly shortly the expected servants arrived with tea she did not want to drink, and food she had no stomach for eating. There were also offers to make up her bed, or another bed, or to bring the doctor, or medicine. Granny Zim turned down these signs of caring, fairly certain Linon was alone weeping, and that First Daughter-in-Law was on her way to the auger.

She waited, pondering everything that had happened.

When she heard the others settling down for the night, she waited a bit longer, until she had thought everything through. Then she slipped out the back way and up to the temple. She located Bu, and tapped her very lightly behind the ear, the way she had wakened her children when in a deep sleep.

Bu's eyes opened wide in the darkness, and she sat up. Granny Zim patted her hand, and bent down. "Meet me in the scriptorium."

She left so that Bu could get dressed and follow her.

Granny Zim went to the chamber where reading and writing was taught, sat down on the instructor's platform, and closed her eyes. When she first met YinYin, it was after the discovery that the demon had always come to hear her play. As if YinYin knew Granny Zim would go to her favorite bridge. No, as if the demon knew where she was. Since that time, that conviction had widened to believing that YinYin had some sort of awareness that humans didn't.

She whispered, "YinYin, come. I need you here. Yin—"

"I am here."

Granny Zim jumped, then patted her own scrawny chest to try to calm her frantic heartbeat. "I didn't expect you quite that fast," she said a little breathlessly.

YinYin said nothing, only waited in silence.

Bu arrived moments later, groping her way in the dark room that was lit only by the blue squares of the open windows through which a scrap of Ghost Moon could be seen.

"Bu. Before we go further, I need to put a question to you. If I were to leave the school, would you wish to continue studying with the school, or with me?"

Bu, still soggy from restless sleep and worry dreams, whimpered, "I don't understand."

"The words are simple enough. I believe that I might have to leave the island. No, no exclamations about bringing bad luck with my words. We haven't the time. First of all, I could have died at any time these five years. People my age die. Usually before we are ready. It's not bad luck to say so, it's the way it is. So. If I must leave, would you rather stay here at the school, a place you know, and at which you have earned respect, or follow me, though I cannot promise safety, or even life. Though I am hoping of course that the worst does not prove true."

In the darkness, YinYin's eyes glowed with tiny pinpoints of red, and when Granny Zim's gaze turned that way, the red extinguished.

Bu said, "I would follow you."

"Why?"

"Because…because you make the qin sing the way I want to make the qin sing. There are other very good players, but the qin doesn't sing for them."

"It doesn't sing for me, either. It's an instrument. My skill does all the 'singing,' which I expect you're still too young to see as a very trite metaphor. No, no apologies. I understand your meaning, and further, I very much want to keep teaching you, because I am convinced that you can make the qin sing, too. Perhaps even better than I can."

Bu dropped her head, still uncomfortable with compliments.

A short breath, and Granny Zim said, "The fact is, YinYin

is a demon. I feel—"

"I know," Bu said softly, almost too softly to be heard.

"—that a definition…what?"

"Chief Musician Zim, I said I know."

Granny Zim fumbled the cap off the flame stick waiting beside a lamp, blew the embers within to light, and used it to kindle the lamp. Now she could see both young faces. "You knew?"

Bu's squinting gaze slid from one to the other. "I… guessed. But I thought, YinYin is a friend. If she doesn't want to say, I ought not to ask."

Granny Zim winced. "How did you know? Does anyone else?"

"I don't think so," Bu said. "I'm the one nearest YinYin. And I never noticed anything, not really, until she gave me my crystal. Then I saw her eyes with red in them. At first I thought it was a reflection, but then I saw it once or twice at night, with no light around. And once, when Cricket jumped out of a bush at us, with candied haws he'd brought up from the city when he was sent for tea, I was looking through my crystal. I was behind YinYin, you see. I always follow her, so I know where to step. Her braid turned into *smoke*. Then a blink and it was a braid again. And sometimes she smells like, oh, like a winter wind, a little. I like that cool scent in the summertime. And I saw in one of the scrolls, that those were the signs of a demon."

"This doesn't disturb you?" Granny Zim said.

Bu said, "Should it? YinYin has been with us every day since we auditioned, and nothing has happened, except us learning every day. She is better than I am in method, and she gave me a very precious gift. Is that not a friend?"

Granny Zim said, "Very well. Another time, I might like to discuss your thoughts on friendship."

YinYin spoke for the first time, "As would I."

"But not now. The fact is, through circumstances that I cannot change, I am going to have to leave the temple, and take YinYin with me. There is someone who also knows about YinYin, who will sooner than later make trouble about a demon amongst us if I do not."

"Where will we go?"

"That remains to be seen. If you are to come with me, I want you two to pack your things, and meet me on the street in front of the medicine shop. Can you do that? If you decide to go with me, I need you to do this well before dawn."

"Medicine shop," YinYin said, in that passionless voice. "I know the way."

"I'll follow her," Bu quavered. "But…can we help you? Where will you be, Chief Musician Zim?"

"Get used to calling me Granny Zim. Whatever happens next, we will no longer be in the temple hierarchy. 'Granny' is a respectable term for old woman, within and outside of the family. Try it."

"Granny Zim." Bu bowed, and YinYin mimicked her.

"Go."

The pair left. Granny Zim blew out the lamp, and when her eyes had adjusted again to the darkness, she made her way out. At least her feet knew the path, after all these years. It was only now that her decision began to affect her with reality, and tears threatened as she mentally bade farewell to the room she had known since she was ten years old. She continued to bid every familiar pillar and wall and round moon door farewell, saving three low bows for Suanek's eternal serenity, within the temple.

Then she trod back down to the Zim household, sharply aware it was for the last time.

She found the light on in the upper room. Her daughter was there, with her elder two sisters-in-law. "We found you gone," Linon said. "We hoped it was not…"

"I'm too stubborn to give up a moment of my life, old as it is, by a dramatic gesture," Granny Zim said. "I've no intension of hurling myself off Ghost Bridge because of a setback." It sorrowed her to see how all three relaxed. "But you're not going to like what's coming next."

"Mother, I can live with the idea of your demon," Linon began. "I have to accustom myself to the idea."

"Maybe you can, but you know who won't," Granny Zim interrupted. "That white-eyed wolf will hold YinYin's presence at the school over our heads forever. Which would cause a lot of innocent people grief. It's *that* I cannot abide. I need to leave. With the problem. Except, I'm concerned about you."

Linon and First Daughter-in-Law exchanged glances.

"I went to the augur," First Daughter-in-Law said, flushing. She knew very well that Granny Zim was more skeptical than not about his auguries. "I told him nothing. He cast the sticks, then said something about fire and metal in the wrong spheres, and cautioned me not to eat inward-heating foods until Ghost Moon is full again. He said I personally ought to be safe — the elements were in balance for me personally — but I must only trust those whose affinities are for water, metal, and earth. Everyone knows *she* has an affinity for fire and air," First Daughter-in-Law finished with faint triumph.

Granny Zim was tempted to point out that it was an easy guess that Third Daughter-in-Law was concerned somewhere with the dilemma that sent her eldest daughter-in-law seeking advice, as Third made trouble regularly, and everyone up and down the street knew it. As for that prediction of fire and air, the augur probably knew everyone's birth lines. But Granny Zim suppressed that, her heart panging unpleasantly over the realization that this might be the last night they all saw one another. The time for arguing about the truth of augury was past.

It was clear her daughter thought so, too.

"We've been talking half the night," Linon said. "And finally decided to come to you since sleep was impossible, and sure enough, you were not even here. Here's my suggestion. Agree to her terms. Let her adopt in. I'm going to see to it that her training as my assistant leaves her with little time to be seducing this and that family member to turn them against one another."

"*Very* little time," First Daughter-in-Law said grimly. "Also." With a gesture toward Second Daughter-in-Law, she said, "We are going to dedicate our lives to making certain that Sister Linon outlives her, in spite of the twenty-three years between them, even if she has to make it to a hundred."

The knot in Granny Zim's heart loosened a little at these words. "You are good children, all three of you. I'll leave it to you to explain to my sons as you see fit. I've only one request." She turned to First Daughter-in-Law. "Say whatever you need to, to the instructors. I believe with me gone, Third Daughter-in-Law will not soil what she expects to be her own nest by mentioning demons, especially if YinYin is gone, so no one can examine her to prove her accusations true. The school will survive. It is as well that the tradition is to choose the new chief among them."

The others nodded; Granny Zim was not the first Zim musician to be trained there, but she was the first to rise to the rank of chief.

"Then you are taking the demon with you?" Linon asked, sounding relieved.

"I am. And Bu. Whose training I will continue, as long as I am able."

"She's a good child," First Daughter-in-Law said. "Will there be trouble from her family?"

"Not they," Granny Zim said, with a dismissive gesture. "Though I've never met a one, I know children. Bu was essentially thrown away to survive on her own. Though her birth mother might harbor regrets. But time heals all wounds. As for the rest of them, I learned some things about Bu last winter, when she caught that fever. She talked more than she had since she came. I believe there was a second sister, the sort who made Bu sniff out the good mushrooms from the poisonous ones, and do all the work picking them, when the two were sent out during the rainy season. Then she'd claim she'd done her share."

"Another fire personality," First Daughter-in-Law commented sourly.

"Remember, my husband was fire," Granny Zim countered with a small laugh. "Fire and earth. And he was the best man I ever knew. My point is, don't give the Lum family another thought."

She went to her writing desk to grind some ink, as up at the temple, Bu whispered to YinYin, "I need to visit Suanek. Only a moment."

"Why?"

"I need to light incense. For Second Mother. I don't know…if I can again."

YinYin said nothing, but accompanied her, and waited, no more than a shadow, as Bu lit incense, then uttered prayers of supplication to Suanek to grant her mother safety, health, and happiness. She prostrated herself, head to the floor, three times three, and then the two of them stole out as quietly as they had come in.

ELEVEN

As promised (said the storyteller) we are now on our way to meet some heroes and villains.

It was a little frightening, as well as exciting, for Bu to be standing on the nearly deserted street, waiting for Granny Zim. She made out the blobs of the two moons, one a slice as it sank, the other larger as it rose.

The east had begun to blue when Granny Zim emerged out of the darkness, accompanied by two other women swathed in cloaks. Silently the women gave one another tight hugs. "Remember what I said about their playing when the searchers come," Granny Zim whispered to the taller, and when she turned to the other, the tall one came to Bu.

"Take care of her, will you, child?"

Bu could not see into that hood, but she swallowed in a dry throat. "I will do my very best."

The figure handed Bu a bulky carryall. As Bu pulled it over her shoulder, she heard the soft hum of strings — a qin!

YinYin was also given a bulky carryall that uttered discordant notes, and the two women melted into the shadows between the medicine shop and the tea trader's.

Then Granny said, "Pull up your hoods." And when they had, "Come."

To Bu's astonishment they made their way not to the east end's inlet, which led toward the tiny island of her birth and where Bu had assumed they were going to hide, but down the street toward the harbor. It was slow going. Granny was not fast, and Bu and YinYin were burdened by awkward carryalls. Bu's crystal banged against her waist in her sleeve pocket as she tried shifting the carryall around to ease the thump of hard corners against her ribs and back. Finally she put her arms behind her and wrapped them around the bag. That helped.

The smell of brine strengthened, as did the light. They kept walking, nearly alone; Bu could not see the furtive eyes behind shutters and cracked doors peering out at them, but Granny could, and she was glad that she had insisted they pull their hoods over their heads. Why? She laughed at herself. It would soon be all over who had left. But at least no one knew who they were now, or why they were there, and dared not interfere.

Bu's thoughts flitted like stirred moths around a light. Were they going to slip into a boat? Bu had never learned to row. Questions piled up behind her lips but she kept her teeth shut against them. Think of the music, she scolded herself. But the music, until now her most faithful companion, seemed very far away indeed.

When they reached the pier, Granny Zim stopped. Bu blinked past strands of hair from her hasty braid, and peered seaward. Was that a boat coming? She heard the rhythmic splash of oars. Who? Rescue? *Enemies?*

Presently the pier jolted as something bumped against it. Following the jolt, the clatter and ring of armor and weapons and heavy boots, and tall figures loomed out of the fading darkness.

One said, "Grandmother? Where is the headwoman I met yesterday?"

He used the book language, only pronounced differently. Bu suppressed a weird impulse to laugh at how odd the word sounded in that accent.

"I wish to speak to your commander," Granny Zim said, also in the book language, her voice thin. It was Chief Musician Zim who spoke, despite the age in her voice.

"Why?"

A couple of snickers, and a guffaw from those looming figures in the murk, were quickly muffed when the red-cloaked one glanced back, the long red fabric swinging about his boots.

"May I inquire the purpose, Grandmother?" the man

asked, still courteous.

"I am a Zim. You met my daughter yesterday. We have been headwomen of this island for two dynasties. I want to see the treaty paper."

"Army General Panheg brought it himself yesterday," the man said. "Your headwoman did not ask to see it. He remained on board the capital ship today, and the treaty records lie with Fleet Admiral Zhali."

Granny Zim hid a pulse of relief; she did not want to see the treaty so much as to discover if these invaders even knew about it. Then they really did consider themselves legal, in some wise. She hoped that meant there would be no outright looting and killing once their search was over.

"I can send you to the capital ship," the man continued. "The boat is returning anyway. But I warn you: it will be the fleet admiral's choice whether or not you will be permitted to come to land again."

"I will take that chance."

"And these?" A hand waved toward Bu and YinYin.

"My attendants."

"I see." The man called something in another dialect down to the boat. "My coxswain will take you now."

Granny Zim turned to Bu and YinYin. "Into the boat, children."

Poor Bu! At twelve, she had been terrified to be rowed some three hundred paces. This was a far greater distance, toward the invading ships, and an utterly unknown future. She hoped toward a future. But there was no comforting promise of a life among nuns if she did not want what lay ahead.

The boat bumped and jolted over the water, which occasionally sent cold sprays to sting her face. She shivered, mostly from fear, clutching the qin in its bag close as if to steady her.

At length they neared what appeared to be a towering brown mountain: a ship, rocking on the water. Incomprehensible shouting presaged a kind of platform being let over the side. Clinging to the ropes supporting the four sides, the three were hoisted to the deck, where another red-cloaked figure in glinting armor said, "Who are you?"

"I am Zim Li, Chief Musician at the temple. It is my daughter who is headwoman. She is not old enough to remember the last time imperials showed up. I wish to speak to your...your fleet admiral," Granny Zim said in the book language.

Bu was so grateful she understood it! Granny Zim was so clear—unlike these others, with their odd accent.

"Follow me."

They were led to what appeared to be a hut in the center of the ship. Inside this was a room that smelled of cabbage and ink and something that reminded Bu of metal—she had never sniffed sword oil.

They were led to a gray-haired man wearing even more elaborate armor. He sat behind a desk. "You are?"

Granny Zim repeated what she had said before, then added, "Do you have the treaty paper?"

"I do," this man said in a wry voice. "Are you questioning our credentials?"

"I want mainly to have assurance that there will be no wanton looting. And I'd hope that your end of that treaty will be kept."

The man uttered a dry laugh. "If you are referring to the patrolling of these waters in search of pirates, the fleet admiral is seeing to that. Your treaty—and many others—were... elsewhere, during the various difficulties at the imperial capital. However, his imperial majesty..." Here the man turned, clasped his hands, and made a short bow in a northwestward direction. "...has entrusted Army General Panheg and me with reestablishing matters..." His voice trailed away as he hunted through a small pile of scrolls at the side of the desk, and then pulled one out. "Ayah."

He was silent as he read, then he glanced up. "It states that the temple fosters musicians amongst the nuns, yes."

"I taught them," Granny Zim said. "I am here to offer myself in place of any of my students you might wish to take away from the temple."

Bu found it difficult to follow this conversation, as she was still mastering what she thought of as the book language. And the man's accent was so very difficult to understand. But it seemed that Granny was endeavoring to protect the school.

"By tradition, we only take the most promising among the novices, before they make vows. How is swapping the old for the young a good bargain?" the man asked, still sounding mildly puzzled. "Forgive my bluntness, but I am a warrior, and we are blunt men. Your age against the longer lives of the young and vigorous seems a fool's bargain. Why are you really here?"

"I am the better bargain if you are seeking those with skill. Those novices on the mountain are barely beginners. We only hold auditions every ten years, and we're a few years into a new cycle. None of them have any skills save music, and that is still rudimentary. Whereas I, who direct the entire school, could begin another school. At least in the old days, I understand that the imperials valued music?"

"That is true now," the man said. "Interesting! I have matters to attend to, but I will test your skills, and talk to my captains about what and who they find up at your temple." He turned. "I take it these are your servants?"

"And also my best two novices."

"I could consider the offer of a pair as a gesture of good faith." He snapped his fingers, and Granny Zim, Bu, and YinYin were led out again, then down a narrow ladder and past a series of what looked like horse stalls, only with fitted doors.

They were gestured into one, and the door was shut. A tiny hole high up let in the weak morning light. The room was bare, except for a narrow sleeping platform down one side that would fit two lying straight, three at a squeeze. At one end lay folded blankets. Two trunks opposite proved to contain items of clothing that smelled like men. Bu shut them quickly: it seemed they had been placed in a room belonging to others.

"May I ask a question, Chie—Granny Zim?"

"Ask."

"Did I understand correctly, the offer of a pair referred to YinYin and me? If so, what does that mean?"

Granny Zim rubbed her eyes before speaking. "I believe he was, on the surface, acknowledging our cooperation, but his tone, his wording was a reminder that disposition of the two of you is his right, not mine. But worry not. I expected as much, and we will have time to work on that."

Granny Zim sat on the sleeping platform, continuing in island dialect, "If I'm not mistaken, someone in my family will be spiteful enough to try to sell off my novices for her gain. What I said just now will emphasize our connection with the temple, though we teach men as well as women, and very few remain once granted mastery. She got half of what she wanted, but the other half—my bowing to her, and her future control over me through threat—was denied when I left with you, YinYin. She cannot prove there ever was a demon if there is no demon. Ayah, enough of that. Bring out those instruments, and let us get them tuned. Oh, this air is sodden with water. It's going to be a challenge to keep the strings from going sour…"

At her gesture, Bu and YinYin carefully opened the two carryalls, and withdrew a qin from each. Even in the weak light, Bu recognized Granny Zim's own qin, and one of the better test qins from the hall. There was also a test zither, a side flute, and a notch flute. At the bottom, neatly folded, were a pair of robes for Granny Zim, a brush, and an extra wooden hairpin, plus a packet of precious tea—a last love gift. The sight of it made Granny Zim's throat close.

Bu and YinYin put their own meager carryalls aside, and waited expectantly for orders.

In that weak light filtering down, Granny Zim looked old and tired. "I will admit that I don't know if this was a good idea. If I possibly can, I'll give you a future. But YinYin, you must be very careful."

"Yes."

Granny Zim pressed her fingers to her eyelids. "At my age, it is not good to exert all through a night. Needs must! Now, you two, especially Bu, what comes next ought to have been a lesson in the eighth or ninth year. Not that your skills are lacking, it's the intent. Our aim is to shape you, through discipline and the wisdom of the ancients, into mastering true music, with true intent. What some call pure, though a more practical way of expressing it would be, using our skills with the intent to express what is best in our hearts and minds."

Bu bowed over her hands, novice-style.

"We strive to train you to be your better selves as you master the power of music. Because it *is* powerful. You know that. You breathe it with every breath, you dream it, you express it with every note and every silence between notes. But music can also be used to ignite other emotions, what they call entertaining. It can be used to ignite battle lust on the field of war. It can *influence*. What you're going to hear me do is play to bring out emotions—in fact, to control the emotions—of my audience. Specifically, this imperial fleet admiral, and the army general, if he is there."

Enlightenment struck Bu all at once. "Music that gladdens, music that saddens, and music that maddens," she whispered.

"Yes."

Bu was not certain what to say. When she glanced at

YinYin, she recoiled at the glow in YinYin's black eyes.

Then it was gone.

"Let us tune the strings, and use the time we are given to review some lessons..."

Because they did not know when Granny Zim would be summoned, and if she would be expected to play alone or with the two accompanying her, they spent the time as they would at the temple, working very softly at lessons.

The summons, when it came, was for Granny Zim alone, but she insisted on her novices being there. The imperials assented, ignoring Bu and YinYin as beneath notice. As servants.

The space was the worst sort—in a noisy galley with too many people, and wretched sound. Granny Zim glanced around as Bu and YinYin placed the qin, and she tested each string again. Then Granny Zim turned to the fleet admiral, who sat on a small platform, at one side a man also in glinting armor, though dissimilar as far as Bu could tell.

"What would you like me to play?" Granny Zim said.

The captains in the background continued talking, laughing, and eating.

Fleet Admiral Zhali said, "I expect you only know the ancient songs, all that about the core tones and the five elements."

"Twelve pitches, corresponding to the two moons, talk, talk, talk!" shouted a red-faced captain. "Our tutor used to go on about that. Tedious beyond bearing."

The fleet admiral said in a tone of reproof, "The ancients are always worthwhile."

"This old strummer can play the ancients for the venerable military commanders," Granny Zim said, plucking out a chord to test sound. "Or, name a newer song, if the esteemed company prefers that, my poor skills will attempt to please you." Bu had never heard Granny Zim use the mode of the lowest rank, though she had been raised to speak that way to Madam Lum and the elders.

"Would you even know what's sung at the imperial court?" one of the captains retorted. "What about 'The Last Hyacinth,' or 'The Butterfly Scarf,' which is older?"

The army general spoke for the first time. "Those are romance maunderings, better left to the scholars and boys with three hairs in their mustaches, who write bad poetry to impress the sleeve dancers. Do you know 'The Battle of Two

Ancestors Hill'?"

Granny Zim had been watching the two commanders in chief as these songs were named. "How does it go?"

The general waved at one of the captains, who obediently hummed a melodic line in a pleasing voice, each note true. Bu immediately recognized middle-tone mode, that is, the middle of the five tones that form the core of music. Formed around quick, military-sounding triplets, the ballad melody was easy enough to catch. There was only one variation before the refrain.

Granny Zim plucked out the notes that the man had sung. Bu thought she would say, "This is predictable," or perhaps more politely, "This is a common adaptation of a typical mid-tone mode," as she would have said to the novices. Instead, she said, "How is this?"

And she began to play, maintaining a steady, stirring rhythm that several in the room tapped on the edges of their plates with eating sticks, or thumped wine cups on the table. The fleet admiral bobbed his head, and the general smiled.

Granny Zim played it through twice, and then tried another ballad, an ancient one celebrating Liad II. At this familiar tune, half the army captains joined in to sing.

Bu smothered a nervous giggle at their accent, which sounded incongruous to her ears, and schooled her face as well as her posture. Her attention stayed on Granny Zim, whose face turned most often toward the two on the dais, but Bu sensed that her mentor listened to them all. She wished she could pull out her crystal to see Granny Zim's face. But what would that tell her? She closed her eyes to listen.

When that ballad ended, Granny Zim began another ancient martial ballad, dedicated to an early emperor, and gradually opened out to the full seven tones, though keeping the melodic line. Then, her left hand maintaining the basic melody, she began adding triplets, at intervals of threes, in a high register, for birds. Slightly lower, and modified, for children. Then she worked in new melodic phrases in intervals of fives, which were the most common for people—one melody for men, and its complement for women.

Bu was so involved in the music building and building that at first she was unaware of the company's gradually intensified listening. Still the melody strengthened. Now intervals of sevens, and here and there an unexpected fourth that created a sense of urgency, yet in the background, the military melody kept repeating.

A crescendo, and more fourths, angular and even harsh: war.

The birds disappeared first. Then the children. The men followed, and the complementary melody—the women—shifted to the fifth tone mode, the lowest: mourning. Both Granny Zim's gnarled hands swooped and plucked with relentless precision, evoking a swarm of heartbreaking sound as she brought out the raw emotions, sometimes deeply buried or half-forgotten, of loss, and grief, and finally, a glimmer of hope.

Bu could not see eyes glistening, but she heard suppressed emotion in the listeners' breathing. And still the song did not come to an end, but altered back to smooth, pretty thirds and fifths, suggesting the immanence of peace. And finally it closed at the high register, with the birds.

The last notes vibrated on the air, each plucked true, then faded.

Then a thunder of genuine applause.

TWELVE

THE FLEET ADMIRAL LED the praise, smiling widely, while the army general remained silent, his face expressionless. Granny Zim bowed. No telling, yet, what that army general's hidden reaction might mean for the future, but he had been listening with at least as much attention as had the fleet commander. She had seen it through the tension in his shoulders, and she was certain that tomorrow, after his raiders went through the temple, he would be questioning the leader of the raid. If First Daughter-in-Law could be trusted—few better!—those raiders sent to the temple would hear little but jangling strings, stuttering warbles on the winds, and clanks from the bells. Third Daughter-in-Law wouldn't get two tinkets for tuneless warblers. Granny Zim could not protect everyone from being taken away, but at least she could attempt to preserve the school's novices, who were her responsibility.

The fleet admiral summoned one of the orderlies, and the three, with all their belongings, were soon enduring another choppy journey over the dark waters to a different ship. This one a troop ship, which had numerous divisions in its belly. Granny Zim was given a very small cabin to herself in the upper area, with a small window in the hull that fit tight as a shutter. It let in light and air. Bu and Yin were put in a cabinet even more cramped off hers, with only a tiny air hole.

Bu relaxed a little when an orderly showed up, this time

with blankets. It seemed that nothing dire was to happen if they were given blankets. Another orderly brought tea, and pancakes stuffed with chives, garlic, and greens, along with unfamiliar spices that tasted odd, but hunger adds relish to new tastes, and Bu devoured her share.

Granny Zim picked at the meal, then said, "Do you understand what I did?"

Bu swallowed hastily, her mouth watering. "You played a song about war, but from the eyes of those who do not fight."

"Very good, but before that." And when Bu hesitated, and YinYin remained silent, Granny Zim said, "I asked for what they wanted to hear. The fleet admiral's responses told me that he likes traditional better than the newest fashion. All I got from the army general is that he guards his dignity. He had someone else sing, rather than singing himself. And then?"

"And then you gave them a ballad in full sevenths, about war, but I think you wanted them to think about those not fighting the war?"

"Those usually destroyed by war, yes. And those left at home. Also, a reminder that some of them might never return home."

"But at the end, you offered the melodies of peace."

"Which is quite traditional. The fleet admiral's reaction was the more freely expressed, but surface, like light on water. I suspect that the army general's impressions were deeper, and for reasons I have yet to discover, he did not want to display them."

"What does that tell you, Granny Zim?" Bu ventured a question that she never would have put before others in a class.

"A good question that requires time before I answer. I need to learn, if I can, which of those two has the greater influence, though it seems by their sitting together that their powers are divided equally. The navy conveys, and fights at sea, the army goes into the islands and takes the tribute. Fight if they must. It could be worse, for these do not appear to be bent on conquering, or suppressing—though I might be wrong."

"If the islands defend themselves?" Bu asked, a scrap from her reading surfacing in her mind.

"Then all those weapons get used. We can do nothing about that." She pushed the dish away, swallowing a couple of times, and breathing sharply. "Let's tune the instruments, and we'll begin with venerable 'Ospreys'—always suitable..."

Granny Zim found it impossible to eat because the ship's constant heaving made her dizzy, especially when the winds came up later in the day. But she had been prepared for discomfort. The year Teg took her along with the fisher fleet, she had suffered miserably the first week or two.

When the orderly returned, before Bu thought to pocket the uneaten pancakes for in case, he said nothing. Presently an elderly doctor appeared, his long gray beard indicative of Granny Zim's age, if not older. He prescribed bitter medicine steeped with great chunks of ginger. It helped.

They retired to a restless, worried, uncomfortable night full of the creaks and moans of wood, strange odors, and snatches of worry dreams. The next morning, Bu woke alone to thunderous noise and the timbers shaking around her. Panic seized her until she comprehended a cadence. Storms made equally wild noise, but never to the paired-beat rhythms that, ironically (so Instructor Ding had said) you actually did not find in all nature's noises, in spite of the "natural rhythm" name. Rhythms belonged to humans and creatures that had hearts and desires. (That last being utterly incomprehensible to many, if not most, of the novices, but they were used to assuming that their elders knew what they were talking about.)

"Fear not," Granny Zim said when Bu emerged from the cabinet. "I believe that noise is the military up on the deck rehearsing various things with weapons. I saw similar exercises each day, in all weathers, on my husband's fishing fleet, for they had to be ready for pirates at all times. Tell YinYin when she gets back from the privy," Granny Zim added as the orderly knocked and entered with breakfasts, "that that noise is nothing to worry about."

The cheerful young orderly said, "You mean Panheg's tigers? Oho, no worry as long as you stay out of their way, but don't go up there in the mornings, or you're likely to lose an ear before you can blink!"

YinYin turned up then, and offered to pour the tea. The orderly left, chuckling, and Granny Zim hoped that whatever gossip he carried back to his commanders reported two ordinary novices who kept to their place, serving the old strummer.

Bu had not slept any better than Granny Zim, who was still looked pale and ill, but she drank ginger-medicine and imposed order on the chaos of their lives as they worked through a lesson. After the midday meal she could barely look at, she said, a little faintly, "I believe we can rest: there is likely to be a summons again."

Granny Zim and Bu returned to bed. YinYin disappeared like smoke.

The summons came that night, as Granny Zim had expected. This time, she told Bu and YinYin to play accompaniment by repeating the melodic phrases, as she embellished them with building emotion and virtuosity. This time, the fleet admiral nodded his head, smiling, and at one point, he leaned down to address an aide, who also smiled. Whereas the army general sat very still and expressionless, his gaze almost unblinking as he watched Granny Zim's hands.

Afterward, she asked Bu to rub those hands, which trembled and shook. The tendons were tighter than the qin's strings. But she was pleased with the outcome ("I think the army general is the one I need to influence") and so it went on the third day, when the audience had swelled to all the naval and army captains. This time, there were no requests—the audience waited expectantly, and Granny Zim began with light, vigorous rhythms sure to appeal to military tastes, but gradually guided the music to excavate deeper emotions, and then bring them back safely to the shores of brightness and humor with bird phrases. It was a concert aimed to please a general audience, but Granny Zim had worked in querying fourths, seeking and asking without finding. As she played, she watched that army general from under her eyelids.

The fourth day they woke to the ship moving in a different manner, and discovered that their islands, so unfamiliar when seen from the sea, had vanished. They were on their way somewhere else.

Granny Zim did her best to hide the sorrow in her heart when Bu and YinYin joined her that morning. She had not been able to give any of her grandchildren a farewell, much less her sons, who would arrive to the unpleasant discovery that she had departed with the tribute raiders—unless the imperials got to them first, when they went to sell their pearls before sailing home.

"Granny Zim, are you very ill?" Bu asked, after listening to Granny Zim's harsh breathing.

"No, no, merely missing home, now that we have put out to sea. I hope the school survived," Granny Zim observed as she gazed out at the gray-green ocean. "Ulp! Bu, please bring me more of the ginger medicine. I wish…"

Bu leaped up, staggered, and went to the corner, where the orderlies had set them up with a kettle over a coal-holder to boil water, a pot, and cups.

Granny Zim turned away from the window, her eyes betraying that she had been weeping. "I have to admit the hardest of all is not knowing if my efforts achieved anything — if they took any of the novices, or how many. It's too much to hope for that they left them be."

YinYin said, "They took Cricket. No one else."

"Cricket?"

"Cricket?"

Granny Zim's and Bu's exclamations collided. Then Granny Zim leaned toward her, murmuring urgently, "I don't want to know how you know. I probably would not understand it anyway. *Where* is he? How was he when you saw him?"

"He is in one of the big ships," YinYin said. "He was not happy when he was in the boat, but he is talking with two of the others taken away. I think he knows them, as he calls their fathers uncle. They are from the east harbor. And I saw that they sleep shoulder to shoulder on the platform down in the ship."

"Friends from his days as a beggar," Bu ventured a guess. "He always makes friends if he can. That's the first thing I learned about him."

Granny Zim thumbed her eyes, then said, "The night we had to leave. You spoke about friendship."

YinYin said, "I am still trying to understand what it means."

Bu felt both of them looking at her, and ducked her head. "It's not for me to say. The ancients are wiser. They say it better."

YinYin said, "But they also say so many different things."

Bu considered. "I'm still reading what everyone else read when they were small. It's a bit like, ayah, like gathering a lot of little rocks in order to make your own mountain, isn't it?"

"Try to express it," Granny Zim said. "We have the time. More time. Breakfast seems rather late today."

Since Granny Zim had asked, Bu struggled to define something she was still exploring within the safe boundaries of music. "It is such an easy word to *say*, friend. Some of the girls were friend-ly, but I never felt comfortable in their presence the way I do with you, YinYin. Especially those whose words were sweet when they spoke to me, mostly before the instructors. And sweet to one another's face. But when that person went away, the words turned sharp. I always expected it would be the same when I went away."

"It was so," YinYin said.

I did not want to know that, Bu thought, but she kept that to herself. "It was easier to be in Tensi Yi Nis's company, in a way. She despised me, but I knew it, and so there was no falsity, in which a person cannot trust anything they hear." She turned to YinYin. "Are we friends? We don't talk about things the way the other girls do. But that's all right, because I'm not good at talking. I know that we eat together, and we fixed each other's braid in the mornings. And you brush hair so nicely. If I shut my eyes it felt a little like the way my mother did it. Sometimes that was the best part of the day, except when I practiced and it went well. Is that being a friend?"

Instead of answering, YinYin turned to Granny Zim, who said, "If it feels like friendship, then I guess it is. It always seemed to me that people could have different types of friendship with different people."

She hesitated as the water wash-splashed against the side of the ship. Then she said, "My husband Lu Teg and I were betrothed from the time I was born. He was five years my elder, but we played together as soon as I could walk. He had many friends. He watched out for me all through our childhood, and after I was accepted at the temple at ten. The first auspicious day after I earned my mastery, we married, and we still stayed friends. He served as my idea of friendship, the other person you were happy to see each new day, who knew you, who trusted you, and whom you could trust." She tipped her head, gazing out the window, and the pause of reverie became a silence that the other two did not break, until Granny Zim roused, then said briskly, "We're going to take 'The Moth in the Wind' through all twelve chromatic scales this morning. Let us see if we can get through the first two before they remember us and bring the porridge."

Bu ran her hands over the familiar qin, her mind going back to the discussion. It seemed to her that what Granny Zim was really asking was, did YinYin think about friends and friendship?

What would a demon think about such things? Bu

hesitated to ask. Words were too much like meeting others' eyes through the crystal. It was intrusive in a way. And it could be that demons simply didn't have the word *friend* if they even had a demon language.

Did they have the word *demon*?

Everyone who had heard the simplest sutras knew that there were five kinds of immortals, just as there were five kinds of creatures. From there more divisions came, having to do with the earthly elements, none of which she understood. She didn't have to. Geomancy and augury and matters of Essence were very much of the unseen world, and she was struggling to understand this one, which was where YinYin and she had to live.

If they were friends, perhaps it was an act of friendship not to ask about such things? YinYin might be half-immortal, or even whole immortal, only why would she be so poor? The more probable explanation was some immortal blood. Either way, she was an orphan, having arrived barefoot, with a single garment, so there could not be a happy story there.

Bu was so involved in her thinking that she started when the familiar rap sounded at the door, then the orderly entered with the food basket. "Very sorry to be so late," he said.

"Is there a problem we ought to know about?" Granny Zim asked.

The orderly had strict orders to treat the elder with all the respect due to a skilled master, so instead of snapping that it was military business, not theirs, he muttered, "I must hand this in and go, but I will just say, we're having to turn the entire ship inside out." His voice sharpened to bitterness. "On top of regular duties. Just because that carrot-nosed old augur insists that a demon got on board. Now we have to search through all the tributes taken last haul, before we land at the next."

He sniffed, and muttering curses under his breath, left.

Granny Zim turned to YinYin. "You must stay human, YinYin."

"I will stay human."

Bu portioned out the porridge, her own middle boiling like porridge with sudden worry. She followed Granny Zim in getting the breakfast down, drinking a pinch of the precious tea that Headwoman Zim Linon's daughter had sent as a gift, and then determinedly turning to lessons.

The search party gave a perfunctory knock shortly before noon. A sailor poked his head in, glanced briefly at them, waved a much-battered Essence paper around, and when nothing happened, banged the door shut again. They heard the clump of the sailor's and his armed companions' retreat, then Granny Zim said, "Do Essence wards work against you?"

"Some," YinYin said. "It…it is like a wall, a little. Most do not, when I am human. I am better at being human now than I was."

"Stay that way," Granny Zim ordered. "If you want music, work harder at staying human than you ever have."

YinYin put hands together and bowed in assent.

THIRTEEN

WHEN A SKINNY TEENAGE orderly returned at sunset with supper, Granny Zim said, "We were told they searched for a *demon*. Is it *true?* I hope they found it and sent it away!"

"They didn't find anything, Grandmother," the orderly said. "Word is, it flitted away when the augur did the ritual over the command ship."

"Good, good, good. We will sleep well tonight," Granny Zim twittered.

"So will we," the young orderly commented as he stacked up the dishes from earlier, giving them a gap-toothed grin. "It's been do this, do that, all day, never did our backsides so much as touch a sitting mat. Ate while running."

He vanished on the last word.

There was no summons that night, which enabled Granny Zim to rest her hands. Bu knelt by her bed platform and massaged her hands, her arms, and her shoulders, in the way that they had all learned to do for one another when lessons had been especially arduous. When Granny's breathing eased, "I hope they leave us alone now," Bu murmured.

"I do not." Granny Zim's eyes flashed open. "I do need the rest. I've let myself get lazy, these past years, only playing as long as I liked. It is good for me to work myself up to concert time and effort, for I am very certain it's going to be needed sooner than later."

Bu accepted the mild rebuke with bowed head, and used it to redouble her own efforts, in spite of the sodden air, the endless pitch and yaw, and her own worries about what might happen.

That began a new pattern. Bu's stomach had not liked the motion, but she got used to it after a few days. YinYin remained silent, as Granny Bu had instructed. And at times, when Granny Zim rose and had to make her way hand over hand along the walls to the privy, she peeked into the tiny cabin to see Bu oblivious in slumber and YinYin lying very straight, eyes open.

Once they'd finished their work of a morning, and the thunderous cadences of the military drill on deck ceased, they were allowed to walk on deck if the weather was good. YinYin stayed in the cabin, apparently unbothered by being confined. She'd lie on the narrow bed platform that she and Bu shared, so still it seemed as if she'd turned to stone.

Bu longed for air, and went out to explore the ship. At first she was very self-conscious walking about alone when other tribute girls were in the charge of matronly military servitors. These women kept their charges walking in line, and though the girls could chat, they could not stray. Bu was the only one permitted to walk about alone, from which she guessed that Granny Zim had been granted a special status, which extended to her attendants.

This was the pattern until they came in sight of uneven bumps on the horizon. When the fragrances of soil and fruit and wood drifted over the water from those conical green hills, she was deciding she might dare to try her crystal when one of the aides came around to say that orders had been handed down for everyone to return to their cabins until further notice. Bu sensed alertness in both army and navy people.

Bu moved as hastily as she could, and when she reported to Granny Zim, the latter nodded. "They're readying for invasion. Maybe it will be as peaceful as the one at our islands, which I am the more convinced was deliberately arranged to happen when the men were away."

"Do all the islands have fisher fleets?" Bu asked.

"Some have trade fleets. Some have their own military. That's my understanding from many years ago. You know how seldom anyone but our few traders come to us."

They turned their attention to the wind instruments until noises from Granny Zim's open window drew them to peer out at boats full of warriors departing, escorted by four warships, the rest ranged in a line. Bu stared through her crystal, relishing the wind-rippling banners and Essence streamers, the severe lines of the sails, and the fascinating geometry of the ships. She glanced at the faces of the warriors until they had dwindled to little figures. Some were tense, others joking back and forth. Armor and weapons glinted coldly, and she withdrew, not wanting to think about those weapons being used.

Lessons resumed. It was very nearly dark, the sun a smoldering ball in the west, when the first boats began to return. Bu sensed a change in the sharp voices hallooing unintelligible shouts back and forth as wood groaned and sails clattered and banners thwacked in the wind.

The first boat drew into view, its crew and passengers glowing in the lurid light, which revealed bloody bandages on some, and at the back long figures covered by cloaks, including their faces.

Bu backed away, throwing her crystal down, and wishing she had never touched it.

"We're going to need mourning songs," Granny Zim said. "Get the zither."

The fighting went on for four days, and then the boats stayed ashore. When they returned after a week, they were full of prisoners.

"They won," Granny Zim said, her profile bleak as she peered out. "They will have killed the island's leaders, and taken every able-bodied male as well as comely young women. The Turtle Islands will probably need a generation to recover."

"The Turtle Islands? Is that not…?"

"I believe we have gone north. This is the kingdom where the Tensi clan are court nobles." Who else but a king would fight the imperials? Granny Zim thought, but kept that to herself.

Bu smothered the sorrow in her heart. Yi Nis was unpleasant, but she did not deserve whatever news was going to come to the school.

Granny Zim was also thinking of Yi Nis. Be a leader, child,

she thought, shutting her eyes. *It is in you. And your clan will need leadership.* "Let us begin with 'The Lotus Pond' to prepare in case we are summoned. It is the purest of the mourning songs…" And they turned to practice.

The summons, when it came, was to a different part of the command ship. The audience was smaller, the single figure on the dais the army general, looking grim, his gaze flinty, a bandage at one shoulder, his arm hanging loose. Bu squinted around, noting bandages on most of the listeners. Each wore undyed headbands of mourning.

Granny Zim had chosen a number of mourning pieces, both traditional and newer, often called for at island memorials. All three played, YinYin confined to maintaining the central melody on the side flute, which she played with exactly the right slightly breathy, somber lilt. She drew no attention during this first appearance before many eyes. Those eyes were mostly looking inward, at the chaos and carnage of a fierce battle.

Bu provided shimmering glissandos up and down the chromatic scale as Granny Zim's qin plucked at every nerve between heart and head with merciless, no, merciful precision, because she was doing her best to empty that well of grief.

Army General Panheg never reacted outwardly. His face might have been carved from stone as he slowly drank. Granny Zim watched, and altered a melodic line, which Bu reflected. Granny Zim's entire body engaged as she brought forth ever more powerful chords, evoking windswept crags and snow-topped mountains as the wind howled down the canyons, and the wolves howled with the wind.

She evoked funeral boats gliding along the river, outlined by the golden glow of lamps as the fallen were returned home to lie with their ancestors. She evoked mothers and wives, brothers and sons, bewildered and lost, drawing close around the one who would never see their faces again in this life.

The army general drank steadily.

The few captains had gone silent, some weeping openly, when she shifted mode entirely and the music offered benediction by weaving New Year's melodies through, in reminder of the great bridge between the moons whence souls would cross to their new lives.

She did not finish this mourning performance with spring melodies, but gave them sustained chords of peace, echoed by the zither, and a last, soft, very soft repeat of the funeral melody on the side flute, which ended on a long note before fading into a whisper.

Silence met them as Bu surreptitiously rubbed her fingers against her thighs. They had played at performance pitch for a very long time; until now, performance pitch for the novices lasted scarcely a quarter of an incense stick.

The silence continued as they were taken back to the troop ship, where they saw the tail end of a great reorganization caused by the massive influx of prisoners being forced down into the hold, and locked there.

When Bu ventured to the deck the next day, no one stopped her. But she found a great change: part of the great deck was taken up with people sitting in rows. From the low rumble of voices, this crowd was entirely made up of men.

She instantly began to backtrack, suspecting that the army had decided to do more of their practice, but then a familiar voice rang out, "Bu! Lum Bu!"

"Cricket?" She paused, unsure whether to go backward or forward.

A familiar tall, thin blur emerged out of the mass, crowing a laugh. "There you are! I wondered if you'd been swallowed alive by a kraken. Or thrown into the sea as a spy."

"A spy?" she repeated as teenage boy laughter snickered and whooped around Cricket. A couple of figures joined Cricket.

"He's joking," one said—in the accentless language of home. Then a murmur, only part of which she caught, "…another like Brick?"

"Brick is all right, just a little slow. Who isn't, at times?" Cricket laughed again. "Lum Bu is one of the smartest and best of all of the novices."

"Oh?" someone drawled, and Bu's nerves chilled because she sensed someone looking right at her.

Bu had heard that tone before within the last year or two, but never toward her. It had something to do with *flirting*, which she knew some novices had begun doing. The tone sliding up a couple notes in the chromatic scale meant sly approval, and the other tone that began at fourth-tone and slid down was disparagement.

This new voice had used the latter.

"I told you, we were temple novices," Cricket retorted quickly. "Would you molest a sincere novice, and risk nine lifetimes of bad luck? This here is my *Little Sister* Bu."

"Oh-h-h-h," two voice chimed together.

"So you two ugly mutts remember that," Cricket added, but his voice wasn't sharp, or angry. That was the change, she perceived: Cricket had in the past been quick to a kind of flashing anger, but that anger had dissolved. Or maybe spread, the way fire does, if you back away from it, and it warms a room?

"I'll remember!" one said.

"She's safe from me! Not so much as a wink, much less a flower. Or a kiss." That was the other.

"Good. Also, I may as well tell you, she's half-blind, so she can't see your demon-spawn faces, or she'd be running off screaming."

The other two laughed again, and Bu caught a chortled mutter about a fierce squint, the rest too quick to catch.

Cricket turned back to her, still with that same tone of warmth-through-the-room. "Are you with the chief musician? Of course you are. YinYin, too? That's another sister, boys. You'll probably meet her." And in a lower voice, "A lot like Brick, if you know what I mean, but *quiet*, not slow. A fearsome musician."

While Cricket spoke, he took Bu's hand and tugged a little. She followed willingly enough, passing through narrow gaps between the seated figures, who squeezed up to be obliging. They had nearly reached the rail when he tugged again, and everyone sat down. Bu followed suit, by long habit now dropping neatly, knees together, back straight, butt on her heels, hands on her knees.

The boys with Cricket saw this smooth, neat posture, and sat a bit away from Bu, according her a modicum of respect without being aware of it. This was the respect they'd show a monk or nun. Though Bu's robe was sadly wrinkled from having been washed by hand from the rain barrel opposite the privy, and folded in Granny Zim's window to dry along with Granny Zim's and YinYin's robes, she moved like the nuns, who always handed out food on the festival days, and blessings as well.

"We heard about you," Cricket said in an undervoice. "That is, we heard there were a couple of followers with the old musician whose playing slapped Old Panheg down and made him weep on the deck. You know his favorite son died there on the Turtle Islands? He was the captain in charge, his first command. Some snot of a prince shot him before he even finished talking."

Bu was going to protest that no one had fallen sobbing to the deck, but the conversation moved on, a quick river.

"They called it something else," spoke one of the boys who Bu suspected were sons of the wharf "uncles" that she and YinYin had heard that Pig Year after Bu first came to the temple.

"The imperials might have wrote down a different name, but the people call it Turtle Islands. We had three of them at the temple, all silk-born. My guess is, in ancient days someone saw a giant turtle, and thought it signified luck, or something."

"Or something," one of the boys said with an impatient flick of his hand. "Who cares?"

Cricket spoke up. "Bu, did I introduce them? This here is Sanddab, I don't know why, because you can see that he doesn't have two eyes on one side of his head. Or maybe you *can't* see."

This essay into humor was met with honking guffaws.

"He's in some wise a cousin of mine. And that there is Little Toe. He's also a kind of cousin."

"Both our mothers ran off together," Little Toe said, his voice deep.

"Can you believe it? He was the smallest baby anyone had ever seen."

Bu peered at the large form of the young man to Cricket's left as Cricket swept on, "This here is Brick." He slowed down, speaking slowly and a bit loud as he indicated another large form sitting nearby. "Brick is not one of us, meaning from Fig Islands." Cricket leaned closer, whispering, "But he's one of us in that he's a street rat. They found him down south somewhere." Then loud again, and distinctly, "Say hello to Little Sister Bu, Brick."

"Huh?"

Bu blinked at Brick's vague form—how was she expected to tell any of these new people apart?—and then Cricket was off again. "I'll wager hundred to one you never thought to see me again! But the dragons came up to the mountain, and they weren't going to leave without one of us."

"One?" Why one?"

"Because they already had the Chief Musician and two of you. They *say* that when islands cooperate, they take only a certain number, and since you and YinYin were gone, and things were no fun, I said to myself, why not me? I told them I played the drums best, and here I am, in the dragon army."

"All of us are," Sanddab said. "Better than a beating from a drunk uncle for dinner, which was our usual. I've already had more meals, and costing me nothing, than I've had since we went around begging at New Year Two Moons."

"That's right," Little Toe rumbled. "Isn't that right, Brick?"

"Huh?"

"You have to talk slower," Cricket muttered. "They talk strange in the south, but at least he can understand us. Not like imperial."

"At least *you* understand imperial," Sanddab retorted.

Bu said hesitantly, "Is that what you call the book language? Imperial?"

"They told us it's what everyone speaks northwest of us, in the big islands," Cricket said.

Thoroughly overwhelmed, Bu said, "I ought to go back. I've practice to complete."

"You're still doing lessons?" Cricket asked. "Of course you are, if you're with the chief. I would stake a hundred taels she'd be having you playing all five modes in the middle of a dragon attack. Say, did you bring instruments? Of course you did, or how would you do lessons. How about a flute? We could have some fun, if you come tomorrow. We have to live on the deck now, because all those wretches they took off Turtle Islands are locked down in the hold."

"What are they going to do with them?" Bu asked, her ready sympathy overcoming her reluctance to remain without permission.

"Army General Panheg hasn't seen fit to report to us," Sanddab began sarcastically, but Cricket punched him in the arm. "It's said by most that they'll be sold off. So will you," he added unexpectedly, "but it's supposed to be a different sort of thing. You'll be sold for your skills, not as slaves."

Bu suppressed a grimace. She'd been wondering about the future, which at least had been foggy. That allowed for hope. Being sold was a frightening prospect, but then all her life she had expected to be put where the elders wanted her put.

FOURTEEN

"I WILL COME BACK here if I'm permitted," Bu said to Cricket, and threaded her way back, ignoring the occasional comment or question thrown at her, most of which were in incomprehensible dialects. No one troubled her other than these comments; the entirety of the crowd on the deck there was overseen by military people either roaming about or peering down from the tower structure.

When she rejoined Granny Zim, she told her everything, then ended, "I suppose I must remain here, and no more walking?"

"Only if you wish to," Granny Zim responded surprisingly.

"Then…I might go visit Cricket again?"

"I encourage you to do that. He was always resourceful, with quick ears. We might learn things from him. For example, discovering that the army commander lost a son clarifies much for me. I will ponder that, if we're summoned again." She patted Bu's hand. "As for the flute, take it! You should begin learning every scrap of music around you as you can. The days of meeting new people from every rank of life will help in whatever fate brings next. And try not to worry. I intend to get us into as good a situation as I can contrive, and as long as we are at sea, I can work at it."

"A situation such as?"

"The very best would be some noble who wishes to be known as a patron of music, poetry, and so forth. Courtiers pride themselves on their elegance, which includes wide knowledge of the arts. That extends especially to their wives. The imperials are peculiar in their ways of life, I learned: the men compete in the halls of government, and the women in the palaces and gardens."

"Why do they not let the men go out to sea to do military things, and leave governing to the women?" Bu asked. Fig Islands life seemed so much tidier.

"I can answer many questions, but not that one: to question their ways is to grab a boiling kettle. We must accustom ourselves to what we find, if we cannot have what we want. I seek the wife of a duke or a count who is wealthy enough to give us room to begin a little school, which would in turn provide a future for you, as a teacher."

A teacher! Bu was instantly apprehensive. She was so very ignorant! But teachers must have been young and ignorant once? At least so frighteningly exalted a fate, which she knew she did not deserve, lay somewhere in the hazy future.

Right now? She was to learn whatever music people sang or played—as she had when YinYin took her to hear those rice farmers and their beautiful round singing.

And so, the next day, she ignored the sun's glare under a ceiling of little white puff-clouds, and the stifling heat, and ventured onto the deck.

Cricket and his friends appeared to be on the watch, for she hadn't gone ten steps before they called out to her. When she joined them, Cricket said, "Some of these other poke-noses here don't believe we were really temple novices. Want to prove them wrong?"

Bu had brought the side flute. She slid it out of its cloth bag, feeling very strange. This idea of exposing her music before others, without the protection of Granny Zim's superior playing, disturbed her in the same way as eyes meeting eyes through the crystal. But being asked to play was also comforting, for at least she knew what to do and how to do it. "What would you like to hear?" she asked.

"Play anything," Sanddab said, which was no help at all.

Cricket said, "There's always the ancients. They kept us pretty much to that. But I've heard some newer things the warriors sing—"

"How about this?" Bu's mind went to the military ballad

that they had learned the first night. If Cricket and his new companions were to be army people, then they might like something similar to what their commanders liked. She took a moment to breathe properly, set her fingers, and played.

Cricket began tapping his hands on the deck to the rhythm, and as others picked it up and slapped their thighs or the deck, he used his fists, and shifted from the deck to a barrel, bringing forth different sounds. Bu adjusted to his rhythm, and on the second round, a few voices began singing the ballad.

At the end, a number of those gathered on the deck had moved closer, sitting shoulder to shoulder. They clapped, and a couple of people shouted from the crowd, naming songs she was to play next. She didn't recognize any of them, but having seen that rousing melodies pleased them, she began another, as Cricket pulled eating sticks out from his belongings and resumed drumming on the barrel lid.

She played until her mouth dried, then said, "Teach me the melody and refrain of some of your songs, and I will practice them for tomorrow."

"You can learn them in one day?" someone scoffed.

Bu could not hide her surprise. Was it arrogant to admit to it? "I can try."

"Don't listen to her. She'll do it," Cricket said. "We both will. We're used to it. That's what we did at the temple all day."

Then a cacophony of voices broke out, some singing tunelessly. No one seemed to know how to keep true pitch, but Bu guessed from what she'd been taught about the rudiments of melody, and said, "Is this close?" She sang one, then another back, and heard enthusiastic, "Yes, that's the one!"

She listened, sang back, and tried melodies until she was startled to discover the sun was already sinking. That night, she practiced them all with YinYin, even though Granny Zim thought YinYin ought to stay in their quarters, cramped as they were.

The next day was much the same, except that two of the young men brought out bamboo flutes that they had made themselves, and one had a battered eruh with terrible strings that had to be years and years old.

Bu hesitated to point that out, but Cricket clapped his hands over his ears. "No! That's torture. Those strings have to go."

"I can try to fix them," Bu offered softly, sensing profound disappointment in the way the eruh owner slowly took his precious instrument back. "I just need a knife, and I can also try to repair these strings. They have been weakened. The sound won't be pure…"

He pushed the eruh into her hands. "Can you? It used to sound good, when my da played it…"

That night, she sanded and oiled the eruh, using the small amount of supplies that Granny Zim's First Daughter-in-Law had included at the bottom of the carryall. Bu reworked the strings as best she could without the glue they dipped them in before the second tightening. By morning, they were far from the excellence demanded by the school, but at least they could hold a note true for a heartbeat or so.

Bu took the restrung lute back, which was joyfully received by its owner, who exclaimed, "You just saved me half a silver tael, little sister! I shall gladly be your donkey in our next life!"

And so it went.

She played and sang and learned. Both she and Cricket did their best to fix the rough instruments others brought out from time to time, which Bu sensed were precious to the owners. Granny Zim even disclosed some extra strings so that Bu could restring a lute whose strings were not even silk, as well as old and dull. "I'm trusting that we will be able to replace our own strings once we get to land. In the meantime, we are buying goodwill."

"I did not know new recruits had influence," Bu marveled. "I'm happy to share strings, until I can get some silk and make us some if we cannot buy them, but—"

"Influence is not always direct, my child. No captain, much less a commander, is ever going to ask those boys for their names, much less their opinions. However, a good commander keeps an ear to the wind, and your songs are spreading to the sailors, for I've heard some singing along with you when they work directly above me. I believe the other ship has even instigated singing, for their voices reach us across the sea between us when the wind is right."

The weather was increasingly warmer, and these young men had little to do once they had been put through a morning of hard training. Their afternoons were spent there on the deck, out of the sailors' way. They lived there day and night, tidying their tightly-rolled blanket beds along the hull by day. So far it hadn't rained, but Cricket told her when she asked that if it did rain, they'd share what waterproof coverings that the ship contained. "Or if it's warm enough, some of us will go right out there and let it pound our clothes. They throw buckets of seawater over us after we're through drilling, as a way to wash. We can rub the salt off our skin, but there's no getting it out of our clothes. I itch something fierce," he added, scratching at his armpit. "And, the regulars keep telling us that many's the march in a downpour they've made, and we're to get used to it."

Army life sounded horrible to her, but Cricket remained cheery. He and his companions mostly played gambling games or chatted, and seemed glad of any entertainment. Especially by Bu and Cricket. Bu marveled to discover that compared to the playing and singing she heard around her, she and Cricket were to them as Granny Zim was to the novices.

Music was what she had to give, and she found that giving it to people who enjoyed it filled her with joy, and though she played and sang and played some more, she was never tired.

More hoarded instruments appeared, all needing tuning if not mending. It would never occur to her to despise these poor, much-battered instruments, most of which had never been much good when new. Her absorption, as if she handled gold, her neat, careful fingers, and above all, her pleasant voice, gradually drew the mass of recruits into a single crowd, their singing carried over the waters to over ships. Once in a while, from the other troop ship, they heard people pick up melodies and echo them. She had become "Little Sister Bu," and there was nothing said about scrawniness or squints.

It was exhilarating for Bu to hear genuine welcome in greetings when she reappeared each day. If her life was to be like this, she thought at the end of the second ten-day, she would light incense and pray that things would never change, once they reached their destination.

Each night for the following ten days, she shared what she had learned with Granny Zim and YinYin. Meanwhile, there were no more summonses. Granny Zim only cackled and said, "Gives us more time to work on lessons. The better we get, the better our chances at the other end."

Granny Zim was feeling well enough to eat again, but she refused to come up onto the deck. "Bu, you keep going alone," she said. "If they all see an old grandmother, they'll go silent, and then, far as hearing anything of interest is concerned, may's well draw water with a basket."

"What do you wish to hear? Are you planning something?" Bu ventured to ask.

"I'm planning many things. But the first is to rescue Cricket from the army, if I can. Ayah, if only one of those two commanders would call for us again. Then I could ask for Cricket, and once they hear him, surely they'd give him back. I was sure I hadn't failed with that general, but I could be looking at dragonflies and seeing dragons. At least time is on our side."

Bu was not certain that Cricket wanted to come back to lessons, but as he had not said so directly, she kept her opinion to herself.

Anyway, as it transpired (so the storyteller said), time was not on their side.

Two days later, as Bu emerged from the hatch into the open air, she caught sight of a string of boats off in one direction. She screwed up her face trying to make out what was going on as she wished she'd thought to bring her crystal.

It looked like they were sending a lot of people over the side into boats.

"*There* you are."

That was Cricket, his thin form emerging from behind one of the masts. "I daren't lag much longer, but I had to speak to you." He ranged up close to her, so close she could see the blur of his features, and even a flash of the broken front teeth that his father had knocked out to make him look more pitiful as a beggar. "Listen, Bu. Word is, they got pigeons from the imperials last night, and the troop ships are to take the tribute to land since they're full up with those wretches down below. Two more ships are on the way."

"But aren't you part of the tribute?"

"We're already in the army," he explained, with no regret evident in his voice. "If we do what we're told, we get paid after a year, same as the regulars. Captain told me at dawn that I'm wanted for my drums. Which means an easy life, banging out meal calls, and parade, and the like, so don't spare a thought to me." He flashed a grin. "I asked if they could send my cousins with me, so's I can teach 'em imperial. I can watch out for them that way."

Bu was surprised at the regret she felt. But it was clear he did not feel any regret, so she ducked her head in a nod.

"We're off to one of the warships right now, and I have to run. I hope the fates allow us to meet up again. But here's what's important. I wanted to ask you to keep watch over Brick, will you?"

"Brick?" Bu repeated, then remembered the big, silent boy who'd camped on the deck with Cricket, Sanddab, and Little Toe. "What can *I* do?"

"You won't have to defend him. He can do that, sort of, if he sees a fist coming right at his face. But he's slow. Up here." Cricket tapped the side of his head. "You and YinYin, you showed me that people like that aren't simple. Nobody could be simple who could play the bells the way she did at our duet test long ago. And you with that squint, all your luck obviously skipped past your eyes but you got it all in your fingers. Watch out for him as you can. If you're kind to him, then the wolves might back off a bit from making his life harder than it is. Like, tricking him out of his share of the food and finding it funny. I know what it's like to try to sleep while hungry—"

"Cricket!"

"Coming, Captain Nang!"

"Of course, I'll try," Bu said promptly, her ready sympathy kindling. But she doubted very much she would be able to do anything significant.

Cricket gave her a brotherly pat on the shoulder, and pelted off.

Bu was going to retreat, but remembered what she'd promised, and so she ventured toward the somewhat smaller gathering on the deck; though she knew the captains and commanders were overseeing orderly movement, she was still a little afraid.

But when the sea of faces turned to her, and the recruits made way for as they always had, she remembered what Granny Zim had taught about presenting the face you want seen. She smiled as if Cricket and his friends were before her, and said, "Shall we give them a proper farewell?"

A shout of agreement met that.

She played the first melody of the Farewell Song that the women of the Fig Islands sang from the wicker bridges and along all the higher pathways when the men sailed off for half a year or more. Everyone grew up hearing it, though most of the instructors at the temple considered it vulgar.

Bu lowered her flute and began to sing. She was alone at first—then she remembered that no one else would know the Farewell Song. She almost abandoned it, then decided that this was good practice in maintaining her performance face. She deepened her breath and strengthened her voice, which carried, sweet and true, out over the water.

Then an echo returned in three loud, ragged-toned male voices: Cricket and his two wharf-rat friends singing back with more gusto than grace.

On the refrain, ones, then twos, and then fives joined in from the troop ship, as—like most folk refrains—the words and the melody were simple.

A fine body of sound rose as the last boat reached the warship, and it rattled down its sails to begin its journey elsewhere.

Bu could not see that. She drew a breath, and, mindful of Cricket's wishes, began to play one of the oft-requested favorites, a military ballad that was easy to march to.

Many sang, and others thumped the deck with fists and feet, and under cover of a song they knew well, Bu sat down next to Brick, whom she identified because he always sat in the same place, his back to the hull below the rail, knees up, hands propped on his knees and dangling loosely.

"Is there anything I can do for you?" she asked very slowly and distinctly, remembering that he understood a dialect that Cricket had said was akin to the Fig Islands tongue.

"Huh?"

"I said, is there anything I can get for you, or do for you?"

He turned his head. She felt him staring. Then he turned away, and she, sensitive to movement even when she could not define what she perceived, felt a wall of apathy rather than bewilderment.

The song was ending. She moved a bit away, and began another round of songs. Before she finished, she crouched down next to Brick and tried again, "Is there anything I can do for you?"

"Don't bother with Brick," one of the teenage boys said, his voice cracking as he laughed. "You know how he got his name? He's got brick between his ears."

Brick didn't even look at Bu, just stared off into space, his jaw hanging loose.

Bu gave up. Maybe Brick did not want to draw attention, which would surely attract more trouble. She had felt the same way when she was small. It was never a good thing if her elder sisters noticed her. They were sure to stop quarreling with one another and start in on her in a group. She got up and returned to Granny Zim's quarters, and reported that Cricket was gone.

Granny Zim gave a short nod. "I expected that," she said heavily. "I hoped he would try from his end, but all these days passed by, and he never did."

Bu exclaimed, "You mean, he doesn't want to come back?"

"Answer that yourself, child. Did you hear any regret?"

Bu considered, and finally admitted, "No. I was looking for it, and maybe saw some. But he seemed content to go."

"The two of you came at the same time, and for much the same reasons, but you discovered your passion. He has passion, but I was never certain it was for music. He might not even know what his passion is. Many don't, their entire lives."

"Does everyone have passion?" Bu asked.

"I think they do. To greater or lesser extent. Passions, like anything, can be terrible. Most often I think they are small. Maybe as small as wanting to be certain of the next meal and a place to sleep. Add Cricket's name when you pray, and perhaps Heaven will keep him safe. Let us resume with the lute, which we've been neglecting…"

Bu kept her promise and went to the deck the next day. She had saved out the largest of her two spiced pancakes. After she got a pair of the deck recruits playing their bamboo flutes to a popular song, and everyone looking at them as they sang along, she crouched down beside Brick. This time she didn't say anything, just pushed the pancake into his hand, and then moved away quickly. She hoped if she drew attention away from him, he would eat it before whoever it was could see him, and trick him out of it.

And when she went below late that afternoon, Granny Zim greeted her with, "We've been summoned again. Apparently they want you there, too."

FIFTEEN

"THEY WANT ME?" BU asked, fright widening her eyes.

Granny Zim chuckled. "I know not why. Those at the top seldom trouble to give reasons for orders to those beneath. But at a guess, your music, or rather how those young recruits on the deck have responded to it, has gained notice. This is a good thing, Bu. Be modest, respectful, and keep your answers strictly to what you know—which is music—and you cannot be wrong."

Bu was still worried, though she knew Cricket would tease her for cowardice if he were there. YinYin did not say anything, as usual, which Bu found comforting.

Granny Zim had Bu play on the zither, and YinYin on the side flute as she played her qin. This time, they were alone with the army general, who was eating his dinner as they entered his airy quarters on the third floor of the central structure above the deck. He gestured with his free hand toward three cushions, and kept eating as they settled and began to play.

They'd performed two more ballads when he waved at the waiting orderly to take away the dishes, except for tea. Then the general said, "Very fine playing, child. This one must be your best, eh, Chief Musician?"

"She is, O Esteemed General."

"And you decided to play to the new recruits? What's your

name?"

Bu sent a frightened glance at Granny Zim who gave a sharp nod.

"Bu. Lum Bu, O Esteemed Army General." Bu said in a tiny voice, ending on a note of question—as if the mighty general would go into a rage at her temerity for laying claim to the Lum name.

But he was not the least interested in the Lum name. "Speak up, child. You've a voice when you want to be heard; I know that was you, singing to the recruits being sent as reinforcements. A very fine voice, too. What do you want to do?"

"Want...to do?" Bu repeated witlessly. "Esteemed Army General," she added to the deck.

"What made you decide to exhibit your skills among the recruits, or did you not know that they haven't a copper-piece between them until they receive their first pay a year from now?"

Bu blinked, and for a moment there was a glimpse of a thoughtful expression instead of the disfiguring squint. Then the squint was back, and Bu said, "I...I never thought of that. It was discovering Cricket among them. Ah, he was another of our novices. He invited me to play, and I got permission from my tutor."

Army General Panheg remembered the young drummer; he'd had to sign off on a shifting of the roster, replacing the drummer who had died in the initial clash. Not wanting to remember anything of the bloody Turtle Islands battle, he gazed past Bu to YinYin, sitting quietly at Granny Zim's shoulder. "And you? We have yet to hear from you, novice..."

"YinYin," Granny Zim said. "She is newer than Novice Bu."

"What do you want to do, Novice YinYin?"

"Teaching, O Esteemed General," YinYin said in that same flat, small voice she always used.

General Panheg looked past Novice YinYin's square, unprepossessing face to Granny Zim, and said, "I like your military ballads, but that is all the regimental musicians give us. What else can you offer tonight?"

Granny Zim had prepared for any eventuality, and they began with the traditional "Osprey" and progressed to spring airs. Granny Zim watched obliquely. The man seemed restless. Was that how he wore grief, or was it merely his wound bothering him? He still was bandaged over his left side, which meant he had taken a serious blow, or more than one blow, besides the invisible knife of losing a child.

Granny Zim began another traditional spring piece in praise of virtue and heroism. The general listened, eyes closed in a shuttered face. If she could not break past that wall, then had her skills dwindled with her age? She abandoned spring for another heroism melody, "Three Lines of Geese across the Sky", one very old indeed. It did not need to be sung, for the poem was part of the Thousand Poems young imperials memorized in their scholarly training.

> *Far from his scattered flock*
> *A wild goose flies*
> *Dusk in the hollow ravine*
> *No pond, dead grass,*
> *Nowhere to rest, a mournful cry*
> *One moon west, one east, darkness between…*

The poem went on to celebrate and mourn the virtuous heroes who died young without knowing their fame. The qin sustained the haunting chords as the zither played with the melody, bringing out spring flowers, birds, animals — but the angular fourths subdued the sweet, familiar thirds and fifths, bringing out the restless, seeking spirit, a reminder that this young life would never experience the delights of spring…

Still that wall! Granny Zim frowned, plucking the first three notes of the forlorn melody "The Widow At The Gate" but then Bu surprised Granny Zim by reversing those three notes, and changing the song to a gallant wanderers ballad. Gallant wanderers! That was sure to displease the general. It was a silly song featuring a goat as the wandering hero, accompanied by a donkey and an owl. What a moment to suddenly gain boldness, after all this time!

Rather than rebuke her novice before their single listener, Granny Zim played the background, as YinYin echoed the main melody. The general's face gradually eased, and at the end, he merely looked tired instead of carved from stone.

"Thank you. All of you are very skilled. That will do for today."

They filed out, and Granny Zim used the time it took to return to their quarters to examine her spark of anger that this half-trained girl would dare to change the music on her own.

It was a fine reminder that everything had changed. Everything. To pretend that she had the authority of the Zim family, headwomen for generations, as well as the prestige of the temple school, was to shout into the wind. She had insisted that Bu address her as Granny Zim. No titles. She had also insisted that Bu learn common ditties, and even practice them—absolutely forbidden before. She had emphasized that they were now floating toward a future she could try to guide, but could not guarantee.

So when they were back in her little cabin, she said quite mildly, "You took the lead, Bu."

Bu threw herself to the deck, forehead to the warped wood. "This ignorant wretch would rather die a thousand deaths than presume. It's just that his breathing… it was… it was…"

YinYin spoke up without being addressed, so very rare an occurrence. "Two of my kind waited for him to, ah, to invite them in."

Chill flashed through Granny Zim, and Bu's head jerked up, though she still crouched on the deck.

"Stop that," Granny Zim said irritably to Bu. "Sit properly. YinYin, you are not referring to Bu and myself, but to two demons—two of your kind, that is? What term is best, if demon is not correct?"

"Say demon," YinYin responded. "It will do. Human language to my kind is much like the tweet of birds to humans. There is emotion, if not meaning. You know an angry bird from one calling to its mate, even if you do know what is said."

Granny Zim hmmmed as Bu slid to her cushion, eyes huge. "Then two demons waited for what, precisely? Where? How?"

YinYin's form blurred here and there, mostly around the head, the carefully cultivated hair dissolving into wisps of night-black smoke. Then, with an effort Granny Zim saw, and Bu sensed, the demon firmed up. "I am still learning about human passion. I think we are made of passion. Passion is…hunger?" YinYin asked, hand to stomach. "Not there." The hand shifted upward to the chest. "Or here?" To the forehead.

"It can be," Granny Zim said carefully. All her ire had vanished before a far greater concern: she had no control over this turn of events at all.

"That man. His passion, it is…" YinYin's eyes glowed red. Then a blink and they were black again. "I am still putting words to meaning. He wants to end pain."

"I heard that," Bu whispered. "In his breathing. It was

terrible. That's why I thought, we must change the song. I was afraid that 'The Widow at the Gate' would…"

"Would what?" Granny Zim asked. "My intention was to break that wall, so he could permit emotion to escape. That would be a release for him, and a triumph for us."

Bu's face scrunched. "His breathing, I…It sounded so like my father's before he died."

"Oh." It was Granny Zim's turn to frown.

YinYin turned Bu's way. "When we looked at the ships in the harbor. And I put a piece of myself inside you, to make you see. You said, you must remain yourself. Even though you do not see. I took that as right. Your actions as a human, they are right actions."

"You show good judgment," Granny Zim interposed, wondering where YinYin was leading the discussion. "Bu can be trusted for that."

Bu was going to deny any such thing, but YinYin said, "Bu has passion for music. I understand that. It is like my passion. Bu has the passion, and learns the music, and is a right human, without…"

For a heartbeat YinYin's form completely dissolved, billowing like a cloud of smoke in which horrible red eyes and gnashing teeth and claws rent the air. It nearly filled the entire cabin, and as Bu and Granny Zim fell back, Bu crying out and Granny gasping, hand to her chest, in less than a blink, YinYin was back to the form they recognized. "Destroy," YinYin said, in that small, flat voice. "Bu, you do not destroy. Not with words. Not with hands and thoughts."

Bu folded her arms, shivering.

Granny Zim said, "I think I understand. Demons can, and do, enter humans, then?"

"Yes. I did it. With Bu. A tiny part of me. I could live there and grow. I could make Bu see everything. I could put my skills in Bu. I could draw the Essence out of her, then out of all who hear. Bu said, she must be…" YinYin pointed at Bu. "Herself. Though weak. Bad eyes. Learn slow. I do not take Essence to give strength, sight, skill."

"I see," Granny Zim exclaimed. "You have decided it is not right to devour Bu from the inside, even if it will make you stronger?"

"Yes! I am learning the right words," YinYin exclaimed. "It is very difficult."

"You are very young?" Granny Zim asked. "For a demon,

I mean?"

YinYin pondered this, then said, "My kind. There is no time. I see the Fire Mountain and its dragon. I am small. No. Not small. I am weak. If I devour Bu, I get stronger. If the two of my kind enter that man, who wants no pain, but who is very angry, and full of sorrow, then one can devour all his humans through him. Become very old. No, become very big. No, become very power. Power-ful. Full of power. Destroy so many humans. King of Underworld turns eyes toward them, because they are like what you call a god."

"I believe I follow. Then what you two sensed…" (And I did not, in my arrogance, Granny Zim reflected.) "…was him at a peak of emotion in which he would do anything to kill the pain. Because he cannot let the emotion free."

Bu said, "His breathing was so very painful."

Granny Zim turned to YinYin. "What can we do to protect him from being devoured by these two demons?"

"I eat them," YinYin said.

"Ay!" Shock rang through Granny Zim.

"I need Essence," YinYin explained. "It is very difficult to get Essence by human food. If you humans eat one grain of rice, then another grain of rice, you very slowly become not hungry. It is that way for me, with human food." YinYin's voice was thinning out, as if the effort to maintain the human body and express human words had a severe cost.

"You sound as if you are tiring. If demons get tired. Maybe in that form?" Granny Zim asked.

"Yes."

"Then one more question, because I don't think I can sleep if I do not ask, at least. You are learning to draw Essence with your music?"

"Yes," YinYin's voice was rough, almost a soft growl. "Metal."

"Ayah! Through the bells?"

"Bells." YinYin dissolved then, clothing and all.

SIXTEEN

"Is YinYin gone?" Bu asked, peering around as she fumbled her crystal from her carryall, which was where she had put it when she decided not to reveal it on deck.

"If I comprehend correctly, I believe YinYin went to clear off those two demons she sensed," Granny Zim said, proud that her voice only trembled once.

Bu manipulated her crystal with practiced ease and peered around the tiny cabin, sorrow harrowing the knot of fear in her heart at how very old and tired Granny Zim looked. However her eyes, as black as YinYin's, gazed back steadily, sharp and observant.

A little reassured, Bu tucked her crystal away as Granny Zim said, "She might still be here in some sense. I believe we cannot assume that demons are confined to one place and time as we are, but as she just took a great deal of effort to tell us that her motivation is benevolent, I think we might as well assume that whatever she is doing is a right thing, and be glad of it."

"I *am* glad," Bu said. "I didn't want her to go away. Except she said her passion is for bells, and we don't have any bells to practice with."

"We'll do our best to include bells in our music school," Granny Zim said. "In the meantime, the more YinYin learns about how sound makes music rather than noise, the better.

She first appeared to me while I was playing my qin for myself. If she wanted loud noise, she could manifest during thunderstorms. Or shouting arguments, for that is another type of passion."

"Anger," Bu said, and her thoughts arrowed to their playing for the army general. "I think I am beginning to understand 'maddens'," she admitted. "To really understand. I've seen how music, ayah, shapes emotions. But what YinYin said about how that army general was ready to invite demons in—and I could hear that in how he breathed."

Granny Zim said, "I believe your hearing is sharper than mine. That aside, it seems that I have much to learn, too. It's good to learn, at my age. Though I know how powerful music can be, reminders are necessary."

Bu pressed her arms across her middle. Memory echoed the terror of that sudden sight, the lightless cloud filled with red eyes and teeth and claws. She wondered if all those eyes had been real eyes—but how could they be, without a body to rest in? Symbols? "Granny Zim, when YinYin gave us that demon shape, did you see many glowing ember eyes, and teeth, and claws?"

"Swords," Granny Zim whispered. "Knives."

"Symbols, then."

"I believe so. Our minds offered us images we understand for the destructive chaos that YinYin mentioned. Let us rest, for I have much to think about."

Bu agreed with that! She was too tired and worried to think about washing out their second robes. Tomorrow, she promised herself, and carried the cups back, afraid she would never sleep—but as soon as she wrapped up in her blanket, she dropped into dreams.

When she woke, YinYin was there next to her, lying straight on the platform, eyes open. Even to Bu's sight, YinYin was somehow brighter. More solid.

Bu sat up, and when YinYin turned her way, Bu whispered softly, "Did you...eat those demons?"

"Yes," YinYin said in that small, matter-of-fact voice.

"They are dead? Gone?"

"Their Essence is in me. They will learn with me."

Granny Zim sat up. "I don't think demons can be killed," she said, her fingers working her meager braid then pinning it up in the married women's knot. "How many have you absorbed, YinYin?"

YinYin stilled. "Six. They, too, learn."

Somewhat unsettled, Bu rolled her blanket and got ready for the morning.

The orderly appeared a short time later, and as usual, did not glance at YinYin twice.

On the surface, everything was as usual. They ate breakfast—Bu surreptitiously saving out one of her pancakes—and then set about the day's practice.

When they finished—when Granny Zim had to rest her hands—Bu went to the deck, and once again found a chance to slip her pancake into Brick's fingers. She did not know if he'd eaten the previous one, or thrown it away, or gave it away. Or if it was taken from him. She tried to be stealthy, then drew attention away from the silent, slack-jawed figure as she brought forth the songs she had been practicing.

This began the pattern over the next stretch of days.

The sky clouded over, raining off and on. With the moons hidden, it felt as if time had suspended, and they sailed into eternity, for there were no islands at all between the small clusters they had left, and the mass of greater islands west of them, where the imperials and their foes lived.

Army General Panheg had shifted his command to the troop ship and its two warship consorts for the journey back to the imperial island. He began drinking again, summoning the three of them once, twice, and then every night. He did not even know what it was he sought, only that music both hurt and healed in a way he could not describe. His was a lonely pinnacle. He could not unburden himself to anyone. But he could lose himself for a time in memories when surrounded by the exquisite skill of these three musicians, whose music now expressed matters of spring, both in old songs and new, chosen and played with unspoken compassion.

Nothing changed as day followed day, until one afternoon, when Bu brought her usual offering and found a moment to slip it to Brick, she was startled when he pushed it back into her hand. Not violently. But insistently. His blurred face swung her way, and he slurred, "Eat. You eat."

It was the book language, barely comprehensible.

"No, that's for you," she whispered.

"Yours."

"It's fine," Bu said softly, as distinctly as she could. "I had half. And I'll get a supper tonight. It's plenty for me. You need it more than I do. I know they make you work hard. We can hear the thumping on the deck…" She realized she was babbling the way she would have with Cricket, and shut up.

Then, sensing attention her way, she rose, as a tall figure approached. "Ho, little sister, if you want a man's attention, you can do better than Brick-head there."

"He's from our neighboring islands," Bu explained. "Should we not all try to be brethren if we can?"

"I'll be a brother, or anything you like, ha ha ha."

Others laughed as well, and Bu sensed them surrounding her. She kept her performance face steady, though that laughter hurt her ears and her heart bounded about behind her ribs like a frightened hen. She said, "Will you sing with me?"

She asked innocently, but there was nothing innocent in his, Oh, we'll sing real good," followed by crashing laughter.

"Everything all right over here?" That was a new voice, one aware of its authority, calling down from the rail of the superstructure's second floor. The laughter ended abruptly as Bu peered up, recognizing the red cloak of a captain.

Bu said, "We're just trying to figure out which ballad to sing as a duet. Do you have a request?"

"You might try 'The Three Heroes of Sweetbreeze Harbor' and then I suggest you run along. That line of clouds out there is bringing thunder, if I'm not mistaken, and these sorry jackals are about to get their stinking clothes washed for them."

But bowed, her hands together, and began the now-familiar song on her flute as she stamped the rhythm on the deck. The young man who'd approached her began singing, soon joined by better voices. After which Bu obediently retreated below.

She was back the next day, with a stuffed biscuit.

Brick didn't speak to her again, and she continued to bring him half her breakfast, until the day the smell of land reached them. Then the cry and caw of shore birds, as word passed through the ship: Mt. Lir sighted on the horizon!

"Now is the time to wash our best robes, and stretch them out as much as we can as they dry," Granny Zim said briskly. "We need to look as tidy as possible for whatever lies ahead."

Everyone not locked up was on deck the next morning as they drifted on the tide into the broadest harbor the small islanders had ever seen. Granny Zim stood between Bu and YinYin, both with loaded shoulder carryalls. Bu used her crystal to study this new land, which was dominated by a mountain that made their own mountain look like a hill. The top actually vanished within a ceiling of heavy gray cloud.

A series of splendid rooftops dominated the harbor from the foot of that mountain. Rank after rank of tile roofs, each corner lifted heavenward, with tiny figures on each. Below, parallel to the shoreline, more modest roofs, in rows. "That is the city, is my guess," Granny Zim murmured.

"And those grand roofs, above the high wall?"

"A palace. Perhaps even the imperial palace."

"Oh." Bu tried to study the roofs more closely, but at that moment the high voices of girls more or less her age rose around her. While she'd been staring, the tribute girls had come forth, standing neatly in lines, the matrons at either end. Some of the girls suppressed giggles, and whispers about what they hoped; by now they understood that they would become palace maids in various departments, depending on their looks as well as their skills. After ten years, they would be released to marry if they liked, and there might even be pay. Not a few had come to the conclusion that that was more than life would have offered them on their various home islands.

Behind Bu male voices rumbled, punctuated by cracks of nasal laughter, so many of them teens not much older than she was. Judging by snatches of overheard talk, their future seemed to be military in one way or another. It was those miserable wretches imprisoned in the hold who would be going to the mines, or hard labor on roads and the like.

The ship jolted. Bu turned along with all the others, to see that they had come alongside a pier, and sailors were busy making the great ship fast, except for the slow rise and fall on the tide.

"Make way! Make way!" bawled orderlies.

People squeezed up. Bu, still peering through the crystal, spotted the gleam of an elaborate helmet topped by a feather crest. Several red capes followed that helmeted figure. He trod down a ramp to the pier. Bu recognized Army General Panheg, first to disembark. He strode up the long pier to the wharf, where an enormous pavilion had been set up. It was open on the sides. The red roof came to a point, with a dragon banner flapping in the rising wind; a spat of rain splattered Bu's cheek, and a murmur ran through the waiting crowd, silenced by sharp commands here and there.

Thunder rumbled in the distance, ignored by the sailors directing groups of burly wharf workers, who ran up the ramp and into the ship, then began reappearing bearing what looked like big, heavy chests. One, two, three, four … an apparently unending stream of them.

"Tribute loot," Granny Zim whispered in the Fig Island tongue.

When at last the chests had been carried off the ship, down the pier, and then loaded on waiting wagons, more rain stung the waiting tribute people.

A captain appeared out of nowhere, motioning to Granny Zim and those around her, including the rows of girls. "Move along. Don't dawdle or wander," the man bellowed.

Granny Zim led, moving spryly enough. Bu tucked the crystal away; the rise and fall of the ship, and her own steps in a counter rhythm, made it impossible to look through the crystal without causing vertigo.

The ramp was frightening, as it moved constantly under their feet, but they reached the pier, which also seemed to be moving. It wasn't. Bu stumbled, peering desperately at her feet. Granny stepped very carefully, YinYin at her shoulder. YinYin alone seemed untroubled by vertigo.

A blue-white flicker erupted into a clap of thunder that drove half the islanders to their knees before a sudden burst of hail slanted at them. All was confusion as imperial guards stepped in to take control from the debarking army and navy, forcibly muscling gawking locals out of the way—most there to count what they assumed were chest of gold and gems, and to catch a glimpse of pretty girls before they were swallowed by the imperial palace, or interesting prisoners on their way to the execution ground. The guards herded the tribute people into one of the buildings along the outer edge of the imperial guards' end of the palace before the wretched prisoners, locked down in the hold all this time, were brought up and harried through the hail-sharp deluge straight to the prison.

The swarm in the warehouse was quickly pushed and bellowed into a manageable mass, at which time the various palace department chiefs, who usually picked and chose from the pavilion in an orderly fashion, found themselves chivvied into doing their sorting in this crowded environment. Sharp voices bounced off stone, an unfamiliar shape of sound that had Bu wanting to put her hands over her ears.

She was jostled and bumped from either side until without warning she found herself facing a tall woman whose voice snapped like a whip: "The two girls are ugly. Send them to the kitchen. The old woman can go out to the—"

A red-cloaked captain interrupted her, "Those are the musicians Army General Panheg designated for the palace."

"Put them in the pen for now."

"The pen" turned out to be a small enclosure that smelled strongly of horse, divided off from the rest of the hall by a low rail of the sort that would keep horses from wandering.

Granny Zim murmured as they took possession of the far corner, "Next comes the vital test."

SEVENTEEN

BU PULLED OUT HER crystal when she heard some of the deck boys' familiar voices among the low rumbles of men gathered in the main part of the hall, which seemed to Granny Zim to be some sort of gathering place for military parades to assemble when the weather was bad, judging by the stacks of banners and streamers in the far corners.

"Are we in danger here?" Bu asked Granny Zim.

"I think not. I think we're being tidied out of sight until more important people, or matters, are seen to while the storm persists. Here, look this way. From the different uniforms of those hatted captains, my guess is that they are going to pick and choose among these boys. Some no doubt destined for the local guard, and some for the other types of military."

As they watched, guards in shiny chest armor divided the assembled recruits into groups. At the other end of the hall—a few paces from where Bu stood—more guards, or servants, rolled out carts of what appeared to be wooden weapons.

Three guards separated, each holding a wooden weapon. Three recruits were sent down the hall, one to a guard. Each recruit was given a wooden sword. The guards barked a word of command, and then struck experimentally at the recruits.

The recruit closest to Bu struck back bravely, his sword meeting the guard's. Clack, clack, clack! Then the guard swung a bit harder, and knocked the weapon out of the hand of the recruit. "Not bad," said the guard. "Go over there." He pointed toward the opposite wall, where the other two already stood.

Out came the next three. Once again, wooden swords were issued, and the three guards swung. One recruit swung wildly, missing the guard's sword entirely. The second responded with a respectable defense, and managed to keep hold of his sword. The third recruit threw his hands over his head to protect it, the sword dangling awkwardly from his fingers.

Laughter rose from the waiting recruits, as that hapless boy was sent to stand with the waiting servants. It was clear what his fate was to be. Bu studied his face through the crystal, hazarding a guess that he was not all that disappointed. I'd rather push carts and carry things, too, Bu thought

The next set came out, and all three strove to attack the guards. All three lost their weapons, one in two strikes, one in four, and one made it about six before he uttered a yelp, dropped the sword, and wrung his hand. They were all sent to join the group at the wall.

As Bu watched, that group swelled slowly. Another four joined the servants, two so small they clearly had not begun on their man's height, and one squinting in a way that sent a pang of familiarity through Bu.

The smallest group was made up of the ones who'd managed to hang onto their weapons. One boy was very good, so good everyone clapped when his bout ended. Bu was going to turn away when the next three were sent, one shuffling open-mouthed. Was that Brick? She'd never seen his face clearly, but that mouth hanging open vacantly seemed familiar. He took up the practice sword, letting it hang limply. The guard raised his sword and struck, Bu wincing in anticipation.

Brick raised the sword in a clumsy arc, and managed to deflect the blade. Again, from above, another sloppy arc, barely keeping the blade from his ear. The guard sped up a little. Brick waved his blade as if poking a hive of biters, and the guard's blade slid along it. Once, twice, three times — each time, Brick managed to preserve himself from getting hit, though more often than not by a finger's breadth.

The guard lowered his blade. "All right, someone managed to pound some learning into you," he said. "Though I wouldn't keep you at my back for a hundred gold. But rules are rules. You're now the grays' problem…go over there."

As he waved a gloved hand in dismissal, the red-cloak next

to him strolled over, and without lowering his voice, said, "Sending that one to the grays?"

"That's the rules. He held onto his weapon. Though I can't imagine what they'll do with him. Put him on the pilgrim gate, maybe?"

"No, no, he'll be the latest rat stuck on the Weasel." This guard snickered as the first one gave a quick bark of laughter. "Anyway he's not *our* problem."

Brick had to be hearing that, Bu thought with sorrow and indignation, since she could. But Brick slumped off toward the small group without any reaction, where he stood alone, mouth still hanging open.

"Bu? Do you know that child?" Granny Zim asked. In spite of the unwashed night-black hair hanging lankly down his back, and his gaping vacancy, he reminded her of Teg, but taller and broader through the chest.

"He was Cricket's little brother, in a way."

Granny Zim hmmmed. "Of course Cricket would look out for him. Oh, I do wish we had not lost him to the army." She sighed, and whispered a charm of protection for Cricket; if anyone could survive his fellow man, it was Cricket, but arrows have no eyes.

At that moment, a servant in dove gray appeared, and summoned everyone in the horse pen to form a line and come along. Bu tucked her crystal away and hitched the carryall to the other shoulder, for it was beginning to cut into her flesh.

Thus began a long walk in such roundabout ways along high, plain walls, that Bu finally figured out they must be in servants' corridors, which jigged around three sides of important buildings. No straight paths for the likes of them. But at least the way was covered, rain roaring to either side.

Granny Zim was beginning to grunt softly at each step by the time they finally reached a building whose stone had been washed in pale yellow, like so many of the ones they'd already passed. The group came to a halt. "Musicians through that way. The graywings will take you to where you're to go."

Granny Zim, YinYin, and Bu waited as the group passed on out of sight.

Bu had noticed by now that the palace servants all seemed to wear gray. One set of guards had been in shades of gray, including gleaming half-armor; she'd soon learn those were the imperial guards. Lower servants wore dove-gray, differentiated by edging and sashes of a slightly grayer gray.

Darkest of all were these new ones, who wore hats with stiff arms reaching to either side. To Bu, these hats resembled swords, and the way the servants in that dark gray glided silently seemed a little sinister.

"Follow me," a mellow voice instructed.

"Denatured," Granny Zim whispered, barely a sound.

Bu had seen some sort of reference to that in her reading. She was going to ask what that meant, but the servant glanced back, and she turtled her head into her shoulders, hefted the carryall anew, and followed silently.

They were conducted to a tiny waiting area and left alone. It had one small round window that looked into a garden, and a bench. Nothing else. Bu grunted with relief as she carefully set her carryall between her feet.

"I can carry them both," YinYin said.

Granny Zim shook her head. "No. One each."

Ah! Bu's gratitude at the offer dissolved. Of course that would draw attention.

"Surely it's not much farther," Granny Zim said more mildly.

A teenage girl in the ubiquitous gray appeared at the door. Her clothes were different from all the others, a robe of dull gray over an under robe of dove gray. "Please come," this girl said. "The Chief will see you now."

Granny Zim's hand closed over Bu's, giving a warning squeeze. Alarm burned through Bu. The test—whatever it was to be—was beginning now, apparently. Mindful of her posture, she bent to pick up the carryall, to have it taken from her hands by a servant in dove gray. YinYin's was also taken. The two servants followed behind, carrying the bags, as the girl led the way down a corridor that smelled of wood oil, and string glue. Bu was surprised by the prickle of tears under her eyelids at these comfortingly familiar odors.

They passed rooms with wooden doors shut tight against sound escaping, though Bu's ears detected a lute. Eruh. Zither. Practice chambers! The hall ended in a sizable room lined with cushions, where a cluster of people waited on a low dais before a sound-screen rich with a riot of color. Two of these waiting people were gray-haired. So much gray in this bewildering place, Bu thought, as the middle one beckoned to them.

"Grandmother," this man said to Granny Zim, speaking slowly and precisely, as if she were hard of hearing. Or of understanding. "Please sit. I apologize for the unconscionable long walk."

It was very polite, proper address to an elder, but he enunciated so very clearly that Bu suspected that intent lay behind it. He used that accent that she knew by now was considered "pure" imperial speech, but she had privately decided it sounded like frogs croaking, with so many word endings swallowed in a guttural r-r-r-r.

"I am certain you are very tired, and have come a long way. From which island?"

"Fig Islands, Esteemed Chief Musician," Granny Zim said, hands together, as proper for addressing one whose rank is higher than one's age.

"Fig Islands! An evocative name. I'm sure it must be very beautiful there."

"Thank you, Esteemed Chief Musician." Granny Zim bowed with utmost dignity, and Bu knew her instinct was right; this chief musician, while on the surface speaking politely to set them at ease, was implying that they were barbarians. She'd already experienced some of that attitude aboard the ships.

She kept her back straight, hands on her knees, as the chief said, "First Apprentice Xia Chi." It came out sounding more like *Shyacharr*. "Bring the venerable musician a…what would you prefer, Musician…"

"Zim, O Esteemed Chief Musician," Granny Zim said. "This undistinguished one bears the insignificant name Zim Li. Whatever instrument your exalted self desires to hear, this old strummer will attempt to play, though it must be confessed that the old often prefer the old, and the guqin is my customary instrument."

"Mine too, mine too," exclaimed the chief. "First Apprentice, fetch my qin, and please offer it to Musician Zim."

"No, no, I would never presume," Granny Zim said, palms out. "I do have my instrument with me, such as it is…"

"Ah, but after toilsome travel, what instrument is at its best? If you will honor us by attempting one of ours, it would gladden my heart."

It wasn't spite, Bu thought. She knew all the varieties of spite. She had heard them from her earliest years. This chief was not antagonistic, but he was very sure of his rank, it seemed. He wanted them to understand their place at a lower level, just as he sat on an instructor's platform, with that beautiful sound-screen behind him. And Granny Zim was getting more humble by the moment, a sure sign that she sensed the challenge.

A tall boy who sat at the side of the room, quiet and unnoticed by the three at the north end of the room, went out, and returned carrying two qins, one above the other, balanced on each hand. He bowed, without tipping the qins to the slightest degree, and handed one to his chief, and the other to Granny Zim.

Who did not touch it. "This old wretch must apologize in advance for infirm hands," she said. "If it is permitted, one of my novices will tune it. Bu?"

Bu flushed at attention shifting to her. What was Granny Zim's purpose here? There was some message, or maybe it was merely that she wanted to see what Bu thought of the qin before she played it.

Bu bowed from where she stood at Granny Zim's shoulder, knelt to shift the qin's low table, and tried to hide what a relief it was to be off her feet at last, for she'd been standing since dawn—and then had carried that heavy bag for what had seemed twice the length of Fig Island. She ran her hands over the instrument, dreading to discover it was a howler or a screecher, but the wood was sound, beautifully preserved. She tested the strings, finding one minutely off. The tuning pegs were carved in acanthus blossoms, smooth to the touch. It was a beautiful instrument, joyfully ready to sing.

Granny Zim saw that in Bu's quiet face, as Bu resettled the table before Granny Zim, and then returned to her stance behind Granny Zim.

"Do you wish to postpone our informal duet?" the chief musician asked.

"This old strummer begs forgiveness for troubling the Esteemed Chief Musician, and assures him it is merely a question of age and infirmity," Granny Zim said. "Which time only worsens. These old hands to require a moment or two to warm to the task, for which I beg pardon."

"No, no, I quite understand. Let us begin simply, with the fundamentals…"

Simple, Bu discovered can be defined very differently when the intent is a contest without actually being named as a contest. He began with ritual pieces, very advanced to Bu's ears. These were new to her, introduced by Granny Zim aboard the ship. The next two, even more advanced, shifted between the three forms of the seven-toned scale.

Granny Zim echoed them, plucking and strumming to match his touch with such precision he could be playing both instruments. It was pure method. Still as a pool. No ripples or splashes of sunlight, no breath of wind or sound of birds or scent of blossoms.

Bu heard the moment Granny Zim's hands eased — and so did the chief musician, for he launched into "The Five Scholars" with powerful grace, pausing at the end of the first melody.

Granny Zim echoed him precisely, still withholding all expressive embellishment. He played the refrain, shifting modes suddenly, and lifted his hands. Granny Zim mirrored him, precise to the last pluck.

"Now, let us indulge ourselves with a duet," he suggested, and launched into something that Bu had never heard, and judging by the slight tilt of Granny Zim's head, she hadn't either.

But she pulled the central melody from it, and began a counter-rhythm, at a playful, dancing pitch that echoed and then ventured into an exploratory dalliance with that central melody, playing it backwards in the higher registers, and maintaining it steadily in the lower shimmers of sustained sound.

The chief musician's brows lifted, and he stilled his instrument, but Granny Zim played on. Her eyes closed, and she shifted into the chromatics, evoking not just dance, but full ritual, with the melody shifting down a mode until it became a memorial cadence.

The chief musician gave a short nod — but Granny Zim was not done. Her eyes were still closed, and still she built, and built, and here she brought in the Farewell Song, its simple melody so heart-catchingly poignant that Bu had to hold her breath as she was struck with remembrance of all those wives and sisters and mothers and lovers on the wicker bridges and the walkways and the rocky cliffs that overlooked the harbor, and the dangerous seas beyond. It was a folk song — surely these imperials would know that immediately — but presented in a form that brought forth the full range of human emotion: Granny Zim said, without speaking a word, that the small islands had their beauties, too.

Then she shifted back up to the simple thirds and fifths again — the dance. She brought the piece to a close, laying her hands in her lap.

The chief musician said after a lengthy pause, "You are affiliated with one of the temples, I take it?"

"Suanek, O Esteemed Chief Musician," Granny Zim said.

"Chief Huazi will do," the chief musician said. "It seems I am in the presence of a master. What was your rank?"

"The temple honored me with the rank of chief musician, Chief Huazi," Granny Zim said, her manner easing from that ritual abasement.

"Ayah! The temples are known for the purity of their teachings, and their discipline, for they play for the gods instead of for a capricious audience."

"It is so," Granny Zim said, bowing again.

For the first time, the chief musician lifted his head, and Bu's nerves prickled: he was looking at her and YinYin. "And these? I gather you brought two of your students?"

"We call them novices," Granny Zim said. "Though temple vows would be some years off, and our musicians don't always remain with the temple. Their concentration has been entirely on their music, and a certain amount on the classic writings."

"It remains only to test them to see where they fit among our own students, and then we shall proceed," the chief musician said. "First Apprentice? Summon Merit North Three to conduct our new colleague to a suitable chamber. The students—novices—may go in with the lower dormitory. You must be exhausted after your journey. We can evaluate the novices come morning."

"This troublesome nonentity begs forgiveness," Granny Zim interrupted here. "But might I keep one of my novices to attend me?"

The chief musician hesitated, then remembered that the message about these musicians had come from Army General Panheg, who, as everyone knew, was kin to the emperor, and a lifelong favorite.

"It can be arranged, until a more suitable attendant is appointed."

Bu knew what this meant: Granny Zim was going to keep YinYin away from others, if possible. Bu would be alone.

Eighteen

After a whirlwind of names belonging to similar blurred faces, and a bewildering twisting and turning of similar narrow passages, Bu found herself in a dormitory not unlike the temple dorm where she had spent so many years. Only here, they did not sleep on mats on the floor, but on a platform, in well-spaced rows. Moreover, each had a trunk of her own.

"Once they've placed you in the ranks," a soft-voiced girl a little taller than Bu said, "you'll get clothes. There's a set for warm weather, and a set for cold, plus court slippers and outdoor shoes for when there is snow."

"Court slippers?"

The girl's head lowered, and she seemed to take in Bu's worn sandals, woven of fig fronds, for the first time. "Every floor is tile, and swept twice a day," the girl said slowly. "We wear indoor and outdoor shoes. Court slippers are for indoors. They are soft, so that we disturb no one when we walk, and they do not carry in the dirt from outside."

"Thank you," Bu said meekly.

The girl hesitated, as if she would speak, then she gave a slight shrug. "That bell moments ago? That is the summons to supper."

Bu was quite hungry by then, though a lifetime of training kept her silent on the subject. But the girl seemed to find a modicum of compassion, though their relative ranks had yet to be established, for she said a degree more warmly, "You have not eaten yet?"

"A pancake at dawn."

"Ayah! You must be starving. Things probably seem difficult, but—assuming you remain with us—you'll get used to it. The main thing to remember is, though we will point out the golden road, which is the fine tile with gold as the central color, you never tread that way unless summoned by a graywing."

"Graywing. Is that the ones with the hats?" Bu gestured to either side of her head. "I thought I heard the one who took Chief—that is, Granny Zim, addressed by a number?"

"Don't you know imperial history?" the girl asked as they began to walk.

Bu was going to say that she knew there was a war on, and that the "imperial" designation was not accepted by many of the neighboring big islands—thus the wars—but that, perhaps, was a sore subject? When in doubt, ignorance was always safer, so one of the kinder instructors had said when Bu first joined the temple school. All you lose is face, rather than something more dire if you act on a very wrong assumption.

Bu was used to believing that she was so lacking in face that she was invisible, unless someone sought a target. She said, "We Fig Islanders only began studying the ancients a few years ago."

"Ah-h-h-h," the girl said, sounding amused. And superior. Everyone loves to be the one who knows, Cricket had said once, when talking about the silk-born boys.

"Before our dynasty, the graywings were far more powerful, and did terrible things. There was an awful battle, and most of it was right here." The girl waved down at her swiftly moving feet.

"Here?" Bu asked, peering at the clean-swept ground.

"By that I mean, not this spot precisely, but the imperial palace. Most of them were executed, and at first the new emperor declared there would be no more graywings, but they are so *useful*. However, when they become graywings, when they lose their…you know." A vague gesture below her waist. "They also give up their birth name. If they have names among themselves, I don't know. They take on the name of the building them are assigned to, and their duties go with how they are ranked. Our building is called The Garden of Celestial

Merit, though we all call it Merit North or Merit South, for there are several buildings with the Celestial designation."

"Merit North is different from Merit South?"

"Yes. The theater players train on the south side. You won't see them until you pass the test to become theater musician."

"There are so many buildings," Bu observed. How would she learn them all?

"It is confusing, but the names are clues. The government buildings are Glorious, and the forbidden buildings are mostly Heavenly, but you'll never see *those*. At least, for *years*. If it even happens. Merit North Three, whom I think you met, is the daytime graywing assistant to our Chief Musician. Here we are!"

Bu had begun smelling delectable aromas. She followed her guide into a long room, then stopped, stunned by the array of choices before her. It was probably ten or twelve dishes. Of course she could not see the components of any of these, but she could see a tempting variety of colors, and there were the mouth-watering smells. To someone who had been given one dish, with two or three simple ingredients and maybe a side of nut cakes, for the past four years, this table full of heaped platters seemed unimaginable riches. Was she permitted to try them all? Or was there a rank limit?

She decided to do whatever her guide did, which was to take a little from five or six different offerings. After this, Bu sat down where she was pointed to, and ate. The choices were all savory, sweet, and peppery.

Once she'd eaten, exhaustion settled around her head in waves, rather like sinking underwater. She fought it off as her guide took her to the privy and the bathing chamber, where steaming hot water mixed with cold channeled from the river. This was more like the temple, where hot springs mixed with diverted water from a waterfall for bathing. She moved as close to the hot water as she dared, and felt all her aches dissolve.

Once she was clean, and dressed in her second tunic, she climbed onto the platform, and though some of her new roommates were waiting to ask questions, they could see that her eyes barely stayed open. She slept within a breath of lying down.

The next morning, she braided her hair rapidly, and perforce wore her now sadly wrinkled second tunic. She could feel eyes on her, but the others were also hurrying to dress. No one said anything as she followed her guide to the lower level, where the students seemed to be about the age she had been when she auditioned at the temple school.

She headed for the back out of habit, and the instructor permitted her to sit among those with the lowest class rank. Bu saw that these were children of ten or so, but shrugged internally.

The instrument of this lesson was the lute. There was one at each low table, along with a scroll. Bu ignored the scroll out of habit as the instructor put them all through easy warmups, while talking about the basic modes. The lessons were all so well known to Bu that she could concentrate on the language, and how familiar terms were pronounced here.

Gradually the exercises became more complicated, newer students dropping out until only Bu was left.

At the end, the instructor, a kindly-sounding, balding man, said, "I see that you are very well schooled in the ancient fundamentals, Student Lum Bu. But are you not schooled in expression?"

Bu rose and bowed. "O Esteemed Instructor —"

Someone giggled, whispering, "That accent is so funny!"

"Student Sha Lai, you may go into the court and write out Kanda's Ten Admonitions about children's manners. Student Lum Bu, continue your thought, if you will."

Bu bowed as the admonished student departed, head down. "At the temple, these novices must learn method before expression is permitted. This ignorant novice apologizes if she has erred."

"Ah!" exclaimed the instructor. "With us, it is the opposite. We are first of all palace entertainers. We must learn to please those who might not deign to tell us what they want, but leave it to us to divine. In fact, we could be called musical augurs," he finished smiling. "Eh, children?"

The children, obeying this signal that their instructor had essayed a mild joke, gave polite chuckles before saying in unison, "Yes, Instructor Barin."

Bu said, "Shall this undistinguished novice attempt to play with expression?"

"Student Lum Bu, repeat 'The Monk on the Rock,' but please demonstrate what you've been taught of expression?"

"May I add variations?"

"If you are so moved, please do!" he said, his voice a

reassuring smile.

It was of course a test. Bu would rather have played on the qin, but this was good exercise, she decided. She took a moment to settle herself, searching her mind and heart for what to say through a quiet chromatic practice piece like "The Monk on the Rock."

Oh, there it was! She shared her discovery in discovering that emotion could cascade through music, but as she scaled upward, there was the awareness of music's effect on others. She altered modes until she sensed the tenor of the class around her listening more closely. She played to them, offering all the joy she had found even in simple rhythms.

When she reached the end, she finished without flourish and laid the borrowed instrument down.

The class stunned her by clapping loudly. Instructor Barin said, "You have been very well taught indeed. I will report to Chief Huazi that you have already mastered the fundamentals that we learn in this class. For the rest of the morning, will you demonstrate your learning as we finish with refrain heads?"

Bu bowed acceptance, and though the rest of the lesson covered fingering in simple modes that she had passed beyond during her first year, she showed no sign of boredom or tedium. The Instructor, watching her thoughtful expression when her eyes were closed, suspected that either the teaching in those outer islands had surpassed the imperial palace—it was possible, though unlikely—or here was a young Talent. Moreover, one who had no hint of arrogance about her.

At the midday meal, some of the younger students gathered around her, trying to talk over each other with questions—some just wanting to hear that hilarious accent again, and others wanting to know if the islands had fought and lost before she and her two companions were taken away—but she bowed in all directions, apologizing profusely, insisting she had to visit the privy. Once she'd shaken the questioners, she made her way to the refectory shared by every rank of musician and student. She found YinYin sitting alone, as Granny Zim had been invited to the table at the head of the room, where the instructors and the chief musician sat.

It was a relief to be able to eat in silence once more, as she considered the morning. Had she made any mistakes? Not intentionally.

After the meal, she and YinYin were summoned by another student. All looked alike to her. They traversed a courtyard with potted flowering plants that gave off a heavy perfume, and entered the same chamber Granny Zim had been tested in. There was scarcely time to greet her before the chief musician addressed Bu and YinYin.

"Your chief agrees with our assessment. You two will be attending the advanced level in the mornings, and in the afternoon, you'll join the lower level in deportment lessons. After which we will assess your knowledge." He made a motion as if using an ink brush.

Bu sat upright, startled. This was the first time she had ever been told her deportment was at fault. Her surprise was easily visible. The chief musician said, "There is another standard for the imperial palace, and many regulations."

There was nothing to do but bow acceptance. And because it was now time for afternoon lessons, Bu and YinYin had to follow their guide a bit of a distance to the deportment class.

The instructor's sharp voice was Bu's first sign that this was going to be difficult: it was that same woman who had said so loudly that they were too ugly for anything but the kitchens. Bu was used to being called ugly — that had almost been the first word she learned as a baby, scorned by the older sisters who resented having to watch another unwanted sister who ought to have had the wisdom to be born a precious son. Being a person who couldn't see faces, Bu never thought about anyone's looks. She evaluated people mostly by voice, and this woman's voice reminded her of sharp, metallic tools.

As she followed YinYin into the room, Bu sensed the stares of a lot of strange children, and felt awkward and stiff.

"You are late," the sharp-voiced woman snapped.

"If this unworthy may be permitted to speak, Venerable Instructor Halma, we have just come from Chief Musician Huazi, who begs your indulgence and requests your expertise in tutoring the newcomers," said their guide with a low bow.

"I see," said Instructor Halma, in a slightly less frigid tone. "Very well. You two, sit at the back. You will have the example of the entire class to emulate as you repair your ignorance."

Bu and YinYin went to the bench at the back wall, where Bu sat in relief. Of course she couldn't see anything, but at least she was safely out of sight.

Or so she assumed.

The class was in the middle of practicing bows. Instructor Halma rapped out incomprehensible titles, and stalked among the students as they rose and bowed to various degrees, then knelt down again. Only what were they doing with their hands?

Bu stole glances at YinYin, and copied her hand movements—this bow required hands in sleeves. That bow required hands together. Another bow with hands on knees. Bu was a little late with each movement.

Then the instructor snapped, "You. Tribute cull. Why are you watching the only other person in this room as ignorant as you are?"

Gray flowed as the instructor bore down on her. "You! What are you looking at her for? You've an example at the front of the room, whose precision is the example you must emulate."

Bu blinked, face screwed up, but then the woman snapped, "Hands out!"

Utterly lost, Bu shot her hands out, palms down. Then white pain took her breath away, and she fell to her knees. Hot throbbing on the back of her right hand belatedly signaled that she had been struck, hard, with some kind of thin stick.

"Stop that ugly squint," the instructor blared. "If you affront the least of the imperial family with that hideous face, we all will suffer for it!"

Bu opened her mouth, but all she could do was gasp as she cradled her hand against her chest.

YinYin said, "Instructor Halma. Lum Bu has weak eyes and cannot see that far."

"Cannot see? Why didn't you say so!" the instructor's loud voice had not abated, implying Bu was at fault. "You're to report that to the graywings. In the meantime, do *not* squint. It does not improve your vision nearly as much as it distorts your face."

Bu's eyes had filled with tears. She widened her eyes lest that stick come out of nowhere again.

The instructor said stiffly, "Let the sting of that remonstrance serve to remind you to break that ugly habit. And next time, put out your palm, if you do not wish to be struck on the top of your hand. Ignorant barbarians!" she added in a hissing under-breath, and stalked back to the front of the class. "Now, the bow to the emperor when he passes by and has not addressed you…"

So it went, up, down, bow, hands this way, that way, kneel, face down, face to the floor, over and over and over. Bu gulped back the tears, wondering if she would ever play another instrument—but by the time the class finally ended, the agony was mere pain, and she could move her fingers again, though it hurt.

The reading class was next, and this time, YinYin went to the front and said to the instructor, "Lum Bu cannot see to read without her crystal."

"A crystal?" the instructor repeated. He was a short man with a round face and a thin topknot. "A crystal? Not a crystal eyepiece? Let me see that."

Trembling, Bu pulled it from her sleeve with the uninjured hand, prickling all over with awareness of being stared at.

"By all the gods! So primitive a thing, it is quite uncut! Ayah, but I believe that will aid in finding a crystal eyepiece that will facilitate…"

Bu gradually grasped that the imperials had crystals cut in such a way that a person could look through them and see more clearly. These were kept for everyone's use, there in the room where they studied reading and writing. Unfortunately, none of the ones in the box helped her. A glance through one of them made Bu's eyes ache. The rest were wrong to varying degrees, and all of them far too weak.

The instructor said to Bu, who trembled lest she be judged having done wrong, "I'll speak to the chief about sending you over to Supplies, where the eyepiece-maker works. It might be that he can duplicate what you see in your crystal."

Hearing this very nearly overcame the throb in Bu's hand. A crystal that she could use when needed?

She managed to eat with her off hand, very clumsily, and later that evening, when she returned to the dormitory, she discovered that her roommates were horrified to a person. They promptly made a pet of her—something she had never experienced. One girl insisted on daubing Bu's hand with a precious salve.

"That's Hard-Ash Halma," someone else said. "She is the *worst* for the tiniest infractions of deportment."

"If you like, *we* will drill you on all the routes we're permitted to use, the ones we dare to cross when we can, and the ones you'd do better to avoid forever," said another girl.

"And unless she makes you turn your hands down, which only happens if she's already remonstrated at least once, always put your palms up. Putting your palms down like that is seen as a challenge. As if you are insisting you are right. Do you see?"

"I did not know," Bu answered. "Thank you." She turned to the circle of blurred faces. "This ignorant outlander thanks you all."

"It's all right, all right." A hand patted her shoulder. "Outlanders don't know any better. Any reasonable person remembers *that*."

Much comforted, Bu lay with her hand curled under her chin. The salve was mildly effective. Mostly it smelled like herbs, a pleasing aroma, and Bu slept.

The next morning, when she arrived at breakfast, YinYin was waiting at the door. She intercepted Bu, and took her back out, and into a new hall—to Granny Zim's new chamber.

Granny Zim's breath hissed in when she saw the purple bruise on the top of Bu's hand. "I wish I had been there," she said. "Though I expect it was probably better that I wasn't. Bu, I am sorry."

To Bu's utter horror, Granny Zim bowed over her hand.

"No, no, no," Bu stuttered. "It's all my fault—so stupid—I ought to…"

"You ought to nothing. How could you possibly know any of the rules they all grow up knowing?"

"But you don't know either," Bu said with a watery attempt at a smile.

"That is true, but I should have remembered what I lost sight of: to these people, no matter how skilled I am, or you are. Any of us. We are, and always will be, tribute slaves, as that Halma Dak said. I wish I could take her stick to her own hands! I thought I could…ayah, it matters nothing, what I thought, because I was wrong."

"It's really not that bad today," Bu said, anxious to soothe Granny Zim, whose voice trembled with regret. "When it first happened I thought I would never use it again, but Instructor Halma apparently knows exactly how hard to hit people, or so the girls in the dormitory said. I'll be all right. And I do want to learn music, and they said we could be among the advanced students. And I'm to get a crystal eyepiece for seeing!"

"That," Granny Zim said, "we can do in any number of places far less dangerous. I'll find a way to get us out, as soon as I can."

Bu said, "Dangerous?"

Granny Zim sighed. "I think you're too young to remember any of the truly bad hurricanos?"

"I've heard about them. And I remember the way to the

cave we were to hide in, but we never used it."

"Yes, that's correct. Hurricanos are rare — we renew the charms against them without fail, and one of the matters I trusted our augur in was predicting them, as he was correct both times he said one was coming. The worst aspect of them is that they often come twice — they blow past, then there is a quiet time, but if you dare to go out, you're sure to get caught when they come right back again. They are very vicious that way."

YinYin said, "There are many of my kind in them, devouring all the lives the winds put up."

Granny Zim said, "Thus the term demon winds. Here's what's important right now. The truth is, as tribute, we are the property of the emperor. It is only he who can release us or not, at his whim."

"Oh," Bu said, her head turtling into her shoulders at the mention of so terrible and exalted a figure.

"I will try to arrange an interview, once I understand how best to put my request that we be sent somewhere far from this palace. This city. This island, even. But this is what you need to remember. No matter how comfortable it is here, how grateful we will be to get you your crystal eyepiece, while we are here, we are in the center of the hurricano. The center is *never* a safe place."

NINETEEN

AT FIRST, BU WAITED apprehensively for that interview to happen—and she prayed to Suanek every time the bells rang, to protect Granny Zim. It was very like waiting for a storm to strike. Bu startled every time she saw a graywing, and when her first patrol of imperial guards appeared while she was on the way back from the nondescript set of buildings the others termed the Household Department, her knees turned to water, and she waited to hauled off to execution before a thunder-browed emperor two or three times the size of a human man, for some obscure infraction.

The patrol passed by without a second glance, and she managed to get her shaky legs walking again.

Her third morning, she and YinYin were issued new clothes, including underthings, soft socks and inside slippers, and most important of all, two sets of an over-robe of the same soft gray the other students wore, but with a narrow strip of silk at the edges. Real silk! It was a slightly darker shade, and signified that she was among the upper level of the music students—which meant, she was sternly admonished, that she could be summoned to play in the background should certain lesser members of the imperial household send for music.

"But it won't actually happen," one of her dormitory mates earnestly told her. "The competition is so very fierce for even for so low a position. Everyone wishes to be noticed."

"Why?" Bu asked.

The girl stilled, clearly disconcerted. "Why what?"

"Why would anyone want to be noticed? Everywhere around me, especially in the deportment class, we're told not to draw notice, or terrible things will happen."

"Notice for anything but playing. It's good to be noticed for playing well!"

"Or looking good while playing," someone commented.

The original speaker scowled the commenter down. "If there is not a theater piece being played—for only the seniors advanced over to South Merit will play for those—the court is permitted to hire us if they wish to have music at a court function. Or, if the emperor gives them permission to summon us. If you please them, they might tip you. Some of them throw gold around as if it was water. And there are other ways to become a favorite," she added, saw Bu's total incomprehension, and scorned her for being stupid.

But Bu wasn't stupid. She'd observed the beginnings of flirting at the temple school, though such things were considered a breach of the temple's peace, and so those who wanted to flirt had to do so when they had free moments away from the temple.

The subject was back again that first week, when Bu's dormitory mates gave her a precise rundown on who was the handsomest among the upper ranks of the music students— with a few thrown in from the scribes and the arts, as especially toothsome examples.

Not that everyone agreed. An argument that Bu suspected was not new broke out over whether Xia Chi, first in their rank, was handsomer than Ji Hak, another of the seniors. Bu already knew who Xia Chi was. He was the one with a voice like the perfect bamboo flute: pure-toned, earthy, a little breathy. She wondered what he looked like, not that she would ever dare to stare.

She asked the second night the subject came up, "Do the boys know that you rank them? Do they rank you?"

"Of course they do, ha ha!"

"And we love to tease them by saying we have a list, but we won't tell them who is on it," another said.

"As for their list, ayah, it was always Sun Rose at the top. Always. Until she went off at New Year's to be a concubine for one of the Grand Princes."

"If she's clever, there will never be a proper wife,"

someone else put in.

Bu was just as glad to contemplate that she would never be on any "list."

She was regarded by the masters as a Talent, albeit ignorant of the ancient writings, and of palace ways. But then she was a barbarian from the outer islands, so what else could be expected? She was also kind, earnest, grateful—and very boring, decided those who sought different qualities in potential friends. Or connections. Or rivals.

Bu was happiest in the morning classes, immersed in music. The best part of those mornings was class with Granny Zim, who had been invited to serve as the instructor for fundamentals (method, at the temple school).

Granny Zim kept her opinions strictly to herself. She could see Bu's happiness, and she knew that YinYin was still absorbing human ways as much as the music. Granny Zim disclosed nothing of her own discoveries—that out of all the masters, only three were devoted to music for its own sake. Everyone else thought mainly of what would please the imperials, court and family, and their highest goal appeared to be playing background for the theater pieces. The imperial music school strove to produce the best stage and entertainment musicians: for the one, the players were the focus, and for the second, the social occasion for which they provided popular music that was not to interfere with the purpose of the social function.

It was as different from the temple goals as Ghost Moon from Phoenix Moon.

On the fifth day, Bu was sent to the Household Department. At the very back was an interesting workshop whose room was filled with implements she couldn't quite make out, the sounds not music but the taps and chinks and tinkle of tools working with metals, minerals, and ceramics. The smells sharp and unfamiliar.

The eyepiece-shaper was an old, sparse-bearded man who mumbled to himself as he worked. He had her hold her crystal so that her sight was sharp, then he drew a precise picture of her hands with the crystal in them. Only when he had sketched every plane on the rock did he let her lower her hands, then he explained that he would look through as she did, and reproduce the effect he saw.

She ran back so as not to be late to the afternoon deportment class that she dreaded. There, she had to remind herself not to touch the silk she wanted so badly to finger for its softness. To keep her eyes open and not squint.

Meanwhile, at night, her dormitory mates kept their promise and drilled her on palace customs. This bow for this person, these words if she accepted a tip, these words if she refused a tip.

"Why would a musician refuse a tip? Is that to be done if one makes an incorrect note?"

Bu couldn't see expressions, of course, but she sensed some communication going between the two girls who were coaching her. One said, "If you do not wish to become a favorite, or if you suspect a request coming that you do not want to be obliged to fill. If you don't refuse by preserving their face, then you've really stuck a straw up a tiger's nose!"

"'Oh esteemed and honored imperial highness,'" one girl intoned, falling to the floor and banging her forehead repeatedly. "'This unworthy wretch would rather die a thousand deaths than defile so generous a gift with these undeserving hands.' And bow yourself out, nose to toes so you catch no one's eye, as fast as you can." She leaped up, head bowed low as she scurried backwards a few steps.

"But it'll be *at least* a year before any of the masters summon you," the high-voiced one said comfortingly.

The wry voice added, "They won't want to risk being taken for the hen as the phoenix rises behind them."

That girl was shushed from all sides, to which she said, "Why not say it? Xia Chi did. I heard him. He said both Lum Bu and the other one are Talents, and he'd back them against half the masters."

"He was drinking," someone else said. "It was the rice wine talking. And you ought not to be following the boys over to the Chrysanthemum Garden."

"It was my free night, too. And Ji Hak was with them."

Free nights? Bu caught at that. Would that be the same as festival days, when lessons were suspended? Where would she even go?

The next day, a graywing materialized out of nowhere to tell her she was summoned to the Household Department. Her heart jolted against her ribs at his appearance, and didn't stop banging until he vanished again.

She ran all the way. When she reached the crystal worker, she was given a round piece of clear crystal, fitted into a metal holder. If she held it a finger's breadth from paper, she could make out characters without having to bend down to the paper! And if she held it to her eyes — not too close — she could see details at a distance. It wasn't perfect. There was a fuzziness still, and things seemed curiously flat, but she was so grateful to have anything that she thanked him over and over, insisting it couldn't be better, and so she left with her new tool in her sleeve pocket. Though she kept her crystal for when she wanted precision.

Writing was still difficult, as she still must do it one-handed, but at least her reading was slowly improving. She didn't really need to write. No one at this imperial music school minded her using her voice as her aid to memory, rather than writing down the notations the others memorized.

She wanted to use the crystal eyepiece to look at people's faces to help her learn to tell them apart. There were so very many of them! The temptation was to see if voices matched faces. Like First Student Xia Chi. Only what if she got caught staring? She knew it was rude to stare, but the idea of being caught at it by him seemed especially terrible.

Her solution was to avoid anyone she was tempted to look at.

She struggled with that dilemma for a few days, until a new matter claimed everyone's attention: word was whispered around that no less than a grand princess was to join the zither class.

"A grand princess?" Bu asked, mentally sorting through the daunting number of important titles requiring their own special bows. "That means, she's a daughter of one of the emperor's family?"

"The emperor's favorite sister," one of the girls said, and everyone briefly clasped hands in the direction of the imperial palace. Bu was still learning that references to the family, the orders, or something personal pertaining to the emperor required this salute, whereas general mentions did not. "The youngest princess. He sent an entire battalion to protect her when the troubles broke out, during the last generation."

"The daughter of that princess will join us?" Bu asked. "I thought we were not permitted to see any of the imperial family. That is, the princesses."

"That is true of the *imperial* princesses. No one sees *them* until their wedding day, and then they always go veiled. But the *grand* princesses are sometimes seen within the palace. And of course princes can go anywhere they please."

The grand princess was there when they filed in to the zither class. A special cushion had been arranged right up front and center. The students flowed around her, sitting on the more modest mats in rank order. Bu got a good look while the princess was facing forward. She did not wear gray, but layers of something that looked soft as clouds, in gradations of silver, blue, and white, and her long fall of hair was pinned up at either side with golden hairpins worked with pears and jade. The chief difference, though, was that the princess's right-hand picks glinted with gold, whereas the students either used bamboo picks or their nails, if these were long and hard enough.

Tenth Grand Princess Rathlan diligently performed warm-ups with everyone else, her lower lip caught between her teeth. Bu's quick ears caught falsity in the second through fourth finger plucks, and her slide was uneven, without the slightest shimmer, but her thumb and first finger plucks were vigorous.

The instructor said, "Student Lum Bu, please come sit by her highness and demonstrate 'The Dragon's Five Talons'?"

Bu shifted to the seat next to the grand princess and settled her instrument, then aligned herself properly, though she'd noticed that many of the higher ranks of students neglected aspects of proper posture in favor of what they considered graceful poses.

She flexed her hands, and arced her fingers in the correct manner, plucking with precision so that the string rang bright and true. She didn't use picks, but her nails. Her left hand pressed without adding undulations to the wrist; instead, as she performed a slide up the frets, she added the shimmer of vibrato. She was so focused on correct performance that she failed to register the princess turning on her cushion, tossing her long, flowing sleeves back, and then resting her chin on her fists as she watched Bu.

At the end, she exclaimed in a high, clear voice, "I do hear a difference! There really is a difference!" She smiled around with an air of discovery.

Everywhere her eye landed, instructor and student bowed alike. Bu belatedly, when she perceived all the dark heads nodding like blossoms in a breeze.

The princess laid a finger to her lips and bent studiously over her zither. She didn't speak for the rest of the lesson, and when she left, students and instructor bowed her out.

One of the younger students slipped out after her, then popped back in to say, "She's gone, and so are her servants."

Everyone began talking at once, until the instructor rapped twice for silence. "Do you think any of the imperial servants will be pleased to hear all your wild speculation? Tenth Grand Princess Rathlan deigns to grace us with her presence for this week. If report of your speculation reaches imperial ears, do you imagine your lives will be more comfortable?"

The students chorused a denial and an apology, and were dismissed, Bu to marvel over the fact that she had seen an actual princess. It seemed it was nearly as uncommon for her fellow students.

That night, Granny Zim also had a first experience. Chief Huazi caught her at the end of the qin class for the upper ten seniors, who were sharpening their technique. "We've been summoned to play for a court dinner by the grand prince," the chief said. "He likes at least three qin for volume of sound, behind the full range of instruments."

Granny Zim bowed, her curiosity whetting.

The experience was both enlightening and exasperating. A court dinner was very different from a proper concert. Their playing truly was background entertainment. You would think, she reflected sourly, that people who spoke so much about valuing the arts would actually give them a little attention? Would they talk and toast one another and tell jokes through a poetry reading or recitation?

The great dragon dais was empty, but the servants had set golden dishes and exquisitely arranged food for the emperor just the same. Next step down on that elaborate dais was a single figure who had to be the grand prince, a sizable man with an iron-gray topknot encased in silver and pearls, and a long gray mustache on either side of his mouth. He led the talk, and whenever he paused, his guests were sure to stand and offer long, flattering toasts. And yet Chief Huazi had cautioned the players not to permit any silence, but to go from one piece directly to another. "Don't expect applause," Instructor Barin had cautioned as they walked down long corridors toward the elaborate building the feast was held in.

Applause there was not. The musicians softly played the entire time, until Chief Huazi divined from signals too subtle for Granny Zim to catch that it was time to bring the music to an end. Sure enough, the grand prince rose, nodded in all directions, and said in his genial voice, "Wishing you all good rest and excellent days, I will depart first."

He stepped down toward the side hall, rather than walking past all the guests' tables to the main door. This side exit was apparently was oblique permission to keep enjoying themselves.

The grand prince passed close to Chief Huazi, his knee-length sleeves flowing as he tossed a tasseled, silken pouch to the chief, which clinked promisingly. Then with a flourish of those sleeves, and a swing of the long jade ornament at the grand prince's belt, he departed, a graywing running ahead and calling for his palanquin.

Did the musicians give concerts anymore, or was music centered entirely on the theater? It seemed insulting to ask, but maybe that was only from the temple school perspective? "I want to get out of this place," Granny Zim whispered to herself in the island tongue as she returned to her chamber, and stared down at the three gold coins in her hand. "Before they ruin us all three."

TWENTY

IT WAS AN ODD thing, Bu thought at the end of the week, how something you had no part of could still fill your heart with pride. She sat in the seventh position in the winds class, and used her crystal eyepiece to take fierce pleasure in the enthralled expressions on her classmates' faces as YinYin played one of the imperial school's flutes made of silver.

There had been no silver flutes in all the Fig Islands. There had been very little silver. In YinYin's hands, the silver flute produced a bright, clear sound evoking stars on a very cold night, whereas the wooden flutes reminded her of the scent of soil in spring. Bu liked wooden flutes. But she was used to them. The silver flutes were new to all three of the Fig Islanders. They required a different touch, and their best expression dominated the strings, calling for different musical approaches.

"Very well done. The best," the instructor said when YinYin finished. "I think we will all agree that Student YinYin has an affinity for the silver flute. Student YinYin, I will speak to Chief Huazi about your beginning to train for the theater. All the dramas now have flute parts, but we've a scarcity of players for those parts."

The seniors clapped politely. YinYin stood impassively under all those eyes.

The grand princess did not come to the zither class that

day. Bu was secretly relieved—until, just before supper, Bu was startled to be summoned by none other than an imperial page. Of course she must go at once. At least it was not far, and there were no more classes.

The page took her to a garden a short distance away, bounded by high yellow walls. Two guards stood at either side of the round door, but they did not move when the little page, who couldn't have been older than ten, led Bu inside. The princess sat on a bench under the shade of a redbark tree, near a profusion of potted orchids that gave off a heavenly fragrance in the summery air.

Bu performed the correct bow very self-consciously, then stood before the princess, who sighed. "I can hear the difference between your playing and mine. I've been trying all week to carry what you do to my practice of 'The Merry Beggar', but my playing never sounds as good. Is it the instrument perhaps at fault, and not I?"

Bu bowed, and began one of the deferential nothings that she had been drilled in by Instructor Halma and her dormitory mates.

Grand Princess Rathlan glanced around, then interrupted. "Do not tell me my playing is divine, or go on about how clever I am. I know I'm clever. I'm clever enough to recognize that my playing is mediocre, despite always hearing how heavenly my playing is. I've heard that all my life from my mother, my imperial uncle, even, and of course my maids and my tutors. I believed it. Which is why I thought that performing Sixth Imperial Princess's new favorite song would be the perfect birthday gift. But after a week of very hard work among you, I still do not sound nearly as fine as you do. Why?"

Bu said slowly, "O esteemed grand princess, this lowly outlander is not yet trained in the proper speech for one so exalted."

Grand Princess Rathlan eyed Bu, who wished she could pull out her crystal eyepiece to see the princess's face. Though she could hear frustration in the beautifully modulated voice. "I comprehend. You're afraid to give me the truth. No one gives me the truth, except my twin, who isn't even my true brother, and he can't tell me *why* I sound bad. Or *his* brother, who is *deaf*."

By now Bu had gathered that, like various grand princes and princesses, not all the imperial princes and princesses were still alive, and in the case of several of those imperial princesses, were married off to distant royalty. Yet they still maintained their rank and number in the imperial family. Bu did not know which not-a-brother was meant, or if he had musical training.

When unsure, bow.

"I *want* you to tell me what I am doing wrong."

Bu bowed again. "This unworthy student wishes the grand princess to understand that her exalted fingers have learned a deft touch on the zither, that ought to please many."

"But?" the princess demanded, frustration sharpening her voice.

Bu's ready sympathy overflowed with her need to always speak truth about music. She mumbled to her toes, "We temple students had to spend months learning merely to breathe correctly. And then we had to strengthen our fingers with exercises before we could touch an instrument. And then we had years of drills that train us in precise use of forward pluck, backward pluck, with and without pick, and in slide, and strum, and vibrato. In how to sustain a note though we played so softly that the sound is felt more than heard."

The grand princess sighed. "Go on. Though I'm beginning to see what no one wanted to tell me—that in fact, my tutors lied to me with pretty words."

"This unworthy one wishes the grand princess to recollect that the intent of those lessons might have been different. That these tutors might have been hired to train those of imperial birth, in an incense-stick or two of time each day, to look well while playing. To play softly and easily, without the necessity to spend weeks—months—learning the precision of pluck and touch."

Grand Princess Rathlan snapped open her fan, and plied it slowly, its long silken tassel swinging as she contemplated Bu's words. "Are you discreet?" she asked suddenly, then snapped the fan shut, and twirled it as if throwing something away. "Don't answer—of course you will say yes. Who doesn't? There are reasons why 'The Merry Beggar' needs to be far better than I can play it. I think we're going to have to plan a bit of a subterfuge. Be ready for a summons tomorrow, and bring your zither. The auspicious hour for birthdays is always Fifth Dragon when we're to have theater after, so you must be here tomorrow, at Third Dragon's third bell. I will have a maid waiting. What's wrong? You look as if you're being sent to Execution Square."

Bu stuttered, "This ignorant outlander has not been promoted past the first class in deportment...Instructor Halma..."

"Oh, I've heard about that white-eyed wolf. All my maids are terrified of her. I'll make things right with Chief Huazi. He never gives *us* trouble, and he outranks Deportment Instructor Halma."

Bu was forced to bow acquiescence, and the princess waved her fan in dismissal.

Bu slipped back inside, her heartbeat galloping when she found a small cluster of her dormitory mates waiting at Merit's outer door. "What did she want?" one asked.

The princess could not possibly want discretion more than Bu did. "She just asked me a lot of questions about the fundamentals of the zither," Bu said evasively. "Oh, I am so hungry. Please forgive me, I hope there's something left..." She motioned toward the dining hall.

There was plenty left, of course. Bu sat with YinYin, and when she was certain no one paid them any attention, used Fig Island dialect to tell YinYin what had happened.

YinYin said little, which Bu found comforting. She dragged out bathing until her skin wrinkled, and then, grateful that she no longer had to scrub her clothes, she retired to the dormitory where she found half of the girls asleep already. She curled up and shut her eyes, but dread kept sleep at bay for half the night.

The grand princess had been a reasonable person, within what Bu imagined was a princess's view of the world. Bu had not been given a choice in whatever was to transpire the next day—but then this music school was in truth a department that served the imperials, just as the Household Department was. Choice was not in question. The students were eager to perform. How could she have avoided this situation she was not ready for?

Before breakfast, YinYin appeared at Bu's dormitory with a summons from Granny Zim. Overwhelmed with relief, Bu hurried with YinYin to their master's chamber.

"Why didn't you come straight to me, Bu?" Granny Zim asked, and then, seeing Bu's anxiety spark, patted the air between them. "No, no, a foolish question. I know you. You surely thought you would be disturbing me. I wish I could cure that worry, but we are as the gods, and our parents, made us." Then she scowled, and said, "Tell me exactly what happened."

Bu did.

Granny Zim scowled deeper, and Bu waited in trepidation, though she sensed that Granny Zim was not faulting her. But the entire situation made her uncomfortable. "I thought so. It was your instructor who drew that princess's attention to you, and of course you must obey. And do your best."

A new, more horrifying thought burst upon Bu. "I … was put into a trap?"

"Possibly. I won't attribute motive without having been there, and I do not know the person. It might be a trap for us three, the outlanders. We are not part of this community yet, and we were placed above many who have been here longer. We've talked about different motivations; for most, the goal is performance, whether privately, for personal advancement, or the prestige of being part of the imperial theater."

Bu said, "The girls talk about the one, and the instructors about the other. I still don't quite understand either of them."

"That's because island life is so very different. For the first, our men are gone such a large part of the year, that the taking of concubines is not practical—though some of the men do seem to have friends, even families, in other harbors. It's always been a subject we don't discuss. As for the theater, I assumed that this was akin to our festival plays, but I'm beginning to perceive that there is an enormous difference."

"Yes," YinYin said.

Granny Zim turned to her. "Is this shared performance on stage something you wish to pursue?"

"I will learn it. I want to learn *everything*."

Granny Zim nodded. "Then I will do what I can to aid you in that. As for our situation now, I know now that there are a few among the senior students who cannot hear the difference between our methods and what they thought of as fundamentals. Most of these are students whose entire motivation is to strive to gain notice, on their way to better things."

Bu understood that. She had heard as much in the dormitory.

"There are no doubt those who wish to see us fail, even if by saying or doing the wrong thing, regardless of our music."

Bu's eyes stung.

Granny Zim sighed. "Bu, you must remember that this is a dangerous place, in spite of the beautiful gardens, and all the servants who take care of our laundry, and the excellent meals.

I enjoy those things, too. But I still want to get us out of here as soon as I can; while I don't expect attack with swords and hordes of armies, it is ambition that I am wary of. It is dangerous when the ambitious see you as a target to overcome, just as the warrior does."

Bu bowed in acquiescence. "What shall I do?"

"Nothing. To act differently from expected would also draw notice. I will abase myself before Huazi, and request—very stringently—that neither of you, and I'll try to include myself, are to be called on as examples before any visitors, including imperial family, in future classes or demonstrations. I'm sure I can get Instructor Halma to back me in this request. I might not like the way she teaches, or how much she relishes her punishments, but at least with her there is no praising the apples while stealing the peaches."

"Do you think he will excuse me from having to meet the grand princess's page?"

"I will try, though it might be you will have to obey. I'm going to make certain that it is the last such incident, if I can. Go about your day as if nothing were amiss. And if it comes to pass you must do whatever it is the grand princess has planned, be circumspect during, and especially after. That is, no matter what you see or hear, do not speak a word about it. Lie if you have to. You surely have noticed how much they gossip about the imperial family."

"Yes," Bu said, thumbing her eyes. "I can understand talking about one another. They did that at the temple school. But why talk about people we will never see, much less meet?"

"Because whims affect us all. They have the power of life and death. That makes them interesting, and of course they get talked about. But I am certain you've noticed that when people talk, the smarter ones notice who is talking as well as what is said. Do *not* be the root of a gossip tree. It can do nothing but harm."

TWENTY-ONE

Bᴜ ᴍᴏᴠᴇᴅ ᴛʜʀᴏᴜɢʜ ʜᴇʀ morning classes in a fret of nerves. Anything having to do with the mysterious and all-powerful imperials was a bridge of knives and swords. However, one thing she knew she could rely on was her music. She used all her lesson practice time to work on the grand princess's song, until her fingers knew it so well that she could open her heart to the instrument.

No message came to relieve her of that appointment at the garden gate.

When Third Dragon rang, she took an early bath, and put on a fresh tunic. The zither she had used for practice was waiting for her when she went to the storage area. She took it, and used a roundabout route to cross to the Garden of Serene Contemplation.

That same little page was waiting for her. "This way," piped the page, and so began a rapid journey along the edge of the garden. The entire area was walled off, but Bu could see the tops of trees and smell the fragrances drifting from various gardens large and small before they reached a splendid building whose tiles glowed in the westering sun. Bu put her crystal to her eyes, making out the guardian statues along the up-tilted eaves. The roof was in layers, an impressive structure partly shaded by beautiful trees. Bu wondered if withered or yellowed leaves were nipped away before they could offend imperial eyes—everything was so orderly and perfect. Even the profusion of orchids growing in huge pots of porcelain, gold-edged and painted in brilliant reds and blues.

The servant entrance was all the way on the other side of yet another high wall. Being in the company of a page, Bu had no reservation about peering through her crystal. She used the stone YinYin had given her, as she knew how to get the sharpest image.

They entered through a storage area that Bu was learning was typical of structures in the imperial palace, and through there into a kitchen yard, where people were busy at various late-afternoon tasks. Through one side of a kitchen area, and then through a carved door into much finer rooms. This one had a tapestry of Suanek on one wall, and opposite that, potted plants that gave off peppery-sweet scent. The beams holding up the roof had been carved with twining leaves, and there were more trees and leaves painted at the sides of doors. Peach trees mostly, Bu saw, sweeping the crystal back and forth. Green and peach and hints of gold being the dominant colors.

Through that room into another equally large—and Bu stopped with a jolt when she saw that the room was not empty. In the center was a couch, on which lay a young man in layers of black and gold and red silk, embroidered with dragonflies and climbing roses. As Bu stared, startled, he raised one hand, tapping the air three times, then bent his fingers in what appeared to be some sort of signal or code. Behind his couch stood a tall young man whose broad-shouldered lineaments were vaguely familiar.

Was that Brick? Bu turned the crystal toward him. He wore the gray and chest armor of the imperial guard. At his side hung a sword. He stared back at Bu with apathy; was there recognition? Ought she to speak? No, there might be rules about servants and duty, and anyway, they could not be said to have conversed, and it was so uncomfortable to be *stared at*. Surely he'd feel it, too.

She glimpsed a third figure before palming her crystal and tucking it away. The third young man never looked up from where he sat hunched over some sort of board with markers on it. His over-robe glowed like a twilight sky, a deep blue embroidered in lucky yellow-fish with long streaming tails, amid graceful reeds. The board had been worked in tiny squares. Belatedly Bu wondered if she was seeing a Circle board, one made for imperials, for those pieces had been carved from jade.

Bu bowed, though no one paid her the least attention. A bow seemed safest. She squinted around, trying to find the page, who'd vanished. She was on the edge of panic when a figure in shades of rose with accents of blue and green floated in on tiny steps, golden chains in her headdress swinging. "There you are," exclaimed Tenth Grand Princess Rathlan.

The young man on the couch groaned, "I've been here for—"

"Not you, Lir. And why are you even *here*?" As she spoke, she slapped her palm lightly on the Circle table, whose legs were carved like elongated egrets. When the young man seated there glanced up, the princess wound her finger in a circle, and the young man turned a thumb toward the one the princess had called Lir, still stretched out on the couch.

Lir (here, the storyteller added apologetically, "This is how the fourteenth imperial prince was known to his cousin and his closest brother—and how he thought of himself, so I will presume to use it) said petulantly, "Because I needed a rest on the way to Sixth Sister Sua's gate to the underworld. Shortest distance, here to there." And he groaned loudly. "I'd never survive the journey from my own gate to the underworld."

The princess sighed. "What happened? No, I don't think I want to know."

But Lir was waiting to tell her, or to tell somebody. "Pig pen. Behind the Jolly Sailor. Jolly! Never saw a worse set of jackals in my life."

"*Another* harbor gambling den? I thought you were forbidden to go to those horrible places."

"It's fun. Except they fouled the dice. I could hear it. Upset all my numbers, and when I called them on it they set the door thugs on me, and after they tried to break every bone in my body, they threw me in with the pigs out beyond the alley." He groaned again.

"You probably deserved it," she said, but not at all sharply. "I know you. Of course you baited them."

"They almost killed me! Probably would have, but Brick here turns out to be handy with a chamber pot."

The princess turned to Brick, who stared into space, mouth hanging open. She was astonished to see that Rathlir's latest bodyguard seemed to have lasted more than a day or two. Unlike all the others. But, despite his handsome looks, he didn't seem as if he had the wits to give a report. She turned back to her cousin. "A chamber pot?"

"It was right there, and it turns out, if anything comes right at him, he doesn't let it get past. Even more, he's *quiet*. I want to keep him."

"I'm sure the Imperial Guards will be thanking all the gods for that," the princess retorted. "As well as the imperial ferrets. How many bodyguards have you gone through this year?"

"*I* am not at fault," Lir stated with as much dignity as was possible in a person lying flat. "They get themselves transferred. If you believe Vo, they stab themselves in order to avoid being ordered to guard me."

"*I'd* stab myself if I had to do anything with *Vo*," the grand princess replied. "But your tongue doesn't help. And your laziness. Lir, if you're going to ride in my cart with me, then you have to be silent right now, for I have to rehearse my present for Imperial Cousin Sua, and we cannot be late. Remember, after the gifts, we're to have Chapter 29."

"And that is why I'm here," Fourteenth Imperial Prince Rathlir stated.

"I do trust you got Imperial Cousin Sua a gift? Imperial Uncle won't like it if you turn up just to watch the latest chapter, without a *suitable* gift."

"Poem. I wrote it for Zhuori, but Imperial Father won't know that. Change a few words, and it's a birthday poem."

"You don't know what he knows and doesn't know," cautioned the grand princess, whose worry sounded genuine to Bu.

The imperial prince shrugged, his silk rippling, then he held up a highly polished hand mirror, reflecting the table behind him. After which he dropped the mirror onto his stomach and jabbed the air again, making odd signs.

The princess beckoned to Bu, who stood where she'd halted, clutching the zither to herself with one hand and her crystal eyepiece with the other. "Sit in that corner — ayah, what is that look? Do I have a spider in my hair?"

Bu had been squinting, unsure whether or not to risk using the eyepiece and possibly meeting someone's eyes. But then she remembered Instructor Halmas's dire comments about how ugly her squint was, and how she would get everyone into trouble by affronting the imperials, so she widened her eyes. From the princess's startled exclamation, apparently that looked worse. Her face flooded with color as she bowed and retreated to the corner she'd been pointed to.

The grand princess blinked at this odd behavior, but she could see how terrified the music student was. And the girl had been earnest, with no arrogance or oily obsequiousness, so she bit back the instinct to laugh and said, "At Sixth Imperial Princess Rathsuanek's palace, there will be a screen set for you to play behind. You're going to play 'The Merry Beggar', and I'm going to dance. If we're not to be late, we need to go through it a little before I must depart."

Bu set up the zither in the corner as the grand princess practiced slinging out her sleeves. Bu did her breathing to calm her nerves, which jangled like broken strings. Then she made minute adjustments, and sent a chord shimmering into the air. The zither was ready to sing of youth, and hope, and spring.

Bu shut her eyes and played.

The grand princess danced, buoyed up by the glorious cascades of sound.

At the end, Prince Rathlir sat up. "You. Music student. Are you playing for the theater troupe tonight?"

Bu scrambled to her feet and performed the proper bow for an imperial prince as she said, "This undeserving beginner is not ready for performance."

"Ayah! If you're not ready, then I'm a—"

The grand princess interrupted him unceremoniously. "That was so beautiful. Again. Can you make it sound less…less… no, I speak wrong. Let it be that wonderful, and if they listen more than they look, it will still be good enough for Imperial Uncle, which is all I ask."

They had enough time for Bu to play it through twice more, then the little page was back. Bu had to grab up the zither and scurry after the child, as the Princess poked the young man in twilight blue and gestured toward the door.

"That was very very very very beautiful," the little page said breathlessly, as soon as she and Bu were safely in the narrow servants' corridor. "We were all listening from behind the door. I never heard it played so beautiful."

"Thank you for your kind words," Bu said. "Can you tell me something?"

"If I can, O Musician."

"I am only a student musician, no rank," Bu said scrupulously. "I think the one person was playing Circle?"

"That was his imperial highness, Twelfth Prince Rathtan. He plays often with his imperial highness, Fourteenth Prince Rathlir."

"How could he play..." Bu halted, remembering the mirror, and the jabbing. "Was that was he was doing with his fingers?"

"Yes," the little page said. "They talk with their fingers. Their imperial highnesses sometimes play without seeing the board." She looked around, then said, "This way. We have longer to walk, but Grand Princess Rathlan's cart is very slow, and they have to get both the princes in. We will arrive first."

The grand princess's palace was on the other side of a garden from the First Imperial Princess's palace. As the page had promised, Bu arrived first, and was handed off from servant to servant, taken along a bewildering set of angled corridors, and then settled on a cushion, with a proper low instrument table behind a great screen decorated with flying cranes.

Bu could see nothing beyond, of course, but she heard voices. They all spoke in that gargled accent, their cadences smooth and almost musical, very formal, full of compliment and titles and self-deprecating comments.

At last the grand princess arrived. At first Bu did not recognize her, for she had spoken to Bu quickly, briskly, with only a little of that cadenced lilt. But now she spoke slowly and formally—and Bu was startled to discover that she, and the two princes, had to be greeting no less a figure than the emperor. He was actually in that room! Bu wondered that the air did not catch on fire around her lowly self.

She spread her fingers and flexed them, breathing against her nerve storm causing her hands to go damp. That would be fatal indeed! But all she could think was that she was not supposed to be there at all. It was supposed to be at least a year, if not more, before she was judged fit to be in the exalted presence of those people beyond the screen.

At least they could not see her! And then Bu reminded herself that music was like the screen and the carvings to them. Entertainment. Background. No one would notice her.

It was that thought that sustained her as the birthday ritual slowly unfolded. The unseen, unknown Imperial Princess Rathsuanek received everyone's good wishes, there was the smell of incense and a prayer, and then the gifts began—in rank order. Bu, listening avidly, soon began to determine by the comments and compliments which gifts were genuinely welcome and which were acknowledged politely. If she had not been told that this was a birthday celebration, she would have thought it was a competition, for she could detect undertones of tension in those formal, cadenced flatteries, thanks, and denials—this was after everyone waited for the emperor to voice his comment on each gift.

Once the emperor's consorts and several aunts and uncles had presented the imperial princess with her gift, it was time for the imperial princes and princesses to make their offerings. And then, finally, it was time for the grand princes and princesses.

When the steward called for Tenth Grand Princess Rathlan to come forward, a servant appeared in the doorway next to Bu's corner and waved at her.

She began to play.

Her doubts and fears fell away as the beautiful instrument responded to her touch. The spring song swelled and flowed, and Bu heard the hiss and swish of silk, and the soft tap of the grand princess's slippers as she danced.

When it was over, the servant was there waiting. "It is late," he whispered—Bu wondering if she was about to be blamed for that. But then she saw a cluster of people in strange costumes waiting to take her place. Each wore a mask with distorted faces. The drama's latest chapter! This was what everyone was waiting for.

Bu picked up the zither, clutched it to herself, and followed the servant out, dodging the rush of people to set up the theater without making their imperial audience wait.

A new page stood at the back door to conduct her along the arduous route back to the music building, and there, the page pulled from her sleeve a pouch. "I am to give you this, and tender the grand princess's compliments," the page said.

Bu bowed, and said what was proper—glad of the lessons, if not the way they were taught—removed a coin from the pouch to hand to the page, who gave her a brief smile. Off the page flitted for the long return to the imperial pavilions, in hopes she could catch a glimpse of the last of the performance.

Bu returned the zither first; the night graywing took charge of it without comment. Instruments were often returned far later than this.

"Where were you?" Bu's dormitory mates demanded when she reached the dormitory.

"I was summoned to play for the grand princess, who did a dance."

"In the *Golden Lotus Zither*? I heard the imperial court was to see Chapter 29 tonight!"

"I don't even know what that is," Bu said truthfully. "I was only there for the one dance, as a birthday gift for an imperial princess."

"Whom did you see? What did they say?"

Bu remembered Granny Zim's admonitions. "I saw nothing. I was behind a screen the entire time."

"Did they give you a tip?"

Bu pulled the pouch from her sleeve, and remembering an incident from a few days ago, she said, "This is my first time having money. I would like to celebrate, but I don't know where to get snacks for us all."

As she hoped, that instantly changed the subject. The girls argued about which bakery was the best, and Bu finally surrendered a portion of the coins inside the bag to the two most insistent girls, who promised to bring delicious things the next time they got free time to go out.

The rest thanked Bu for thinking of them, and everyone was in charity as they settled down to sleep. Bu let out a long sigh of relief, grateful that the worst was over.

TWENTY-TWO

GRANNY ZIM SENT YINYIN to summon Bu the next morning.

Bu gave a complete report, after which Granny Zim hmmmed, rocking back and forth on her cushion. Then she said, "And you left the moment you were done? It is well. Better than I had hoped. This grand princess is at the very bottom of the imperial family rank, which means limited authority, and her intention seems to have confined itself to providing an adequate gift for her cousin. If she forgets your name, even better."

Bu thoroughly agreed: she wanted only to be overlooked entirely by everyone outside the Garden of Celestial Merit, so that she could concentrate solely on her music.

Granny Zim had three days to begin to believe there would be no consequences of Bu's trip into the forbidden territory. Then one rainy, wild afternoon, she had just finished a class on chromatics to discover one of the emperor's graywings in the doorway to her classroom.

She had learned that the gradations of gray worn by all imperial palace servants, from cooks to guards to scribes, corresponded to importance. The Emperor's Own (sometimes called "imperial ferrets" where no one else was around) wore black. In a peculiar reflection of that—considering that the King's Own had been chosen specifically as watchdogs over the graywings—the highest rank of graywing, those permitted in the emperor's presence, wore a gray so dark it was nearly black. Their hats with the stiff wings were black.

This graywing was garbed in the colors of night.

"His imperial majesty summons Tribute Musician Zim Li," this person said in the unexpectedly mellow voice they all used. Though it was pleasant to the ear, their appearance was enough to strike fear into the most stolid heart.

Granny Zim took a moment to breathe her body into submission, and rose, not caring how much she tottered. The graywing waited, motionless and patient, and when she could trust her knees to carry her, she gave her master's robe a tug over her skinny chest, and ran her finger under her silken sash to smooth wrinkles.

The graywing took her along unfamiliar corridors. Here and there she glimpsed spring-green trees towering over the tops of high walls, until they crossed over an arched bridge and into the back of a building with crimson columns and fine tile eaves, with many guardian statues on each. These had to be charmed, but they didn't seem to keep YinYin out. She'd have to ask about that.

The room she was taken to could have encompassed the entire Zim house, including the wicker bridges over the two cascades from which they drew their water. There were only two occupants, besides silent servants standing motionless against the walls at either side, hands folded, eyes lowered. But those ears registered everything, Granny Zim was very certain. And how many hidden eyes on guard?

The graywing led Granny Zim to a cushion on the floor some thirty paces from the dais and its enthroned figure. Granny Zim knew better than to stare; a brief glance disclosed a white-haired man whose topknot was enclosed in gold. He wore a long, loose silk robe over several layers. This over-robe was embroidered with fire dragons, each with five outstretched talons. On a cushion at his feet sat a woman perhaps Linon's age, from the softness of her jaw. She wore a beautiful headdress of gold, with gems and pearls that complemented her silver-streaked black hair. Her over-robe was twilight blue, embroidered with tiny butterflies. She plucked at a qin in a way that made Granny Zim's skin crawl with the urge to take that instrument away and tune it, but the woman seemed unaware, her gaze remote.

Granny Zim's bony knees thumped down onto the cushion and she pressed her forehead to the floor, uttering the greeting that she'd been told was appropriate when summoned by an emperor.

His voice was rusty with age. "Sit up, sit up. I don't make anyone my age or older kneel unless they are sinners."

Granny Zim pushed herself upright, and sat back on her heels as the emperor leaned down, and cupped an age-spotted hand around the silent woman's cheek in a tender gesture. When she looked up, he gave his head a small shake, and she lifted her hands away from the instrument, looking a question. He opened a hand toward the door, and she rose, made a brief bow with immense dignity, and walked away without once glancing at Granny Zim.

The emperor said, "My consort is deaf. Or did you know that?"

"This ignorant outlander knows nothing about his imperial majesty's august family," Granny Zim said.

The emperor sat back with a wince and a sigh. "They made her learn to play though she's never heard a note. She feels it through the strings. Most of the time they don't seem quite the right note, but I've gotten used to the sound over the years. I find it comforting. Though nothing like the performance your student gave from behind the screen for my sixth daughter's birthday."

He paused, and Granny Zim suspected she was supposed to be grateful for this reference to Bu, though she didn't trust it. She uttered some words of deferential praise.

He said, "My nephew Panheg Sanhi made some extraordinary claims about the music from your faraway islands. It seems he spoke no less than the truth, judging by what we heard the other night. I'm curious to hear what her master's play is like. You may use my consort's instrument."

No doubt he considered that a rare accolade, but it took all her control not to react with the extreme doubt she felt.

She started to hoist herself to her knees, then fell back when a graywing flowed from somewhere behind the columns at the side, picked up the qin, and laid it before her. That's right. You didn't approach the Presence unless bid. Then there was to be no table? Ah, the guqin in ancient days was said to have been laid anywhere.

She settled it properly before her; at least it was beautifully made. Though she apparently must do without a table, she would not, even if her life depended on it, play those strings as they were. She tested one and tuned it, apprehensive of a barked order to begin. To her surprise, the emperor seemed content to wait, though she could wish him elsewhere, no doubt awaited by his numerous minions, instead of staring at her as if he had nothing else to do.

At least the tuning pegs were tended by someone, if not the deaf consort; they held properly, and when Granny Zim tested them again, she breathed out. It was better than she had permitted herself to expect.

What to play for an emperor? She'd been told that one only answered questions. It was not done to address his imperial majesty first.

What was his mood? She was not supposed to stare the way he stared at her. Ayah! Why not give him the Fig Islands farewell song, a piece of heart-haunting beauty? It had been written with that intent, to remind the men of home. This piece, played here, now, would be ironic, even if only she understood the irony.

She breathed in, and played.

That hall had been built for sound, she discovered. She adjusted her play accordingly, permitting each note the full head, belly, and tail. Each note blended exquisitely with the fading tail of the previous, and she smiled to hear the rich sound reaching from wall to wall. Oh, how she wished she were home again, seeing her grandchildren chatter about their day. Drinking tea with her daughter. Going over the trivial matters of the temple students with First Daughter-in-Law!

All this pent-up emotion imbued a song written for poignancy, and when the last notes faded away, her inward focus returned with a jolt. She remembered where she was. And with whom.

The emperor's breath hissed in. Then his eyes narrowed. "I should probably summon Panheg Sanhi back, to hear why none of your theater players were included among the tribute numbers?"

"If your imperial majesty pleases, this outlander must point out that there is no theater in the Fig Islands. There are festival plays that last an evening, always the same ones each year. What appears to be imperial theater is not known in the Fig Islands."

The emperor's eyebrows shot upward, Granny Zim noticed in a brief, covert glance. "Temple music," he mused. "Our temple music is not...eh, I'm minded to try an experiment. First Graywing."

"Sire." A shadow at Granny Zim's side.

"*The Golden Lotus Zither* has a few more chapters to go, if it follows the customary form. That would give them over at Merit enough time to put together a new piece. I want the Fig Islanders to lead the music for the next."

The graywing bowed and flicked a glance at Granny Zim. She understood her interview had been concluded—now that the emperor had upended the entire schedules of both Garden of Celestial Merit schools.

She performed the low obeisance once more, and followed the graywing out, her emotions veering between relief and annoyance.

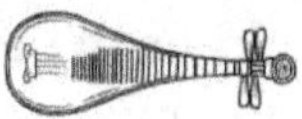

Chief Huazi managed to hide his reaction to the new imperial order, saying only, "We shall have a new schedule by morning. I will send a message over to Chief Yne Rilap in South Merit."

Over breakfast the following morning, Bu and YinYin were also summoned to the chief, who said evenly enough, "It appears that the emperor has issued instructions for a new theater piece. You two apprentices will be reunited with your Chief Zim for the duration. Chief Zim?" He turned to Granny Zim. "I am also to send over any of the seniors you feel have learned a sufficiency of your musical discipline."

Granny Zim could see how badly the chief musician was feeling about this oblique demotion in the way his gaze remained on his instrument. She bowed low, intuiting that to say anything would only worsen the situation, and then the chief added wryly, "Good luck."

Granny Zim bit back the retort forming on her lips—I expect I will need it—and summoned the girls with a look.

Because this was deemed to be an experiment, no one was going to shift from North to South to sleep, only to work. Bu followed Granny Zim's thin, bent figure across the great courtyard between the two sets of buildings for the first time. Now and then she had heard cadenced shouts coming from across the high walls, but she had never had a glimpse of what went on inside.

The chief of the players was a tall, willowy man of maybe fifty years. He regarded Granny Zim from under slack-lidded eyes, giving no hint of his thoughts about the imperial orders. He said only, "Welcome, Chief Zim. Permit me to conduct you on a tour."

Bu kept her place behind Granny Zim, next to YinYin, trying to be unobtrusive as she used her crystal eyepiece. She would have been immediately lost had she not, for the players' buildings were completely different from the musicians' rooms with their thick walls to limit the clashings of many instruments in practice.

There were a few thick walls, behind which singing could be made out. Otherwise there was a lot of open space filled with color: long swaths of fabric, and so many props. In one of the yards, Bu was startled to see children leaping and twirling and doing things she would have thought impossible, such as balancing on their hands, their feet rapidly twirling a sewn ball in the air.

They were finally introduced to the theater musicians, who were rigidly polite on the surface, but whose wall of resentment was nearly palpable.

The tour finished in one of the large rooms, as Chief Yne Rilap swept his sleeves and over-robe back with a gesture, and dropped gracefully to a cushion. One long hand invited Granny Zim to the cushion opposite. YinYin and Bu stood at her shoulders.

"Of course we are always developing new pieces," Chief Yne said. "Before we discuss these, might I put a question or two?" And when Granny Zim bowed acquiescence, "What pieces do you know? Probably the older ones, like *The Student and the Swan*. Or *Three Roses for the Beauty...*?"

"Neither of those," Granny Zim said.

"Neither?" Chief Yne remained inscrutable, but disbelief raised his voice a half-note.

"We know the plays for teaching writing in the *Dialects of Enlightenment*, and we know Mana Ta's *Five Festival Plays*, such as 'The Nine-Tailed Fox and the Thief.'"

Chief Yne passed a hand over his face. "You do know those are primarily for the instruction of children?"

"They are popular on our islands," Granny Zim said. "Everyone knows them. Knows what is coming, and sing along. It's our way of venerating the heavens before we begin our feasts."

"I see. Then let us commence with a very simple piece that is a bit more modern—no older than three hundred years—

and learn one another's ways." The only emotion he betrayed was the sardonic dip on the words *three hundred years.*

A young student was sent to fetch scrolls. Bu's ever-ready worry deepened at the thought of struggling through a scroll while in the presence of those disapproving musicians, but Granny Zim patted her hand. "Do as you always do," she murmured.

The silent musicians were all there, with their instruments, waiting in a unified silence when Granny Zim, Bu, and YinYin joined them, each with an instrument: Granny Zim with her qin, Bu with the zither, and YinYin chose the silver flute. The theater musicians had no scrolls before them, unspoken testimony that they knew this old piece well.

The atmosphere slightly eased when Granny Zim glanced at the scroll, and then began playing the melodic line without any hesitation. Bu hummed softly, committing it to memory, and on the refrain, joined in. Yin added the flute when the scroll called for it.

They played through a scene, then stopped, and the atmosphere was slightly less hostile. Then Granny Zim said, "Are there notes for expression?"

"Please explain what you mean, Chief Zim," Chief Yne said. "Are they not in your scroll? I believe I heard you play them."

"Is this not the, ah, what we call the method — the fundamental?" Granny Zim asked. "Shall we try it, so that I can explain what I mean?"

Chief Yne nodded to an assistant, who brought in some players, all dressed in loose clothing much like rice farmers, except the fabric was very fine. They moved to one end of the room, which Bu saw was divided off at either side by hanging fabric. This was a stage!

Chief Yne nodded to his musicians, who began to play the prelude. At first, everything was fine. Granny Zim and Bu came in when they were supposed to. Then the players began to move about and sing, and the musicians behind Granny Zim softened their volume.

Granny Zim and Bu quickly did the same. Then the preliminary exchange ended, and an aria began, accompanied only by the qin. The player danced very slowly as he sang. And when Granny Zim began to add expression, the singer halted, and turned to Chief Yne. "The cue for the sword?"

Chief Yne pressed a long forefinger to his forehead, then

turned to Granny Zim, and bowed. "The flourish you added was very fine, but it replaced the sword note. The cue."

Granny Zim looked down at the scroll, then up, enlightenment clearing her face. "Each of these notes is a cue, is that it? So the expression is always the same, written in?"

"Exactly. The gestures and choreography can get very complicated. Everything must be exact, especially when there are many in so small a space, or they collide with one another." He sighed, and everyone remembered the emperor's orders. "If I might request the Chief Musician to play something for us, something from your experience?"

Granny Zim acknowledged that here was another proof of the schools' different perceptions of music. "This is what I played for his imperial majesty." And she gave them the Farewell Song. This time, the emotion that came forth was bewilderment—that sorrowing awareness that as one's beloved sails away, there is nothing one can do except pray for their safety, and resign oneself to what fate has in store.

At the end, Chief Yne said, "I believe I begin to understand. If this is an example of your form of music..."

"It is."

"...it appears to me that players and singers are extraneous. The emotion that we bring through our rehearsed actions, the warp and weft of song and action, and known symbols our audience is familiar with, for you is entirely here." He tapped his head.

Whispering among the musicians acknowledged that. Bu caught disparaging phrases—ignorant outlanders—and admiration as well.

Chief Yne said, "We've been given orders to combine our arts, but we were not told how. Permit me to bring my wife over. She used to be First Dancer, but since she retired to teach dance, she also choreographs."

"Are we breaching proper form?" Granny Zim asked.

Chief Yne smiled. "There must be a hundred different styles for theater pieces, depending on where you come from. Two hundred. Song and dance, the oldest form, probably arose out of what you do, only with temple dancers responding to what they feel."

"Song and dance," Granny Zim repeated with a dubious look.

Chief Yne smiled wryly. "I realize stating it that way calls up pleasure house song and dance girls and boys. Their purpose has dwindled to a single thing. But our history shows that song and dance were the first forms of worship, before ritual was set down. Let us see if we can reinvent the old temple song and dance and make it new."

TWENTY-THREE

BU HAD BEEN WARNED never to sing, lest she end up sent to a pleasure house. Perhaps this was a legitimate threat somewhere, but she soon came to understand that the theater singers' training was as precise as anything her fellow musicians learned at the Fig Islands' temple. When playing a string instrument, each note must have three parts — the initial pluck, crisp and true, called the head. The belly was the sound brought forth, and the tail was the string's hum as it faded. Precise playing required knowing exactly where belly gave way to tail, so that the two sounds would weave.

It was the same with singers. Each note had the same three parts. And while one was concentrating on singing, there was also movement. Lots of movement. At the height of a scene, two or more characters might be enacting a sword battle, in no more than six or seven paces of space, while performing a complicated duet. She recognized very soon that there was no chance in Heaven, islands, or the underworld that anyone was going to snatch her away and expect her to do either of those things.

The players' day began before the musicians' did. By the time Bu woke and came over from the north building, the players had already put in a hard morning of physical exercise meant to build their strength and keep them supple. Then came rehearsal, and training, more rehearsal, and more

training. If they had no night performance, they got free time —
and many of them went outside the palace to dance some
more, flirt, and have fun.

Since Bu and YinYin had no classes currently, they were
free. "Come with us," cried the merry dancers. "It's more fun
in a crowd. And if you find someone you want to be alone
with, we don't mind!"

Bu's humble attitude was the second thing the theater
students noticed about her. The first was the enchanting way
she and the other two played. Chief Zim was an elder, to be
treated with distant respect. YinYin was quiet, and tended to
respond to questions with a flat stare and a soft, "I need to
recopy my music," or some such.

But Bu? The dancers decided, much as the upper level
girls' dormitory on the north side had, to make a pet of her.

First it was her eyebrows they insisted on fixing.

"What's wrong with my eyebrows?"

"Nothing, if you want to look like two caterpillars crawled
onto your face and died."

"ShiShi is right. You have a nice forehead. Why hide it
behind those hairy things, and that nun's braid?"

"But it is unfilial to pluck away what my parents gave me."

"Don't let me hear unfilial. Do you think *me* unfilial, who
burns incense to my poor father every new Ghost Moon?"

"Little Sister is right! Didn't your mother cut your nails? Of
course she did, or you would have arrived looking like the
demon bride from Ghost Island! If you were home, she would
be teaching you to shape your brows, and make yourself fine.
And even in your islands you must know that if your parents
groom you a certain way, then you keep doing it, for *that's*
filial!"

Bu did not want to say that if she had been home, First
Mother would have married her off already to one of those rice
farmers' boys who used to torment her, caterpillar brows or
no. "But I am unmarried. This braid is proper."

"The braid is, but a part in the middle, tenting your
forehead? Ayah! A braid off each temple, so simple, gives you
so much brighter a face! And that's before you weave a ribbon
or two into the side braids..."

Then there was actually leaving the palace.

Walking out with the girls revealed a completely different
world. The girls showed her how to string her crystal eyepiece
on a ribbon for easy access, and Chief Yne readily assigned

wooden tallies to everyone so that they could pass in and out the east gate, used by servants and deliveries. It was also where letters to different players and dancers were delivered. Bu discovered that the theater players never left the palace before stopping to see if they'd received admiring poems or a flower or a fan.

"The most popular is Grun Tham," Bu was told. He was First Player Apprentice, which meant he was the best of the students in singing as well as the astonishing movements the players made on stage.

When Grun Tham went out, a crowd of young people from all over the imperial city was sure to gather. Bu learned through the other girls' enthusiasm what handsome was. She did like looking at his face when everyone was together for training. It was such a symmetrical face, with a broad smile, and dark eyes that reflected the glowing lamps. He wore his beautiful soot-dark hair loose down his back, the way unmarried scholars did, the silky side locks pulled up in a small topknot and tied with a long, floating ribbon.

His clothes were as fine, his sleeves as long as he dared — wide sleeves were very much admired, but limited to the nobility — and a tassel with love knots at his narrow waist. His voice was as expressive as an instrument of wind, especially when he sang. Though in her heart, Bu preferred Xia Chi's voice, with its undertone of kindness.

Those first few forays were short, due to uncertain weather. The girls seemed to be content to walk up and down a street full of tea places and pleasure houses whose downstairs rooms shone golden with lamps, and from which music and a hubbub of voices spilled out.

The music was entertainment music; by now Bu understood the difference. It was not badly played, but there was no true emotion in it, no inspiration. The flourishes were all the elementary phrases of expression that she had learned her first two years at the temple school. Those flourishes had been meant to train the fingers and the heart, but here, it seemed, they were an end in themselves. Music here on the imperial island did not express anything beyond the conventional: love song; mourning song; mountain song; work song; seasonal and harvest songs. Music was there as background to the arts of dance and song and movement, or it was decoration, like the tapestries, the calligraphy scrolls on walls, and the pretty, painted paper lamps.

That week slowly settled into a routine. Granny Zim drilled her two students before breakfast, continuing their temple education. They now had mastered eighty of the two hundred techniques with each hand, and would test next on the next twenty of the single-hand techniques. Granny Zim also had them working on the next hundred, which was mastering two-hand figures of escalating complexity.

Then Bu and YinYin were excused to practice with the players as Chief Yne's wife, Rao Ri, slowly began assembling a new play taken from extracts of extremely aged scrolls. Yin played wind, Bu strings, and certain seniors of both the theater musicians and the seniors from the north building played with them, learning by example, as Granny Zim taught method to the rest.

Gradually a sense of excitement inspired them, taking the form of a heady conviction that they were inventing something new. The emperor would be the first to hear it, of course. If he approved, they would be able to present it to the world.

Granny Zim then discovered, at the end of that first week, that she was expected to report progress to the emperor.

There were two emotions she liked least: anger and fear. She felt both when the imperial graywing appeared, and she understood that she must abandon her carefully planned day, and toil across the expanse of the forbidden palace, along tedious high walls that all looked alike, in order to…what?

This time the empress was there, sitting next to the emperor, who half-reclined on his throne. The empress wore an even more elaborate headdress than the deaf consort had. It was gorgeous, and imposing, but Granny Zim wondered what it must feel like pressing down on skull and neck.

The empress raised a gold-framed crystal eyepiece to watery brown eyes. Granny Zim briefly met that slightly enlarged eye with her own gaze, her mind leaping to her third night, when she discovered a scroll whose tag was a different color than most of the rest. She had been given permission by Rao Ri to read anything in the theater archives, in order to better understand the plays.

She had hummed the melodies, liking them very much; they were brisker than those she thought of as imperial island songs. Lots of thirds and fifths, played for harmony, in a fast rhythm that surely must have been vigorous on stage. The title was only *Spring Garden*—without the usual references to philosophy or the noble arts—and the arias and dances appeared to be centered around different flowers.

But when she began to carry it out, the little graywing in charge clasped his hands and exclaimed, "Oh, no, no, no, that one, it's much better for it not to leave the archive."

"Oh?" Granny Zim asked encouragingly, but he only took it carefully from her hands, and trotted back among the high shelves to replace it. When she asked Rao Ri later, she shut the door before answering. With a quick laugh, she said, "That is not an imperial theater piece. It was popular elsewhere, and a troupe dared to bring it to the city. One night only. I'm just too young to have been there, but I heard about it some years later. What a clamor!"

"What was it about?"

"The empress and harem duels. That's the only word for them. Scandal trailed after the empress for years. Until the war. Of course she's old now, and all her children, her daughters and her two adopted sons, died in the troubles..."

Granny Zim blinked herself back to the present, seeing what were still beautiful features beneath the sag of time, and the lines that experience carves into the face.

The empress said, "I was not able to attend my daughter's birthday festival." Her voice was cracked, almost a caw, and Granny's first thought was, *Here is a woman who knows what it is to scream grief into a pillow lest it be heard* as the empress went on, "I want to hear the music the others spoke of, but from the master, rather than the student."

And here came a graywing, carrying a zither.

Granny Zim bowed, taking the time to breathe her annoyance away. To the imperials, this was her purpose. She said, "This old outlander will attempt to reproduce her student's interpretation of 'The Merry Beggar' but it is hoped that her esteemed imperial majesty comprehends that no two performances are ever alike."

The empress's eyes narrowed, then she said, "You do not write them down? Is it that the notation is unknown at your temple?"

"Your imperial majesty, the fundamentals are written in the temple scrolls. These are what we call method—very like the fundamentals we are honored to study in the imperial palace. But expression is the feeling the player brings to the piece, usually inspired by the listeners. There are times when a master has begun to play and those who can write down the notes as they are played do so, aware that they are in the presence of a great piece. These might be added to studies, but it is understood that even if the piece becomes a part of method, expression will be evoked by the player."

"Am I hearing an indirect claim that you might not play as well as your student?"

"Your imperial majesty will be the judge of the success or failure of the piece. This old strummer makes no claims beyond her attempt to fulfill the command with which your imperial majesty has graced her." Granny Zim bowed again, thinking that she'd managed to get that out pretty well, considering her lack of experience in court speech.

The empress uttered a quick breath that might have been taken for a laugh. The tiny gems on delicate golden chains hanging from the phoenix headdress winked in the light from the windows high above. "That accent of yours is a reminder that things truly are done differently in far parts of the empire."

Though the Fig Islanders in no way considered themselves part of this empire, they had acceded to its demands as the reed bows to the ground in high winds. Granny Zim bowed as well, and then tested the strings.

While she did so, the emperor reached over for a cup, his fingers trembling. A graywing flowed to his side and gently pressed a cup into those fingers. The emperor drank, then sat back as if the act exhausted him.

While she completed the tuning, Granny Zim recollected Bu's practice, heard once. She called up the central melody and its front and back refrains, and began to play to the empress.

It was a song of spring, but Granny Zim was not a child of spring in either birth or in years. Neither was the empress. The searching fourths that emerged from beneath the dancing harmonies in thirds questioned a world in which the young died first, and for what? The senseless wars of men, that the women at home could do nothing about? Questions that might be asked by those young men so far away as they faced the prospect of their bones growing cold in a distant land, from which no one known to them could bring them to the ancestral burial ground and have at least the small comfort of recalling their names in generations to come. Only, would they ever know, once they had passed over the bridge of stars to a new life? At least they would have that new life. And so would the old, after the burden of remembered pain was washed away, leaving the sweet hope of a new beginning.

The empress's eyes closed as the beautiful melody searched, then soothed, her heart. When the last note had died away, the emperor grunted as he straightened up, reached over, and gave her hand a path. "Very different from what she played to me. It's like an augury."

The empress opened her eyes, revealing only a very slight moisture along the lower lids. She said, "I comprehend. Tribute musician, your music is a garden in which lotus, and roses, and peonies, grow side by side with the bitter herbs of healing. This song is a rose, and your student's a rose, but every rose is different. A miracle in its own right."

Granny Zim bowed and muttered a deferential denial. Empty words, but they had to be said.

And the empress accepted them as polite ritual. "I look forward to what you and the theater bring for us. It will be all the more valuable in that there can only be this one performance, and that the next will not be the same."

Was that dismissal? Yes. Granny Zim bowed yet again and withdrew, and there was the long journey back again, as she shed one worry for the new set: would the players and dancers be able to adjust to not having the same exact cues at each performance?

She found all the theater musicians and players waiting — the chiefs dressed well in case they were summoned — and called them in to report her imperial conversation, and what it implied. It was quite late when she finished, and went back to the north in hopes of finding a biscuit or two to eat.

YinYin was waiting, those black eyes steady in the darkness. "Bu went out with the dancers. But she is not back yet," YinYin said bluntly.

Granny Zim's heart jolted painfully. "Where is she? Can you…?" She waved her hands as if dissipating smoke.

YinYin turned her head, gazing into the distance. Then she abruptly dissolved, leaving Granny Zim alone.

TWENTY-FOUR

BU DISCOVERED THAT SHE loved borrowed clothes.

The dancers and girl players knew which of the baskets and barrels and shelves of costumes could be borrowed for an evening stroll. There were two dancers in particular, Nightingale and Spring, who found it to be immense fun to treat Bu like a live doll. They fixed her face and her hair, and then brought out swathes of cheap silk (which looked insanely costly to Bu), held them against her, then whipped them away again, until she was robed in bright green over pale yellow and sand-colored, flimsy under-robes, with a flame-colored sash to match the ribbons in her braids.

Bu would never have paired green with flame, but together the contrast created a flicker effect that she kept running her fingers over. A borrowed pair of embroidered slippers made her feel like a princess; her sight was too poor to see that the slippers were threadbare. They were soft on her feet in their worn socks, and to her untutored eyes gorgeous.

The dancers also corrected her walk and her manner of holding a fan. Bu listened seriously as she did to every sort of correction, thinking that if she behaved the way the dancers did, she would remain unnoticed in a crowd.

Walking along the streets where all the local young people congregated delighted her, once she became accustomed to it. With a group of others, she did remain safely unnoticed.

She also concentrated on breaking the squinting habit, which she had learned drew the eye. The crystal eyepiece now hung around her neck for easy access, and she could even wedge it between her cheekbone and her brow ridge, changing eyes when one got tired and achy. She knew what perfect was. She retained that memory of the harbor that day long ago, when YinYin put demon smoke into her so that she could see.

The day that Granny Zim was summoned to play for the empress, the schedule was upended when Granny Zim could not teach her classes. Everyone rehearsed the day before's lessons, then the dancers and the music students were dismissed while the masters waited to find out if they would be summoned.

The social butterflies among the dancers promptly annexed Bu, dressed her up as well as themselves, and ventured out. At the gate, while one sorted through messages, the others loitered, talking and laughing, until a teenage page appeared. They recognized him for an imperial page.

"His imperial highness wishes to know if First Apprentice Grun Tham is coming out tonight?"

"The senior players are all being kept in," Nightingale told him. "But we are all here if his imperial highness wants to play!"

The page nodded shortly and sped away.

"Why did you say that?" Spring poked Nightingale with her fan. "Didn't you recognize him? That's Mayfly, one of Prince Weasel's pages."

"I know that," Nightingale retorted, tossing her braids back. "I think Prince Weasel is fun."

Another dancer put in, "As long as you are smart enough to leave if he gets wind in the brain." She twirled her fingers around her ears.

Spring shrugged. "He's only that way when he gambles."

"Which is all the time," put in a fourth dancer.

"Especially now that Zhuori at the Chrysanthemum Garden says she's sick and won't come out onto the stage if she sees him."

The girls (except for Bu, bewildered by this fast exchange of gossip, as usual) laughed, and they set out walking.

By now Bu had heard enough gossip about the imperials' young generation to have put together "Prince Weasel" with the battered prince she'd seen lying on the grand princess's couch as he played Circle in a mirror.

She also knew that there were four entertainment houses most popular with the palace students and the nobles their age. The Chrysanthemum Garden was full of fine art, scrolls calligraphed by great poets, and very expensive. The nobles and imperials went there, and very popular entertainers, such as Grun Tham, who never had to spend a tinket. The only gambling permitted there was Circle.

The Four Roses was livelier. It was cheaper, which meant artisans' apprentices and merchants' offspring could go there. Also those further down the social rankings (like dancers) if they were pretty and good company, and amenable to whatever invitations were extended. It was open to all kinds of entertainment, including the types of gambling frequented by those high in rank.

The dancers at Chrysanthemum Garden were the best, and paid the best; the Four Roses paid less well, and there weren't any dancers at Honey Hive or The Golden Rooster, just indifferent music, lots of liquor, and more gambling opportunities. "We *never* go *there*," Spring assured Bu with a pout.

Bu liked walking about, looking at the glowing lamps and listening to the chatter around her, as long as no one ever noticed her. And she loved watching the dancing. It had not occurred to her to put herself forward in any way—she was content to let the others talk and laugh and flirt with strangers.

But Nightingale and Spring had other ideas.

They set out in a group, pausing to buy candied haws. Nightingale insisted on treating Bu, though she still had most of the coins she'd been given by the grand princess— everything she had not spent on honey cakes for the musician students in her dormitory.

"You don't have to," Bu said seriously. "I have coins in my pocket."

"I insist! It's such a delight ever since you came among us. You are as sweet as a bunny, but your playing would put the celestial phoenix to shame!"

Bu blushed, thanking her, and accepting the sticky treats. She did love candied haws.

They kept walking, and presently Spring said, "Here's Chrysanthemum Garden. Should we see if Zhuori is dancing?"

"It's always lively there," Nightingale said, linking her arm with Bu's. "Don't you think, Bu?"

"I do," Bu said. "I like it there very much."

"Not if it's poetry night," one of the girls remarked from behind them. "Unless the pretty scribes are let out."

"Those boys are all snobs," Spring said with a pout. She walked on Bu's other side. "The dancing is best at Chrysanthemum Garden. And you like to watch dancing, Bu?"

"I do!"

"Then let's go there."

One of the other dancers said, "But we just heard Mayfly say the Weasel Prince is let out of the palace again. You know he'll go to Chrysanthemum Garden first, and if he does, Zhuori won't be out."

"And what happens then?" Spring goaded.

"Oh, sure, Owner is more likely to let others on stage — if you have enough to bribe him. Do *you* have ten golden taels? I don't think there's a single golden tale between us all!"

"We have something better," Nightingale said with a smile. "Bu."

"Me?" Bu's crystal eyepiece dropped with a slap against her silk-covered bosom. "I can't dance!"

"No, silly bunny, you can *play*."

Bu stopped short. "Play? But..."

Spring sighed, casting her eyes skyward. "Lum Bu, it's not forbidden. They might even hire you. In fact, I am very sure that, if we can get you on that stage, Owner will try to keep you by throwing gold coins at you."

"But I don't want to be hired there," Bu said nervously. "I'm just a student. I have so much more to learn. And if — when — that is, I thought one day to be a teacher."

Spring groaned theatrically. "There is so much wrong with all that, I don't even know where to begin."

"Yes," chimed in another.

Nightingale held up her free hand. Unlike Spring, she could see the fear that Bu never quite hid. She was ambitious, but not cruel. "Let's talk over here," she said to Bu. "Spring, go see what's what, and come back and tell us." She made shooing motions toward the others, who took the hint.

Nightingale drew Bu under the eave of a fabric shop, still open to catch the eye of wandering young people with money to spend.

"Look at me, Bu," Nightingale said. "I know you're half-blind. Use your crystal. Really look at me." She paused, as Bu peered timidly into Nightingale's face. Beneath the excellent rouge, and the artfully plucked brows, was a round face, a thin nose the opposite of Bu's mushroom blob, a low forehead enhanced to look higher by her mouse-ear hairstyle, and a determined mouth. "Do you see me? Though I still can wear a girl's hairstyle, I am no longer your age. Come Sky Wishes Day, I can wish as hard as I like, but I will still turn twenty — and that means if I'm not selected for the theater, I'll be turned loose. That's fine if you have a family to go to, but my family is too poor for me to come back. That's why they sold me to the palace in the first place, to get tax relief for the three years a daughter brings. But my ten years are nearly over."

Bu was beginning to understand how that worked. Though she was called a tribute person, a good part of all the other imperial palace servants were in a sense tribute people. Not quite slaves. That was for one's lifetime. Those poor wretches taken off the Turtle Islands were slaves until they died. The tribute people, including girls (and sometimes boys, though most extra boys went to the army) could regain their freedom in ten years, if not hired permanently at that time.

"I want Zhuori's place," Nightingale said, still low-voiced. "I tried once before. I was too young, in all ways. Too impatient. Not enough training. I'm too tall for the theater dancers, who must never be the height of the players, but being tall is not such a matter on the street."

Bu's brow furrowed. "What about Zhuori?" Then flushed, because that was not even remotely her affair.

But Nightingale uttered a small laugh. "Trust you to ask about that. You may not realize it, as your eyesight is what it is, but she's thirty-two. Dancers have to be young. She's angry right now because she tried to trick Prince Weasel into taking her in, but he didn't bite. What boy not far past twenty, no what *prince* of not far past twenty takes in a favorite when he can dally with anyone he sees? She reached too far, but there are tens and tens to take his place. She just has to be less ambitious and more practical, and she will get a comfortable life."

Bu nodded.

Nightingale said, "Would you not like to see me succeed?"

Bu said, "If I can, I will try."

"Good. Let's go back to the others. Be thinking in that phoenix brain of yours about 'The Merry Beggar.' It's very popular right now, and I've been working up a dance to it. I think I can match it to your cue-less style. My dance will please the eyes, but reach them *here*." She laid a fist against her breastbone.

Bu was not being asked to do anything forbidden. Instead, she was being asked to help someone who had been kind to her ever since her arrival. She squashed down her trepidation, and walked with Nightingale to meet the others, who loitered outside the well-lit entertainment house, chatting and flirting with passers-by.

Spring turned, saw the triumphant lift to Nightingale's chin, and clapped her hands lightly. The two of them went in ahead of the others to find the owner. They were still arguing when the rest of the crowd, Bu among them, caught up.

"Here she is," Spring said, pointing. "She truly truly is the best. A fairy from Heaven! I promise you've never heard anything like her."

"She can be Suanek come again, but it's twenty gold if you want to audition. I have my standards. And if the audience doesn't like you, out you go, no more chances."

"But we don't have twenty gold. We will never have twenty gold," Spring wailed, crossing her arms.

"Is that my problem?" the owner retorted. "No. It is not. My problem is pleasing my customers, and if I didn't set a hard limit, you girls would pester the life out of me."

"Let her play," a new voice interrupted from behind. "Zhuori is sick so often, why not give someone new a chance?"

Bu knew that voice! It was the couch prince from the grand princess's palace. And there was Brick at his back, his flat gaze drifting over the crowd.

The owner hesitated. Everyone there knew why Zhuori wasn't dancing, but it never did to antagonize a prince. Especially when fault—if fault there was—appeared to be divided pretty well between the two of them.

The owner hated letting twenty gold taels go by, but a prince was a prince. Even an annoying one with a dubious reputation. At least he wasn't drunk. He bowed low, biting back extreme irritation, and said, "If his imperial highness desires it to be so, what can this poor proprietor do but acquiesce?"

Bu said softly, "I do not have an instrument."

"They have them here," Nightingale said quickly, waving a hand. She was already mentally reviewing her choreography.

Bu worried that the musicians here would not want to share their instruments, but a word and a look from the owner swept that away. One of the musicians, reflecting that the dancers were palace trained, guessed that the musician might be, too, and if coins were being handed out by the prince to see new dancers, he might be as generous to a musician. "You may play my zither."

Bu bowed her thanks, ran her fingers over the instrument, which was plain, the wood worn, as if it had worked for more than two generations of players, but the strings were new and tight, the pegs excellent. It hummed with vigor.

By the time she had settled off to the side, as far back as she could in hopes of not being noticed, Nightingale had stripped out of some of her outer layers, and loosed the mouse ears so that her hair flowed about her. She had planned for this day, and so wore a dance costume beneath her clothes. The wood of the stage was smooth as silk, so she could dance barefoot.

She moved out to the center of the stage, and struck a pose as Bu closed her eyes and considered Nightingale. She would not think of all those others out there; if she kept her eyes closed, it was very like playing for the imperial family, mercifully hidden beyond that screen.

She began simply, so simply that at first the audience, many with the owner's good rice wine in them, began to rustle and whisper and scoff, but Nightingale twirled and snapped out her sleeves like wings, and the talk silenced.

Bu caught the movement, and smiled. Here was youth, and hope, and joy in music; she echoed that snap with an extravagant glissando, and the duet began. Because it was a duet. Bu echoed Nightingale's pleasure in dancing, grateful that she had been learning to see what dancers accomplished during the past week's experiments. She had a long way to go to truly play well for dancers, she was certain—and so, after the refrain, she closed her eyes again, let the song bloom within her, and trusted Nightingale to echo her.

Which she did. It was frightening and yet exhilarating to let emotion rather than cues dictate her moves. She was trained so well that she had any number of steps in memory, leaping and twirling and sweeping and pausing to pose and smile as the zither filled the air with butterflies of sound.

When it ended, the entire room erupted in applause. Bu left Nightingale to bow to the audience and pick up tossed coins and flowers and fluttering ribbons of beautiful, heavy silk. She thanked the musician for the loan of the zither, and slipped down through the back way, and around in search of those she knew.

"What did I tell you?" Imperial Prince Rathlir exulted. "I ought to have laid a bet, a hundred to your twenty."

"And so his most esteemed imperial highness would have won," Owner said. "Truly, his taste is as exquisite as his exalted birth." As Owner bowed and uttered that and like flatteries, his attention was elsewhere—he was determined to get to that zither player and flatter her into a firm contract. But where was she? Nightingale was alone on the stage, sweeping up the largesse.

Bu had seen the owner looking around. Afraid that she might be the target, she pressed farther back into the shadows beneath the stairway to the gallery, where she waited for Nightingale to show her the way out, when a voice briefly reached her from the hubbub, "…you'll have no longer than two breaths to attack before the grays charge in."

It was low, but precise, cold with intent. Then it was subsumed into the general noise. The hairs on the back of Bu's neck twitched with the undertone of threat.

The grays, she knew by now, were the imperial guard. That meant something to do with the imperials, and there was only one of them in sight—that she knew of.

She peered around a jointure in the stairway, her crystal eyepiece wedged between brow and cheekbone as she swept the crowd. There was the prince. Why did they call him a weasel? She looked at that broad, high forehead and the angular face coming in to a pointed chin. Weasels on Fig Islands had been considered lucky creatures, because they kept the rat population down, but to Bu they had been vague brown shapes, sinuously swarming up the tangled trunks and roots of the fig trees.

She heard his voice rise in a laugh, "Come on! I'll play any two of you. Won't look at the board—"

She would never approach him directly. Ever. But there was Brick—who, if he did not protect his assigned prince, would be executed. No defense possible.

Bu slid around a stack of barrels, and, seeing the owner's back turned as he peered into the shadows on the other side of the room, she eeled her way through the outer ring of the crowd, making for Brick. The top of his head was easily visible above the others.

She reached him, and softly touched his sleeve. He twitched away, then peered frowningly at her, mouth open as usual. "I hear something," she whispered, and repeated what she'd heard.

As soon as the words passed her lips, she felt stupid—it was not at all informative, maybe not even a true threat—and she was going to apologize and slip away when Brick grasped the back of her borrowed clothes, catching her hair painfully under his fingers, and slung her unceremoniously out the front door.

As she landed on the entry steps, tears springing to her eyes, screams and shouts erupted inside. Then a stampede of frightened people crushed together in the doorway, trying to get out first. Bu had a heartbeat to scoot back and cling to the pretty carved railing of the entry stairway before the bottleneck broke and the shouting crowd stampeded past her, feet trampling the folds of her robe.

Inside clashes, clangs, and shouts rose over the noise of the fleeing customers, followed by the ruddy flicker of flames.

Bu sobbed, the sound completely subsumed into the noise, until a cold hand tugged at her, and she looked up into YinYin's face, fires reflected in black eyes—and behind them pinpoints of ember glow. Bu's grip on the rail loosened, and YinYin's strong arms fended off some of the wild, fleeing people in hauling Bu to her feet.

"We will run," YinYin said, and Bu stumbled willingly into the darkness of the street, and away.

TWENTY-FIVE

"BUT HE *DIDN'T*," BU said to Granny Zim later that night, once her many cuts and bruises had been treated. "I was *right there*. Imperial Prince Rathlir did *not* set fire to the Chrysanthemum Garden, or attack anybody. I don't care what the rumor is. I am a witness to what happened."

Granny Zim raised a hand. "I understand. But I still want you to keep silent even when the wagging tongues around you are wrong. Let someone else correct them."

"But it is not just when someone takes the blame for a terrible thing he did not do. People *died!*"

"They died of wounds, not fire," Granny Zim said.

"I know! And he did not even have a weapon!"

Granny Zim closed her eyes. "You have been trained to see and speak the truth, which was simple in our islands. Or simple enough," she added, scrupulous herself. "However, right now, this is an imperial matter. That means it has to do with those in power, and in matters of power, the truth can seem as bent as an eating stick stuck in water. It's safer not to chatter at all about such things."

Bu bit back a sob; while she had been waiting her turn for the physician, dancers, players, and even the youngest of the graywings attached to the theater, had either passed through asking questions, or excitedly repeated what they had heard. All of it wrong, Bu wanted to say, but YinYin had brought her to Granny Zim first, and Granny Zim said, *Keep silence.*

"Bu, what you have to understand is that it *never* goes well to get oneself involved in power disputes. Did you say anything while you were being wrapped up?"

"No. I obeyed your order to stay silent." Bu shook her head slowly. "Even when Spring came to tell me Nightingale was found with a broken arm, and nearly burned in the fire!"

"At least it was not a leg," Granny Zim said, keeping her opinion of Nightingale to herself; while she faulted no one for ambition, she was furious at that girl for dragging Bu into her schemes. "A dancer's arm will heal without further trouble. I feel badly that fate placed her there, but it could have treated her much worse. No doubt that owner will offer compensation—perhaps a position, if what you say is true about her prospects. Do not worry yourself over Nightingale."

"I won't," Bu said miserably. "Though I hate seeing her lying in bed like that. I saw her, before they sent me out."

"The doctors will have filled her with medicine that makes her sleep, so that the bone will set properly."

"That's what Chief Rao said," Bu whimpered, wiping her eyes. "But I overheard her saying that the princes were hauled straight before the emperor, which sounds so terrible, and oh, it seems so unfair that someone who did not cause the disaster should be taking all the blame."

"He's a prince," Granny Zim stated. "He can do such things, and nothing dire will happen to him. Some graywing no doubt is delivering a bag of gold at this very moment to the owner of the shop, who will soon be telling anyone who asks that the prince was not even there. The gossip will die away."

"But the dancers say that the emperor hates him, and he's sure to be confined yet again, and it wasn't his fault—"

"—and 'yet again' means he's caused plenty of trouble before. Bu. Being confined to a palace in which an army of servants attends to your slightest wish is not the sort of penalty that causes me tears of grief," Granny Zim retorted tartly. "You did what you thought was right. And you escaped injury. Perhaps you ought to refrain from dawdling about the streets just because those hen-witted dancers flatter you into following them…"

Granny Zim saw in Bu's fresh cataract of tears how much these words hurt her, and relented. "Ayah, I am old and stupid! I forget. At your age, it is to be expected that you would enjoy going out into the world. There is no fault in being young! But perhaps it is time to concentrate on what we are doing here. There are many opportunities ahead for exploring the outer world. Remember, we still have the emperor's order —" *at our necks* " — to be fulfilled. And so much of what we are doing is new. There are going to be new rehearsals, probably longer rehearsals, until we are certain of the new way of proceeding."

Bu wiped her eyes and nodded soberly.

Granny Zim sighed. "As you've probably noticed, the players are having the most difficult time, as they depend on precise cues, and our music is impossible to provide these in the manner they require."

"Grun Tham said yesterday that the emotions are like catching wind, or bottling fire. Is that what he means? He didn't seem displeased."

"I noticed. I think many of the apprentice players, especially the young ones, rather like the challenge. They relish the call for direct emotion rather than the highly controlled false emotions of their plays, wonderful as those are to watch."

"Oh, they *are* wonderful. I should like to see a whole one, instead of pieces."

"In fact," Granny Zim said slyly, "I think it might be very useful for you to observe the senior class in their rehearsals, to really get a grasp of what they do, and how they do it. I've seen some of those youngsters rehearse the same three or four movements over and over and over. Very much like our taking apart method in both ends of refrain."

Bu agreed, and Granny Zim was relieved to see her much calmer. "Now, go back and get some slee —"

A respectful knock at the door interrupted the word. Granny Zim hesitated, for it was quite late, but then a second, more insistent knock caused her to nod at Bu, who sprang to the door.

Outside stood one of the graywings, who said, "Student Lum Bu is summoned."

Granny Zim was longing for her own bed, but she grunted herself up off the cushion, saying, "I am coming, too, as her master."

"It will be as the captain decides," replied the graywing, calm and melodious as always.

Captain? That did not sound good at all.

At least there was no long, horrible journey to some dank

prison. They crossed to Chief Huazi's outer room. The chief sat there, along with the theater chiefs. Tea had been brought, Granny Zim noticed; the imperials seemed to want a veneer of politesse, of civilization, over incidents that were not the least civilized.

Bu began trembling when she laid eyes on a figure in a long black tunic over black trousers, sashed at the waist, and cut up the sides for riding. This man appeared to be about thirty, maybe a bit younger, and he offered Bu a smile.

"Come forth, Student Lum Bu," he said, not at all threatening. "I am here to investigate what happened this evening at the Chrysanthemum Garden."

Bu sent a wild-eyed glance Granny Zim's way.

"You must tell him what you know," Granny Zim said, in an attempt to calm poor Bu down again. "It's gossip that I forbid you to share outside this room."

Chief Huazi nodded in approval at that, and the theater couple echoed it, Rao Ri saying, "I wish Spring had half your girl's sense. She seems to have seen the least yet has the most to say."

The captain of the Emperor's Own said cheerfully, "Oh, speculation is inevitable when something happens, but it ought to die down quickly enough once we establish the truth."

Bu was thinking of that bag of gold that Granny Zim had speculated about, then she drew a deep breath. "I—this student knows very little."

"Begin when you first sensed, saw, or heard something amiss," the captain encouraged. "Even if it was a single instant. Every bit is helpful in building a picture."

Bu's testimony began as a tangle of half-finished sentences, with frequent backtracks as she tried to be scrupulous, but the captain was patient, and gradually her viewpoint—limited as it was—emerged. The salient point was that voice she had heard while she hid under the stairwell.

"Did you see who spoke?"

"No."

"Did you heard that voice at any time after that?"

"No."

Tears started again when she got to the part where she clung to the stairway as people stampeded by, nearly trampling her. She was a forlorn figure standing there, trembling from head to foot, a bandage on one wrist, and a blooming bruise on her cheek, where her head bumped against the rail that she then clutched.

At the end, the captain said, "Thank you, Student Lum Bu. You did very well. And … I would follow your master's advice about gossip." He nodded a dismissal.

Bu turned to Granny Zim, who indicated the door. Bu escaped gratefully, and Granny Zim said, "Do you need me to stay?"

The captain said, "While there are no imperial orders, while I have the senior staff gathered here, I want to reiterate the sensible advice you appear to have given your student. From what the young dancer saw before she was thrown down and trampled, she got in the way of at least one hired assassin. However, that fact is to remain in this room. Use whatever means you have to encourage your students not to discuss what was to all appearances a mere altercation between drunken patrons."

The chiefs all bowed as they murmured compliance, and the captain rose from his cushion and left, the tea untouched.

Granny Zim reached over and picked up his cup; a lifetime of abhorring waste prompted her to down it. The warmth, the fresh taste did restore a semblance of civilization.

"Assassins," Chief Yne said slowly. "Not many can afford to hire them."

Except imperial princes. The words hovered there, thought but unspoken.

Chief Huazi sighed. "Are we to see a repeat of what happened thirty years ago?"

Granny Zim set the cup down, aware that what, for the islands, had been rumors of civil strife leading to the fracturing of the empire had been immediate for all three of these people. She sensed residual fear. "I told Bu that I want her to see some theater so that she will better understand how music and players, script, cues, and the stage all fit together," she said.

Chief Yne's fine brows rose. His wife nodded slowly, and Chief Huazi smiled, hands on his knees. "We can see to that at our end: time to resurrect some older plays, which our seniors will prepare the music for. We've summer festivals to think about…"

TWENTY-SIX

I DID PROMISE HEROES and villains, did I not? (Asked the storyteller, as the innkeeper brought around more to drink.)

We have already met a few who might be heroes, or villains. Which is which it is not for me to say. You will have to decide.

But first let us move away from Granny Zim, who discussed new plans over tea, and YinYin, who walked in the darkness, resolutely holding to a human form due to some very potent charms installed at the intersections of the imperial palace, and Bu, who slipped into troubled sleep.

Let us briefly visit the emperor, who glared down at his twelfth and fourteenth sons—Rathtan, son of his favorite consort, and Rathlir the youngest, and the most troublesome.

No, the most obviously troublesome.

He let the silence build, glaring from his throne as they knelt there. Not that silence would disturb TanTan, who lived in a silent world. It was Rathlir who was sweating, as the emperor waited for reports with more substance than the wild rumors that had first dragged him out of bed.

Oh, Rathlir, he was thinking to himself. Kanda said that man's face is reflected by water, his fate in the stars, and his luck in his children. It is the same for emperors. Seven living sons out of fourteen, and every one of those seven trouble in some way or another.

It was the first four deaths that still hurt the worst, after all these years. For it was his much cherished First Prince—the Crown Prince—who had proved to be the most unfilial and devious, though Second Prince had been just as bad, readily overseeing the deaths of the third and sixth as if they were rats in the walls, and not brothers, with whom they had played as children. But then Second Son had mimicked his brother in everything.

Why couldn't his clever, talented, beloved first son have waited? He would have inherited it all—and at a much more sober age than twenty-two. *If I die tomorrow,* the emperor mourned as he stared down at his youngest without seeing him, First Son would have been not quite fifty. A good age, still strong, but sober. Certainly sober enough not to have gathered the most corrupt and self-seeking among the courtiers, promising anything, as he had at twenty-two. The same age Rathlir was now…

At least, he'd often comforted himself, Rathlir was too lazy to be devious.

Enough. He signaled for a graywing to bring more tea.

He'd drunk half of it when one of the Emperor's Own entered silently, bearing a written report. The emperor frowned when Rathlir glanced up.

The prince hastily lowered his gaze in a semblance of humble regret, and the emperor read the report, which combined the testimony of both Imperial Prince Rathlir's and Imperial Prince Rathtan's bodyguards, plus the proprietor of that damned house the brats all fluttered around like moths to fire.

The most interesting by far was the shortest, that of Lir's new guard. Who had actually managed to hang onto a position no one wanted. But what was this? Girl. Zither. Said something about an attack in two breaths, just before the new guard saw the first of the assassins, who seemed to materialize out of the air.

There were many unanswered questions here, but for now, it seemed that for once it was really not Lir's fault. He, according to three separate witnesses, had (as usual) been in the middle of bragging about his Circle prowess, offering (as usual) to stake ridiculous amounts of gold against himself.

"Go away," he said abruptly. "Confined to your palace until this disgusting mess is cleaned up."

He watched Lir elbow TanTan (so he was known to his

brother and favorite cousin, though he knew himself by a sign, not a sound) and turn up his thumb, at which both prostrated themselves with all the outward signs of filial propriety and then exited with more haste than grace.

Was it a mistake to relax the rule and let them live together? The rule had been strict for centuries: no sons of different mothers to share a palace. Far too much violence in imperial history. Dynastic history, he corrected mentally. There was little evidence in the Kun family archive that brother had attacked brother, or cousin against uncle, with quite such enthusiasm before great-great-great grandfather Kun had come to the dragon throne.

They had broken the rule because there seemed no way to bring TanTan out of the apathy of his infancy, until he saw Lir and Rathlan when the latter's mother had brought them on a visit. He had actually smiled, for the first time. So they were brought again and again, and the two babies got TanTan to crawl, and to walk, and to talk with their hands. The three had been inseparable since then…

We will leave the emperor to his reminiscences as we shift to the northwest end of the imperial palace, the opposite corner, more or less, from the Garden of Celestial Merit where Bu slumbered so fitfully.

Here, Grand Princess Rathlan paced back and forth in the outer salon of the princes' palace, ignoring the refreshments the steward had ordered servants to bring. She was not budging until the boys returned and told her what had happened.

Noise heralded their arrival, the two bodyguards separating, one to roam the outer building and one to come inside lest there be waiting assassins.

"What happened?" she demanded, the moment her cousins entered the room. She threw her hands out wide for TanTan's sake: question.

"Lan! Why are you here?" Lir demanded with brotherly familiarity. Born on the same day (though one in the morning and one at night), Rathlan and Rathlir had been called "the twins" since that time, as their mothers were close friends, and his mother died soon after his birth.

Lir flicked his elder half-brother with the backs of his fingers, and the two exchanged glances, then TanTan patted his sleeve, and pretended to draw a knife out to throw.

"Assassins?" the grand princess asked in shock. Then she

said, "Where was Vo?" She pointed out the window, and struck her backside, which was the sign among the three of them Eleventh Imperial Prince Rathvo, loathed by all three.

"He was there," Lir said grimly. "I wondered why he offered to accompany us. Said he wanted to see Zhuori dance, and when she wouldn't come out because I was there — which he knew very well was likely to happen —"

"Did you ever sleep with her?" Rathlan asked wrinkling her nose. "She's *old* under all that paint."

"No!" And TanTan opened and shut his fingers three times — *grasping* — as Lir said, "TanTan's right." He clasped his hands toward his brother in their sign for *you're right.* "Anyone could see she didn't want *me,* she wanted me to bleed gold. Fun to flirt with though." He grinned.

"You mean, fun to take her away from Vo."

"Saved her from grief, is the way I see it," Lir said.

"Go on about Vo. He said he wanted her to dance, though he knew she wouldn't come out if you were there?"

"Owner said she was sick, of course. Then Vo said loudly that there was nothing to stay for and headed for the door. I thought we were done with him, and then that girl you brought was there. She stunned everybody with 'The Merry Beggar' again —"

"That's the garbled news my maid heard," the grand princess exclaimed. "There was something about a dance so brilliant that it caused a fight and a fire, and you were in it. I was afraid that Zhuori had got to you at last. I never thought of assassins."

"I don't think anyone did," Lir said.

The grand princess bit her lip, then said, "Not that I want anyone's innocent family exterminated to the fifth generation, but did they have charmed weapons?"

"Not that anyone told us," Lir stated, looking toward Sanhu, who stood impassively.

"Oh, it was too much to hope for that there were, and that Vo hired them. Because we know he would if he could."

"Who could prove it? *They* started the fire, and vanished once Brick and Sanhu got between them and us."

"You ought to have smelled rats in the walls the moment Vo said he was going with you." The grand princess whirled her hands in signs as she spoke, and TanTan smacked his fist to his palm, nodding vigorously.

Lir hissed a long-suffering sigh. "Here's the elders all

making me copy out Kanda on brotherhood, and Mother Empress insisting that we make peace, and I thought, if Vo wants to come along with us, I won't be the one to say no—"

"He's *always* going to be evil," Rathlan said, with the conviction of someone who had nearly been pushed into a fire at the age of two, when Imperial Prince Rathvo was five. All the adults had insisted it was an accident, but the grand princess could still see so very clearly the narrowed eyes of intent in her cousin's face, and the fingers spread on his two hands as he came at her. It was her own instinct to duck away that had saved her, she was sure, followed by a servant plucking her away by her clothes. Though everyone else remembered her stumbling toward the fire, and Rathvo protesting he was trying to save her.

She still didn't understand why someone seemed to be born evil. Was it really the stars, or his birth on a metal day? But her own mother was also born on a metal day, and she was a bunny to everyone. The emperor's favorite sister.

Lir did not trouble himself to question. Vo's unrelenting covert cruelties were a condition of life. "So gossip got all the way to your palace that fast?"

"You know Ginger," the grand princess said complacently. "She got everything out of Mayfly."

"That maid of yours is faster than the imperial ferrets for news," Lir commented.

"You ought to be glad she's loyal to us. So Brick saved you? Did he use a chamber pot? I have to go find him and ask. See if I can get an answer besides *huh?*"

"Don't harass him," Lir said as he started toward his bedroom, rubbing his knees.

"It's not harassing to *tease* him a little. I've a weakness for phoenix eyes—which are wasted on him."

"Just leave Brick alone," Lir retorted. "He's put up with me for a month, and he's quiet. I don't mind him around at all. And if you chase him off, it will be the imperial ferrets in here. Also, I'm pretty sure he really did save my life tonight, didn't he, Sanhu?"

Sanhu spoke up from his position by the wall, from which he could see everything, "It could be said that way, your imperial highness."

Lir grinned at the guard, who had been with them since they were teens permitted to have their own palace. "You just disapprove because he's tribute. Wasn't trained up with the rest of the grays."

"If I may be allowed to speak, he's sloppy, your imperial highness. He got between your exalted self and the point assassin because he tripped over his own feet," Sanhu said, still disgruntled because he didn't manage to kill much less capture any of the three black-clad, masked assassins. At least they had not succeeded in harming either prince. But they had been far too adept at using hapless patrons of the entertainment house as shields, and then obstacles to aid in their escape. "Brick did stay in position. And stamped out one of the fires." Then, as if that grudging admission was too complimentary, Sanhu added, "He's just stupid." This was not said in a cruel way, more matter-of-fact. Sanhu, a painstaking individual, did not think that a head of brick was an attribute for an imperial guard.

Lir grinned at his two co-conspirators. They liked stupid, because that meant there was one less mouth blabbing everything they did and said.

Then his wandering mind caught at a stray fact. "So the gossip isn't me, so much as 'The Merry Beggar' and the dance?"

"That's what Ginger said. Claimed the usual—a goddess come down from Heaven, a fairy dancing."

Lir shut his eyes. "I thought so, too, but actually, I believe it was that girl's playing rather than the dancer's talent. It was that same girl you brought over, who plays like no one I've ever heard before. She even made *you* look good."

"Thanks to the virtue and good fortune emanating from your imperial highness, this poor untalented cousin must deny the undeserved compliment," Rathlan lisped, performing a low bow, every line of her body mocking. "You're the stupid one. Go to sleep. I'm going to tell Ginger to find out where the girl is playing next."

TWENTY-SEVEN

THE TENTH GRAND PRINCESS'S maid and Rathlir's page were accurate in their reports of talk along the main street south of the imperial palace. Many wanted to hear the new, charmed music, and others to witness the new, charmed dancer.

The owner of the Chrysanthemum Garden fervently helped to spread the gossip as it would draw custom, unlike any reports of mysterious assassins springing up in the middle of his common room. While his house was closed anyway, he sent his workers out to propagate the talk about the new fairy dancer. Meanwhile he hired an army of workers to eradicate the damage as quickly as possible. A closed entertainment house was not bringing in money.

His being able to hire those workers was enabled by a modestly clothed, quiet individual carrying a jade tally who offered him a handsome remuneration to keep Imperial Prince Rathlir's name from whatever explanation he provided to the curious, which he knew better than to betray.

And so, while his house was restored and his workers praised the new dancer all up and down the street, he himself ventured over to the imperial palace gate to request an interview with Nightingale. The latter expertly toyed with him just enough to secure a good deal, but when asked who her mysterious accompanist had been, there he was balked: Nightingale readily gave him Bu's name, but it seemed the girl either would not, or was not permitted, to come out.

Nightingale told him, with her eyes cast down modestly, "I first must dance in one more theater piece, the new one we are preparing for the emperor. Then estimable Chief Rao says she will consider my time complete."

The owner departed content, having heard the words Nightingale wanted him to hear: new theater piece, emperor.

Nightingale left the interview content, as she had gotten what she wanted: a future, at least secure for a few years, and in the immediate sense, she would still dance in the new piece. She had to be seen in it, because every scrap of music was so enthralling, so very different from anything they were used to. Those with long sight among them bloomed with anticipation. This was something that was going to be talked about by *everybody*.

As for those within the Garden of Celestial Merit, there was one last very brief reference when the chiefs met very late behind a closed door one night, as Bu slept with phrases of music weaving into her dreams, and YinYin walked through the night's deepest shadows, struggling to grasp the Golden Point of Balance: what could be more powerful than a state of constant equilibrium? Was it even possible?

"My esteemed colleagues," Chief Huazi said, with bows toward Chiefs Yne and Rao, and then lowest and longest to Granny Zim. "I am impressed by everything I hear and see. Truly, these fragments promise a piece fit for his imperial majesty." Here, he clasped his hands and bowed toward the dragon throne. "However. I ask only to learn, but are you bent upon using only ancient scrolls and plays from the archives? Is it that your music can only be adapted to such?"

"The music can be adapted to anything," Granny Zim stated.

"I can understand the inclination to choose among the plays in the oldest archive," Chief Yne stated. He paused to study both doors, which remained firmly closed. He lowered his voice. "We have a saying, *two centuries for safety and three for obscurity*, for no one wishes to be thought, ah, presumptuous."

Chief Huazi suppressed a shudder of memory. In his young days, only someone very sure of their position could write a play illuminating current events, unless these lauded those on the throne. He said, "I do understand the instinct to draw on old stories. They are safely about long-dead figures."

Chief Yne said, "The problem is, pretty much everything in certain of the very ancient scrolls was in effect a lesson for this or that emperor."

Chief Huazi rubbed his chin, where in his grandfather's day, a sparse beard would have been straggling. "There are others so obscure that they are difficult to comprehend now. Such as an entire piece exhorting against the wearing of brocade."

Ayah! Everyone thought of the beautiful brocades now firmly a part of required court robes.

"Then there are the ones that promote ancient customs that are no longer considered wise, such as having to drink the cup dry at every toast, instead of only toasts to the emperor."

"Ah-h-h."

"And," Chief Rao put in, "there are so very, *very* many plays warning of the dangers of ignoring divination."

Chief Huazi snapped open his fan to hide his wince, and Chief Yne looked away. Granny Zim's mind went straight to the infamous Ban Erno the Traitor, whose auguries had brought about the civil war that had happened right here.

She said, "This old outlander will probably deserve nothing but scorn for her temerity in speaking before this august company, but there is one way we temple musicians were very well supplied, and that was with very old *temple* plays. They might not be very good. In fact, most are what could be termed wooden—little more than elders preaching to children whose only response is gratitude for the teaching."

"Please, Chief Zim, if I am hearing a 'however…' I trust you will speak," Chief Yne said, bowing as his wife leaned out to pour more tea for Granny Zim.

She bowed her thanks, then said, "There is a play I've in mind. We used to perform it every Ghost Month when I was young. It was called *The Swan Fan*. The play is not very exciting, but the music is excellent, and embellishments such as we practice now could make it superlative. And no one could claim it's been done too often."

The two men bowed at that; the faraway Fig Islands might be regarded as old-fashioned to the point of barbarism in all other respects, but if Chief Zim said the music was "excellent" then it must be extraordinary indeed.

Chief Rao gasped. "Ayah, I know that one. I did not know there was music associated with it! It is a teaching play among us. We used to have to copy it out when I was very small. It's all about filial obedience, as I recall."

"The setting," Granny Zim said, "is from the days when lovers-fans, or swan-fans first became the fashion among those of high rank. It being very expensive to weave silk fine enough to be pasted to either side of a fan, hiding the sticks altogether. For back then, only the wealthy could afford fans with two sides."

"It is that way now, for the finer silk fans," Chief Huazi murmured. "I remember my grandfather was very proud of an old fan with only one side painted. It was a prize from when he was a student. The calligraphy had been written by a famous scholar."

When no one had anything to add to this fond reminiscence, Granny Zim went on. "For a time, so I read, the royalty and nobles gave lovers' fans to one another as a sign of love. Fidelity. The pictures on them in those days always being pairs of birds or animals who choose one mate for a lifetime."

"Ah, I'm beginning to see," Chief Yne said. "Go on."

"Its message is, as Chief Rao explained, about obedient children, drawing of course on Kanda's lessons about filial behavior, but at the center is the respected grandfather and grandmother, who could be taken as symbols for the emperor and empress," Granny Zim said, thinking rapidly. "The long speeches about filial obedience can easily be illustrated with more dance, and we can weave in a pair of lovers to give it a semblance of a story."

Chief Huazi rubbed his chin. "And the ending?"

"If we want a sad ending, one or the other is betrothed at birth to someone else, so they obey and swallow their grief for a lifetime..."

"...and if we want it to end well, they are both betrothed from birth to someone never met. They chance to meet one another masked, exchange poems and flowers, then discover that they each fell in love with their intended without knowing, thus emphasizing the wisdom of parental choices, and the reward for obedience, propriety, and virtue being lifetime happiness." Chief Yne laughed. "A story only done ten thousand times, with little variation."

"But it's how the story is told that matters," Chief Rao finished triumphantly. "We have three glorious dances already worked on—the poetry reading, the girl's coming of age, and the ancestral worship dance, that I took from other plays. But all three can easily be adapted to this story."

Chief Huazi bowed toward Granny Zim. "I concur. The music you have given us for the ancestral worship dance is so beautiful."

"That is actually Bu's first composition," Granny Zim said. "It's still a ladder of familiar island combinations, but that's how composition starts, and she brings so much emotion to her variations." Granny Zim strongly suspected that Bu was thinking of that mother who had let her go at the tender age of twelve.

"Someone raised those two girls of yours right," Chief Yne exclaimed. "The one is so modest she is barely noticed, and the other so humble and so good-hearted that her nature calls out to the good in others."

Granny Zim was not about to talk about YinYin, still assembling a human façade. After delving in the richness of the archives here, looking for writings about demons, it was becoming apparent to her that in her profound ignorance she had been arrogant in thinking that a handful of years—even tens of years—would transform a demon to human. It seemed it would take more like hundreds of years. YinYin was still more a reflection of human traits than a human person.

But YinYin's true passion was music. And YinYin was capable of great things, that Granny Zim would stake her life on.

She said tartly, "I would not raise a chicken the way Bu was raised. She flinches if a person coughs suddenly, and she is still so starved for praise that she's like a small child when she hears it, her mouth flapping like a fish."

"Better than those who hear too much empty admiration," Rao Ri commented, eyes rolling northward, toward the forbidden areas of the imperial palace. "My theory is that troublesome children begin that way amid too much flattery and praise."

This very oblique reference to Imperial Prince Weasel was quite daring, but it was late at night after a long day.

"One can assume that a similar upbringing was given to all in a similar situation, and yet they differ so vastly when they reach the age of reason," Chief Yne observed mildly, pulling the subject away from imperial princes.

"That's easy enough to explain," Granny Zim said, reaching for the safely of generalities. "This person's sign is earth. That one is under the influence of earth, and so his fortune depends on getting there. Fire can produce earth, as earth can multiply wood—it merely needs wise interpretation of the auguries to counter bad influences."

She halted when she perceived a sudden tension. She looked with surprise into the faces around her, mentally reaching back. The word 'auguries' had done it. Again, what had been distant news for the Fig Islands was within living memory of these folk: specifically, Ban Erno the Traitor, whose false auguries ignited the civil wars that tore apart the empire thirty years ago, a fire still blazing in the northern islands.

She had managed to stumble into a subject far more fraught than a spoilt prince.

After a pause that began to stretch to a silence, Granny Zim said, "I beg forgiveness beforehand, but I have a question…"

The other three hesitated, each hoping the other would answer, because surely the question arose out of the word *auguries*. Chief Huazi bowed; Chief Zim was his elder, and a superlative master who deserved all his respect, so he would never speak a word of remonstrance. Instead, he excused himself as politely as possible, claiming the late hour.

Chief Yne got up to follow, and Granny Zim said, "Please. If the emperor sends another summons, which I expect will happen, I do not want my ignorance bringing trouble to everyone."

Chief Rao touched her husband, saying, "Get your rest, Rilap." She walked him to the door, and when he was gone, she looked in both directions, and said in a low voice, "It's the Minister of Rites Ban Erno you want to hear about?"

"If you please."

Rao Ri poured out more tea, then said, "First, you must understand that even referring to the name is forbidden. The entire family was executed. I won't say it wasn't undeserved, in the sense that all were complicit. Ban Erno turned out to have made his astonishing auguries because he had spies all through the imperial palace. It was his wife, who headed the embroidery department where my sister works, who collected the information. Their son took bribes, and … ayah, I've told it backward."

"I think I might hazard a guess? He was able to make auguries that always came true?"

"More than that. By the end, the Crown Prince scarcely took a step without Ban Erno telling him what to do. He collected secrets, bought and sold other secrets, all of which enabled him to cast predictions that were always precise. And so the Crown Prince tried to overthrow his father because it was written in the stars. Ban Erno was to become the new Right Chancellor, with a dukedom. But it was those secrets, many of them very old, hidden by the most powerful and corrupt that brought about the war, because it involved so many old houses. When they received word ahead that they had been condemned to nine generations, their islands threw down the imperial banners, renewed their ancient kingships, throwing trade and tribute into chaos, and here we are."

"I understand. You do not have to say more."

"Now the augurs are not permitted to come out of the Divination Department at all. The only reason they weren't all put to the sword was because the *old* Minister of Rites had been regarded as the rebirth of Kanda in his wisdom and selflessness. The very opposite of Ban Erno, whose accumulated wealth from all those secrets turned out to be a king's fortune all on its own. It was whispered he had his eye to the dragon throne itself."

"Thank you," Granny Zim said, bowing before rocking herself to her feet. "We have a saying in the islands," she added with a grunt as she hoisted herself up. "The deadliest poison of all is power. And gold is second. Not an observation I'll make outside this chamber."

Rao Ri laughed under her breath, and the two parted for the night, relieved that at last they had a name for the new theater piece, which would conform to safely ancient framework.

Granny Zim said nothing of this conversation to YinYin or Bu, of course; the latter was deep in her studies, enchanted with the new lessons in composition. Everything she had always wanted to say, and could not, found its expression through music.

The following day, Chief Yne announced the name of the theater piece, and said that he could conduct auditions for the roles of The Young Scholar and The Noble Maiden.

Granny Zim was considerably surprised that these auditions were not confined to singing and acting, but after each performance, the chief asked questions. Grun Tham stood at the edge of the stage, hands behind his back as he said, "I have learned through the three pieces we have already that we must not merely know the cues, which we use to *mimic* feeling, we must know the sound, which *inspires* feeling. Our art is emotion embodied in sound: the music, our voices. From the two, art is born."

Everyone clapped, and Granny Zim caught sight of Bu staring up at him enraptured. Oh, oh, oh. Was her crush on gentle Xia Chi already transferring to this highly polished jade ornament of a boy? Who had obviously prepared his "spontaneous" speech well ahead. What will be will be, she reminded herself, knowing that she was now looking at who would be playing the role of The Young Scholar.

The girls were lining up for their audition when once again, Granny Zim was summoned to the imperial presence.

TWENTY-EIGHT

OH, TEG, GRANNY SENT the thought outward as she toiled on painful joints across the vast expanse of the imperial palace. *Are you seeing me now?*

During those raw, painful years after her sons had come home without him, she had spoken to him only in the ancestral shrine. Though he was not buried there. But surely his soul would wander home, would it not, before going on? Or would he stay and wait for her?

Gradually she'd gotten into the habit of speaking to him when she sat alone at the Suanek's Way wicker bridge. Now that she was so far from home, she swung between wondering if he'd followed her, or if he'd gone away long ago. Sometimes she hoped for one, then the other. *Here I am, on my way to talk to the emperor. Remember when we laughed over his defeat? At that time all it meant was no more tribute visits. Ayah! Look at me now! But I will not get angry. There's no use in it, and probably danger. I will think about Bu instead, who has finally discovered spring flowers of the heart, though she hasn't said anything. She might not even be aware of what she's feeling.*

Poor Bu! No doubt unsettled by Xia Chi's kindness and his compliments on her music—all very decorous, always within sight of the elders. But to Bu, it has to be worse than kissing in public. Far safer, so her sixteen-year-old reasoning probably went, to yearn after Grun Tham, who had his pick of boys and girls, and who will never give Bu a second glance. She could enjoy her yearning without the terrible threat of reciprocation. *Remember us at the same age? How the first touch of the hand meant all the world had changed?*

"If only people could skip the ages of sixteen and seventeen altogether," Granny Zim sighed under her breath as she winced her way after the gliding graywing.

While she was on her way, the emperor brooded.

The graywings had divested him of the heavy formal dragon robe he wore only before the court, and escorted him by palanquin across the magnificent garden to Golden Dragon Pavilion, where he could rest his back. There, his personal attendants eased him into a much more comfortable dragon robe for personal interviews such as this next one.

His steward announced her imperial majesty the empress. At his assent, her entourage aided her to a divan, and she dismissed the maid who would have begun fanning her gently. That served as a signal for the crowd of silent attendants to bow themselves out.

The two were alone. She said, "My honored emperor, I think it a mistake to confine those boys yet again. Lir always breaks out in some way the moment he's set free. It's as if he cannot help it any more than can an arrow halt itself when released from the bow."

"I know," the emperor grumbled, trying not to cough as his fingers ran along the edge of the heavy silk tied at his bony right hip, then touched the sash at his waist. Loose again. In spite of all the imperial physicians' efforts—and their assurances that he would live many more years—he was getting scrawnier. "I don't know how else to keep that pair of rascals safe. If it really is Vo behind those assassins, this is a troubling first. What is amiss with that boy?"

"You won't believe me if I tell you what I believe."

"You always come back to his mother. You never liked Consort Rajai, before she even gave me that boy."

"True. That little-girl lisp has irritated me since you married Kouhan Rajai, but that's irritation. Many people irritate me, but I don't think them venal. She is different. I still think the overdosed purgative that killed Li Sian was quite deliberate."

They both thought back to Lir's birth, and his lively mother insisting on rising immediately afterward to attend a party. Of course she caught a cold. Consort Rajai, who had insisted on visiting Consort Sian in her bedchamber, had pressed a family remedy on her, tearfully explaining later that everyone in the family took it with no ill effects, and how could so dear and so vital a person not wake from a simple medicine meant to purge the cold from the body?

The emperor didn't believe Consort Rajai capable of evil. Silly? Yes. She was so small, so unthreatening, always welcoming with delicious desserts if he went to her palace. It was true he found her breathless lisp and her caresses cloying after a short time, but that was not *wicked*. She was doing her best to please him. How could he fault that?

Rathvo, however, he was not at all certain about. Vo was handsome to look at. All his sons were. To an extent, he amended with a vivid image of Lir's foxy chin and those wide, restless eyes. He did look rather like a weasel. A handsome one.

Vo had his mother's sweet smile. But he had a sneaky way about him. Always had. "I overlooked Vo's boyish pranks because I wanted Lir to learn how to deal with him," he said finally. "I need the next emperor to be able to deal with islands full of Rathvo."

"Lir does not want to rule. Vo does," the empress said.

They both knew that Vo protested devotion and modesty. He could quote Kanda's rules about filial obedience without a falter. All the boys could. They were taught to, and the elder three — dull, plodding, and earnest, just like their placid cow of a mother, contentedly sitting at her tambour day and night — meant it. They were filial, and did their duty in an earnest, plodding way. But even those three had noticed the resentment, the *hunger*, in Vo's sideways glances whenever any of his brothers and sisters had received the slightest sign of approval, even right after he got his share.

"He's like his mother in the fact that whatever you've given him, it's never been enough," the empress stated, and the emperor had to concede that this was true. Consort Rajai was the most cloying when pleading for more pearls, more bolts of the best silks, more of this, more of that, for both herself and her "poor son."

He grunted agreement, then said, "Here's what's important. If my ferrets discover that Vo's been treating with some assassin sect out there, he's going straight to a tower up at Snowy Peak Fortress, until I'm dead, and beyond worrying about it."

A graywing tapped at the door, and called just loud enough to be heard, "Chief Zim is at the outer door."

The empress signed to her waiting maid to give her a hand in rising, and she started out, her long silken train hissing over the floor. "I will say only this: find something for Lir to do."

She exited before he could retort, *But what?*

The emperor hauled himself upright, scowling at the shining floor. He had made the error of forcing his older sons to work together, thinking that that would create a bond between them. It had with his own brother, whose absence still knotted his heart.

He had not made that mistake with his second family. Each son had been put to different tasks that did not overlap, and each daughter was, or would be, married off as soon as possible, to weave the empire back together by alliance. The girls, in a sense, were taken care of—except of course for his niece Rathlan, whose mother had promised her she could choose whom she would marry. Which was why she was still loose at twenty-two.

What could he do with these younger sons, each with greater problems than any of the others? There was Vo, who wanted to own the world, but hadn't the temperament to say it straight out—or to rule well should he get it. There was sweet, silent TanTan, who they had discovered was bright, even brilliant, but deaf as a rock. There was poor Jin, who lived in a world of ghosts, and spent his days making paper birds to hang from the ceilings of his palace. And there was Lir, who only wanted to gamble…

Granny Zim entered, and put herself through the joint-cracking obeisance. As she did, she took in the tension in the emperor's thinned mouth, his furrowed forehead, and in the line of his shoulders beneath that exquisite robe.

"What progress can you report, Chief Zim?" the emperor said as he gestured her to take her place on the waiting cushion.

"If it pleases your imperial majesty, this talentless musician and her superlative colleagues at the Garden of Celestial Merit have chosen an appropriate play, to which our poor outland styles are being brought."

That much she had practiced on the way through the palace doors.

"Name?"

"*The Swan Fan*, if it pleases your imperial majesty."

"Is that the same one we had to copy out for our tutor when I was barely getting my adult teeth?"

Granny Zim recognized this question as rhetorical, and bowed from her cushion. "It was deemed proper to select a well-respected piece from the ancients, your imperial majesty."

"'Music is that which moves us from the internal; rites are that which affects us on the external. Music brings about harmony. Rites ensure obedience,'" the emperor quoted. "Kanda was quite firm about both music and ritual. But do I need lessons in the virtue of either?"

Granny Zim bowed once more, back and forth, the wind through the trees. "No one would dare assume such, your imperial majesty. It is just that the dearth of theater pieces in such places as the Fig Islands has caused plays like this one to stay in practice, and each iteration adds to the music."

"It is your music that is extraordinary. What I cannot determine is how it flowered there and not here at the heart of the empire."

Might your wars have something to do with that, she wondered.

"I have even looked back at Kanda's admonitions, the first of which is that music without the rituals would be uncultivated. Kanda insists that we adhere to ritual and music not because it is helpful and convenient for society, but because he believes them essential to the harmony of Heaven with earth. Is it truly the influence of the temple that makes your music so transcendent?"

Granny Zim said, "This humble seeker dares make no claims to transcendency. It is taught within the temple that harmony and order bloom within the heart, as flowers bloom outside. But to reach harmony, music should not contain any falsehood. Shall this old outlander play the introduction? It begins when the Chart of Sun's Return finishes for a year, and trees begin to bud."

Her guess that the emperor might want something both soothing and uplifting to the spirits was correct; he gestured to a graywing, and Granny Zim was brought an instrument. This time a qin.

Ah, and such a very fine instrument. She inadvertently smiled as she gently touched the strings. Fine, and recently tuned by an expert. She rippled the strings, evoking the burbling of spring waters, and sank into memory as she played. It was Teg she saw, when they married as teens, before the ships sailed south. Oh, the poignancy! Played upon her favorite instrument, the music swelled, filling the vast chamber.

Each pluck and chord showered the emperor with sound, bringing forth an upwelling of memory. Of old emotions and thoughts long buried. He was already regretting the past, but the purity of the music washed away any remaining bitterness. He closed his eyes, permitting the harmonies to flow over him, but when it ended, the weight of the invisible mantle that he never truly escaped was there to enshroud him once again.

He murmured ruminatively, "Kanda is excellent on the stewardship of the ruler, inspiring when he speaks of the two types of courage, though he never truly understood the emperor's view." He had not meant to muse out loud, but when he glanced down at Chief Zim's face, he saw no bewilderment there, and he paused. "You know something of ruling? I was told your islands make no claims to kingship, overt or covert."

"That is true, your imperial majesty. If your Heaven-blessed eyes saw the size of our biggest island, which perhaps might fit into this palace with plenty of water around it to spare, your august majesty would laugh at the idea."

"There are smaller islands whose banners make preposterously large claims. I am very aware of the old saying: a king abroad, emperor at home."

Granny Zim bowed, surprised at the drift of this conversation. Ayah! She meant win her freedom—to go somewhere and begin her school—which meant not antagonizing the most powerful person in the nearest hundred islands. "This ignorant outlander makes no claims to knowledge outside her very small sphere, your imperial majesty. It can be said that the Fig Island chief is a woman, who merely wears the title *headwoman*. There is no banner, throne, or court. Even so, there are tasks of stewardship that must be considered for their consequences."

"That is it exactly! Kanda speaks of virtue guiding day to day decisions, but he did not appear to comprehend that the emperor does not merely think from day to day, but from dynasty to dynasty, century to century."

Granny Zim bowed anew. She suspected she had the underlying question: when he'd asked if it was the play their tutors had had them write, in a sense he was asking if *The Swan*

Fan was aimed at that errant prince who had eluded assassins earlier in the week.

No, he was asking about the humble pear tree while thinking about the exalted mulberry. Or, to be more blunt: he was asking, indirectly, about educating princes.

She considered her words, picking and choosing her way as if she walked barefoot upon the shoreline over hidden rock shards and the remains of spiny creatures. "This old strummer recalls, your imperial majesty, that Kanda did make distinctions when he spoke of education. It seemed he divided people into categories. Persons in high status. Persons in authority. Persons of exemplary living. Persons of talent. The highest of all, if this old brain recollects properly, was the sage. These were to be educated by encouragement—to steep oneself in the loftiest poetry, history, ritual, to exercise the body in archery and horse, and—for us the most important— to play and compose lofty music."

"Correct," said the emperor. "Go on. I'm so old, the king of the underworld keeps looking up in my direction, so I can say what I want without fear. And so can you," he added.

He could say that, but could he tolerate hearing her true thoughts? She did not trust his words past the breath he expended in saying them.

He went on, "I'm curious what you were taught, out there in your faraway islands."

"Then, your imperial majesty, there were the categories that required admonishing teaching, beginning with petty persons. This list began with the *you ought nots*. Some of those were obvious, such as proscribing drunkenness during the daytime, which should be given over to study, but included oddments to ignorant islanders such as refraining from wearing brown or dark red embroidery at the borders of robes, or red or purple in everyday clothing."

The emperor raised a hand. "It seems we learned much the same. The texts recopied and carried to far islands such as yours seem not have been altered as much as the language came to be." He decided not to venture a joke about the hilariously flat twanginess of her accent. That accent emphasized how very far from insinuating entanglements in the current conflicts this outlander was. It freed the conversational path in unexpected ways. "Do you have children, Chief Zim?"

"This humble mother was granted by the heavens three sons and a daughter, your imperial majesty."

"And these sons are no doubt talented and exemplary?"

Granny Zim hesitated. Was he hinting at regrets? Who knew what an emperor thought might be regrettable — or what she could say about it. Ayah, she would tell the truth regardless. "Two of these sons are considered dutiful, filial, and are respected in their leadership. The third … he obeys his brothers, but if there is a task required by duty and a tempting game on either side of a path, he invariably will turn toward the game."

"And what did your husband do about that, Chief Zim?"

"His solution, your imperial majesty, was to give him more nets to repair, and the hull to scrape free of barnacles."

The emperor laughed quite heartily at that, and Granny Zim knew the interview was over.

The emperor gave the sign to the graywings, who removed the qin and the old musician, leaving him free to return to his palace. But halfway along, he changed his mind, and glanced at the graywing pacing alongside his palanquin. "To the empress's pavilion."

The bearers sidestepped with practiced smoothness, and headed off in another direction, winding through the imperial garden until they reached the empress's splendid palace alongside the emperor's.

He found his empress in her bedchamber, her headdress gone, her mostly gray hair combed out and lying in a long fall nearly to her knees as she knelt to welcome him.

He gestured her to rise, and sit next to him, the floor-length sleeves of her favorite celestial blue spilling over his gold-embroidered robe. "I know what to do," he said. "After this new theater piece is presented, I will send them all off on a pilgrimage to Kanda's island, to lay offerings at his ancestral altar. Perhaps that will cultivate a semblance of sense in Lir and Vo."

TWENTY-NINE

"IT IS THE DELIGHT of this humble little sister's life to discover that Esteemed Elder Sister Aisin favors the silverleaf tea," Seventh Consort Rajai cooed as she sat on a little stool at the older woman's feet.

Consort Diar Aisin never missed a stitch as she smiled on Second Consort Kouhan Rajai, who then went on to lavish praise on the embroidery. It was an utterly predictable piece depicting silver-winged orioles amid their hanging nests in redbark trees, so often given to young girls as suitable for training nimble fingers and noble minds. In a word: boring.

But Consort Rajai continued to practice her flattery on the elder consort, famed for her placid temperament—and for her dullness. She had once been handsome—nicknamed the Dancing Fairy among the emperor's consorts—but four children in nearly thirty years had added to her flesh. No one would take her for a dancing fairy now.

However, everyone visited her, and if you could get her to talk she always knew the latest imperial gossip. That sometimes included tidbits it would have been better to keep to herself. Such as now.

When Consort Rajai could not dredge up anything more to flatter in that dreary embroidery, she veered toward a subject sure to please Consort Aisin: her three sons. Consort Aisin was as credulous as she was insipid. She seemed to truly believe those dullard sons of her were qilins of brilliance.

Rajai won a slightly wider smile for all her hard work, and then Consort Aisin said, "Perhaps your Rathvo will return to a similar position. Our dear emperor is always thinking of our sons."

"Did you say 'return', beloved elder sister? This silly featherhead of a little sister was not aware that her son was to go anywhere?"

Rajai was aware of a thrill of fear. She ought never have listened to that cursed cousin of hers, who had read far too many of those worthless tales of the criminal Jong Siang, leader of the hundred and ten 'gallant outlaws' of the outer islands. Cousin Ye and his Brotherhood of the Invisibles! Invisible indeed—half the city had been talking about their blundering attempt at the Chrysanthemum Garden. She knew the rumors had to have reached the emperor.

Consort Aisin said, "I thought you knew? Ayah, I forgot, it was to be a surprise for the younger boys. Once the new play comes before us, our dear emperor is sending them to make a pilgrimage to Kanda's shrine in the company of tutors. Surely it means they will be awarded a position within government on their return." She set a stitch, then gave Consort Rajai a fond smile. "Your Rathvo might even come to work under one of my two. Rathkanda was telling me they need two more assistants over at Imperial Works. And Rathliad would welcome him at the Secretariat. He'd go in at the ninth level, but steady work means steady promotion. Look at those two, second and third ranks, and Ratha a governor with his own garrison!"

Consort Rajai forced a smile as she squeezed out suitable words of gratitude and thanks, but inwardly she fumed impatiently until at last the bell rang the first hour of Horse.

That was her signal to rise and make her departure, promising more gifts for her admired elder sister. She was respectfully bowed out of Consort Aisin's pavilion to where her cart waited. Here she looked around and commented brightly that it was such a perfect day, she might enjoy the air and walk through the imperial garden before returning to her lonely pavilion. The cart was dismissed and she trod down the path, and through one of the round arches that divided the harem's portion of the palace from the imperial garden, leaving her two maids to wait there for her return.

She had not walked long before she spotted her son loitering over one of the arched bridges. Though no one was in sight, the grays knew everyone who entered the imperial garden. Mother and son took their time meeting up, as if this were a chance encounter rather than an appointment. Consort Rajai suppressed her annoyance that Rathvo's rank still did not permit him to visit her but the requisite once a month, on his and her birthdays, and on festival days.

There was nothing wrong with mother and son walking in the imperial garden, at least. They had established their enthusiasm for healthful walks as soon as Rathvo was granted his own palace on Princes' Row; Consort Rajai had trained him from an early age never to reveal anything before servants, save only his mother's Nanny, whom she'd brought with her from Kouhan Palace.

Consort Rajai said, "Did you know that Imperial Father is sending you to Kanda's Island on pilgrimage?"

Vo's eyes widened in surprise. "I did not."

"That goose Diar Aisin revealed it. The empress must have told her, and she forgot it was a secret."

Vo's mouth thinned. "Imperial Father is going to pack me off without my knowing?"

"If she had it right, it's not you alone. You're to go with Rathlir and Rathtan. I don't know about Rathjin."

Vo said with conviction, "He's insane. They'll never let him out of his pavilion."

"You're to go with tutors. I'm thinking this will be your chance to get rid of them without watching eyes."

Vo's lip curled. "Mother, Imperial Father will undoubtedly send ferrets as well as an army of grays, and probably half the navy as well, seeing as we'll have to cut through the Inner Islands on our way west. I won't be able to scratch my nose without being seen. Not that I would try anything anyway, if I were with them."

"Why not? It's a better opportunity than doing anything here! I'm still furious with my foolish Cousin Ye and his 'invisible' Invisibles. I want to cut his throat when I think of how they botched *everything*. You're still under suspicion—and yet you gave him that expensive charmed spear."

"Why do you think I'm so careful? I'll deal with them once I'm on the dragon throne. Best of all, it will be legal, too." His smile showed his straight white teeth. "Thanks to Imperial Grandfather, Uncle Ye and his Invisibles are now breaking the law, possessing charmed weapons. But first I must become Crown Prince, and that won't happen if there is any suspicion attached to my name from now on."

"Then this pilgrimage to Kanda's Island becomes a missed opportunity."

"Not … if, say, that ship sinks in an unfortunate accident."

Her eyes widened. "Is that not a danger for you, too?"

"I won't be on it," he retorted. "At least, that's my idea at this moment. I'll be too sick to go—I'll break a bone if I have to, so that I must remain behind. Then suspicion cannot possibly point to me. But I'll need Nanny to probe that pirate nephew of hers—"

"Nanny is afraid of him," Consort Rajai observed, not seeing the rare blooms that scented the folds of her robe as she passed by. "However she's more loyal to me than she is to that family of hers. I'll get her to send a message to her nephew."

"Do. Thanks to Imperial Aunt Aisin's wagging tongue, we have time to plan, at least. They won't begin the new play until we've seen the last chapters of *The Golden Lotus Zither*, and I've heard there are ten more."

Consort Rajai slipped her arm into Vo's and patted his hand fondly. "Dearest Vo! You inherited your father's capacity for knowledge, but you got the Kouhan cleverness."

The two parted at the gate to the harem, Consort Rajai promising to send Nanny to visit her relations, and dispatched a page to inquire, after suitable flattery, about the new play.

Interest in the new play spread a little farther each day. Both the emperor and the empress speculated about it, wondering how it would differ from *The Golden Lotus Zither*, which was still popular. *The Swan Fan*, though a very old ritual play familiar to all, was going to bring something new and special to delight the senses—everyone was sure of it, after hearing the rumors about the music at Chrysanthemum Garden that was so heavenly a fire broke out spontaneously.

Bu was the happiest she had ever been. She dreamed new variations and combinations through the night, and woke each morning eager to get right to work. Each day was filled with making music, or talking about it. She did not know that Granny Zim had decided that Bu was going to do most of the composition on this new piece.

Granny Zim was right in believing that if Bu knew she was the chief composer of this iteration of a familiar piece, she would panic. Granny Zim presented each aspect of the evolving piece as assignments for Bu to practice on her own. Bu tackled these joyfully with her voracious desire to learn, and brought them back to Granny Zim once she'd polished them. Granny Zim then took Bu's pieces to the others.

She also began having Bu listen to rehearsals, casually asking her opinion. Bu quietly expressed her thoughts, which Granny Zim then carried to the chiefs and masters after Bu was not there to hear her words offered as directives. Granny Zim would tell Bu eventually—once they began final rehearsals.

It was going to be a success. The brightness of voices, the spontaneous, heartfelt exclamations of approval from the imperial musicians, made that much clear. YinYin played, and practiced in her usual silence, but one night, after an evening of putting actors, dancers, and music together for the first installment of *The Swan Fan*, YinYin said to Granny Zim, "Harmony and order are accumulated inside as flowers bloom outside. Such music—this music—cannot contain any falsehood."

"That," said Granny Zim, "is the true definition of vulgar music: containing falsehood, though it can be for perfectly harmless reasons. Such as 'mere entertainment' as in singing of love when there is no love in mind or heart. It has nothing to do with the birth rank of musicians or listeners."

YinYin drifted away, which Granny Zim knew by now meant the demon would meditate, perhaps translating human words, and concepts, to however such things were understood in the unseen world.

Granny Zim was as content as she could be, given that she had yet to find a way to get Bu away from the influences of the imperial court, before she was tainted by her proximity to those drawn to the center of power.

She knew that even the most timid bird eventually flies the nest.

She did not know that Bu's heart was already in the air.

It would be wrong to assume that Bu had resented Granny Zim for her exclamation against the vagaries of young people the night of the assassins and the fire. Granny Zim had promptly professed herself wrong. Bu heard her regret and sincerity. And she respected Granny Zim far too much to go away angry. But she had been hurt, which made her hesitant to talk about personal matters. Such as the girls in the dormitory introducing Bu to the delights of storybooks at night before they slept. The girls took turns telling the stories that they had read many times, most of which had to do with either adventure or romance. Often both.

Bu adored these stories, and she was learning a lot about the mysterious, enchanting world of love and romance. When one or another girl brought out a precious book to pass around, if Bu had finished her tasks, Bu put her crystal eyepiece in her eye and read, enthralled.

She also thoroughly enjoyed the group crush on handsome Grun Tham. Bu admired all his fine features, his voice, his excellent performance, right along with the others. Granny Zim was correct in her assumption that Bu had no desire to gain his return notice. But what Granny Zim failed to notice was the gentle, gradual friendship developing between Bu and First Apprentice Xia Chi. It was with him, after zither class, that Bu exchanged opinions about music. Those comments gradually led to actual conversations as they lingered outside the classroom door. Bu didn't think to mention these conversations because she talked about music all through the day, when she wasn't playing it.

The next time Granny Zim was summoned to the imperial presence, the chiefs dismissed the musicians early, for little could be achieved without her observant eye and Heaven-blessed ear. Bu agreed to go with the others into the city because she had errands in mind that had *nothing* to do with entertainment houses: she wanted a storybook that she could share with the others who had so generously shared with her, and she also wanted to look at fabric. She wanted a pretty robe of her very own.

When the young people filed singly past the imperial guards at the gate, Xia Chi happened to be directly ahead of Bu—and he happened to glance back, and seeing her replacing her wooden tally carefully in her sleeve as if it were the finest jade. He said, "Are you going someplace in particular, Student Lum Bu? I know the streets pretty well."

"I want to go to a bookstore, First Apprentice Xia." Bu would not presume to use his full name. She added quickly, "If it the least out of the way, please don't trouble yourself."

"It's no trouble, because that's where I'm going, too," he said. "I can show you the best of them all. Old Vinyi brings in not only old scrolls, but plays, with music notations, from far to the west."

"The west," Bu exclaimed. "What kind of music have they there?"

"I've only heard an example or two from travelers off ships in the harbor. I've no idea how good they are, or if they are representative. It was lively but noisy. For example, they put seeds inside of gourds to shake and pound. And they have loud winds made of metal."

"I think I might like to hear it," she said doubtfully. "Just to compare."

"Perhaps they have as many varieties as we have," he commented, and smiled. "I might once have claimed our music superior, but I know that would make you laugh. Your Fig Islands versions of the sacred rituals makes our music at Merit sound like noise."

Bu blushed and disclaimed a little, but they both knew it was true, which made her uncomfortable. He saw that in her ducked head, and mercifully changed the subject. "I wonder if some of our musicians have moved away from ritual because of its familiarity."

"Do you think familiarity becomes noise to listeners?" Bu asked, grateful for the shift in their conversation that she didn't want to end just yet.

"I don't, but I've heard it said. So many are always wanting something new."

Bu nodded. "I've heard some say that the old music is boring. Tedious. That included some back in Fig Islands, though I don't find that true at all!"

"Before he retired, Old Master Guoteg once insisted that we young students don't truly understand Kanda when he teaches that ritual's sacred ceremony is not just for cultivating the ear, but it is a reminder in that it goes back to the origin of human nature."

Bu said slowly, "In the temple, we were told that fundamental for Kanda is not the individual's inner being, but rather a standard that both transcends the individual and helps to shape us."

"The rites and rituals," Xia Chi said.

"Yes," Bu agreed—in her enthusiasm, some of her shyness slipping away. Her fluting voice, usually barely above a whisper, rang with conviction as she exclaimed, "And that makes music and ritual *essential,* not just important."

"You will find no disagreement from me." Xia Chi raised a hand, fingers pointed skyward. "Music is the harmonization of Heaven and earth; the rites order Heaven and earth."

"Yes!"

"What I've had trouble understanding is Kanda's insistence that harmony is by necessity the unification of plurality. It seems so obvious that it almost seems pointless. Of course you need two, or more, to make harmony."

Bu's mind returned to the shipboard, when she and YinYin were alone with Granny Zim. How important it had been for YinYin to discuss that very thing.

Bu said, her voice quiet again, "I think—this silly student believes—that is, I could be wrong, but..."

"Please continue, Student Lum Bu. This foolish student labors to understand."

She bit off a protest that he was not foolish, not at all. That would be so...so *personal*. His easy tone, his warm smile, removed enough of her doubt for her to go on. "Granny Zim taught us that when we say that music is the harmonization of Heaven and earth, and the rites order Heaven and earth, the reference is not merely to one or more instruments creating a harmony. Though that is a part of it. It means, where there is harmony, and order, all living things are in accord. Ritual gives us the path, and music the promise of what the path will bring us to."

"Thank you for your enlightenment," he said with a low bow and a smile.

She was too afraid of appearing presumptuous to see his gentle humor. "Oh, no no no! It was not I. It was Granny Zim, in our lessons, during the ship journey..." Bu was afraid she'd said too much.

Xia Chi said with a wince of sympathy, "Please forgive this awkward student if the question is unwelcome, but to have to leave your home like that. Is it very difficult?"

Bu considered all the things she could say, and wouldn't. Second Mother, who had cried to see Bu go away, would remain a tender memory enclosed in Bu's heart. Her days at the temple seemed impossibly far away now, and she would never refer to those dear—and occasionally painful—days.

Instead she said, very quietly, "We learned to carry our homes with us. N-not like a turtle, but...the memories. Our customs. Our language, and our foods."

Xia Chi was struck silent, for this answer seemed unutterably sad, and he knew he could not fix it for her, or for anyone ripped from their homes in tribute. Her answer was sad, but also wise.

He resolved to write a poem and set it to music. If only for himself; he was not certain he had the temerity to offer it to her, who he admired so much.

THIRTY

THE SWAN FAN'S STORY is old, so old that everyone knows it well, the storyteller pointed out.

Here, the scholars among the audience rolled their eyes. The young master looked impatient. The elderly auntie nodded in agreement as others glanced at the gloomy windows, and then back.

The storyteller said, "Being a very thinly disguised temple ritual aimed at teaching the young, it was not expected by anyone to extend past a single night's performance, unlike customary plays, which can have upwards of fifty chapters—many of these with much-repeated themes from the same, and other, pieces…"

As Granny Zim took her place next to Bu and YinYin, she had to admit that, much as she longed to remove these two from this prison of a palace, it was secretly gratifying to see all those people out there with their golden headdresses, their silken robes flowing like jeweled water, embroidered with peonies and dragonflies, thistles and tiny birds. The clothing denoted those most high, but the faces, even those furrowed with age, shone with the expectation of children awaiting a treat.

She would do her best to give it to them.

She took in the musicians at either side, fingers poised, breathing steady. She glimpsed the bright colors of costume at the wings. Behind them, the painted backdrop indicated a dilapidated inn: the Modest Maiden's father, on his way to a new governorship, was traveling with his family, none of whom wanted to leave their old home.

It wasn't until the final rehearsal when all was put together that it occurred to Granny Zim that there was yet another layer to this ritual in the form of a play, a lesson that dealt with those forced from their own home and hearth. Kanda had certainly known the cost, wandering from island to island as he had his entire adult life. Ah, so be it. If the emperor had objected, he'd had plenty of time to speak.

She struck the first chord, and sent it rippling into the air of the hushed room.

Grun Tham, tall, handsome, every muscle lessoned, appeared out in his tattered robes and in between one step and another becomes a starving student. He shivers, clutching his precious scrolls to him, for he is on his way to the imperial city to sit for the Imperial Examination.

The new governor's family huddles around the fire, forced to this humble inn by a storm. The opening music evokes the storm, contrasted with the inner theme of safety within the family circle, then fades, and the heroine's voice rises in song.

> *Swift the cruel eagle, dark the woods*
> *Rough winds on old lattice windows*
> *When shall we find our new home?*

Then she spots the Student, and being a modest girl, quickly closes the lattice, though the inn is no longer quite so forbidding.

> *But then I see him, bent over his scroll,*
> *Bare toes peek from worn shoes, elbows at sleeves,*
> *Yet his eyes shine with Kanda's treasures*
> *And now the curtains are kingfisher blue,*
> *The woods filled with green frogs singing.*

It was the emperor's whim to surround himself not with his consorts, or his elder sons, but the youngest ones, on cushions at his feet. The consorts whose children that did not include smiled anyway, long-trained court habit, as did the few unmarried princesses left in the imperial palace.

Grand Princess Rathlan sat with her mother at the right of Rathjin's mother, the single favored girl. Hardly a girl anymore; Kouhan Rajai gave her a dismissive glance and then looked quickly away, careful to preserve the drooping demeanor of a dutiful, though worried, consort.

Those two elder sons (the eldest being at his garrison on duty), seated a step below the emperor, smiled as well, as good-natured as they were dull and dutiful. They had gotten into the habit of regarding the younger sons as puppies, a habit that persisted even though the puppies were now grown men.

The emperor kept a light hand on Jin's shoulder. It was very rare that Rathjin left the safe realm of his pavilion. He sat between the emperor on one side and his mother on the other, who watched ceaselessly for any image, movement, or color that might startle or disturb him. She could never predict what might cause him to cover his face with his hands, for she did not believe in the drifting shades that he saw everywhere save his own palace, where the charms surrounded him with peace: she sometimes thought sadly of the mad grandmother the family had never spoken of outside the home, living happily barefoot in a nine-level pagoda in the middle of the Sea of Heaven's Peace. Back when it was safe enough to make the Journey to the Clouds to see the orchids, she had strained to glimpse her.

The emperor glanced down at TanTan sitting side by side with Lir, as they had since they were little boys, small square backs below round heads of fine black hair. Now those squares had lengthened and broadened across the shoulders.

TanTan's fingers rested on the worked wood of the dais, where he could sense the pulses of the percussives, enhancing the rich color and stylized movement of the dance. TanTan loved plays because the graceful movement, the symbols and colors each told a story, even if it was not quite the story the music gave to the others. His mother, seated beside the empress, did not touch anything. She enjoyed the splendidly elegant, constant movement.

Lir had sighed before putting on formal robes, which constrained him into formal behavior. He loved plays that promised action, which *The Swan Fan* most assuredly did not. He'd had to copy it, and similar instructive plays, countless times as a restless youth. But this was a different *Swan Fan*. He ought to have guessed that, from hearing that tribute musician's student play "The Merry Beggar" so well that night weeks back.

On stage, it's time for the student to discover the Modest

Maiden, who with her sisters is dancing to ward off the bitter cold.

> *He sings, enchanted.*
> *Autumn wind strip the ash trees*
> *And bring the whirring wings of grasshoppers*
> *Above, white horses prance cloud to cloud*
> *And arrows of geese clear the mists*
> *Through the whirl of wind-whipped cassia leaves*
> *The ripple of your dancing cloak*
> *Is like the forest owl garbed as a tree sprite*
> *I watch, though my flowered mat grows chill*

After Teg's death, Granny Zim had ceased to consider whether or not the music she made might be art. For her, Essence, so vital to life, flowed only when she played. That lesson had been breathed in by Bu, whose brilliantly played zither complemented Granny Zim's disciplined qin, weaving the evanescent emotions of youth around the sagacious Kanda's exhortations about the importance of family to harmony, order, and civilization.

> *I watch the night birds flit to the river*
> *To drink and frolic with the water-borne moons…*

The performers concentrated on their cues, their moves, their music—but some, during pauses, dared to dart sideways glances at the imperial family to see how they were taking this play. Those whose interests revolved around the doings of imperial princes and princesses counted those figures on the cushions at the seat of the emperor. Wasn't one missing?

Oh, surely that was the one everyone whispered was ghost-mad. Except wasn't that Rathjin, the one with the unfamiliar face, entranced with the musicians off to the left, away from where the Student and the Maiden are discoursing around the hearth, as the Father and Mother watch benignly?

> *Beneath the curving eaves, where swallows nest*
> *She sings like the laughing-thrush and dances like the*
> *osprey in flight*

On stage, the Father discovers that the Student, though threadbare, comes from a distinguished lineage, and promises that if the Student does well on the Imperial Examination and thereby obtains a good appointment, the Maiden will become his wife. But first he must leave, and face the dangers of the long journey.

The melody of the ritual was picked out on the bells, at first barely discerned beneath the Maiden's dancing winds, the Student's longing eruh, and the Father and Mother's benevolent strings.

The Maiden accompanies the Student to the gate, where she is permitted to bid him farewell. Her song drenches the listeners with warm rain and the scent of flowers, the melody a mother's caress, a lover's lingering glance. His farewell song strives and stamps and drums to the rhythm of blood. It's he who must toil against fate, and nature, and the vagaries of other men, if he is to return worthy to marry her.

Everyone there knew the rise and fall of that melody from old ritual, but everything around it was new. New and yet familiar: the known melody partook of discovery, and of familiarity, and weaving the two together it was neither. The eyes of the elders stung with remembered emotion as the Student sends lingering looks back from the gate. And the young, vital with first feelings of romance, were swayed into easy tears as the Maiden's anguish drags her back to obedience, her steps too slow for the drum and the flute, but her harmony, in blending the two, soars above that of her sisters as she prays for the Student's safety.

The music swept into a refrain as on the stage, clouds scudded across the sky, and dancers twirled back and forth with symbols of Ghost Moon parting and joining again, indicating the passage of a year.

The Student returns in triumph, wearing his new robe of a fifth-level official, and the wedding dance reaches the rafters. Everyone is on stage, dressed in red and gold as the couple are wed.

The melody is there, rung in the bells, as the music swells, sweeping emotions into the empyrean.

And YinYin, who has been watching the aimless drift of Essence from the skies, from the stars, from the seas, from the distant chanting of several different temples, and from the sacred redbark trees surrounding the ancestral hall, sees how Essence emanates from the intensity of emotions: the exhilaration of the players and dancers on the stage, the musicians learning to open their hearts to their music, led by Lum Bu, who is apparently unaware of the gates to her soul opening to an infinity of Essence as her skilled fingers weave it together into a tapestry that casts benediction over them all.

> *We lie by the open window where Phoenix Moon gleams*
> *At midnight there are no voices*
> *But within the gauze curtains a pair of smiles*
> *Even when the ice on the pond is thick*
> *Our hearts will still be like the pine and the cypress*
> *Evergreen, our branches twined evermore.*

YinYin drank in a part of that tapestry—a very small part! For there were ever-vigilant watchers in all corners of this palace—and strengthened the whole.

Yes. *This* was the power of music: it wove Essence, extending its influence to all who hear. YinYin gave them Bu's longing for the sweetness of passion, and Granny Zim's exhortation to peace, and felt that emotion intensify as it crashed over them.

The last reverberation of the bells—echoing the temple—died away, and a hush descended. Then the applause, fervent from most, self-serving from one or two whose hearts were too hard to permit the music entry. Exhilaration—enchantment—thrill—tears—yearning. Rathjin blinked at YinYin, fascinated by the coruscation of color around this one person; his father and mother only saw that he was happy, and rejoiced.

The emperor sighed, trying to hold this echo of the young man's strength of feeling. But it was already fading. He wished for one very intense moment he could lock them all up, and keep this music solely for himself. He could compromise by cherishing Chief Zim, and by making it difficult for his theater to take their entertainment even before the nobles, at least for a time, by demanding another such play as soon as possible. And he needed one. He needed that sense of strength as well as the scouring of the higher emotions, leaving him a semblance of peace.

A semblance.

He closed his eyes against the empty cushion where Rathvo ought to have sat. Then he loosed a heavy sigh, knowing that by the time his palanquin reached his pavilion that he would not sleep until the interview was over.

And so, late as it was, he summoned his chief graywing, and spoke out the expected order.

Within a very short time, Consort Rajai prostrated herself before him.

He said, "I take it you knew about the secret orders—orders known to no one else—about my wish that the youngest imperial princes make a pilgrimage to Kanda's shrine?"

She hesitated, about to deny it, for she had prepared a very dramatic scene centered around her surprise at the orders, followed by a mother's passionate impulse to disobedience, driven by the need to nurse her extremely ill son.

Thinking quickly, she spoke, her well-trained voice throbbing. "Honored and beloved imperial majesty, please forgive this foolish, fearful mother, whose only child is so very ill. I was not going to raise my voice against your imperial majesty's wishes—who would know better your cares for your beloved sons?—but last night three water dragons came in my dreams, sorrowing that should my son be taken from me while he is feverish, the result should be an ocean of my tears. The only thing this good, obedient child desires is to please you, but my dear imperial husband, I beg you to blame me for wishing to keep him home."

"Three water dragons, eh?" The emperor said sadly, wondering that she had not chosen to claim nine. It was as he had predicted—but there was no triumph in him. He had lost so much already, and Vo, though as twisted as a snake hiding in the grass, was still his son. "Granted, granted," he said on a sigh, and flicked a glance at a graywing, who noiselessly went out.

Consort Rajai might have paused had she seen that look, but she remained in that posture of abject submission, forehead to the floor. She dared not show her face lest some sign of her triumph reveal itself; though she was almost as clever as she believed herself to be, and quick to observe and to react, the crystal eyepiece her lifelong anger and resentment had shaped caused her only to perceive that the emperor was sad. Of course he was sad that Vo was sick, and would miss that benighted pilgrimage.

She had won. Vo would not have to get on that ship. "Your graciousness shines down upon us all," she said, and smiled all the way back to her palace—until she saw the two imperial guards waiting there, with Nanny bound in chains, a yoke about her neck.

"Before you're locked in the Cold Palace," the captain of the grays said to the former Consort Rajai, omitting all honorifics, "you may say your farewell, for you will never again see either this traitor, or your son, in this life."

THIRTY-ONE

"BUT EVERYONE SAYS THAT Vo went on a ship all by himself, early this morning, and that it's going somewhere else, not on the pilgrimage," Grand Princess Rathlan protested the next day, with the fearlessness of someone who has always been indulged by the emperor.

She had rushed all the way to the emperor's palace, where he was in the process of being readied for court by the graywings. Directly south, on the other side of the imperial gardens, the courtiers, hatted and robed, carrying their jade tablets of rank, bowed and strolled or deferred in a slow and deliberate dance as they assembled at the Hall of Glorious Harmony.

The empress, who had shared breakfast with him, listened in silence, reflecting that it was a miracle that so spoilt and willful a princess as LanLan had a good heart. She could have been so very much worse.

"Everyone says?" the emperor repeated, frowning.

The grand princess had heard it from her maid Ginger, whose cousin worked in the kitchens at Rathvo's pavilion. Rathlan knew that while she could safely blame rumors on others in the family and the emperor would forgive her, it would be a very different thing for a servant.

"He was yelling loud enough to be heard from Mt. Lir," Rathlan said blithely. "I was going to have breakfast with the boys, and wondered what all the shouting was; there was something about Ice Fortress?" Seeing that the emperor really was displeased, she bowed her head, and dropped her tone to apology. "I do not mean to pry, Imperial Uncle. I only wondered, but when I arrived at Lir's and TanTan's, and found them being packed up, and they told me that they too are to embark, though on a different ship, I thought, if there was supposed to be a place for Vo, but that changed, cannot I have that place?"

She then threw herself to the floor at his feet. "The palace will be so *boring* if they go and leave me behind! I'll die of the tedium!"

The emperor did not at all like hearing that his palace, which boasted the very best of everything, was boring to his sister's girl. "Does your mother know you are here?"

"N-no..." She peeked up. Had she gone too far?

At this, the empress intervened. "It seems to me, dear niece, that without the company of the imperial princes occupying your days, you might use the opportunity to better yourself with study, and to think about marriage."

Rathlan looked up from the floor, her gaze soulful. "I could study ever so much if I went with TanTan and Lir. Would it not be auspicious for me, for us all, to make the pilgrimage together?"

The emperor gave a snort, which caused a fit of coughing. Graywings sprang to his side, and the empress leaned over worriedly to rub his back, but he waved them all off. "LanLan, I pity this husband you're to find, for unless he turns out to be one of my tougher generals, I know who will be ruling your palace."

Rathlan lifted her head a little farther, eyes wide with hope. "I may go, then?"

The empress quashed her with a frown. "The only young woman among so many men? And do not waste your breath mentioning your maid. You seem to forget you are no longer fifteen. Twenty-two is a very late age to be marrying. You need no further objections against you..." She remembered then that Rathlan could pick her own husband, and sighed.

The emperor glanced her way. "Once LanLan chooses someone, *I* can negotiate the marriage contract. No one will give *me* trouble." He turned his frown to the grand princess. "Her imperial majesty is correct, though. Sending a young woman your age alone is harmful to your reputation."

Rathlan could see from both imperial faces that they were considering the princesses. Fatal! Rathsuanek would treat her like a maid. Rathtak was as dull as her brothers. Rathnon was sweet, but she would never survive—she couldn't bear riding in a boat on a flat pond, and Rathyi, the youngest, was a spoilt brat, and everyone would expect *her* to be entertaining Rathyi, who would be throwing tantrums right and left if she wasn't constantly the center of attention.

"I know," she said quickly. "We could use entertainment. There are lots of women at Merit Garden. Many of respectable birth."

"Ship space is limited. We were already going to send a musician or two—"

"If my very dearest and most beloved of imperial uncles would consider a suggestion from this talentless and stupid niece, let one of those musicians be that girl, I forget her name, who plays like a fairy! You remember, she played for me when I danced to 'The Merry Beggar' for Sixth Imperial Princess's birthday. Send them both. Aren't there two of them from the Island of Music?"

The empress said, "One of them is the aide of Chief Zim, who is an elder and frail. It seems their temple does not have servants. We might try to put a new servant in with Chief Zim?"

"Don't," the emperor said. "Chief Huazi said she will have no servants about her, that she keeps temple ways. I don't want her the least uncomfortable. She's got to be older than I am. But there is no one who plays better…"

He considered the girl, who, Chief Huazi had reported, had been raised by nuns. A nun would be delighted to make a pilgrimage to Kanda's shrine, surely. "Yes, we will do that. The wagging tongues will be stilled if so respectable a girl goes along with you, as well as your servants. We were already going to send the best one of Huazi's students. I want the senior musicians here, working on their next piece."

The emperor had spoken; it remained only to send graywings to see to all of the changes.

Rathlan bowed herself out, told her waiting maid to alert her household, and walked to her mother's grand pavilion that had belonged to the father Rathlan did not remember. All she knew was, her father and the emperor had been each other's closest ally—very much like her, TanTan, and Lir.

Her mother was upset, as Rathlan had known she would

be. But Rathlan stressed the fact that they would be exactly as safe surrounded by escorts and the like as they were at home.

"But there is all that fighting," the Dowager Grand Princess protested.

"And surely Imperial Uncle knows where all that is, and we will sail well away from it," Rathlan said. "Please, Mother. Imperial Uncle gave his permission—and you know, we will be studying the entire time, and of course there will be prayers at the shrine. The empress wants me to consider a husband, which is my filial duty," Rathlan said slyly. "I could pray for one at Kanda's shrine." Rathlan could see that the mention of a husband, which she'd strenuously resisted, was the convincing detail.

Her mother patted her hand. "I would very much like to see you come back inspired to do what every other princess must do."

Rathlan took her leave, knowing that her mother would be shortly on her way to the augurs to cast the sticks about this prospective journey, and then to determine the most auspicious time for departure. As Rathlan headed for the boys' palace, she considered marriage. Still no interest. She spend most of her time with two young men; what use would a husband be? Husbands were apt to give orders, which she would hate. When she was annoyed with Lir or TanTan, she could go to her own pavilion. She wouldn't be able to get away from a husband.

When she passed by Rathjin's pavilion, she recognized Brick on guard. Oh, had the boys gone to visit Jin, to say farewell?

She turned her steps, letting her glance linger over Brick. It was such a shame that those long phoenix eyes were so fine, but his pretty mouth hanging open so doltish. Same with his bearing. He had well-made limbs, but he slumped and shuffled so.

She passed by, squashing the usual impulse to tease him just to gain his attention. To hear that "Huh?" in that deep voice.

She passed inside Jin's pavilion, which had been painted in soft blues, shading toward deep blue on the ceilings, to resemble the sky. Everywhere, exquisitely made and painted paper birds hung on silken strings, each at different lengths. A window was always open, so that a breeze would stir the birds into rustling flight.

Instead of tables and chairs, there were cushions everywhere, half of them with cats curled up or stretched out on them. A couple of cats ambled her way, tails up, and she stooped to stroke them as she passed through to Jin's own room, which smelled strongly of cat.

Here she found the three princes, Jin sitting at the single table, which was spread with paper, scissors, and paints. He was busy folding a bird as Lir said, "It would be fun if we all went. Do you sail? I can't remember if we ever got you onto a boat."

No answer except an absent smile.

Everyone looked Rathlan's way. Jin's smile widened. He really was so handsome. And so sweet, in his own odd way.

Lir sighed. "I guess you really aren't interested, Elder Brother Jin."

Jin kept working. Rathlan knew he could speak when he wanted to. But he rarely did.

TanTan tapped the table, and when everyone turned his way, he pointed at Rathlan and made their question sign.

"I'm going with you," she said, touching her collarbone and then pointing at them, following which she folded her hands together and swooped them through the air like a ship. "I wish all four of us could go! We're to have music, even!"

"How'd you wangle that?" Lir asked.

"Threw myself on the floor before Imperial Uncle," Rathlan said proudly.

"I'd study if it was music," Lir said. "But this morning, we heard it was going to be Kanda and tutors the entire way."

"Musicians as in two," Rathlan corrected. "Won't that be so much more fun? I sent Ginger to pack my things, and that will include my zither. You should bring your flute."

"And have those imperial musicians snickering up their sleeves at how terrible I am?" Lir retorted. "I'm happy to listen. Especially if it will get us out of copying Kanda's *Conversations* yet again." He flicked a glance TanTan's way, and both rose to their feet. "We'll see you when we get back, Brother," Lir said. "And we won't forget to bring something back for you."

The three left Rathjin, whose untroubled profile bent over his latest bird as he traded a large scissor for a tiny one so that he could cut the precise curve of an ibis's beak.

Once they were outside, the princes' guards having separated one ahead and one behind, Lir turned to walk backward from long habit, and Rathlan said and signed, "Did you really think Jin might come with us?"

"He was at the play last night," Lir said, hands swooping for TanTan's sake. "He liked it! You know he does have days when he's like any of us."

TanTan put thumb and finger two finger-breadths apart: *almost.*

Lir shrugged as he admitted, "Almost. Ayah! He looked right at me, and praised the music, and then he added that First Brother loved it, and also that there was a benevolent demon among the musicians."

Grand Princess Rathlan sighed.

"There was also a lot of the usual stuff about metal and the Twelve Houses of the Stars, and some impending change. I didn't pay attention to that, except to be glad that no one was overhearing any of it."

Rathlan sighed again. "I'm sure his servants have been ordered to not hear any treason he blabbers. He has no idea half of his divination babble is treason."

They considered the fact that anyone else but Jin would probably be hauled off for interrogation if anyone heard his mutterings about changing Houses and suchlike. Even mentioning augury was dangerous. But Jin was…Jin, who held long conversations with the princes' eldest brother — the one who had died a few years before any of them were born.

They changed the subject to what they ought to enjoy for their last meal before they had to take formal leave of all their close relations, and at the other end of the palace, Granny Zim and Bu stared at the imperial graywing who had just informed Bu that she would be sailing on the outgoing tide that night for Kanda's shrine in the western islands, and to bring any instruments she thought would entertain the imperial princes and Grand Princess Rathlan.

Bu was in shock. Granny Zim was furious. She wanted so badly to refuse to let Bu go, except what would that do? Once again, fate, in the form of the emperor, lifted its hand and with a casual swat, changed lives, reminding her that she was essentially powerless.

"Do you have any questions?" the graywing said finally, successfully reading the fear-inspired anger that Granny Zim struggled against, and Bu's shock swiftly turning into panic. He added, his gaze on Bu, "Her Highness the Grand Princess Rathlan requested your presence, Student Bu Lum."

Bu blinked; the graywing saw in her transparent

expression that the rumors were true, this girl had no ambition to be flattered.

The graywing then said, "There will be two of you sent on pilgrimage. You will not go alone."

Granny Zim raised a hand, anger sparking to real alarm. "I cannot do without Student YinYin."

The graywing responded with calm dignity, "The emperor acknowledged that. Student Lum Bu will accompany First Apprentice Xia Chi, as the emperor requires the master musicians' presence for a new presentation."

A telltale blush burned up Bu's neck to her hairline. Then she said to Granny Zim, "I won't be here to learn it." Her voice quavered.

Granny Zim's hand trembled as she patted Bu's. "You'll learn it on your return, have no fear. And you will not go without being prepared to further your studies. I have been assembling scrolls for you as I reform your senior years' projects."

"Senior," Bu repeated.

"Are you not seventeen now, or near? And have I not explained that you have already been working well into sixth to ninth year studies? Rest assured on that score. I expect you and the senior apprentice to continue refining your method, and to get much farther along in composition. This will be a perfect opportunity for that."

The graywing, seeing the expected obedience, said to Bu, "Any more questions, Student Lum Bu?"

"What am I to pack?" she asked, her voice thin.

"A trunk is being prepared for you by the Merit Garden staff. All you need to bring are any personal items, and of course your instruments, and materials appertaining."

"That means silk for strings, child," Granny Zim said. "Extra tuning pegs, though they ought to have some sort of wood in their supplies, but I know you won't want to ask. If that is all, we had better be about it."

She bowed to the graywing, who bowed back. Bu hastily bowed, and followed Granny Zim, who began a stream of instructions interspersed with warnings and scattered thoughts on what Bu ought to be practicing.

Bu tried to listen, but all she was aware of was the relief she felt, knowing that she would not be alone. There would be a…she had not the temerity to even think of Xia Chi as a friend. But she could talk to him, the way she had talked to Cricket, long ago on the island. There was no silliness, no fan flirting, or fulsome compliments. She was *safe* with him.

Her thoughts kept coming back to that, and so she was calmer than Granny Zim had thought possible when, later that evening, as wind whipped at hair and clothes, Bu walked away from her, up the ramp into the ship after a row of gray-clad servants bearing baskets and boxes.

The ramp graunched as it was pulled away. The sails clattered down, and above them the dragon banner unfurled, charmed streamers to either side.

Granny Zim's vision blurred. She scolded herself, thinking she ought to be used to the young ones leaving her. Lum Bu was not the first. And she would be back.

But it hurt all the same.

THIRTY-TWO

WHEN GINGER WAS TOLD by Grand Princess Rathlan that one of the musician students would be coming along — "It's the girl who played 'The Merry Beggar' so wonderfully" — Ginger had to bite back a protest. If the emperor had decided to send along another princess, or the daughter of one of the high-ranking courtiers, there would have been a bigger ship, or a second ship, or some sort of reshuffling of the fine suites, and Ginger would have been able to keep her tiny cabin off the grand princess's all to herself. But the news that a tribute girl was selected meant one thing: Ginger was going to have to be cramped up with an unwanted roommate.

That determined her to get their own hierarchy straight from the moment that girl walked on board. Everything Ginger had heard about her was confusing, which in Ginger's view most likely meant trouble: she was like a nun, she was supposed to be a nun but wasn't, she was severe, she was stupid, she was a Talent.

That last one Ginger believed. She'd stood outside the door when the tribute girl first played 'The Merry Beggar' for her highness. Ginger had also heard that Talents could be, and often were, obnoxious.

Ragged clouds fled Phoenix moon as the servants boarded. Ginger made certain to get on board first, to oversee her highness's things disposed properly by the graywing and the under-maid, for there would be no pages on this journey. She raced into the adjacent closet where, sure enough, two bedrolls and two small service trunks had been stowed.

She shoved the second bedroll into the far corner along with the standard small trunk containing Household Department-issued music students' things. She pushed her own similar trunk to the most advantageous spot as a kind of divider, and spread the plumper bedroll out below the window, where Ginger would get the tiger's share of the fresh air. Then she settled her personal things in such a way that claimed slightly more than half the window side of the space, leaving the smaller, stuffy side free. So be it. If that tribute musician wanted a fight, Ginger was ready.

Ginger was always ready. She and her sisters as well as two girl cousins had one by one been sold to the palace in order to ease the punitive debt their fathers had accrued in being inadvertently connected to The Trouble thirty years ago.

The only reason why the family had survived at all was because they had not sold anything but rice to the traitors, who — unknown to the merchants' brothers, both swore — were stockpiling goods for their revolt. If they had sold the traitors so much as a single knife, the entire family would have joined the long line for execution. As it was, they had lost their fine house, their shop, their share of a trade ship, and had had to begin all over again, under the weight of a crushing fine. It was either that or exile.

And girls meant a dowry. Girls could not work at the docks when the trade ships came in. Therefore, at age six, Ginger had found herself in the palace emptying chamber pots, and had had to learn to look out for herself. By the time she'd schemed and bribed and traded her way to serving the grand princess, she had discovered when to tattle and when to stay silent, whom to flatter and whom to threaten before they could threaten you — and above all, to keep her ears sharp as a nine-tail fox in the woods. The grand princess was still talking to the imperial princes, so she sat on the bedroll she'd claimed, arms crossed, and waited. She did not have to wait long.

Graywing Four's familiar voice approached, "…and you will sleep here when you are not on duty, Student Lum Bu."

"Thank you...forgive this ignorant one, but how shall I properly address you?" The girl's voice at least was pleasant — but the horrible Consort Rajai's was even sweeter.

"This one answers to Graywing Four. If there are no more

questions, many tasks await."

"No, no. Thank you, Graywing Four."

Ginger's face soured. A flatterer, eh?

Student Lum Bu's familiar face appeared in the doorway as she stepped over the threshold. She was as plain as Ginger was herself, though taller by a hand, at least. She looked around and smiled when she saw the window. "Oh, this is so much better than I hoped for," she exclaimed.

Ginger, expecting irony, heard it. "Don't blame this insignificant servant, your great and imperial majesty."

Bu blinked, completely taken aback. Did this person not see her student robe? "My pardon, but I am Student Lum Bu," said Bu. "Graywing Four brought me here, so I don't think I am in the wrong place?" She blinked a question, the light from the single swinging lamp reflecting in wide eyes, one of which had a crystal eyepiece poised between brow and cheekbone.

Ginger heard these words and had to reassess. Short-sighted. Definitely odd. Stupid, then? Odd could be trouble, but stupid she could deal with.

"That is your bedroll, and your trunk. You'll have to keep your personal things on top of the trunk."

As she spoke, Bu had already taken out her comb and her book, and laid them on top of the trunk. Then she folded her carryall neatly, and tucked it behind the trunk.

Ginger blinked at that exceedingly modest array of two objects, and said, "Is that all you brought?"

Bu glanced back at her. "Isn't it enough? They told me that the trunk would hold clothes and…perhaps I had better look. Ah! Yes, it's all here."

Ginger's voice was somewhat more dubious than confrontive now. "Where are your musical instruments?"

"Oh, they said that those went into the schoolroom.. When I heard that, I was afraid that this would be even tinier than the little room YinYin and I slept in, on the tribute ship. It was half this size, and no window. This is so much more spacious!"

Ginger heard this, and realized that Lum Bu really was not speaking ironically. Further, it seemed she and irony had never yet met. But she didn't sound stupid. And there had been that marvelous, enchanting playing…

She said, "Is it true you lived in a convent, before you came to the imperial island?"

"It was a temple. And there was a convent," Bu corrected quickly. "But our part was a school, attached to the temple. It had been that way for centuries." She reached toward the bedroll as she fought back a yawn, then withdrew her hand. "Perhaps I had better make sure where everything is, first. I don't want to trouble anyone in the morning, and that graywing pointed things out so fast all I remember are swinging lamps and steps and a lot of rooms here and there, all belonging to other people."

While Bu spoke, Ginger had been thinking, and hauled to her feet. She had made herself thoroughly familiar with the ship when she and the servants had brought the first loads over that afternoon, to ready things for her grand princess. "Come on, I'll show you around."

"Thank you," Bu said, bowing quaintly. "Ayah! This talentless person is named Lum Bu, actually Bu will do, when we are not in a formal situation. I don't truly have a right to Lum."

"I'm Ginger," Ginger said, abandoning the title she had concocted for herself, to be imposed in their own private space. "Come along. The privy is back this way…"

While Bu and Ginger dodged around sailors and servants and guards busy stowing things and tending sail as the ship labored its way out of the harbor, the two imperial brothers got themselves settled into the spacious cabins on the second level of the three-story superstructure aft on the deck of the warship.

TanTan familiarized himself with everything, used to the fact that he would get scant explanation, unless he could prevail on Lir—as flighty as a firefly—to write everything down. He had never been permitted on a ship before, and found everything of interest, from the complexity of sails and charms to the way the escort deck and spear ships were spaced, with scouts sailing quickly in advance.

Lir was as excited as a boy by every detail. He, too, had never been permitted to go anywhere beyond the royal city, and that was always surrounded by guards. He was still surrounded by guards, but at least he and TanTan and LanLan were *moving*. To unknown waters, and away from all the irritating constraints of court!

He was gloating over that to Rathlan and TanTan when there came a rap at the door, and the barrel-chested, pumpkin-headed scribe who walked in was instantly familiar.

Lir groaned. "Master Angka."

Master Angka Nakanda had earned first place in the

Imperial Examination when he was seventeen, and had been promoted three times since then—that in spite of his abject failure to get some education into the youngest three princes a few years before. He had been the last in a long line of master tutors whose successes could be measured only in the fact that the princes could read and write.

Master Angka gave the Fourteenth Imperial Prince a stern look that didn't quite mask the quirk of laughter at the corners of his eyes, as he cleared his throat and held up a familiar sight: a scroll, heavy paper adhered to a heavier silken background, which meant an imperial edict. As if to reinforce the appearance of the Emperor's Voice, a dark-clad graywing stood at his shoulder, tall and silent. The imperial princes immediately recognized one of the emperor's personal staff, there to serve as steward over all the servants—but everyone knew he was also there as the emperor's eyes. And he no doubt had pigeons housed on the rooftop solely for his use.

With a heavy sigh, Lir dropped to his knees, followed by his brother, and Rathlan behind them, in the place of secondary imperial family. The boys' personal graywing quietly laid a written paper before TanTan then withdrew to join the servants at the perimeter of the suite, who prostrated themselves.

Master Angka read, "My imperial sons and my beloved grandniece are hereby informed that their studies will commence on the first morning of their journey, to be held each day until such time as Master Angka Nakanda declares himself satisfied that the day's lesson has been completed to his satisfaction. Written by my hand, their very concerned imperial father." And the master went on to read out, in a sonorous voice, all the emperor's titles, ending with "Son of Heaven."

Lir banged his head on the deck, saying, "This son hears and obeys his imperial father." A little in front of him, TanTan laid his hand on his copy of the edict, which everyone recognized as his assent to obey.

Lir climbed to his feet, saying sourly, "Ought to have expected it. Imperial Father is once again praising us in the west while smacking us from the east."

Master Angka handed the edict off to the waiting graywing, who would display it prominently, then let his smile come. "Your exalted imperial highness did not permit this untalented pedant to finish."

Lir said suspiciously, "Yes, O Pedant?"

Master Angka said, "Your imperial highness is no longer fifteen, woefully — even embarrassingly — behind in the fundamentals of Kanda's thought. That is, I'm certain you are still behind in the written texts, but we shall explore the meaning of those texts with a question posed each day. If the discussion of that question warrants it, reading and especially the copying of texts, can be laid aside for that day."

Rathlan conveyed the gist to TanTan as Lir eyed the master. "That's extortion!"

Master Angka grinned broadly. "It is education, your imperial highness. It is the essence of education."

THIRTY-THREE

THE TWO IMPERIAL PRINCES and their cousin poked all over the tower ship with the lifelong ease of people before whom everyone else bows out of the way. TanTan had to see the crossbow holes, the leathern shielding to protect against fire, and then he wanted to look at the chart, to see how it differed from a map.

Lir followed up to the command center, where Fleet Leader Naoki was speaking to an orderly, "I want the scouts to sketch everything afloat, right down to those fishing junks I can see out there. Get the silhouettes at least. If anything is visible more than two days, they are to board, search, and if necessary, deal with anyone suspicious."

The orderly ran to write up the orders, and send them by pigeon.

Lir loitered out of sight. As usual, he was impatient with details; while TanTan pored over the chart, marveling at features of harbors that were mere lines on maps, Lir swept his gaze over the entire chart, and sighed. "It's going to take twice as long to get there, just because of the barbarians?"

Fleet Leader Naoki bowed. "Our orders, from his imperial majesty himself..." Here the clasped hands and a bow back toward the imperial island, "...are to avoid the Inner Islands altogether."

Rathlan appeared. "The servants are bringing up the food.

I'm hungry!"

The princes left the command center, which freed the sailors to get back to sailing the ship. There was a small dining area in a central room between all their bedchambers. It had been fitted with fine screens depicting snow-topped Mt. Lir and eagles in flight on one side, and on the other, a mountain pagoda above a monk fishing along a bank with willow and redbark. Sumptuously embroidered silk cushions awaited the imperial cousins around a dragon-clawed low table piled with dishes of porcelain and gold.

Conversation was desultory; Lir and Rathlan were aware of people all around, in contrast to the princes' pavilion, where they could dismiss servants to the far wing and revile without an audience.

By the time they had finished the meal, it was very late. It took a while to settle in, with everything so different, down to the lotus-lamps swinging back and forth, scattering shadows and light in patterns. TanTan found that soothing, Lir irritating. Eventually they all slept, and were still asleep when Bu woke the next morning. Long used to moving without disturbing anyone, she rose, dressed while standing on the bedroll, did up her hair by feel, then rolled her bedding up and stashed it neatly.

Outside in the hall someone had left wash water, plus tea for rinsing the mouth. She took advantage of both before going to the privy, and from there, to the schoolroom, which had a single lamp lit. By its unsteady light she located her qin.

She was going to sit down and begin practice when she considered those cabins so close by. Would anyone hear and be disturbed?

She picked up the qin and ghosted out again, and down to the deck, which was mostly open space. Almost no one in view. The sun was barely below the eastern horizon, bluing the sky. She recognized Brick in that dim light, standing motionless at the rail. Had he been on duty all the night through? Instant pity emboldened her.

"Will it disturb you if I do musical warmups?" she asked, joining him at the rail.

As always, it took a moment or two before he turned his head to look her way. His face was in shadow as he gave his head a shake. Then he turned back to his watch, though little could be seen beyond drifts of fog glowing softly in the lifting darkness.

Bu walked quietly to the far side of the rail, sat down on the clean-swept deck, tuned the strings, and began her fingering warmups. She played softly at first, but she was so used to the quiet provided by thick walls and doors, that gradually her volume rose as she bent over her qin to hear the clarity of each pluck, slide, and sustained note.

No one disturbed her until the rustle of cloth and a quiet step brought her head up. Here was Xia Chi, with his qin under his arm, and a pleasant smile, the early sunlight illuminating his face. Bu quickly removed her eyepiece as Xia Chi said, "May I join you? I heard you from the windows —"

"Oh, no," Bu exclaimed, horrified. "I must have disturbed everyone!"

"It was barely discernible," Xia Chi assured her. "And I am used to rising early. But…I was counting as I got ready, and you did not stop at eighty."

Bu blushed. "There are two hundred altogether, but that includes the two-handed techniques."

"Ah, and I thought myself so advanced to have mastered the eighty Chief Zim has introduced us to." He gave her a rueful smile. "Would Student Lum Bu honor this lamentably talentless individual by going through them with me?"

"I would be happy to," she said, privately thinking that she would not dare to presume to correct a senior. Especially this senior.

That resolve lasted through the exercises for two fingers; her natural shyness and reluctance to appear conceited lost to her need to respect correct fingering. When he commenced with the thumb of his left hand, each pluck just blurred enough to twang her nerves, she demonstrated, forbearing comment.

He paused, his gaze intent, and requested a repetition. With equal gravity and politeness, she repeated it. Then again, and finally she put her hand near his on his qin, and executed a perfect pluck.

"Ah, ah, ah," he exclaimed. "That sounds…true."

She smiled with relief, without the vaguest idea how appealing that smile could be in her ardent face, and he worked at getting his thumb exactly right until he repeated her crisp, assured snap.

"That's it!"

Slowly they worked through the rest of the eighty he knew, and he begged her to demonstrate some of the others. That led to combinations. And gradually, the two extended combinations into variations, until the deck resounded with strong, vibrant harmonies.

By then, the imperials had woken, Lir and Rathlan to the expert harmonies, and TanTan to the vibration in the deck when Lir bounded out of bed. A quick breakfast and they were ready to explore the ship in daylight—but when they emerged from their suites, there was a tall, shadowy graywing waiting, with Master Angka beside him, scrolls clutched meaningfully in one arm, the other hand extended in invitation toward the schoolroom.

Lir groaned like a boy half his age, and slumped his way into the already-hated chamber, which was flooded with light, all the windows open to the deck to catch what little breeze there was. It was going to be a hot summer day; the qin music wafted in, sweet and beguiling.

"Why can't we go listen?" Lir tried.

"They will play for your imperial highness any time once your studies are complete." Master Angka sat behind the low table, and shook his sleeves back before reaching for his inkstone. "Your imperial highnesses may begin with an easy copying assignment, or this poor, lowly master could pose a question for discussion…"

"Discussion," Lir said quickly.

"Discussion," Rathlan echoed, knowing that her opinion was never to be sought before court, so why trouble herself over musty texts?

TanTan tapped his lips and wound a hand in the air.

"Very well, your imperial highnesses," Master Angka said. "My question is this: what is a barbarian?"

"It is you, for throwing that at us so early in the day," Lir retorted.

Master Angka only bowed, though suppressing a smile, and reached for the top scroll on the pile he had set down at his table, the oldest and heaviest-looking of all those scrolls.

Lir exclaimed, "I retract that, I retract that, with full apologies." He clasped his hands together and bobbed three quick bows.

TanTan clapped his hands, made the sign for Kanda, and then put his hands in the position for the first formal bow toward the ancestors, after which he flattened his hand in negation.

Rathlan said, "He's saying Kanda claimed that barbarians are those who do not respect the rules of ritual propriety."

Master Angka withdrew the reaching hand a little. "A good beginning. But it is only a beginning."

Rathlan sighed. "I have never put any of those long lists to memory because there was no use in it. They all tell me my only purpose is to marry and give some noble ally sons."

"Would not your esteemed highness preside over your children's education?"

"I'm sure that noble ally husband will do that," she muttered.

"But your highness will surely discuss his vital and valuable labors with him, as her revered imperial majesty is justly praised for doing. If this mere scribe might offer a suggestion, we might begin with simple definitions of words used in everyday discourse."

"In other words, talk," Lir said, bowing again. "Which is better than having to copy out long scrolls."

She scowled his way. "But *I* never said 'barbarian' — ayah, not recently, anyway —"

"That was I, last night," Lir admitted with a sigh. "I know it was careless. I retract it."

Master Angka bowed slightly. "But the word is out there in the air, your imperial highness. The precious words of so estimable a person as an imperial prince..."

Lir scowled, about to retort that Master Angka was arguing for the sake of arguing, but then he remembered a scrap of a lesson from the *Twenty Five Virtues*, and saw the trap yawning right before his feet: if he didn't want to be copying those Virtues — and the last set was very, very long — then he had better scrape his brain now. He hastily finished the quotation before the master could, "...ought to be able to explicate or to defend his utterances, or he ought not to have spoken. I could defend it, but there truly is no defense. That word gets slung around by everybody. We call the Horseboys barbarians, because they're causing us no end of trouble — but I suppose they in turn call *us* barbarians, or why would their king be throwing their warriors against us? For that matter, one of my elder brothers once said that the ignorant easterners we draw tribute from all call us barbarians. Then," he added with a cough, "my most esteemed and respected elders right there in the imperial palace have called me a barbarian dolt at least once a week, or more, as long as I can remember."

"Your response then is that everyone else does it, so your imperial highness might as well mimic them?" Master Angka asked dulcetly, and once again that hand reached for the scroll, almost touching it.

TanTan waved in negation, and sent a glare Lir's way. He smacked his hand on the table twice, left hand, right hand, then made the signs for a horse, and then for Kanda, and this time Lir translated. "TanTan says—and I agree—that the original definition came about because, as my cousin stated, Kanda said that anyone who does not accept the fundamentals of ritual propriety is a barbarian. That has been taken to mean the Horseb—ah, the horse brethren—"

"Your imperial highness might strengthen your position by using their term for themselves," Master Angka suggested mildly.

"The Jun Suai—but that just means 'horse brethren' in their dialect, which is taken from our language."

"Mmm, the evolution of language is another debate topic, but we have plenty of days before us, your imperial highnesses, and I happen to have many interesting ancient texts on that topic." Master Angka reached behind him and patted a trunk carved with laurel leaves. "If his imperial highness the Twelfth Prince Rathtan would grace us by continuing his thought…"

TanTan was smacking the table and gesturing vigorously.

Lir said, "TanTan is telling you that the central tenet of the Jun Suai thought is a man on a horse, with sword and bow, whereas the central tenet of our imperial thought is Kanda's concept of ritual propriety."

"I will accept that preliminarily, your imperial highness," Master Angka said, bowing toward TanTan. "This laboring tutor wishes to put a question to all your imperial highnesses: do you believe that the Jun Suai are incapable of civilized behavior or thought?"

The three looked at one another, Rathlan a little wildly. She had never troubled herself with a single thought about the people making war on the empire, outside of a general loathing. Again, because no one was ever going to ask her opinion. So why think of unpleasant things?

TanTan frowned into the air between the master and his own hands, which had frozen mid-gesture, his fingers tense as his thoughts raced.

Lir sighed. "I think that's a trick question. Of course they are capable of civilized behavior. At least, some of those histories in the archive that old Master Yuak made us trudge through when we were thirteen said over and over that honor was very important to the Hor — to the Jun Suai. I can't imagine that their king, when he threw down our banner, put up his own and called himself a king, suddenly turned coward, and cursed family hierarchy, and defiled ancestral shrines. In fact, I remember one of those records claimed that they have ancestral shrines, but they put them on the west side, not the north, and they speak to the ancestors through shamans, not through prayers. If you're going to say that that isn't civilized because it doesn't follow the Twenty-Five exactly, then bring on the copying."

"His imperial highness the Fourteenth Prince Rathlir need not trouble himself to put words into the mouth of this humble scribe," Master Angka said with a dignified bow.

Lir remembered then that when Master Angka got very formal, he was at his most deadly. Ayah, bang the alarm bells — that masterly forefinger had just touched the Evil Scroll of Doom.

Lir bowed back, hands crossed over his breast as he said, "This ignorant one regrets even the suggestion that his foolish words might be mistaken for the wisdom of the sagacious master."

Master Angka fought to suppress any hint of a smile as he said, "Then I gather that your imperial highnesses and this mere master are in agreement that the meaning at the heart of the Twenty-Five is not bound up in the superficialities of exact wording?"

"We are, O Master Angka," Lir said.

The master lifted his brows, his hand still near that scroll. "Then, if I may pose to the imperial offspring of his revered and esteemed imperial majesty the Son of Heaven, a related question: what is the fundamental lesson the ruler must take from the Twenty-Five?"

A ruler? None of the endless repetitions of the first Virtues, all concerning children obeying parents, would apply now.

Three faces twitched, brows contracting, mouths thinning, as three minds tried to dredge up mostly-ignored lessons from the past. Lir was aware of the swell of music flowing in, ever more entrancing, and he was about to claim that it was distracting, but he was also aware that he hadn't actually noticed it until now.

TanTan knew what Jin would say, and tapped out the signs for the Five Elements, stitching them together as Rathlan translated slowly, "TanTan is saying that everyone, even the ruler, must acknowledge that the natural law is true for all three worlds, from which the Twenty-Five derive…ah, natural law meaning the five elements—metal, wood, earth, water, and fire—conquer each other, in orderly, ayah, order. The last element, fire, then conquers the first, metal, which binds them together in a circle of harmony, reflecting the great circle of harmony that the sun makes through the sky, the stars make in wheeling overhead, and the earth makes in wheeling through the seasons. Therefore the proof for this relationship is everywhere."

Master Angka's hand withdrew a bit more. "That is a considered answer, Imperial Prince Rathtan."

(Phew, he's addressing us directly, Lir covertly signaled his elder brother.)

"But it is not quite the answer I am looking for. It might be an unfair question, but I will pose it anyway: why do we hold the Imperial Examinations at all? Why do we teach the Twenty-Five, not to mention all the other classics? What does the ruler use from those?"

Silence, and even the music had stopped, as outside, Bu and Xia Chi—who had heard through those open windows the imperial cousins' discussion intensifying—had by sign agreed to cease their practice and look over Granny Zim's first lesson, written out carefully.

Then Lir sighed. "All right, bring on the inkstones." He held out his wrists as if they were to be shackled.

Master Angka shook with silent laughter, then said, "Instead, permit this seeker of wisdom to put a last question, which I trust might inspire some further discussion. We have touched on the fundamentals, which I am convinced have lodged in at least a superficial form within your imperial highnesses' blessed memories. We have touched on the fact that the Jun Suai, whether barbarians or not, have organized themselves through history around a different set of tenets, which can include many of the tenets we hold to. But there is still, I suggest, a profound difference in the respective rulers' way of establishing order. The Jun Suai, a warrior society, regard punishment as the corrective for law-breaking."

"Don't we also have punishments for law-breaking?" Rathlan asked, as TanTan looked a question, and Lir frowned.

"We do, but if you chance to look through the archives, you will find that the sage rulers' edicts repeatedly state that the way to govern the people peacefully is through teaching, not through chastisement. Thus the lessons, the rituals, the repetitions. The Twenty-Five are to shape everyone so in a truly enlightened world, we would not have to have penalties because everyone would live according to the Twenty-Five Virtues."

"I think I see," Lir said. "If it's just punishment without reason, it leads to anger and evil thoughts."

"Correct, your imperial highness. Though I suggest a rephrasing: what is the use of punishment without virtuous teaching?"

Lir's head panged. They had stayed up late, and had drunk too much rice wine. But that was a mere excuse. He was quite aware that he had gotten out of the habit of following even so simple a discussion. He clasped his hands and bowed. "I think I understand."

Master Angka looked at the faces, then said, "I take the liberty to suggest, your imperial highnesses, that was an adequate beginning for the first day. The scrolls are here. Not all of them are dull—there are many here that discuss the doings of emperors of the past, good and bad. You are welcome to borrow them and read them at any time. We shall continue tomorrow."

And outside the music started up again, revisiting themes from *The Swan Fan*.

Rathlan sighed as she whirled out. "After all that, I think I need to dance," she said, and ran down to the deck, her ribbons and tassels rippling.

THIRTY-FOUR

BU AND XIA CHI were so convinced that the schoolroom aboard the tower ship must properly be left to the imperials, they sat together on the deck, poring over the first assignment Granny Zim had written out, as the sun rose and strengthened. Gradually the deck filled with sailors, then the company of imperial guards. The two music students crowded closer to the rail while the rising wind threatened to take all their precious papers out to sea.

In spite of these increasing distractions, Xia Chi taught Bu the introductory music for a popular play, then its main themes. As the imperials' voices drifted down through the open windows, Bu softly, quietly practiced that music until it was perfect, while he watched her hands, trying to replicate the unnervingly perfect precision of each pluck and strum.

At midday, Bu flexed and wrung out her hands, then gave into the impulse to play some of her variations from *The Swan Fan* as the discussion above finished up. She was so happy. She had begun the morning afraid of her own self-consciousness, but it turned out that even away from the classroom, Xia Chi was as easy to work with as he was to talk with.

Within moments the grand princess showed up, and when Bu stopped playing, Rathlan waved her hands. "No, no, do continue. We've been cooped up inside, and I need to dance. Play!"

Bu bowed, and played.

Lir lingered in the schoolroom, and presently joined TanTan, who had gone to nose through the scrolls and books the master had brought.

Lir smacked him on the arm to gain his attention. "Why do you think we got that question about the enemy?" he signed. "At first I blamed myself. But. He could have made us copy Kanda about respect for language, and the importance of not being careless with words. I remember copying all that until my hand ached." He grimaced and crouched over his hand.

TanTan wryly signed, "Dropped hints, careless words." He laid his hand on a text, then turned to his brother. "If Imperial Father wins the war. The Horse People come back. He wants us to think. Not enemies?"

Lir pursed his lips. "That's thinking *far* ahead. But then, scholars are always debating what if this, what if that. Master Angka has to keep us busy, and we've nothing but time ahead of us."

TanTan responded, "Tomorrow's question? More Horse People?"

Lir said, "His unspoken point was that all three of us are playing zither to water buffalos about the enemy. He being the zither player, and we three the water buffalos. If we don't want to be copying the *Conversations* about the dangers of ignorance, this water buffalo thinks we must get ahead of his questions."

TanTan smacked the table, then signed, "Our usual way?"

Lir clapped his hands in agreement, and pointed. "You read. I talk. I'll get LanLan to write your scribbles out, and all three of us will think of possible questions so we won't sound like water buffalos tomorrow. *Look* at how much paper he brought! That's a worse threat than any mere warning of a beating waiting for us, and a night kneeling outside the ancestral hall."

TanTan had resisted the toil of learning to read and write the longest of any of the imperial children, until Rathlan and Lir had convinced him that the squiggles on paper corresponded with things in the physical world, beginning with his own body. Eventually that extended to the unseen world. For him, there were seven senses: the five physical ones (including the useless hearing, often referred to in texts), the ones he equated with the mind, or concepts, and the ones corresponding to emotions, or the heart. Once he grasped that idea, he never stopped reading, though writing never came easily. They had gradually developed a method whereby either Lir or Rathlan would take his labored work and expand it into readable form.

Mostly this had fallen to Rathlan, who loved writing. When she wasn't with her two imperial cousins, she was writing letters to her cousins on her mother's side, and to the princesses who had been married off. There were three who always were hungry for news from the palace where they had grown up—and she was vitally interested in the world beyond the confines of the imperial palace.

TanTan returned to rooting through the trunk for anything about the Jun Suai, because once his ignorance about something had been pointed out, he felt it was a hole he could fall through, leaving him bewildered in a world that always seemed ready to carry right past him.

Lir prowled around the schoolroom, occasionally glancing out the window at where the imperial guards moved through military drill, as the marine warriors waited for their turn. Imperial Guard Sanhu Ban, TanTan's personal bodyguard, was at the front, directly across from Imperial Guard Colonel Deg. Lir's eyes strayed to Brick in the back, who shambled his way through in plunging fits and starts. He seemed to have been trained by a water buffalo, but he had saved Lir's life twice. And he didn't blab—at least, he didn't blab to Lir. Who knows what his reports to the grays were like. Maybe he chattered like little sister Rathyi, who *never* stopped yapping and demanding attention.

As he watched Brick wave a heavy sword through the air as if poking a hornet's nest, Lir grinned at the thought of Brick yapping a single complete sentence.

Then someone banged a gong, and the imperial guards dispersed. Time for their meal. They racked their weapons, the colonel climbed to the command tower, and the others went below; it seemed that they ate together, now that the ship was in the middle of the ocean, surrounded by a formidable escort, instead of trading off duty and rest.

Ah! What better time than now?

With his typical insouciant belief that he was welcome anywhere, anytime (except to his brother Rathvo), Lir slipped out and down the stairs to the deck below the weather deck, where crew berthing started. There were crossbow ports here, letting in air, and weapon racks bolted to the bulkheads. This was not an area of fine screens, rugs, or cushions.

He followed the smell of bean-paste-filled steamed buns and broiled fish to one of the bare rooms not far from the sailors' galley. Here, he found the guards sitting shoulder to shoulder on deck mats around a table.

They froze at the sight of him, set eating sticks and half-devoured buns down, rose, and bowed.

Lir waved. "Sit, sit, sit, go ahead and eat. Sanhu, Brick, you know I mean what I say."

Sanhu grunted, jerking his chin down, and the imperial guards unfamiliar with Fourteenth Imperial Prince Rathlir (except by reputation, that is, "The Weasel") sat down, but they sat stiffly as Lir said, "Maybe you heard us up there with Master Angka?"

A quirk at the corner of Sanhu's mouth made it clear that, yes, everyone had heard that blundering discussion. Water buffalos indeed. Shrugging that off internally, Lir said, ""What do you know about the Horseboys, besides the fact that they wear fur hats, and that they want to kill us all?"

Some exchanged looks, then Sanhu, longest acquainted with the princes, said, "Fact is, your imperial highness, there are some of us descended from those who came south from Ryu Island."

"Ryu Island," Lir repeated, mentally poring over the map he'd half-heartedly studied off and on. "Ah! One of the big islands, northeast."

"That's the one, your imperial highness. My family came down from there four generations ago," Sanhu said.

"Mine more like five, but from the big island, your imperial highness," one of the other guards put in, his voice rumbling. "There's never been trouble over us being descended from Jun."

Lir recognized that statement as an oblique question. He leaned against the bulkhead as the ship gave one of its occasional lurches. "And there won't be any now. This is a fishing expedition. Sanhu here will tell you that my brother and I will do just about anything to avoid having to copy out pages and pages of Kanda. Master Angka seems to think we need to know something about the enemy, so here I am, fishing." Lir mimed yanking a fish out of water.

Sanhu grunted. "All I know is what my grandfather told me, your imperial highness. He got it from his grandfather. I don't speak their lingo, but I know the story of the Three Blessed, and something about why my family came south."

"Which was?"

"Drought—bad weather by turns—shamans said Heaven was punishing the Jun Suai, you see, your imperial highness, because they had thrown nature into turmoil by hunting the animals almost to death. Families were starving. Meat being the main meal. Not much else out on the grasslands of the big island. Horses liked the grass," Sanhu added, his sun-seamed eyes crinkling.

"So...they came south, conquering their way?" Lir asked.

Sanhu shrugged a shoulder, considering the skinny, skittish imperial prince from under his brows. He really did seem to want to learn. "I can only relate to your imperial highness what my grandfather said, that until we descendants got into the imperial army, there was no stopping the Jun. They claimed the blessing of Heaven, but aside from that, you put a man on the ground with spear and sword, against a man on a fast horse with an accurate bow, and who wins?"

Lir said, "All skills being equal, seems the man with the spear is dead before the other one gets within range of that spear."

"Your imperial highness has it right." Sanhu turned his tea cup around with his callused fingers. "Though Grandfather said you'd hear from *them* about them being stronger, more honorable, tougher, because they were specially blessed." He grunted indifference. "If you get close enough, they bleed like anyone else."

"Tell me about the Three...Blessed, you said?"

"Your imperial highness, the story goes like this. Three fairies from Heaven came down in spring to sample the peaches planted by the Morning Star. As they gathered them, they met three local boys, and, ayah, spring happened, if you know what I mean. All three got pregnant, and so the king of Heaven forbade them entry for consorting with humans."

"The three had to live among humankind, see, your imperial highness, but they gave their three sons three gifts: the horse, the bow, and the sword," put in the other guard. "I heard a lot of hero tales when I was small."

"Their sons had more sons, and so they became the Jun Suai—Bow-Brethren of the Horse. If your imperial highness wants more about that, I was told they translated that as Lords of the Horse, or horse lords, but that didn't really take down here in the south because lords here are descendants of those who pass the Imperial Examination and earn merit by serving the emperor and getting promoted to green, or purple, or red robes." Sanhu sat back, the cooling tea between his fingers.

Lir knew then that they wouldn't eat until he was gone. He pushed away from the wall, then looked at the others. "Anything else to add? No? Brick, you?" Lir appended, just to hear...

"Huh?"

Lir grinned. "Never mind. We can't all be wag-tongues. Any man who can use a chamber pot as a weapon—first dumping the contents on the worst drunk of the bunch—is my hero."

He sauntered out, and climbed all the way up to the command area, where he found Imperial Guard Colonel Deg eating his meal as he read little strips of curled paper—dispatches brought by pigeons.

Lir paused to glance out of one of the windows pushed open. His gaze caught a hazy bump on the horizon. One island looked pretty much like another to him. What did the world look like to pigeons? More to the point, how did such tiny creatures navigate?

The two commanders spotted him in the doorway, and Deg dropped his paper and his nutcake to salute as Fleet Leader Naoki turned away from the window that overlooked the foredeck, where his marine warriors were pairing off for hack-and-slash practice. Both bowed, faces wooden at this intrusion into their world.

"Return to your meal, Imperial Guard Colonel Deg," Lir said, motioning for the colonel to sit. "This is only a fishing expedition. A question or two."

The colonel sat, clearly taking the motion as a command. He did not pick up either food or paper as he waited patiently, as if he stood on the parade ground, his half-armor with its silver dragon insignia clean and shining.

Equally clean and shining was that of Fleet Leader Naoki, who stood with feet spread, hands behind his back. Parade ground alert.

Lir sighed inwardly, but he was on a mission. "I'm trying to learn something about the Jun Suai," he said. "Part of the tutoring ordered by my imperial father."

At this, both men clasped their hands and nodded toward the imperial island. Lir belatedly did the same.

Fleet Leader Naoki's blank expression altered slightly to interest as he said, "I've been in two sea battles, your imperial highness, both off Benevolent Winds—what they call Jun Gan, who knows why. Did his imperial highness wish to discuss battle strategy, perhaps with an eye to the chart?"

"Maybe at some point. Right now I need to understand generally. Master Angka wants us to learn something, and I'm trying to sniff out what, and more importantly why."

Lir's reputation was known to these two as well, but that had been tempered through Deg's frank talk with Sanhu, the first night the orders went out to choose their teams and prepare. *Fourteen's about as steady as a one-legged drunk in a high wind, but he's honest. If he tells you something, you can believe it, unlike Eleven, who talks out of both sides of his mouth.*

Lir's disarming frankness caused the two to unbend incrementally. Deg said, "I've been in one battle, your imperial highness. We were driven off. They fight hard because they know how to fight, but they also have to fight. There were some reports by our scouts who speak their dialect that if they lose, the captain of the losing company dies in the square. Their king's shaman saw him on the dragon throne, and means to have it."

Fleet Leader Naoki gave another short nod of agreement. "The rumor we heard, your imperial highness, is that their king has also been through two or three shamans."

"Until he found one who sees the future he wants?"

"That is our impression, your imperial highness."

Lir saw that he'd gotten all he was going to get, and retreated, considering all that he had heard. What was Master Angka after? It all came back to Imperial Father, he decided, and went to hunt up Rathlan, who surely had stopped dancing and was hungry by now.

He was right. She sat in the dining area, watching Graywing Four manage to pour tea without spilling, in spite of the constant heave of the ship. Graywing Four, like Ginger being considered part of their inner circle—reporting to their respective superiors what they all agreed on—Lir dropped down, waving Graywing Four to carry on, and asked, "What did Ginger find out about Rathvo?"

"Little more than what we heard: he left on a ship earlier, reported to be going to Ice Fortress, and the Horrible Consort is definitely in the Cold Palace, washing her own clothes. But no one knows why."

"At least he's not *here*. I'll light incense sticks nine times for that. Now, here's what TanTan and I decided..."

THIRTY-FIVE

GRANNY ZIM RETURNED FROM seeing Bu's ship sail away and found little gifts, flowers, and notes of congratulation for the excellence of *The Swan Fan* waiting outside her chamber. As she lifted the basket, she was aware of a sense of misstep, and recognized the cause immediately.

The Swan Fan was Bu's piece. However, Granny Zim had not revealed that to anyone—Bu, because she would have panicked, and others lest someone say something to Bu, and cause her to panic.

"What a dolt I am," she declared as she picked up and threw down a note calligraphed on heavy paper, with a red seal stamped on it. She didn't trouble herself to figure out which imperial consort it came from. She didn't know any of them. She didn't want to know any of them. She wanted to escape them all, but it was becoming clear that escape would be difficult, because she was bound her by her own pride in her skills, and by Bu's budding Talent.

YinYin came in then, and looked in mute question from the basket of notes and gifts to Granny Zim.

"I should have told that emperor *The Swan Fan* was Bu's before he left that hall," Granny Zim declared. "And of course, I ought to have told Bu," she added as an afterthought.

YinYin seemed to consider that, and said, "You asked her how she would arrange each variation."

"That was my method of getting her to compose the whole, with only a little guidance. I thought myself as sly as an old fox. Sly as a decrepit, very old fox, because I out-slyed myself. If I'd thought to blurt it out then and there, the emperor would have kept her here."

YinYin's head tipped. "Do you know for certain?"

"No," Granny Zim admitted. "It's possible he would have been angry, because the order, or edict, was given to me, and he might have got pepper up his nose that I gave the work to my student. I don't know. Ayah! What a fool I am, thinking myself so clever."

She swept the notes together and looked around her small room, trying to figure out what to do with them. The coins, she tossed into her trunk. The flowers could go next to her bed while they kept their fragrance.

Then she looked up, frowning. "You usually come in here if you have something to say. What is it?"

"One of the humans recognized me for what I am."

That jolted Granny Zim so severely her arm tingled all the way to her fingers. She wrung them and flexed her hand until the tingle went away, as she whooshed out her breath. "Who? How?"

YinYin said, "I know which human. I know where it is. She? No. It is a he. I have listened. She—he—told some other visitors, earlier today."

"And?"

"Nothing."

Granny Zim bit back impatience. With YinYin, everything had to go in steps. In other circumstances, she might laugh at the notion that demons, who were creatures of chaos, found humans confusing. But that was not now. "Did you find out the name of this human?"

"Yes. It is called Thirteenth Prince Rathjin."

Granny Zim plumped down on the bed platform. Though she really had paid scarce attention to gossip about the imperial family, a stray fact or two had stuck. "The one they think is mad. But he saw you in your real form? Does that mean he sees the world of the unseen?"

"Yes."

Granny Zim frowned at the wall, then turned. "There is absolutely nothing I can do. If you have to, you know how to be invisible, at least."

"Yes."

"Very well. Let us leave things as they are. I hope you will continue to, ah, listen."

"I will listen." YinYin went out, opening and closing the door with the same meticulous care, as if performing a ritual.

Granny Zim, left alone, sighed out her tension, and became aware of exhaustion pressing down on her. She forced herself to ready for bed while muttering, "Teg, if you're here—and right now I'm believing it more than not, which always seems to happen after YinYin and I have one of these little talks—I suspect you are laughing at this worn old body. I don't feel the justice in aging. My mind is as nimble as it ever was. I'm vitally interested in far more matters than I was when we had youth to squander. And yet, a day like today presses on me as if I wore an iron yoke."

She lay down and dropped into sleep, waking to the stream of a new sun, bringing an urgent press of affairs. She had sent Bu off with the entire list of lessons that she'd been working out for the past weeks. There had been no time to recopy it, but she knew that if Bu returned ("Please, Suanek, look out for my Bu"), she would return with those papers.

Very well, then, she must relinquish the matter into the hands of the gods.

She washed, dressed, wound her thin hair impatiently into a bun and skewered it with the hairpin Teg had given her years ago, then went out to find what looked like everyone in Merit waiting to speak to her.

The graywing was first; it seemed the emperor wanted another theater piece, this one with a story. Chief Huazi was busy reorganizing his seniors. He had been relying on First Apprentice Xia Chi for a great deal, and now must find another as knowledgeable and as diligent. "Xia Chi was so far ahead of the other seniors. May this desperate colleague inquire if your assistant, Student YinYin is as diligent?"

"Chief Huazi, alas, YinYin is slower than a frozen snail at writing, and besides, she has all she can do with keeping up with this old body's requirements. I beg forgiveness, but I cannot do without her."

Chief Huazi had expected as much, but he was in truth desperate, as every class was being reorganized to accommodate the new music. He went off to look at his roster again.

Chief Yne had accumulated many gifts from the imperial family for his players—and criticisms from himself, so once he'd conveyed his compliments he took his players off for a discussion.

Chief Rao had to reshuffle her dancers to accommodate the departure of Nightingale, and the promotion of a couple of slim, silly thirteen-year-olds to the bottom of the rank. Her questions centered around when any new music would be ready, and could she have a few lower students to provide music as she worked her dancers?

They all plunged into new music and old stories, melding the two, as the following days passed. At the week mark, the not-unexpected summons to the dragon throne arrived, and this time Granny Zim was prepared.

By now the chiefs had agreed that when any of them were summoned, rehearsals at the upper levels would halt for the interim as they waited to find out if there would be further orders. It was both exciting and unnerving to be in at the birth of what felt like a new era of music.

The senior music students were dismissed to return to the north side and their regular studies, the players were given a free afternoon, and the dancers were swept off by their chief to work on combinations as a Merit graywing tapped out a rhythm on a drum.

The graywings had been apprised of the schedule change, as always, which meant what one knew, they all knew. That included graywings from other imperial pavilions. Thus, it was not an hour before a graywing from the imperial side appeared: "Student YinYin is summoned to Tranquil Rivers Pavilion, for an interview with his imperial highness, Thirteenth Prince Rathjin."

YinYin, for whom proximate walls were mostly a theoretical boundary, heard the summons spoken at the gate to Merit, and so was there at Granny Zim's little chamber when a page brought the summons.

"I will come," YinYin said.

By now YinYin was quite practiced at the complicated steps of human activities such as opening doors, stepping over the threshold and going through, closing the doors, then walking along pathways, among all the other aspects of mimicking human life.

Even so, it was a new thing for YinYin to take a human interview without company in Granny Zim or Bu.

It was also a new thing for Thirteenth Imperial Prince Rathjin to summon anyone. He had never done so before. He did not socialize, except when others visited him, usually his mother, or Lir, TanTan, and Rathlan. Rathvo had once entertained himself by tormenting Jin, until he was forbidden to go near him unless he was under the imperial eye. Jin had understood at a young age that he was not only powerless, but even those who sympathized with him most didn't believe a word he said. Thus he sent the summons without knowing if he would actually be obeyed.

Jin did not have a bodyguard, as he never left his pavilion. Guarding him was part of the general round of patrols. The passing patrol saw the student go in with the page, and would see the student come out with the page.

He was gratified when the demon that walked in the shape of a teenaged girl entered behind the page, who bowed. Then YinYin bowed.

Jin had planned very carefully, in case the summons actually worked. He pointed behind him to a zither that Rathlan had left behind a year or two ago, and said to the page, "I wish to commission a piece of music for the emperor's birthday. Graywing Seven will attend me. You may wait outside until this music student is finished consulting with me."

The page bowed and withdrew. Graywing Seven, who was used to Jin's ways, said softly, "Does his imperial highness require this one's service?"

"I do not."

"This servant will fetch refreshments." And Graywing Seven left.

Jin had no social chitchat. Alone now with YinYin, he said, "One of your kind infested my Second Brother."

YinYin considered. Silence reigned, as Jin picked up his pen, bent over one of his folded birds, and began stippling the throat of a rainbow pheasant.

"Yes," YinYin said presently—with no honorifics, as no one was there to model them.

But Jin paid no attention to honorifics, which were empty language to him. He was surprised at the depth of the relief he felt at YinYin's admission. "No living person believes me. But Elder Brother gave me to understand that Second Brother was loyal and true until the demon infested him. And caused his death. Though they say it was a poison that rotted him from the inside."

"Yes," said YinYin.

Jin gathered his courage, and admitted to his greatest fear. "I need to know if it is waiting to get me."

"There is no demon here," YinYin replied. "Except me. Some…you might say they are small, were here. I ate them."

"Do you know where that one is? Is there a way to get rid of it?"

YinYin fell silent again, and once more Jin began his meticulous painting. A fingernail's worth of carefully render- ed golden feathers later, YinYin said, "That one is at a distance that I am not strong enough to reach. If it comes, I will try to eat it. It will try to eat me, because that one eats the Essence of souls."

Jin's forehead puckered. "I thought that happened to evil people, that they attracted evil demons. First Brother did not believe that Second Brother wanted to rule. Or that he was his enemy."

YinYin had read enough by now, and listened to Bu and Granny Zim enough, to hazard a guess at the complexity of human emotions that prompted this observation. "It might be that your Second Brother ardently wished to be more like First Brother. So ardently that the demon held out the promise of being more alike, and Second Brother accepted a part of this demon."

"A…part?"

YinYin said, "One time, Student Lum Bu wished to see as other humans see. I put a little part of me into her so she could see. Then she did not want that part, and so I took it out again. But that demon put a part in the one you call Second Brother, and it ate his Essence in order to grow."

"Do you do that?" Jin asked, afraid again.

"No. I eat the Essence of emotion brought forth by music, and I use that Essence to infuse more music, which causes more emotion," YinYin said—repeating the same words spoken once to Granny Zim, for the two of them talked about such matters.

And Jin nodded slowly. "I think I understand. I think I do."

YinYin said, "You asked me to make you a music. I will make you a music."

Jin smiled at that, and YinYin noticed with utter dispassion that he was beautiful for a human, in the same way that Bu was beautiful. It was a beauty that had little to do with the arrangement of outer features, which were to YinYin as lines of bark on a tree. It was the clarity of their Essence, suffused with joy in their art. YinYin often contemplated the power of art.

"I would like that very much," Jin said.

YinYin pointed. "Why all these paper birds?"

"Because birds are nature's purest art, and so free, and I want them as friends, but a bird in a house is in prison. So I make these. For live friends, I have the cats."

"I see the cats," YinYin said. "They can come and go."

"Yes," Jin said, and YinYin reflected that the only one in a prison was this prince, but he did not seem to regret it.

Graywing Seven appeared at the door, bearing a tray of fresh tea and a pile of pastries.

"Student YinYin is going to leave," the imperial prince said.

Graywing Seven set the tray down, knowing that Jin would demolish tea and pastries, and went to summon the page.

The page entered, bowed, and YinYin bowed, then scrupulously followed the page out, as Jin turned to the ghost scintillating in the shaft of light slanting through the window. "First Brother, you were very right," he said. "Second Brother never betrayed you, just as you said." And, after a time, "But you must see him free before you can go to the moons' bridge? I understand, I understand, I would feel the same about TanTan and Lir."

Graywing Seven, tidying in the background, gave a sigh, pitying the gentle, mad prince. At least he seemed contented with his imaginary life — which was more than you could say about a lot of people in the real world, he observed later to his fellow servants in the kitchen.

THIRTY-SIX

"ELDER BROTHER WAS RIGHT," Lir signed as well as he spoke the next afternoon, following their gathering with Master Angka in the schoolroom. "Barbarians again."

TanTan had guessed that finance would follow the general definition of barbarian versus civilization, and had delved into the trunk for scrolls outlining the laws concerning gold, copper, and bronze coinage, and their history. Rathlan was interested in anything to do with people, and had blithely described the *old* definition of barbarian: islands whose people traded purely in barter, which was possible when everyone was known to one another.

TanTan scribbled that coinage was a sign of civilization, because of the implied trust in all aspects of the exchange, which results in peaceful trade. And that was the essence of Kanda's teachings.

"What does that tell us about the Jun Suai, who do not trade in coins?" Master Angka asked, after looking from TanTan's hasty scrawl to the emphatic signs he made, most of which the other two translated in single words or phrases.

TanTan scribbled madly.

Lir was not about to get caught in the "barbarian" trap again. "Esteemed Master Angka." Clasped hands and a slight bow. "My brother Rathtan points out that, according to the historian Mei Ne, they have a very complicated system of trade, built upon the idea that the man on the horse protects the farmer in the field, and so a certain amount of rice donated a year to the rider obligates the rider to keep thieves at bay, and to fight invaders. That rider has to offer a portion of what he collects to his chief, and so on up to the banner commander, and the banner commanders owe to the king. It is a system, according to Mei Ne, built upon defense, not trade, though there is trade between villages and towns. Mostly with us."

Master Angka noted that the fourteenth prince got all that out of the words *trade=horse=farmer=field Mei Ne defense system.* Which argued that Lir was not nearly as ignorant as he seemed to want to appear.

TanTan clasped his hands, ducked his chin in a nod, then tapped a scroll on his desk.

Master Angka bowed back. "Very well, your imperial highnesses, very well. That will do for a start," he said to them both, and they went on to discuss Kanda's words about civilized exchange, which had been taken further by various emperors since then, as well as writers like Mei Ne. Then he let them go.

The following day was as successful, but when the three of them met in their private dining area afterward, Lir was frowning.

TanTan smacked the back of his fingers in his palm and looked a question. Rathlan sighed. "What is it now, Lir?"

"The first day, we skipped past rites. Yesterday, Master Angka pushed us into the Ministry of Revenue. Today the barbarians lasted only long enough to set up a comparison, but we got into the Ministry of Works. It seems to me that 'reviewing the old to learn the new' is a merely a threat, and he has a different intent."

"I'll be happy if you're right," Rathlan said, tapping her heart and miming writing for TanTan, then making the sign for Kanda, with a shake of the head. "I really don't want to be copying out the Twenty-Five over and over. I still dream about the tedium."

"I don't think it's going to happen unless we turn up asleep. Instead, I suspect the intent is to push us into delving into the imperial court's Six Departments, and all their ministries."

TanTan shrugged, flashing two and five fingers, and lifting his palm toward the ceiling in their "better" sign: better than copying the Twenty-Five.

Rathlan eyed Lir in sudden distrust. "You do remember that this study was imperial uncle's own edict. Are you going to refuse to work the way you did when we were little, just because the emperor might be planning to put you in some department at the ninth rank for a year or two, once we return?"

"To refuse would be unfilial. Which is a true act of barbarity," Lir said, hands out. "No, no, no, it's just that studying court was so pointless when we were small, and Elder Brother Vo — and his mother — kept claiming he was going to be the Crown Prince. And Vo promised that unless we obeyed him we'd all be exiled to tiny islands to rule over two villages and their cows as soon as he inherited the dragon throne. Why study? We would never use it."

"If we didn't die before then," Rathlan interpreted TanTan's emphatic slapping of his hand to his chest in agreement.

Lir dropped his fan and rubbed his forehead. "I still wonder what exactly got Vo put on that ship separate from us. If Ginger hadn't seen, I wouldn't believe he or his mother are truly gone. Our biggest threat in our entire lives, just...one morning gone. Like that." He clapped his hands. "I wish I knew why."

They were used to not being told what the emperor did not want discussed. Ginger, and to a small extent the page Mayfly, had been their mail method of finding out what they could. They knew their limitations — even pages could not go everywhere — but if Ginger saw it, it had happened.

Lir waved his fan dismissively. "That aside. I've no objection to filial obedience, which means following Master Angka's lead on this journey, and then afterward, toiling as an under-scribe for a time. Might be interesting, for a time, now that Vo is gone. If he's gone. I just don't want to sit here in the hot weather reading scrolls we had to read over and over ten years ago."

Rathlan said wryly, "Very well for you who remembers every word you've read. I don't. Of course I don't need any of it, either, since I won't even be an under-scribe on our return."

"I don't remember every word I read," Lir said. "That's Jin. But I do remember the gist."

TanTan tapped them both on the arm, slapped his hands together, and mimed that the scrolls in that trunk were all new to them.

Lir smacked his chest and whirled his fingers as he spoke: "I consider all *new* scrolls to be a sign of possible faith in us, in which case I'm willing to be as filial as Imperial Father wants."

"Then we'll continue as we are?" Rathlan said, a hand moving between the three of them, then turning over in question.

TanTan signed agreement.

Lir found it easy to make a little effort, but that left all the rest of the day lying heavily on his hands while he was stuck on a floating box in the middle of the ocean.

He invaded both the guards' and the sailors' berths in an attempt to organize some gambling games, but their captains were abject in their apologies, saying that they had received strict orders about no gambling on this pilgrimage to Kanda's island—nothing could be more inauspicious.

He tried running the perimeter of the ship with TanTan, but that became tedious very fast. He rammed around like a gourd kicked from rail to rail until Sanhu said toward the end of the week, "If your imperial highness wishes, you might consider joining the imperial guards' martial arts drills."

This was not the first time someone or other had attempted to get Lir into martial arts training. He opened his mouth to refuse, but Rathlan said, "Do. Would it not be preferable to plunging around like a goat caught in a pen with a fox?"

"I hate martial exercise," he said as soon as Sano trotted off to join the other imperial guards.

"You hated it because when Ratha did it with you, you were bored, and when Vo did it, you always ended up hurt."

Lir scowled, recollecting the utter tedium of performing lunges and squats over and over. It had been no better when well-meaning Imperial Fourth Brother Ratha tried to demonstrate the purpose. Slow and heavy, he had not been convincing—Lir's attention had gone to the imperial guard who even more slowly tried not to hit Fourth Imperial Brother.

"It's something for you to do," Rathlan said. "There doesn't seem to be anything else while we are at sea. Unless you're going to spend weeks playing pitch pot and Circle."

Lir sighed, glancing toward the upper area of the superstructure where their bedchambers lay. He didn't mind playing endless games of Circle with TanTan, because there was an infinite variety of strategies as well as intriguing mathematical indicators related to common and uncommon moves. Except TanTan had apparently decided he had to read every scroll in that trunk.

The next morning early, Lir dressed in the loose tunic and trousers that were customary for the princes to wear during exercises and came down with TanTan, who began running the ship's perimeter. The guards watched out of the sides of their eyes as the youngest imperial prince approached them, determination furrowing his broad forehead.

Those whose first encounter with him had been on this ship still didn't quite know what to make of the Weasel after these first few days. Like a weasel, he poked his nose everywhere, but as someone said, a prince *could* go anywhere. After Phoenix fourth hour gong rang, he could be heard up in the schoolroom arguing with Master Angka, who argued back, sometimes with laughter. There were no orders handed out, no recriminations either, even when Master Angka was heard to howl with pretend anguish, "Ayah, a turtle would give me a better answer! Faster, too!"

Now here he was at drill time.

Lir bypassed the front row, and went to the back and stood beside Brick.

Sanhu approached Lir, and bowed. "Your imperial highness, your place is first rank."

"*You* know how long it's been since I did anything at the practice court. I'm staying back here so I can see what to do. Carry on!"

Sanhu saluted, returned to his spot, nodded at the orderlies waiting at the big drums midway along each rail, and *boom!*

Thump!

The imperial guards, did a right leg squat-and sweep with the wooden practice swords. Boom! Left leg squat and sweep. Boom! And so on, as the sun climbed higher, radiating summer heat through low, patchy clouds.

Up on the balcony, Ginger brought an umbrella to the grand princess as the first spats of rain fell.

Rathlan waved it off. "If it doesn't rain harder than this, it will feel good. I hate being hot. How can they bear it? If I ask they'll say it's proof men are stronger."

Ginger knew when she could speak up and when it was prudent to assume the silent demeanor of the servant. Right now, her princess wanted company, so she said, "Your highness, they haven't been down at the laundry, watching those women dealing with sheets, which are heavier than stone when wet, and the room is filled with steam."

Rathlan smirked. "The elder princesses say that men faint if they even see childbirth. They'd never survive doing it."

The two looked down at the laboring men with tolerant scorn, and then both turned toward Lir in the back. His face was already crimson as they did squats. They could barely hear him keeping up a running commentary aimed at Brick, punctuated by grunts and "Ow!"s. The guards maintained their usual silence—and of course said nothing about the prince breaking that silence with every breath.

Rathlan eyed Brick's broad shoulders tapered to a narrow waist, and how his sweat-damp clothes clung to sleek muscles. How could someone that well-made be so very clumsy, always a heartbeat late? It was almost as if he tried to be clumsy, it was so consistent.

She turned to Ginger. "Does Brick talk to you yet?"

"No, your highness," Ginger replied with regret. It was rare that she failed to get some response out of anyone.

"He can't be as slow as they say," Rathlan observed.

"He might be like their imperial highnesses," Ginger replied.

Rathlan said, "True. Jin won't speak unless he has something to say, and TanTan can't speak. But neither of them is slow. Lir keeps insisting that Jin is the smartest of all, but he lives more in the unseen world than this one."

And he might not be sure which world he was in at any given time, Ginger was thinking. Nor did he seem to care unduly. All his servants loved him because he was easy, and kind if he noticed you, and they were used to his talking to the air. Some disapproved, saying it was inauspicious—sure to draw the notice of evil—but his servants had taken care of that by bringing in extra charms to ward evil, and hanging them everywhere.

Rathlan was not thinking about Jin, who had been familiar since babyhood. "I find Brick intriguing just because he's so determinedly boring. He doesn't even try to talk to Lir when Lir coaxes and teases like that." *And he's handsome.* But she could not say that. Though Ginger kept most of Rathlan's confessions to herself, Rathlan knew that Ginger was required to give regular reports to whoever asked. While no one would care about scamped lessons, or coins wasted in frivolous ways, anything having to do with men—even something as useless as admiring a brainless guard—would be reason for alarm, especially with Rathlan's mother. She did not want Ginger to have to be put in that position, which would ruin the easy communication between them, so she kept her thoughts to herself about Brick and his phoenix eyes.

She put her chin on her hand, and when the sun peeped out, glaring with unwanted warmth, she reached for the umbrella Ginger still held. "Now I need shade. Look. Lir still hasn't quit. I think he's going to get stubborn."

Ginger thought so, too. She remembered Fourteenth Imperial Prince Rathlir's sporadic ventures into specific martial arts, like archery, and how he'd work at it until he could do it, then he'd promptly lose interest. The last effort had been to catch up with Twelfth Imperial Prince Rathtan, who ran to the imperial practice court every morning, shot arrows for an hour or so, then ran back. The two brothers had shot together, Princess Rathlan watching them often, until Imperial Prince Rathlir could hit the target as consistently as TanTan, then he lost interest. As usual.

A gong crashed Phoenix fourth hour — it was time for the watch change, and for the imperials to go up to the schoolroom.

Lir appeared, groaning with every step, and joined Rathlan, as Ginger bowed herself away: she knew without being told that they were going to want tea in the schoolroom, and ran to fetch it.

Rathlan smothered a grin as Lir joined her.

"I look that bad, eh?" he asked.

"You look like a drunk who just discovered that one of his legs turned into an extra arm."

"That's right, destroy what little face I have left," Lir said, shutting his eyes.

"You haven't any face," she retorted cheerfully. "What's more, you never cared. Are you going to do the sparring?"

"They'd kill me." He groaned. "Just in time for Master Angka to kill me metaphorically."

They went off to discuss the political scene among the early emperors, and the evolution of the Censors under the Chancellery.

They were well prepared about the court corruption and the island strife of those days, which pleased Master Angka mightily — and so he said in a report that flew off by pigeon toward Azure Tranquility Island, where the fleet would stop to resupply in a few days. The message would be sent to the imperial island from there.

The following morning, Lir implored TanTan to suffer alongside him. What could she do?

She caught the sound of a flute running up the chromatic scale. Ah, there were always the musicians. Especially that handsome one, Xia Chi. He was another she liked looking at, though he wasn't as handsome as Brick. He had something of Rathjin's calm, without the inauspicious talk about ghosts.

She found the sound emanating from the tiny storage room off the schoolroom, where Bu and Xia Chi had retired to sit among the boxes and baskets, once the deck had become too crowded.

"What are you two doing in *here?*" she asked, as the music students scrambled to their feet and bowed. "Why aren't you in the schoolroom?"

"This ignorant student understood that the schoolroom was reserved to their imperial highnesses," Xia Chi said apologetically.

"Ayah! *I* say that you can be in there any time you want. In fact, I wish you were in there playing for us during study time," she added under her breath. "I had the servants stow your musical instruments there in particular so you could practice. See? Those extra cushions are for you two."

"But those are silk cushions, your highness," Bu said softly.

"They're just cushions," Rathlan said, laughing. Then her smile vanished. "Oh, I know there are those at home who care about such things, but I can promise you that none of the three of us do. As for the cushions, I am very sure they do not notice whose backside meets them. Come out, come out!"

The two exchanged glances, bowed, and obeyed very willingly, for the closet was stuffy, smelled strongly, and had terrible acoustics.

"Go ahead," the grand princess commanded. "Begin where I interrupted. I want to see how you finger."

They moved out into the schoolroom, and Rathlan sank down on a cushion in a welter of silk and ribbons. She put her chin on her fists, closely watching Bu's and then Xia Chi's methods of pluck and strum, the sound wreathing through the somnolent summer air.

When they finished the warmup exercise, Rathlan said, "That is much more complicated than anything I ever was taught."

"If your highness pleases, these are exercises brought by Chief Zim," Xia Chi said.

"Yes, and I want you to teach me," Rathlan declared. "I want to learn—at least until my imperial cousins stop playing around with the imperial guards."

Bu found her emotions divided between the desire to help, and her longing to spend her time immersed in these challenging new lessons. Then she mentally scolded herself; she was here to serve. She bowed and said, "As your highness desires. We would have to begin with the fundamentals."

"Mmmm… that would take years, and they are so tedious! Just teach me a song. Let's have music with the three of us, and you can correct my fingering as much as you please while we play an actual song. I'll play the zither." Rathlan paused, then smiled brightly. "It sounds like they are done on the deck at last. Tomorrow, then!"

They rose and bowed as she ran out.

Bu turned to Xia Chi. "What should we do?"

"I think we ought to—" Xia Chi broke off when Master Angka walked in, and checked. "Do I disturb you?" he asked politely.

"No, no, it is we who trespass," Bu said quickly, as Xia Chi bowed, and added, "Her highness desired to practice with us, and gave us leave to use this chamber. However, we would not dare to presume—"

Master Angka threw up his hands in protest. "Stay! Please stay. I heard you—I was not far, and the windows are all propped open. We are after all in a very limited space, and we must all share, just as we do in the dining area."

The three bowed to one another, uttering mutual thanks, and the two sat back down to resume the interrupted lesson, as Master Angka located his lesson ledger, and walked out again.

THIRTY-SEVEN

"OUR HEROES ARE IN place. Our villains as well, even if we haven't seen them all yet," the storyteller said, glancing wistfully at the tip bowl. "It is nearly time for everything to change."

"Finally," muttered the young master. "I was promised battles. Where are the battles?"

"Where is the romance?" one sister sighed to the other sister.

The elderly woman did not like Granny Zim left behind. Would she be forgotten, as the old usually are?

No coins rang in the tip bowl.

The storyteller gave up hinting, and resumed the tale, "Once again it was easy to lose track of the days…"

As they sailed on, sometimes it seemed to Bu that they never moved. It was the world that slowly moved around them, distant bumps of islands sliding past, and overhead, the sun rising and then sinking, and after that, the night sky beginning its slow wheel, the two moons reflecting the sun's arc as they revolved away from each other.

The evening before this peaceful rhythm broke, Bu's stomach growled at the savory smell wafting into the lower deck chamber that had been made over to the staff for their meals. Ginger and a kitchen orderly each hefted a bamboo basket in which buns had been steamed. They separated, pulling the tops off the baskets so that people on either side of the table could spear a bun with their eating sticks. No serving platters for servants aboard this ship, which took Bu back to her austere temple days.

She stabbed a bun and added it to her rice and pepper fish, aware of sublime contentment. She was so grateful to be happy. Every day was spent immersed in music; the grand princess's lessons were easy, as she merely wanted to be coached in new songs, and she did not take up the entire day after all. An hour or two at music seemed a natural length of time for a princess whose life so far had been filled with many sorts of lessons of an hour or so apiece, between the ritual visits to various relations.

Bu was grateful that most of her day was spent with Xia Chi, working together on Granny Zim's lessons. Their evenings were devoted entirely to music, which flowed from Bu in her happiness, stirring everyone within hearing; she and Xia Chi had begun sitting on the balcony outside the schoolroom to play once they finished their lessons.

She kept her emotions, as always, to herself. Through listening to the dormitory sisters, and reading of storybooks, Bu had learned so much about romantic love in its many stages. What else could this sense of warmth within be when she heard the sound of Xia Chi's breathing, or felt the warmth of his fingers lingering on a calligraphy brush after he put it in the holder? She understood it now, how all her senses fired at the tiniest touch, scent, sound. She had never expected someone like her would experience even a sliver of romance. Or maybe only the silliest kind — limerence, so the poets named it, as ephemeral as wisps of fog, or the drift of birds overhead.

There was no sign of him feeling the same way. And why would he? She was the Squint, low-born, and he the very opposite. That didn't mean she couldn't enjoy it, secretly wishing this journey would never end.

But it would end. She must impress on her mind as many memories as she could.

As she ate her meal, Bu looked around at the company sitting elbow to elbow as they bowed, beaming, in offering toasts with the first sip of tea, or the tiny cups of rice wine. Bu treasured the elaborate manners, which she understood as careful effort to respect one another's face. It was so important in such close proximity.

At the head of the table sat the aging, long-eared graywing

in charge, known merely as Two, as he was secondary to the imperial graywing chief, first under the emperor himself. Two was austere, precise, but fair in his dealings with the lower staff. Master Angka, at his right, adapted cheerfully to his company. He and Xia Chi—and occasionally Two—were fond of ancient poetry, the older the better. When conversation at meals faltered, they sometimes entertained the staff with quotations.

There was no vestige of romance in the larger dining room above the deck, the windows pushed open their widest to catch what breeze existed. The three imperials abandoned fans and manners, shoving aside the fine serving dishes so that they could spread out scrolls as they tried to guess what Master Angka would throw at them next.

Imperial Works? The Justice Department?

For them, too, the days had begun to slide by uncounted, stitched together by those evening concerts. Sometimes Rathlan played with Bu and Xia Chi, but most of the time she preferred to listen, aware that the two musicians' expertise far outstripped hers. And TanTan, who heard nothing, appreciated the companionable mood that bestowed on him uninterrupted reading time. Oh, that things would stay just like this!

The next morning, the imperial princes tumbled out of bed and onto the foredeck, to discover it empty, save for more sailors than usual. The sun had barely cleared the horizon, but the morning was already blazing hot. TanTan whapped Lir and palmed a question, pointing at the sun: the imperial guards would not be let off their martial arts because of heat? No—it was just as hot yesterday, and the day before, Lir signed back.

Graywing Four scudded down the steps and approached breathlessly, round face shining and damp. "Fleet Master Naoki bids your imperial highnesses a good morning, and requests the honor of your presence at the command center. Where he says you will have the best view."

"Of?" Lir asked.

Graywing Four bowed as he signed, "Your imperial highnesses, this servant knows nothing beyond this request."

TanTan made the brushing motion that exonerated the servant and started up the steps, Lir following. Before they reached the command center, the big drums boomed twice: summons.

With a roar of booted feet and a clatter of weapons,

imperial guards jogged out onto the foredeck below, wearing full armor. They were not carrying wooden swords, but sharp weapons. Also, only half the number was present. The colonel stood at the prow, the others ranged along the rail, facing outward, weapons at the ready.

Up in the command center, Fleet Master Naoki bowed. "Your imperial highnesses, his imperial majesty has honored me with instructions to explain any aspects of the pending exercise, about which your imperial highnesses might have questions."

"Exercise?" Lir repeated—he and TanTan didn't even have a sign for that. The closest he could come was 'military ruse' but that seemed entirely wrong.

"If your imperial highnesses will condescend to grace the southwest with your imperial highnesses' attention, this humble servant believes much will presently become clear."

Master Angka appeared in the doorway then, and after everyone had saluted and bowed to the proper degree, rearranging themselves in the small space so that the two princes had the best view of the sea, Master Angka said to Lir, while using some of the signs he'd picked up over the past days (emperor—edict—master—explain), "His imperial majesty passed an edict to this talentless master to attempt to elucidate certain aspects of what is to come."

Little of that was comprehensible to TanTan, but he was used to haphazard, often belated, and always incomplete communication. He shifted his attention to the ship, which was clearly in readiness for…something. All attention swiveled to the southwest. Five dots broke the serene line of the horizon. TanTan blinked against the dazzle of sunlight spangling the water as those dots resolved into ships.

"Conceal!" roared the colonel.

With a clash and a clatter, the imperial guards dropped to one knee below the rail, as Fleet Master Naoki said, "We are about to be raided by pirates, your imperial highnesses. Or, so they believe." His voice had sharpened, his attention everywhere; Lir appreciated the lessening of the formal language.

To TanTan, Lir signed: "Pirate attack." Then he said to the fleet master, "You expected them? And the guards are hiding…"

"As an extra layer of defense, though the pirates are not to see them. Not to think we are aware at all. Since we are the target, your imperial highnesses, we are using that to our advantage," Fleet Master Naoki replied. "Using a variation on —"

" — the empty fort ruse? One of the twenty-five strategies," Lir said, pleased he remembered that much. Then he turned to Master Angka. "You knew about this? Or did they wake you up during the night?"

Master Angka bowed in the manner he used before teaching, or explaining, and Lir stopped his flow of questions as Master Angka stated, "His imperial majesty honored this lowly master with an edict before we set out."

Lir was completely taken aback, and struggled to explain this to TanTan, as on the sea, the five ships approached, first details of sails emerging from the haze, then the jumble along the rails resolved into pirates brandishing weapons.

When the five ships began to spread out, their intent apparently to surround the tower ship, it seemed to Lir that from both sides behind their ship a squadron of naval ships appeared out of nowhere.

"Where did these come from?" Lir asked, as TanTan pointed, eyes wide.

"They have remained beyond the horizon, your imperial highness, from the perspective of the pirates. Our scouts have been marking them for the past six days." A grim sort of satisfaction tightened the fleet master's voice. "We knew — that is, we were warned to expect an attack, but we did not know where they hid. Or when they would try their raid. But as it is well known that imperial ships bound southward traditional resupply at Azure Tranquility, we expected that this attack would commence in this area. Our scouts sighted them six days ago, and we arranged ourselves accordingly."

The Fleet Master divided his attention between the princes and his ships and men, as the pirates and the defenders drew inexorably toward one another.

Lir watched, fascinated; the ships were all so grand and moved so slowly. There was a sense of inevitability to it all.

TanTan's eyes moved constantly, taking it all in; he signed, "Imperial Father knew." Lir repeated it aloud.

Master Angka bowed. "His imperial majesty did indeed." Then, "At his imperial majesty's specific behest, we will not abandon our studies today, but commence at present. Will your imperial highnesses honor this master by naming Kanda's five virtues?"

Lir bit back the impulse to squawk, *Kanda? Now?* There

was far too much a sense of forethought here. He imagined Imperial Father sitting on the dragon throne at his moment, his eyes narrowed with that look he got when he was about to hand down an edict.

"Benevolence. Righteousness. Propriety. Wisdom. Trust," he said, as out on the water, the pirates became aware that, as they were attempting to flank the imperial warship with its enormous dragon banner, they were now being flanked by low, fast-moving spear ships, two warships at either extremity, and patrol boats as escorts to the spear ships.

"What is propriety, your imperial highness?" Master Angka addressed Lir, his gaze absolutely serious.

Bewildered, full of questions, Lir repeated the signs they'd made up as boys when dealing with these lessons, and TanTan's hands stiffened, fingers slapping in emphasis as Lir said, "Propriety is manifested in respect toward elders. Which includes Imperial Father." Here both boys clasped their hands toward the northeast—as both the Fleet Master and Master Angka bowed in that direction. Lir continued, "He, in turn respects his people. Ah, which is all reflected in ritual and etiquette."

"Excellent answer, your imperial highness," Master Angka said.

One pirate was jerking their sails around in order to sail into the wind to escape, which was a weak move: the pirates had begun with the wind at their backs, so maneuvering lessened their speed.

"Benevolence, your imperial highnesses?"

Benevolence seemed an odd choice now, as arrows glinted in the sun between spear ship, attendant small ships, and the pirate. Two fireballs arced toward the pirate—which launched its own deadly fireballs.

Lir swallowed in a dry throat; he knew now this situation was not a lesson so much as some kind of test. "All moral humans feel compassion for the suffering of other humans and animals, Kanda writes. He states that this is a manifestation of benevolence."

"If this lowly master might invite his imperial highness to honor us with elucidation…"

It was almost like a play, except the smoke drifting over the water made it seem real.

"In that regard, it is said in the *Conversations*, that every person has some things that he would be ashamed to do. Or some forms of treatment he would disdain to accept." He imagined Rathlan echoing, "Or she"—but it seemed she had not been invited for this lesson. "And these are expressions of righteousness."

TanTan had signed along, adding three fingers held up: that made three.

On the water, the first pirate was now on fire, but the spear ship hit it with more fireballs catapulted over. The warship sailed on, the battle clearer. Closer. Human shapes could be made out, first trying to lower a boat, until a fireball smashed it. Then pirates tried jumping overboard—as the patrol boat mariners shot them with arrows, one by one.

This 'exercise' was no mere drill.

"Your imperial highness?" Master Angka prompted.

Lir made an effort to collect his thoughts, for he was trying to find out what prompted his father to make this act of war into a lesson. He clasped his fingers behind his back—fingers that he discovered had become sweaty—as he brought up memory of those arduous long ago classes so pompous, the words almost without meaning to bored boys. But as Lir watched the organized destruction being carried out before his eyes, the old words took on new meaning: "The ruler must extend those instincts outward, Kanda said. The prince who rescues an abandoned dog values all life, and grows to become a king who works to limit war."

War like that happening at this moment on the water? Two pirates were now completely on fire. No, make that three, as two tried to run downwind.

"War." He swallowed. "Which makes people suffer. Wisdom is knowing when to make decisions that affect the lives of so many."

One of the outer warships closed in on a fleeting pirate, and more fireballs arced. Away to the south, the first pirate ship had nearly burned to the water line, as patrol boats closed around it.

"And last, your imperial highnesses?" Master Angka prompted.

TanTan smacked Lir, who signed the words *war—wisdom—decisions—lives.*

TanTan thumped his fist against his chest, and Lir said, "Trust." Another dry swallow; now he could smell the smoke. "Kanda states that three things are needed for government: weapons, sustenance, and trust."

A cough, as TanTan made the sign for Vo.

But Lir had already put that together. The intent of this lesson was not just to demonstrate the reach of imperial power, its subject was Vo. Who had betrayed their trust time and again. Not just theirs.

He'd betrayed Imperial Father's trust.

Lir straightened his back. "If a ruler can't hold on to all three, he should give up the weapons first and the food next. Trust must be guarded to the end: without trust there is no civilization, and without civilization there can be no harmony."

Out on the ocean, all five pirate ships burned. "I hope," Master Angka observed, as Fleet Master Naoki muttered some orders to waiting aides, "the king of the underworld will warn them to choose something other than piracy in their next life."

Lir said, low-voiced, "This has to do with Eleventh Imperial Brother. Doesn't it?"

TanTan pointed to the burning ships, then to each of them, and smacked his hand flat toward the floor: dead.

Master Angka bowed in assent. "If your imperial highnesses will honor this master with their attention for one more question: What is the first lesson Kanda teaches us?"

"Filial piety," Lir stated without a heartbeat's hesitation. Vo had always paid lip service to filial piety. He even seemed to care about Imperial Father, much as Lir was reluctant to grant his tormenting snake of a brother that much.

But those five burning ships out there, as the navy went about exterminating every one of those aboard, argued for taking every aspect of this day's lessons with vital seriousness.

Master Angka said with slow deliberation, "The family is the first society that a child encounters. Kanda teaches us that relating to other members of the family is the initial political life. Accordingly, family loyalty is the basis for learning how to interact with other people generally. When there is no family loyalty, no true filial piety, that is the fault of the elders. If their words, their lives, give way to the rot of evil, then that rot cannot be anything but extirpated."

Fleet Master Naoki raised a hand. The drummers thumped the drums three times, then three times more.

Imperial Guard Colonel Deg roared, "Stand down!"

The guards leaped to their feet, and at a wave from the colonel, withdrew in order, vanishing below to store their weapons and armor. The pirates were gone, their ships sinking below the waves one by one.

Master Angka let out a slow breath, then said, "I believe that will do for today, your imperial highnesses."

The princes became aware then of the intense heat. Hunger. Thirst. It was past noon — time had sped by, though it had seemed slow. They withdrew to their spacious dining chamber, where food awaited them, along with Grand Princess Rathlan.

"Well?" she snapped.

"Kanda," Lir replied. And when her eyebrows shot upward, he and TanTan both outlined the morning, each in his own way. "Filial piety," Lir said at the end. "I guess that is aimed at us. I realize Imperial Father thinks of us as overgrown brats, but we've never been *unfilial.*"

Rathlan shook her head slowly.

TanTan had been scowling, and now he made the sign for the hated Consort Rajai. Then wiggled his fingers for family.

"Rot and evil," Rathlan said. "All that about kings, and consequences. I think I know what happened: Vo tried to get out of coming along. I remember that much. Faked being sick the night of *The Swan Fan.* He'd hired assassins, everybody said, at the pleasure house."

"They were there. I saw them," Lir stated.

"What I'm saying is, he must have been planning another try. Against this ship, with us on it. Which is why he isn't with us. It all adds together — he really did get exiled to Ice Fortress, if I'm right."

Lir had also been putting it together. "He could not have organized that on his own. He was always out there in the garden with Consort Rajai. Didn't Ginger say that Vo's nanny was taken to the imperial prison in a yoke?" He made an impatient gesture. "Doesn't matter. What does matter? Master Angka's last speech about rot, it was aimed at us maybe, but it was about Consort Rajai. Or her family. She had to be the one getting assassins and the like for him, through those shady cousins that he prized so much."

Rathlan gasped. "They were exterminated, the entire family? Is that what you think happened?"

They considered the powerful, wealthy, untouchable Kouhan family — risen even higher after the Troubles: two dukes who governed several islands, and three or four cousins midway in the ranks at court.

"Treason is unfilial," Lir said soberly.

THIRTY-EIGHT

WHEN BU ROSE AT dawn, she was so intent on moving quietly without disturbing anyone that she did not notice the ship's routine altering. She went straight to the empty schoolroom, where she fetched out her precious lessons made by Granny Zin—there was no room for these in the tiny closet she shared with Ginger, so perforce she had to keep them up in the schoolroom.

Next she tested the qin strings, and was about to begin her finger exercises when she was startled by the deep boom of the battle drums calling the imperial guards out. As the sound did not repeat, nor was it followed by any other unprecedented noise, she returned to her drill, pausing when Xia Chi joined her. He'd seen the imperial guards armed and crouched along the rail, but years of habit kept him quiet on the subject. If those in command wanted him to know why, they would tell him. Far more pressing was the prospect of another intriguing lesson, bringing him a step closer to the expertise that Bu demonstrated so dazzlingly.

He and Bu greeted one another with grave courtesy, and they were soon immersed in fingering work, followed by new lessons in variations. It wasn't until the pervasive sting of smoke brought the two out of the schoolroom and down below to the midday meal that she and Xia Chi discovered that the ship had been nearly attacked by pirates! It was a startling reminder of the world out there. Isolation was an illusion. But at least they were safe.

The midday meal was late, and entirely taken up among the staff by speculation about where the pirates had come from, and what various people had glimpsed — which was not much, as the servants had been ordered down below.

Afterward, Bu and Xia Chi returned to their music. Bu wrapped herself in its semblance of security, which was highly embroidered by Xia Chi's proximity. She relished how his own musical voice had strengthened through his increasingly assured playing.

Xia Chi did not permit himself to think about anything beyond the music. Or, he tried not to. Sometimes a thought would obtrude: the graceful turn of Student Lum Bu's wrist in its natural artlessness; the clean sweep of her shining hair in that modest style with the single wooden hairpin; the fact that he had long found her face intriguing, expressive, and not at all ugly. Not at all. Though he ought not to have such thoughts, because his parents had arranged his marriage when he was very small, and while a man could have more than one wife, he knew that harem life was only peaceful if the primary madam was extraordinarily wise and kind-hearted. His betrothed was neither. And while he could spend as much time away from the prospective Madam Xia as possible, a secondary wife — especially one with no family to support her — would not have that freedom. As long as he kept such observations to himself, there was no harm, surely?

The two of them said nothing to each other that could not be heard by anyone, but their music had begun to weave together, warp and weft, romantic ardor pervading every note, every melodic variation.

"I thought they were perfect when they first played," Ginger remarked to Graywing Four as they spread imperial laundry in the sun to dry. "But those two keep getting better."

Graywing Four nodded, pointing over the side, to where the afternoon sun winked and glittered off the water. "The poets would say it with more refinement, but they are like *that*. Where the sun dances in the sea."

That night, the fleet master signaled to drop anchor early, as up and down the fleet the mariners and guards alike were granted time to celebrate their triumph over the pirates. There was still a state of alertness, but the seas were clear.

The day following, the prospect of arrival at Azure

Tranquility replaced the pirates as the topic of vital interest. Imperial guards and navy would each get a watch ashore, so there was much intense speculation about who would go first, as well as what they planned to do with their shore leave.

Bu did not dare to presume she would be honored by Xia Chi's company. She had no money to spend anyway. She might take a walk to see the sights, and hear whatever music might drift into the free air, though she would be better off employing herself making strings, she decided.

Grand Princess Rathlan plied her fan as soon as Ginger told her the news, exclaiming, "At last!"

Lir sent Graywing Four up to say that they would like to stay ashore for at least a week.

Ginger was back first. "Your highness, here is what I heard. They have to do a search and sweep before you get to disembark," she told the grand princess. "And arrange inner and outer perimeter guards, if the imperial guards declare it safe. And then, the fleet master has orders from his imperial majesty to set sail as soon as new supplies are aboard and the tide is right."

Rathlan groaned. "How long will that take? And when will we get there? I long to eat something that is not the same ship's food. And above all, to bathe in a proper spring, and not in a disgusting wooden tub."

Ginger was thinking that the servants looked forward to not having to lug pails of hot water up and down the stairs six times a day—clean up and dirty back down—but that was one of those things she prudently never said aloud. "As for when, your imperial highness, I was told the birds are restless, which means we must be nearing the island, though nothing can be seen yet."

Rathlan sighed. "Get out my zither. I might as well go play with the musicians to get through the time. Though if I could ever pluck so ravishingly, people would be begging *me* to play…"

At the foredeck imperial guard martial exercises, Lir took his usual place beside Brick, and chortled, "Did you hear we're going ashore? You'll be with my brother and me, of course."

No response from Brick.

"Really? Nothing to say?" Lir asked as they did squat-and-lunges. "You can't be disappointed. What would you do with nothing to spend? I know you tribute boys don't get wages for a year. With us, at least the food will be excellent. We can even work something out with the outer perimeter, so you and Sanhu can get a real bath."

No reaction.

Lir gave up teasing his bodyguard. Maybe he really didn't understand anything beyond a threat in front of his nose.

The next morning, Ginger was not smiling when she and Graywing Four brought breakfast. "Your imperial highnesses, I was told this morning that the birds all vanished from the roost," she reported.

Lir lifted a shoulder. "Is that a concern? Will it impede our landing at Azure Tranquility?"

Ginger bowed, her voice returning to the soft cadences of humble servitude, which she only resorted to when conveying information she knew they would hate hearing. "This foolish maid understood the fleet master to have said that we cannot land at all, your imperial highness. That is, not yet. It seems a storm is expected, and we are not to be in harbor when it comes."

"Wouldn't the harbor be the safest place?" Grand Princess Rathlan asked. "*I* certainly would prefer to be in a good, sturdy building rather than this boat."

"We've sailed through three storms at least," Lir added. "I don't see why we cannot just put the ship at a pier. No, don't go ask. I will. I don't have much authority, but what little I have maybe can get us in harbor long enough for the three of us to disembark for some inn—anything will do if there's no convenient palace—after which they'd be free to do whatever it is they want to do while the storm lasts."

He considered changing out of his practical practice garment back into his layers of princely silk, then shrugged off the idea. First, the heat was oppressively stunning, and he knew that within a single trip up the stairs to the command center his five layers would have him stewing, and second, the fleet master and the colonel had been seeing him every day dressed in this manner. He did not think that changing would add to his authority: they seemed to have precise orders. Imperial Father had foreseen, and circumvented all attempts at divergence.

That didn't mean he wouldn't try.

He threw down his eating sticks and ran up to the commander center where Fleet Master Naoki was in the midst of issuing a stream of orders for tying everything down. He and the orderly halted, bowing. "Your imperial highness?"

"Can you take us into harbor first?"

"This wretched servant is desolated to inform his imperial highness that his precious self is far safer well out to sea for this kind of storm."

"What kind of storm is that?" Lir asked impatiently, peering up at the sky, which was mostly blue, except for a haze in the west.

"It is a very inauspicious sign when all the seabirds fly off to hide. Including our trained birds, your imperial highness. The storms that follow are always severe. If we had reached harbor, we would be putting out to sea at this moment, along with the other larger ships, lest we are dashed upon the shore by waves that can reach the height of a nine-story pagoda."

Lir's eyes widened. "Can we survive that at all?"

"This untalented sailor wishes to assure his imperial highness that winning sea room is of utmost importance. Wood floats. We will be in for a very uncomfortable time, but if we are surrounded by nothing but water, we shall ride through."

Lir opened his mouth to issue a stream of questions, then recognized that none of them were any more than a demand for more reassurance, when it was not only plain the man had given what assurances he had to give, he was in the midst of trying to ensure their safety.

"Carry on," Lir said, knowing it was ineffective—and that he was merely another interruption. He took himself off, and not long after he repeated this disturbing news to his brother and cousin, the graywing Two appeared himself, and in the most formal language invited the three imperials to step down below the weather deck, where a space had been cleared for them. "It is deemed the safest place on the ship," he finished.

"I want to see this storm, at least," Lir protested, and his steps lagged as he followed the others down to the weather deck. In the time it took to get there, the wind began to rise. He peered seaward. Had the swells gotten larger? Yes, but they were not the height of a nine-roofed pagoda. In his opinion, those swells would scarcely reach the guardian statues on the upturned ends of the lowest roof. Yet the sea's color had deepened, and grayed, though the sky was still blue.

No, it was blue everywhere but in the west, where he perceived a dark line along the horizon that intensified as he blinked at it. It was growing fast.

The first hint of alarm caused him to close the gap behind

TanTan, Two right on his heels, the graywing breathing fast. The hatch slammed behind Two—and then, before Lir reached the deck, the ship lurched violently, flinging him into a bulkhead.

There was no more floor; the lamps had been extinguished. He tumbled around until one hand painfully encountered the ladder. He clung to it, until insistent hands pulled him away. A voice barely reached him above the muffled roar that filled the world, "This way!"

He crept like a worm as the ship rocked and plunged around him. He lost the contents of his stomach, before a sudden shock of cold water dashed in his face, leaving him gasping.

The ship had righted enough for him to follow the tugging hand until he was pushed over a threshold into a dimly lit space: a single lamp careened wildly, bouncing and spinning, the flame throwing wild shadows everywhere. In that uncertain light he spotted his brother, bleeding from the scalp, with Rathlan clinging to him.

"You know what this reminds me of," Rathlan cried presently, over the constant din. "Hiding from Vo."

"You want to talk about him *now*?"

"Better than thinking about this!" Her voice rose shrilly. She was not far from panic.

If talking about Vo would keep her mind occupied, that might work for him as well.

The ship's timbers groaned. Lir thrust his feet against a bulkhead, Rathlan thrown against his back. TanTan braced on the other side, his eyes wide in the swinging, spinning light. "He did seem all-powerful back then, didn't he," Lir shouted.

"He was!" Rathlan shrieked back.

"He made us think he was."

"He had spies among our servants," Rathlan yelled, remembering when Ginger had whispered a warning to her one day, after seeing the laundry maid stealing out early in the morning, and running down to the servants' entrance at Consort Rajai's. "He always knew where we were."

The easier to torment them, always with some excuse to make it seem to be an accident, or their fault, resulting in no real consequences. That was why Vo had seemed all-powerful. Of course his side of any conflict, even when outright lies, was always backed by his mother, but he seldom lied outright, and never anything that could be proved against him. The worst of it was how terribly convincing he had sounded, especially when they were small. Lir remembered thinking that Vo was right, and the emperor did nothing because Vo was the favored one.

"I think…" he shouted.

"What?"

More water seeped through the slats, splashing them. As Rathlan clawed her hair out of her eyes, she shouted again, "What?"

"I think…after that lesson yesterday…that maybe… Imperial Father wanted us to fight back."

"Fight?"

"Not *fight* fight." Lir waved his forefinger about like a sword.

He signed the main words, but TanTan was not watching. He held his sodden sleeve against the cut in his scalp, his profile, briefly glimpsed, then in shadow, was the stolid, enduring one he'd get when Lir and Rathlan spoke too fast and got sloppy with their signs. Or they'd reached a new sort of experience for which they had no signs. That had happened often enough as they all grew; TanTan would then rely on himself to make sense of the world.

But there was no sense now. He could only endure.

Another groan from the ship, more heaves, and Lir splashed to his feet. "Tell him I'm going," he shouted, pointing at TanTan, who glanced up, flat-eyed with endurance in the silent, upended world. Guilt prodded Lir behind the ribs. "I have to see, so I can describe it to him. I'll come back."

"Come back now," Rathlan keened, but Lir knew there was nothing he could do. At least he could try to make sense of how the ship navigated in so terrible a storm. Would that not reassure TanTan? He knew it would reassure *him*.

He sprang to the door, landing against it with hands and feet as the ship slanted. When it tipped the other way, he wrenched the door open, jumped out, and as the ship heeled back, slammed the door against an onrush of water.

Then he lurched to one of the air holes, which fitted like shutters. He opened one, to discover roiling clouds directly overhead—and as purple lightning flared everywhere, he made out what appeared to be water dragons of every sea and sky hue, tendrils around their brow ridges streaming, shattered water flying off them. Was he dreaming? He blinked—and here an enormous veined wave arched overhead. He slammed the wooden shutter to and slid the crossbar just as that water hit the side of the ship with a juddering thud, throwing him against the opposite side of the passage.

Fleet Master Naoki seemed to be right about the wood in the ship keeping them afloat. But would the ship stay together? Everywhere he looked, water seeped, as the timbers creaked. Lir stood, fingers outspread against a bulkhead, feeling the vibration beneath him, as up in command, the fleet master watched the horizon, gauging that vibration beneath his feet. He understood the ship's timbers, having lived most of his fifty years on the sea; the keel was holding, and the rudder. But he sensed something in the higher, shrieking note of the wood.

That was before lightning branched directly overhead—and struck the mainmast.

THIRTY-NINE

FLEET MASTER NAOKI'S MIND raced as the mast toppled slowly: as long as that mast fell to either side, there were still the rest of the masts, each with its counterweight to hold it in position, and its team to fight to keep the sails from being shredded by the tearing wind. These masts still stood, so they were still likely to win through, but he was at all times aware of the emperor's precious cargo in those sons of his, and his imperial sister's girl. Though so far the ship held, he still must prepare for the worst, for if anything happened to the young imperials entrusted to his care by the emperor, every one of his sailors, marines, the imperial guards, and the servants would suffer the consequences.

He turned to the orderly whose single charge was the human chain to be deployed as a last resort from outside the chamber where the imperials were housed, to the bundles of bamboo sticks that made buoyant rafts. "Get in position," he roared.

That was when a towering wave and a flaw in the wind caught the side of the ship as if a giant hand smacked it, and —

Smash! The mast struck squarely atop the superstructure.

Fleet master and aides stared at each other, wits flown for a heartbeat. The wood overhead bulged, and then, one by one, support planks began to snap like firecrackers. "To the deck!" Fleet Master Naoki roared. "Get everyone to the boats!"

In well-rehearsed order, his staff began fighting their way down the swaying stairway, as massive surges of water battered them from both sides, and gouting rain from above.

Naoki made to go last—but as if to remind him of his duty, which he had failed, a huge slab of roof smashed down behind the colonel, whose voice diminished roaring for the boats and to secure the imperials. Naoki was alone now. He could do nothing, as he felt through the soles of his feet his mighty ship beginning to come apart. Water smashed him against a wall, then the cold was gone as quickly as it had come, and here was his father, hand outheld.

Naoki tried to say that he must stay, though he'd failed the emperor, but he had no voice, nor was there pain; below him lay a body much like his, cut through by a great shard of wood, but in front of him, the stars, and his father, smiling, and there was his grandfather as well...

Though his spirit had fled, his command labored on, their last orders jostling against the instinct to survive. Imperial guards ran through the second story, flushing out Master Angka, who had gone back up to cover his precious trunks with more palm leaves wrested from the sailors. He scurried out, nearly colliding with Bu, who at the beginning of the storm had gone to make certain that Granny Zim's precious lessons and her qin—so lovingly made, and still full of music— were securely stowed.

At that first sudden heave, she was thrown against the trunk, where she lay completely overlooked by the frightened, hurried servant assigned to chase strays to safety below. She forced herself to her hands and knees, creeping by painful degree toward the door, and crouched there, trembling, until the snapping wood from somewhere overhead drove her instinctively out onto the balcony.

Here, a guard found her. She glimpsed a wet face, eyes distended. "Out, out, out," he bellowed, as behind him, Master Angka was flung from rail to rail, his arms clutching his beloved scrolls against his chest.

The ship lifted on a wave, then dove down, causing the mast to lift and smash once again, through the to the second level. The great tower ship shuddered all down its length, timbers groaning on a huge swell. The second level gave way, splinters flying into the wind like demon-shot arrows, and the first floor ceiling began to pop and crack. Bu looked helplessly from side to side, for the stairway had bent outward, impossible to use.

That was when the ship rose on a new swell, the rudder fighting against the surge, gradually losing its battle as the ship turned inexorably sideways. Bu clung desperately to the balcony rail, her feet dangling in air. She twisted her head in time to recognize Xia Chi—coming to find her—flung overboard, straight into the sea.

Bu wailed, the sound lost in the roar until the swell crested, and foaming water struck, ripping her from the balcony and hurling her into the water. Arms and legs fought desperately as up above, Lir tumbled down the second stairway, then caught himself against the rail.

Hooking an elbow around a support, he turned, seeking help—and there was Brick, making his way slowly along the gangway, one hand at the wall, the other clutching…a knife?

Lir groaned. Why would anyone have a knife *now?* Was he planning to chop up the waters? Brick edged slowly toward him, impeded by gouts of water splashing over the rail. He held onto the rail, as water rushed and boiled around him. He vanished completely once, but when the ship began slanting the other way, and the water sheeted off, then he came on again, one hand at the rail, the other clutching the long knife.

Lir watched him, arm still hooked around the rail. The ship swayed so violently where else was there to go? His arm throbbed in time with his heartbeat, and as water smashed him in the face, dousing him, it ripped his fine golden hair clasp free, sending his hair snaking wetly over his face and across his arms.

A crash from the crushed ceiling shook the ship, nearly knocking him into the water. The ship began to slew sideways as an enormous swell built beneath. From behind Lir, on the other half of the stairway, two imperial guards shouted, "Your highness, your highness, this way!"

"I can't move," Lir began to yell back, but they were separated by a blast of water that tried to wring him from the rail.

Then the wave crested, and flung the ship around so violently that Brick, not five paces from Lir, was thrown entirely past him. Lir instinctively reached—and his hand gripped Brick's bony, sinewy wrist. As the ship rose the other way, Lir found himself leaning out as Brick dangled below, legs and arm in the air, the knife dropping away as he tried to grab…more air. Below his feet, the remains of the mast stood like a forest of spears: if he fell, he would be impaled.

Brick's face turned up, and their eyes met for the first time. Lir stared down into Brick's wide, startled gaze. "Hang on," he shouted—as Brick's cold flesh slipped.

Lir tightened every muscle, jamming his feet against the opposite wall. His body twisted, one arm still locked painfully around the rail, which grated agonizingly against his upper arm bone, the strain on his forearm like white lightning.

Time suspended. Their gazes stayed locked as the ship rose slowly, wallowing, and then—as the last of the masts fell, the back end began slowly sliding toward them, planks cracking, and wood flying into the air, to be smashed down by the winds.

A sailor, bleeding badly, howled nearby, "Prince!"

Out of nowhere, a long shape shot at Lir. He ducked, then recognized a bundle of bound bamboo sticks. A raft!

Lir let go of the rail as his fingers, now free, caught at the binding, and he swung the raft around. It smacked into Brick's stomach, and they fell: Lir, Brick, raft.

Lir had half an instant to gulp in air before he plunged into water, his fingers still caught in the binding, which wrenched with excruciating force, then he was out of the water. He slung himself over the bundle. Brick clung to the other end, black hair streaming down his back, blood smeared over his face.

The ship, flung away from them by another slow-rising, gigantic wave, cracked and shattered spectacularly. Lir blinked his stinging eyes. TanTan? Rathlan? Master Angka? He glimpsed people tossed into the water like abandoned toys, but he couldn't follow a one. It took all his strength to cling to the bamboo-bundle raft, which bobbed and spun—and jerked, when a figure flailed past them.

Lir recognized the miraculous qin player, her pale face gasping before she sank again, water closing over her head. Brick stared, then his free hand plunged into the water, and came up with a handful of clothes and hair. He hauled the limp girl up over the middle of the bundle. The girl coughed, retched up seawater, then roused enough to cling to the bundle.

Another bamboo bundle bobbed nearby, and a third. The first was out of reach, but the second shot toward Lir's face, and he caught its binding with his free hand.

"Put the two together," he shouted, not knowing if the others understood.

The qin player, what was her name again? Lum something, Lum Bu, that was it. Trembling violently, she had enough presence of mind to obey, and extended her long, thin fingers to wrench the new raft toward them. Brick reached past her and hauled the two rafts together, which gave the three of them a bit more buoyancy.

A bolt of lightning struck the stern of the ship. Thunder roared around them as the ship's stern smoked as it sank. Here and there people bobbed about, clinging to wreckage. Some floated by, and Lir glimpsed pale faces looking back helplessly as the wind and water took them away again. Overhead the storm crashed and roared.

Though the air was not cold, the water was, at first a relief as it numbed his bruised flesh and wrenched joints. But gradually, insidiously, the relief gave way to numbness, as time passed. His mind drifted, and he fought to retain consciousness as water dragons and wind demons roiled between sea and sky.

Time passed as they floated away from the wreckage; neither Bu, half-drowned, nor Lir, fighting the agony of a fractured arm, was aware of a third pair of legs kicking steadily below the surface, driving them straight into the sea.

Bu lay across the raft, shivering uncontrollably, her mind mercilessly caught on that image of Xia Chi falling past her, falling and falling, until he was swallowed by green waters. She was far too battered and grief-stricken to pay any heed to the prince at one side, and her fellow tribute slave at the other: she watched the indistinct motions as Brick held the two bundles together with one hand, working the other hand into his clothing, then coming out with some sort of token.

He held this token up. Its metal reflected the lightning, but the glow lingered in its face, to her blurry vision looking like a star in his hand, a dim glow that lingered as darkness closed inexorably around them.

With the dimming glow, her consciousness faded, her last awareness catching on small jerks of the raft as Brick began to kick harder, pushing them away from all the floating shards of wood.

Lir held onto consciousness mostly through persistent pain, but the world had become illusory. He could not tell dream from real, but what did it matter? Everything was so remote, oh, so very restfully remote. His soul had drifted off somewhere, watching his body far below. Where was TanTan?

TanTan was the strongest swimmer of them all. Find Rathlan, who was not a strong swimmer...find her...find them and he could sink into the well of darkness...

He scarcely noticed that the wind's howl and the great waves and the stinging rain had gradually lessened. When a shape darker than the emerging sky loomed, he gazed incuriously. This might be another dream. Like whatever that charmed token was that Brick held up. Was that something the imperial guards were given?

Odd. A glow, twin to it, emerged out of that looming darkness, and resolved into voices, the words not quite intelligible. Had the sea's water destroyed his hearing? Nothing quite made sense—until a boat appeared, lanterns at either end opened to emit a slit of light. As it approached, Lir recognized—still in that remote way—a rowboat full of human faces. These were not demons out of the underworld, but men of ordinary feature, two young and one whiskery and seamed.

They reached down, plucked Brick up, and stowed him into the boat. Lir gazed up, puzzled, but his thoughts were far too distant for a reaction as he listened to voices in the boat. Then hands reached down to haul the music student into the boat, and finally, they reached for Lir. Funny, he thought, though the tickle of laughter came from very far away. Uncouth, Graywing Four would say, and Two would frown at this flouting of etiquette. *Princes* always come first. Didn't they know that? But Vo had always promised that when he sat in the dragon throne, Lir and TanTan and Jin would be last... last... last...

Thump! He roused again, gasping as his arm jarred against the boat's wood. Around him, voices speaking far too quickly. That was a harsh accent as two figures bent over Brick's bleeding head. He shook them off. "It'll keep. Let's row."

That was the longest speech Lir had ever heard from Brick, and in that same barbarian accent...No, *northerner* accent... Master Angka would assign a hundred pages of Kanda... Wasn't Brick from the south?

Lir sank back in a torpor as someone began marking time for the rowers. He noticed with brief interest that the clouds had begun to break and move away, leaving the stars of Heaven to shine down once again, blissfully immobile. The moons rested at opposite ends of the sky, one sinking, one rising: Ghost Moon month was nigh.

Someday, he thought drowsily, trying unsuccessfully to

find a comfortable position for his arm, someday he'd remember why that would matter, but nothing mattered now, and he gradually sank into the stupor until shouts roused him again. He looked up, head panging, to discover a ship outlined against the stars. No lanterns save a sliver overhead as the boat nudged and bumped against the hull.

One by one they were hauled up by ropes under their arms, and Lir was dropped onto the deck. He blinked up at Brick standing over him, along with two fur-capped men.

"The girl," a man said, and added a word Lir did not know. Was that horse brethren dialect? "…your fancy?"

"No," Brick said, in that same northern accent. "Imperial musician. Worth a mountain of gold. Treat her like a little sister."

The men crowded around Lir, gazing down. "And this?"

"Him?" Brick said, and added as the lantern light flickered on the side of his face—his sardonic face, no hanging jaw or stupid look. "He's my horse boy. Put him in the hold for now."

FORTY

WHEN BU WOKE, EVERYTHING hurt. Especially her heart. There again was that horrible image of Xia Chi vanishing into the waters. Hot tears welled up and slipped down her cheeks. Though her body ached, the pain in her heart was so much sharper.

A sob escaped, then she caught herself up mentally. Crying was sniveling, and sure to bring more trouble, that much life had taught her. She had to find out where she was, and why, and what was expected of her. Rousing further, she scolded herself. She had survived being thrown into the water, and she did not know how to swim. Maybe, possibly, hopefully, Xia Chi might have also survived.

"You're awake at last?" That gruff voice belonged to a woman. "Let's see what he dragged out of the deep, and how much trouble you'll give. I'll warn you, I don't like trouble."

The woman was very hard to understand. Bu squinted up at her, one bruised hand groping at her neck for her precious eyepiece. The chain was there—but the eyepiece was gone.

Her hand dropped, and she struggled to rise, wincing as every muscle and bone protested.

"Ayah! Aren't you an ugly thing!" the woman commented. "You sure don't look like a fancy piece, but then we all know boys. As long as it's breathing, ha ha ha."

Bu managed to sit upright. The world swayed then resolved into the now-familiar pitch and yaw of a ship. She put her hand to her head, wincing again, as tears sprang to her eyes.

The woman spoke once more, this time slightly less roughly. "Ay, you got yourself a mighty whack. If the rest of you looks like that bruise on your forehead, no wonder you're blubbering. Come on, girl, let's get you out and see what we have to deal with."

Bu discovered she had been put in a tiny alcove of sorts, between shelves of things that smelled of spice and wild onion and garlic. Two strong hands slid under her arms and pulled her to her feet. One sock had vanished, and the other chafed her foot as her clothes, stiff with salt, scraped horribly over her bruised flesh. It was agony to move, but childhood habit forced her to obedience. The reward was coming out of that stuffy cubby into a warm chamber with cooking implements hanging overhead. Smoke billowed from one side: the kitchen?

One of those strong, rough hands pushed Bu onto a barrel top. A shallow cup was thrust into her fingers, and she sipped a very tart, oddly flavored…milk? She had not drunk milk since she was tiny, and that it had been very watery, to turn one portion into two, but this felt good going down, and she drank it all.

"That's right, that's right," the woman said with satisfaction. "Every drop. Good for every ailment, and fresh from the goat, with my own spice added, to put some strength into that flimsy frame of yours. Got a name, music girl?"

"Bu."

"Nice and short. I like that. You'll call me Master Larq. What can you do? My guess is, not much in the kitchen, not with those hands, and that squint. I wouldn't trust you to chop chives, and not season it with a finger or two."

"Master Larq!" This was a new voice, from a girl Bu's own age bearing a couple of vaguely familiar shapes. "I brought *two!* Nolu says, if we break a single string, he'll scalp us and use our hair, but the flute is my brother's."

"Give 'em to her. Let's see if she knows what to do with either."

Two items landed in Bu's lap. She fought against headache as she squinted down. Her fingers found the familiar shape of a wooden flute and quested over the other, a box with strings up a long neck to a bent head. It was like an eruh, and yet not.

"You never seen a horse fiddle? What kind of music girl are you?" the girl commented.

"They might be too ignorant in the south to have such," Master Larq replied generously.

Bu's fingers traveled all over the horse fiddle, exploring its dimensions, then she exclaimed, "These strings. They are not silk."

"Silk! What use is silk? Rots at a touch, squeaks when wet. Those are good horsehair strings, with cedar-glue..."

While Master Larq spoke, Bu righted the boxy lower structure, balancing it on one thigh as she experimented with plucking the loose strings. She ran her other hand up along the neck of the instrument, and very quickly she understood that this was definitely a cousin to the eruh, so its principles ought to be similar. A sharp pulse of mourning for the eruh that had sung under Xia Chi's hands only the day before the storm prompted a flight of notes. Then she found the bow lying next to her leg on the barrel top, picked it up, and drew it experimentally. This fiddle sang willingly, but its song differed from that of the silk stringed eruh—a sound more like the song of the wind playing among ceramic chimes, through trees...

Closing her eyes, she tried the first line of a lament, experimenting with quick adjustments of wrist and thumb and fingers in order to get the best sound from a very different sort of string, and a narrower wooden box frame.

Gaining confidence, she finished the introduction to the lament, and then out came her variation on the convent school's version of "The Cry of the Osprey," but its joyous nature was much tempered by the sorrow Bu could not entirely suppress.

When she finished, she became aware of silence, and opened her eyes. To her astonishment, five people stood shoulder to shoulder around her barrel. Their faces were a blur, so she said, "Did I do something amiss?"

Master Larq, a solid woman, heaved a sigh. "I ought to've known he wouldn't lie to us. It seems we've got ourselves a true musician, eh?"

The crowd around Bu agreed, nodding to each other, then studying Bu, who was about as unprepossessing as possible, thin and squint-eyed under those caterpillar brows, her hair as stiff with brine as her gray clothing. But her expression around that squint and the bruises and scrapes was a shy smile, unshadowed by any hint of calculation or pretense.

"Here." Master Larq pushed another dish of warm goat's milk into her fingers, this one with twice the amount. "You drink this down. Think you could give us another tune?"

Bu's hands hurt—everything hurt—but music was her solace, and of course it had never occurred to her to refuse to play for anyone who wished to listen. "May I warm up my fingers properly first?" she asked diffidently.

Master Larq gave Bu's frowsy head a pat, which for her was an astonishing demonstration of affection. "Little Sister Bu, you play whatever you want. I expect it's going to suit the likes of us."

And she was right.

While Bu, as always, suited herself uncomplainingly to her company, two levels below her in the noisome bottom of the hold, Lir groaned as he slowly came around.

The numbness of the night previous had worn off, and his arm throbbed agonizingly with every breath. The rest of him also hurt, a disagreeable reminder of so many early encounters with Vo.

Something rustled nearby. In the light of a guttering lantern, a rat looked back at him, eyes glittering. Lir groped around, found a rusted piece of wood, and tossed it at the rat, which scuttled away. Rats! No wonder it stank in this vessel. How…when…?

The storm! Flashes of image fought past the lancing pain in his skull: the rail—Brick with the knife. The ship breaking up. Then holding Brick by the wrist. The crack in his other arm. After that, everything was hazy: bamboo raft? The music student Lum Bu? Voices… Northern voices.

Have we been taken by a ship full of gallant wanderers, he mused. Couldn't be pirates, at least. No pirate would haul people *out* of the water. Not unless they knew who he was, and could demand a ransom—could he offer a reward…

The chuff of feet on a ladder broke into his thoughts. Someone was coming. He righted himself, leaning his back against a trunk. He pulled his knees up, and—grimacing—pulled his aching arm across his stomach.

A swinging lantern threw wild shadows leaping over a jumble of trunks and barrels. Lir saw by that intermittent light that he had been dropped onto a kind of platform above the lower hull of the ship. Black, stinking water sloshed back and forth just below him. Lir remembered the rat, and pulled his knees closer.

The lantern approached, carried by…

A familiar figure, tall, broad through the chest, but wearing a northerner tunic and riding breeches, hair pulled up in braids, a headband with some sort of device stitched on it around his forehead.

"Brick?" Lir said.

"Mantai Hoxie. Better get used to it. You're my new servant."

Lir peered up at him, squinting against the headache. "You can talk?"

Brick—now Mantai Hoxie—uttered a short laugh. "That's your first reaction?"

"I don't understand. Were we captured by gallant wanderers? Why would I be your servant?"

"You can either be my servant, or a prisoner on your way to a very public execution out in the harbor at Jun Gan."

Jun Gan—what the horse brethren called Benevolent Winds, the enormous island that had furnished the main of the empire's brimstone.

"You're not worth anything in yourself," the derisive voice went on, strongly accented. "But as a symbol, your very messy death would provide a sufficient back of the hand to your emperor."

Lir struggled to grasp the sense of what he was hearing, and gave up. "I don't understand."

Hoxie had been looking forward to this encounter, wagering within himself whether he was going to hear a lot of threats, or just a temper tantrum. Either would have afforded excellent entertainment.

But he was getting neither. The southerners had been loud and frequent about Hoxie's head being as thick as a brick, but it seemed for thick-headedness, Fourteenth Imperial Prince Rathlir was at the front of the hunt.

Hoxie heaved a short sigh. "I have not told anyone who you are because you saved my life. That means something to us. Also, ayah, a sign, if a small one, that you might not be a yearling after all."

The word for 'yearling' was an old-fashioned one, meaning a treble-voiced boy or girl, that much Lir recollected from his pedantic tutor when he was a treble-voiced boy.

"The gods only know if there might one day be a man inside the silk and tassels. Eh. Here we are. Either you survive, and live a perfectly adequate life as Lir, Mantai Hoxie's horse boy, or you can be flayed at the post as a useless crown prince of the empire that won't stay dead."

Every word generated a new and maddening swarm of questions like buzzing flies.

Lir put words to the most insistent of them. "I'm not the crown prince."

"No, that did present a difficulty. But you can represent one long enough to die entertainingly." Hoxie shrugged a shoulder. "You're down here because it's the only place I could be sure we wouldn't be overheard while we had our talk. If you've finally got the position through that *brick* head of yours, you might as well come along and get started on your chores."

"I think—I'm pretty sure—my arm is broken," Lir said, pushing one-handed onto his knees, and rising with his right arm still cradled across his stomach.

"We'll bind it up tight, and start you on easier tasks. You've a lot to learn anyway. A lot."

"With a broken arm?"

Hoxie uttered another of those short laughs. "Welcome to manhood."

Lir got to his feet, steadying himself against a trunk as he fought back useless fury and protests. He understood that he was a prisoner of war. But Brick, that is, Mantai Hoxie, was keeping his identity a secret. For now.

"Do you know if my brother or my cousin survived?" Lir asked.

"I do not," Hoxie replied with such indifference it effectively silenced Lir.

Hoxie climbed the ladder in three easy leaps, Lir wincing his way up a step at a time in his wake. Welcome to manhood—what sort of posturing was that? Lir thought furiously. Everybody seemed to have different opinions on what constituted manhood. For Kanda, manhood meant the responsibilities of a marriage and a family, and the *civilized* man took his place in the world, contributing to its arts. To his elder brothers it had meant doing what the emperor commanded, no less, and most straitly no more.

To Vo, it had meant the ability to force younger brothers to one's will.

Horse brethren manhood was going to be battle and pain, apparently. Lir could imagine Master Angka's cheerful voice pointing out that the Jun Suai regarded manhood as a test of heroism, which to Lir was simply another way of saying battle and pain. One thing he was sure of: there wasn't going to be any civilization now.

FORTY-ONE

MASTER LARQ'S VISION WAS mildly blurred up close, not nearly as vague as Bu's, so it did not occur to her that anything was amiss until one of her apprentices whispered that Little Sister Bu was stiff with brine.

Master Larq thrust her fists on her hips. "Why didn't she say so? Does she think we're barbarians who don't know how to wash?"

"I think she might be afraid to," was the cheerful answer. "I did ask if she was born in a palace, and what was it like, and she said that she was born in a cottage, then lived in a convent until she got grabbed as tribute. She said she's only been in a palace once, to perform, but she couldn't see anything."

While the apprentice spoke, Master Larq dipped a bucket into the huge tureen of water always kept on the simmer, filling it halfway, then added pure water from the rain barrel.

This she set down in the storeroom, and drew Bu in. Pointing to the bucket, to a comb, and to some worn but clean, neatly folded garments left by former apprentices, she said, "Here! You can scrub the brine off."

"Thank you," Bu said, bowing.

The apprentice seemed to have the right of it. Master Larq stamped out and resumed chopping and stirring while she delivered a comprehensive indictment of those corrupt southerners who treated their women like sheep, and why weren't they raised to weapons as anyone would sense would do?

Bu was no stranger to bathing out of a bucket. Reverting to old habit, she got herself, including her hair, divested of brine, then put her clothes to soak in the remaining water as she drew on the garments Master Larq had given her. These consisted of billowing trousers that tied at the ankle, and over it a heavy tunic with a hole at the top for her head. It was very loose, but there was a thin sash to bind it to her waist, and a pair of shoes not unlike her old sandals, except with the toes turned up. After wearing the soft inner palace shoes for so many weeks, she hoped that her feet would not chafe.

While she went about her ablutions, Hoxie, both disappointed to be cheated of his anticipated tantrum and intrigued to discover what that imperial prince would try next, remembered Bu, and found tasks to do around the ship while he assessed the situation.

It seemed that Master Larq, sister to the shipmaster, had annexed the music student. That was a better outcome than he'd hoped for. But he still had to get at Lum Bu long enough to warn her. That chance came after she emerged from Master Larq's cabin, lugging a pail of dirty water with both hands.

Hoxie took that from her fingers, and as she squinted in bewilderment, he said, "Lum Bu. Your imperial prince is my servant. If you remember that, he might live."

Bu screwed up her face, trying to see him. "Brick?" she said tentatively.

"My name is Mantai Hoxie." He heard footsteps thumping along the gangway approaching, and abruptly turned in the other direction, handing off the bucket to one of the sailors.

"There you are, Little Sister Bu. We're making wild onion pancakes…"

Bu blinked from his rapidly retreating back to Spring, Master Larq's apprentice. She longed for her eyepiece, then tried to shake that longing off. Luxuries were not permanent, that was a lesson she'd had hammered into her very, very early. "Where might I hang my clothes to dry so they will not trouble anyone?" she asked.

"Why, over the rail at the stern, with the rest of our things. You'll see," Spring said, took a speculative glance at that squint, and changed her mind. "I think I'd better show you." She whisked ahead, a skinny sixteen-year-old who wore her red-tinged dark hair bound up in many beaded braids.

When they returned to the galley, it was time for the

midday meal, which was mainly pancakes, spiced milk, and fish skewers. No rice. The crew was served in rotation, much as the imperial navy had done. The ship was under full sail, dashing northward with water splashing down the sides. A tall boy put Bu to work dipping then wiping dishes, a job remembered from her childhood. It was a job she could do by feel.

She finished about the time Master Larq began cooking the evening meal. When Bu saw that, she tried to conceal her dismay as her body ached abominably by then, and she pressed her water-wrinkled hands to her face as they throbbed. Was washing dishes to be her new life?

But when it came time for the meal to be served, along with what smelled like spiced fermented milk, Bu had just taken a few bites of her share when word passed down into the lower level, "Chief wants to see the song girl!"

Bu found herself pushed from hand to hand up to the weather deck. She peered around. Was that his highness, Imperial Prince Lir over there near the prow? With a broom? Then she remembered what she had been told, and quickly turned away, as behind her, a sailor said, "Horse boy, haven't you ever seen a broom before? You're just pushing the salt around. You sweep like this…"

Bu lost the voices as she was drawn into a single-story structure divided into several rooms. Here was a raised table, behind which a fierce-looking man sat cross-legged on a mat, next to…was that Brick? No, what was his new name? Hoxie?

Bu was pushed forward. She turned her attention to the shipmaster, and made out the shape of an eyepatch, above a dark beard. His body was large, and non-symmetrical. When she neared the table, she saw that he was missing an arm. He speared his food with a knife, and conveyed it to his lips.

She bowed the way she'd been taught.

The man said in a very thick accent, not unlike the one that Brick — that is, Hoxie — had spoken in, "So, so, so, I hear you claim to be an *imperial* musician!" He seemed to find the word 'imperial' humorous, the way he drew it out.

"This student is still learning," Bu said, barely audible.

"Here. Let's see what you can do."

"Chief, she plays the horse fiddle. We heard her. In the kitchen. Played it like she'd been at it ten years, but she didn't know what it was."

"Ayah, anyone can play a horse fiddle. Let's see what she

does with a harp."

Harp? Someone thrust something into her hands. Bu ran exploratory fingers over it and discovered a stringed instrument not unlike the zither. But when she looked about for a table to lay it onto, the shipmaster laughed, and the person who'd given it to her said, "It plays upright. See? These are the legs."

Bu's fingers found the pegs worked into the wood, carved in the shape of the hooves of a barking deer. She sat on her heels on the deck, placed the harp between her knees, and bent over it to test the strings. Many were slightly out of tune. But she found the tuning pegs, shaped like antler nubs, and quickly got the strings resonating true.

"Well?" the shipmaster roared impatiently.

"I am sorry to be so slow," Bu said nervously. "Last string…what do you wish to hear?"

"A war ballad or a sea song, of course. Or don't you know any? It's all scrolls and pillows down south, ay?"

By now Bu had learned plenty of ballads, many of which featured wars. She ran her hands experimentally along the strings. Ah, yes, very like a zither, just played at a different angle.

She began "Liad Il at Willow Harbor" with a tentative, experimental approach. The strings responded now, resonating strongly, and as she gained confidence, she added a thrumming variation in threes and fives, and then a countermelody, the Silver Commander Ranek lament in honor of Liad Il's famous wife. By the end, the chief was bent forward, his brows a single line over the eyepatch and his eye. Others marked time, one sailor producing a hand drum and tapping the rhythm.

At the end, the shipmaster turned to Hoxie, saying quite mildly, "You spoke true."

Someone asked, "Can she play the flute?"

Bu turned, hands together, and bowed.

The northerners brought out hoarded instruments from various corners of the ship. Some were not very good, and all were out of tune to Bu's ear. Though she had never been raised to consider her own worth, she had come by tentative degrees to believe that her music would earn respect—and so it came to pass.

This usually gave her pleasure, which enhanced her playing the more, but as the evening became night, she was only aware of the increasing ache. It took concentration to get her fingers to do what they usually did without so much thought, and an invisible band seemed to press about her head.

For the first time in memory she longed for quiet, but this or that sailor would shout, "Do you know this ballad?" And would sing enough of a melody for her to catch it, and play it back.

This went on until Master Larq scowled at the shipmaster, leaned up toward him, and said, "I mislike her looks."

"That squint is like a demon out of the underworld," the shipmaster said with a laugh. "But she plays like she was sent by the king of Heaven."

"Not that." Master Larq squinted herself—but the shipmaster, who respected her temper, held back a comment, and slewed around to fix his one eye on their prize. "Did you get her drunk?"

"Nary a drop."

"Then she's sickening for something, for she's getting redder in the cheeks, but the rest of her is corpse-green."

At that moment, one of the sailors came up to whisper to Hoxie, "Your horse boy has fallen over in a faint."

"Is he faking it?"

"Not he. Kui pinched him, hard. He never noticed."

Hoxie frowned at Bu, and yes, even in the flickering lantern light, her eyes glittered, too bright.

"Toss them both in the after-cabin. Whatever it is they brought north, we don't want it spreading to *us*," the shipmaster ordered.

Bu's concentration had narrowed to forcing herself to sit upright, and to produce note after painful note. Someone abruptly took the reed flute from her hands, and Master Larq hauled her up by her armpits. "Come along, child."

By the time she was pointed at bedding in a small after-cabin, she was shivering. Master Larq bade her lie down, and cast two thick blankets over her. Bu's nose peeked out. In the dim light of a single lantern, she made out another form beside her, completely motionless.

Then she sank gratefully into fitful sleep, waking intermittently with a horrible thirst. Someone had set water near her head, and two cups. It took all her strength and concentration to sit up, pour water, and drink it down a throat that had become as raw as her brine-chafed skin.

"LanLan," Lir muttered. "Water."

Bu stared, appalled. How was this possible? She was alone in a cabin with a man, one of the imperial princes! But as he muttered more disjointed words, he sounded less like a prince and more like a person in pain.

Bu struggled over to him, holding the cup with both hands. His flesh was scorching hot. He choked down water and subsided immediately into sleep. Bu set the cup aside, wondering if she could tell Brick—that is, Hoxie—that Kanda cautioned men and women who weren't related to avoid being in touching proximity. Would there be trouble over her presumption? At least the prince seemed unaware of who she really was.

That was her last thought before she slid into more feverish slumber. For an endless stretch both woke at different times. Lir was so delirious, his arm so painful, that he was convinced that Bu was his cousin Rathlan, only where was TanTan? He stared at the lantern, waiting for TanTan to appear, to explain where they were, and fell asleep again.

When Bu roused next, it was to discover a huge form crouching down, in the act of placing fresh water by her head.

"Brick," she whispered. "No. Forgive me…"

"Never mind that now," he said, looking into averted face as her feverish fingers caught at his sleeve. "I brought water. What else?"

"I should not be in here with…a man," she whispered.

Hoxie smothered the impulse to laugh, which doused quick enough at her obvious distress. "Right now, it's best if I hide his identity," he explained, low-voiced. "Until I figure out what to do. He seems worse off than you. I don't really think he's going to molest you."

That idea was plainly as remote as Ghost Moon to her as she tried to explain what was proper. Also, what was necessary. "If someone could get those clothes off, I could put them to soak. I think the salt is causing his skin to scrape. He thinks he has fallen on rocks. He keeps telling someone named Vo to stay away."

"I'll see to it." Hoxie went away.

Presently Master Larq turned up, muttering under her breath, and coaxed Bu to her feet. After a long, shaky walk, Bu found herself in the pantry again, which smelled comfortingly of spices now familiar. She fell back to sleep, relieved to be alone, while at the other end of the ship, Hoxie got his trusted friend Ma Pao to help him face the task of cleaning up Lir.

Mostly delirious, Lir tried to fight free, but he had no

strength. Pao whispered a stream of colorful imprecations as he wrestled impatiently with Lir's non-responsive, feverish limbs, but at last they got Lir more or less clean, and into Pao's oldest tunic and trousers.

"What do I do with that?" Pao pointed to the pile of salt-stiff, grimy clothes. "You know Peppergreen will see me if I wash out a servant's clothes."

Unsaid, but known to both: what Peppergreen knows, Mantai Sorxu knows. Hoxie looked down at his prisoner, wondering anew what to do. For an entire year, Sorxu had been merely a distant thought because Hoxie was down south, with no contact but his half of the charmed stone pair, Ma Pao holding the other half. Hoxie had been given a single order — to kill the empire's heir — an order he had not managed to carry out, because there was no appointed heir.

Sorxu was going to find a way to use that against him, of course. Hoxie was aware of the silent duel recommencing as they drew ever nearer Jun Gan. When they landed, that meant caution waking and sleeping, and as little revealed as possible. Like, why he'd have Pao washing a southern slave's clothes.

"For now, give those clothes to the other southerner to deal with," Hoxie said heavily. "At least she seems to know what a pail of hot water is for."

FORTY-TWO

As soon as she could remain upright, Bu uncomplainingly washed Lir's clothes, and by the time they dried, Lir's fever was ebbing, leaving him listless, prone to coughing, but aware of the world once again.

It was a world he did not want to waken to. But here he was. The reminder was the intermittent wail of weird singing that he could not shut out, always late at night. He figured if he said anything to remind the enemy of his presence, he'd be stuck with that broom again. He wasn't sure how long he could stand up, much less use his arm. At least—if he kept it still—it did not hurt nearly as much. But it still hurt, and the flesh of his upper arm was heavily bruised from where he'd wrenched his arm around the tower ship's rail.

That weird wailing was music of an intriguingly different form and quality to Bu. The emotions beneath the unfamiliar melody carried an urgency, an awareness of grief, that finally brought her tottering into the kitchen again.

"You look like a ghost," Spring scolded, the beads in her many tiny braids clattering. "You go back and lie down."

"That singing?" Bu asked, discovering in speaking that her throat was raw.

"Oh, that's the shipmaster. When he gets drunk, he sits on the roof pole and sings those ballads, the bloodier the better. No one can get him to come down until he sobers, not even

Master Larq, though she's tried and tried. She's afraid that his howling will call every demon riding the winds."

When music must come forth, Bu knew, it must come forth, but she would never argue. She accepted Spring's scolding meekly, and withdrew.

Presently Master Larq stamped into the galley, bearing a tray of dirty dishes. "Did I hear Little Sister?"

"You did, but she still looks like a ghost."

The tray slammed onto a rain barrel with a clatter. "We'll leave her be, then. Chase that scamp Peppergreen in here. He's always where you want him least, and never in reach when needed. He can see to these dishes."

"He'll just shove them onto Little Sister Bu again," Spring said, aware that she had looked the other way when he'd done it last. But then, nobody liked doing dishes.

"If he does, you let *me* know, and I'll carve his ears down to his chin. He's not to come near her. If the king doesn't want her, she's going to bring such a good price, such a very good price, and as we're taking care of her, I will see to it we get our share," Master Larq said to Spring as she bustled about.

What benefitted Master Larq benefitted her apprentices. The next time Spring brought Bu wash water, she lingered. "I'm going to do your hair in a proper style," she announced — and held out a few of her least precious beads.

Bu squinted from Spring to her palm, bent over the latter, and her eyes widened. "Oh, these are very, very pretty." She glanced up, her brow furrowed. "But I have never worn such ornaments. I think they would be forbidden to us."

"You're done with the south and their demonic ways," Spring said practically. "You do want to bring a good price, don't you, if the king doesn't keep you? And between you and me, you're far better off if he doesn't. The royal camp is said to be a bridge of knives." Seeing that this advice did absolutely nothing to clear Little Sister Bu's troubled expression, Spring added, "You don't want to have to wear this ugly wooden hairpin anymore, would you? It looks like what a night soil slave would wear, and anyway, when I finish, you will not have to comb out your hair on the ride. It'll last at least a moon, probably longer, if you are careful. Now, sit down."

Bu was so used to obeying orders that she sat, and waited patiently as Spring combed out her long hair, divided it into narrow rows, and then braided it, inserting a bead at the minimum of lucky intervals; she didn't have enough beads to give away for all the lucky intervals. But at least these would give Bu some protection, and look well, driving up her price.

Spring loved playing with hair, and seldom got a chance to do it while at sea, her fellow apprentice being a scamp of a boy who would never sit still even if he wanted braids like a warrior. Oh, how she would love to get her fingers in Hoxie's hair! But he only let Pao do his for him.

She chattered happily, and Bu listened, trying to follow the quick flow of accented words, many of which were new. She gathered that the shipmaster was connected to Hoxie's mother's family, and that they prided themselves on their independence.

When Spring declared she had finished, Bu felt cautiously over her head. It seemed like someone else's head altogether, it was so unfamiliar: the curving lines over her scalp between the rows of braids, the way her hair had been braided and bound high on her head, so that a tumble of braids hung down her back, swinging at every move. But not tangling.

After that, they ate, and Bu was planted on a barrel and asked to sing.

This life was not dire. Bu was very aware of that. But she was so very far from Granny Zim, and her precious lessons and instruments! And worst of all was the hole in her heart where Xia Chi's smiling presence had taken up residence.

This melancholy imbued all her music when she played, though she was only aware of experimenting with combining the ballads she heard with what she had learned, as she tried to adapt her posture, and the way she held the instruments, to what felt most natural. As she did so, she was conscious of attempting to figure out what customs had shaped these instruments — how the people felt, how they thought.

Everything she learned, she brought to her music, and the more that music sounded like what the northerners were used to hearing, the better they liked it. The galley crew especially enjoyed having their own entertainment as they performed their ceaseless labors.

A couple of days after she resumed playing in the cabin for the shipmaster and his crew, she lugged her pail of wash water out to deal with her clothes, when to her surprise, a vaguely familiar figure appeared. She squinted. That was the imperial prince! He was much thinner in those shabby clothes of indeterminate color — like hers, castoffs from someone else.

"I'm to learn how to wash out my own clothes," he said

abruptly.

Ingrained habit started her in a bow, but his hand caught her shoulder, hard. "Don't."

She jerked upright, remembering. How was she to speak to someone whose birth placed him so far above her?

Lir recognized the slightly pained bewilderment in her face, and sighed. "Say it. Lir. That's my name until I can escape. Go ahead. Lir."

"Lir," she repeated softly.

"No thunderbolts struck you, right?" he said, his mouth awry.

Not that she could see his expression, but she caught the tone. "I'm sorry," she said.

"For what? You didn't send water demons and dragons to attack us," and when her eyes widened at that unexpected remark, he said, "I see they're making you over into a barbarian."

"Bar—ayah," she breathed. "Oh!" Her fingers flew to her head, then she snatched her hand down, ingrained habit from when First Mother would slap her, hard, for any sign of what she termed "vanity." Such as touching her hair once it had been braided for the day. "Spring says I won't have to comb it," she explained.

"What I mean is, is this life is what you want? I've seen they don't make you sweep or empty chamber pots."

Bu's wide gaze lifted to his, and there was the grief she could not hide. "I want to go home," she whispered—home being wherever Granny Zim was.

Lir had put the question as casually as he could. As neutrally as he could. But the unhidden longing in her face added its burden to his shoulders. Because she was his responsibility—as would be anyone from home who had been captured as well. Aware of its weight, he whispered back, "I'm going to try to free us. Be ready." And then, louder, "What do I do first?" He pushed his salt-stiff, grimy laundry into her hands. The fabric reeked of sick-sweat, and both, so newly recovered, tried not to breathe deeply

She crouched down on the deck, and pushed his clothes in on top of hers until the water closed over the fabric. "You soak them for a time, to loosen the dirt, then..." As she showed him how to plunge her fists onto the fabric, then scrub and wring, she was aware of a shadow passing behind them, then away.

At the end of the lesson, when his clean outfit hung in the

sun next to hers, he murmured, "Don't trust that Peppergreen. He asks too many questions."

Then he walked off before Peppergreen's attention strayed in their direction, leaving Bu to carry her bucket back to the galley. At least Pao was straightforward in his constant insults, Lir had discovered. They weren't even cruel in intent, just observations — "*Another* simple task you don't know how to do?" — usually followed by a cheerful, "You really are slow, aren't you?"

The tasks were easy enough, once he saw how each was done. But that left him with endless time to brood, beginning with cursing that Brick. *Brick Brick Brick.* Thinking the name as an insult, and mentally adding a list of curses, was only satisfying if TanTan and LanLan were there to share them.

He needed an Essence-master to write out some serious curses on really aged Essence paper; speaking curses didn't work, or Vo would have tripped and broke his nose years ago. Did prayers for the safety of loved ones work? He'd pray for TanTan and Rathlan — and the graywings and the scribe master — if he could be sure any gods listened to him, but he suspected that they had decided at his birth that he was a living jest.

If cursing was useless, that left whining, which was just as tedious. He really was a jest. No sooner did they get rid of Vo than here was a bigger evil — and the worst of it was, Hoxie turned out to be the bodyguard who was supposed to protect him!

It was not even satisfactory to imagine complaining to the emperor, because he suspected he would be told that he only had himself to blame. His aunt had warned him last year. "The imperial guard was nearly eradicated during the Trouble," she'd said. "It's been very difficult to hire, and train, and begin to trust, the new guard, and they are always short in numbers."

"But they have plenty of tributes," Lir remembered pointing out — and wasn't *that* the worst idea in the world?

"Yes, but they only take the biggest, the strongest with some training, and those who are not criminals, or angry about being taken from their homes. Many like having the prospect of a better life. Those are too few. Your imperial father realizes that you do not like your activities curtailed, but turning away every guard they send only adds to the strain."

The real jest was, Lir had kept Brick to be cooperative!

Well, and also because he didn't talk.

And here they were.

His mind was heavy, but so was Hoxie's. He kept himself busy, avoiding Lir — avoiding the problem of Lir — as much as possible. This was not a solution, he knew.

With the familiarity of a lifetime of friendship, Pao soon brought it up.

"Why did you have us bring those two aboard? The girl plays well, but I never knew you to listen to music, and she's obviously not your plaything. Nor is she his," Pao added, his narrow, foxy face canted at a puzzle angle. "Though she gives him her second pancake every morning. I've seen it. But she doesn't linger around, nor he around her. Unless that's the southern way? Cold as fish, even as lovers."

"She's probably just a follower of the Snow Crane," Hoxie said dismissively.

"The Snow Crane?"

"One of their gods. I heard something about her having lived in a convent before she became tribute on the ship with me."

"What does that mean?"

Hoxie said with a hint of impatience, "She gave *me* her second pancake on the ship, is what I'm saying. Nothing loverlike about it." Hoxie snorted, then drank from the bowl of fermented milk Pao had brought him. How he had missed the taste! "I was furious at first. Thought she was suspicious of me, or would make me stand out to the imperials. Until I saw that she was half blind. And that her milk-brother Cricket, a street-rat if I ever saw one, asked her to watch out for me before he was sent south with the army. I did not expect any of that. She was right there, and other than my sister, I've never met anyone who was kind without expecting anything in return. I could not let her drown."

"I can see saving her. Spring says she's meek as a rabbit, and she plays like a fairy sent straight from Heaven. But Lir? He's useless. Can't do the simplest task."

Now on his second bowl of the strong fermented drink, Hoxie slid into a reminiscent mood. "I very nearly killed him. The ship was breaking up. I was furious at not having been able to follow orders. But if I'd cut his throat I would have been two steps behind him on the road to the underworld."

"Did he really save your life?"

"He did. It was my weight that fractured his arm for him

but he held on. Ship was upended on a monster wave. If he hadn't held on, I'd have been impaled on the broken mast spikes."

"I guess it was lucky you didn't slit his throat for being annoying as well as incompetent. I'm surprised you waited that long, though," Pao said cheerfully.

Because there was no declared crown prince—the words were there, ready to be said, but Hoxie held them back. Pao's context was not Hoxie's orders. He'd shrugged those off as a matter between Hoxie and the king. His context was immediate, how ignorant Lir was as a servant. It was far less dangerous that way.

Pao was his milk-brother. They'd grown together from infancy in Pao's mother's tent, while Hoxie's mother attended on the king. Milk-bonds were often more important than blood-bonds, which just meant from the same father. A man could have many, many blood-brothers, all more likely to fight for patrimony than not. Sorxu being the prime example. As close as a milk brother, maybe even closer, was your shield-brother, the man who have saved your life on the hunt, or in a tough fight. The best war bands were made up of shield-brethren. It was a sacred bond, one not to be broken.

And yet, the first person to save Hoxie's life was the one he'd actually been sent to kill—for it had become clear after the pirate defeat, while the imperial guard were drinking and talking freely, that the entire exercise was the emperor's test for his future heir. A test. Point being, Fourteenth Imperial Prince Rathlir was probably going to be promoted on his return from the pilgrimage; it wouldn't be the other imperial prince because, being deaf, he didn't talk, which meant that he couldn't be Heaven's chosen, for the emperor *must* have a voice.

Now, what to do?

Unaware that Hoxie wasn't listening, Pao chattered on, describing, in detail, Lir's many shortcomings in the simplest task. He finally ended, "...why I can't believe he saved your life. He's so ignorant."

"You don't have to believe it. But it happened," Hoxie said, annoyed with the perplexing dilemma—with himself. "Could be I'll trade him off," he said finally, deciding against telling Pao who Lir was, much as it might relieve him to do so. He trusted Pao completely—but Sorxu knew that. And he really, really relished interrogations. Best if Pao knew absolutely nothing about Imperial Prince Rathlir, which lessened the chance of him letting drop an intriguing hint before one of Sorxu's spies.

"Then he's got to learn something, to be worth trading," Pao said.

"Yes. That's your job," Hoxie said, elbowing him.

"I know, I know, I know." Pao sighed. "What do you want to wager he's never even seen a horse?"

FORTY-THREE

TO THE IMPERIAL COURT, Hungry Ghost Month was mostly symbolic, Granny Zim discovered. In the islands, with winter coming, there were often many marriages among those who had dawdled too long over spring and summer. With the two moons the farthest apart they would get in the year, and the gradual return of longer nights, it was time to huddle together and perhaps start families before the men sailed in spring.

The poor set out food each night, for passing spirits, then ate that food after lighting incense in the morning, to restore the Essence that might have been eaten by the ghosts.

The time of the year — her own ghosts — lingered in Granny Zim's mind even the triumphant night of the first presentation of *The Jade Palace*, her first chapter-drama.

The story itself was old, of course. Traditional stories were so firmly the fashion that Granny Zim wondered if such a determined celebration of past customs and art was a lingering result of the Troubles. As if hailing past greatness papered over how badly riven the court had been. Not just the court, but its cherished view of itself as the epitome of merit.

This was the kind of question an outsider could not put, alas. If the court discussed such things among themselves behind closed doors, Granny Zim was not invited to hear it in spite of all the plaudits for her talent and wisdom.

That first night, she listened; she would be on stage most

of the second night, and on various succeeding days of the eighteen chapters, two sets of threes, very auspicious for this time of year especially.

She thus had leisure not only to listen to the musicians—and very pleased she was with their improvements—but to observe the court from behind the curtain. They mostly seemed to be enjoying themselves, including the deaf consort, whose wide eyes followed the stylized movements of the actors and dancers.

Granny Zim glanced once at the emperor, but that old dragon always maintained a single expression when he was in a benign mood. He had to be aware that eyes sidled his way intermittently. There were those who would take their cues entirely from him to determine if they had enjoyed the performance or not.

Her attention strayed to those who genuinely loved music, their enjoyment expressed in lifted faces, shut eyes, tiny sways when the rhythm swelled. One of these was that fascinating prince who claimed to see ghosts. Who *did* see demons.

Thirteenth Imperial Prince Rathjin had kept his promise, not revealing YinYin's true nature. In turn, YinYin had been experimenting with creating music for him. YinYin strayed most often to the bells, whose brassy echoes ignited emotions like fire and storm. The bells were seldom played, for they could overwhelm the rest of the instruments, except used very sparingly to underscore dramatic moments.

Granny Zim noted that Jin's gaze shifted between YinYin, the performers, and the shadows to the right of the stage. Did he truly see ghosts? If so, did those ghosts watch the stage? Did they *hear?*

When it was over, and the emperor bestowed a sign of approbation, freeing the rest of court to offer their congratulations and compliments, Granny Zim left Chiefs Yne, Rao, and Huazi to bask in the golden light of noble praise, and took herself over to the side, near the exit the courtiers used.

As before, Prince Rathjin did not linger to socialize. He bowed to his family before withdrawing, trailed by Graywing Seven. When he saw Granny Zim, his beautiful face lit from within—oh, how he reminded Granny Zim of Bu!—and he said, "We enjoyed it very, very much."

Granny Zim knew he included his ghostly brother besides himself. Impulse prompted a question she had not meant to ask, "Is there a ghost around me?"

The prince looked a little puzzled. "I do not see one," he said.

Granny Zim smiled, thanked him for the compliment, bowed, and watched him depart, light shimmering over the apricot blossoms embroidered over his robe, sleeve-tassels swaying and dancing.

If young Prince Jin didn't see Teg, then no one would, Granny Zim thought ruefully. And here she was, talking to him all these years, when he had probably been reborn long ago as a young man, or even a young woman, somewhere else in the world. Or maybe a great cetacean in the ocean—he had loved watching them dance—or an eagle in the air.

He was not with her. So much for assuming that his soul would wait for hers to join him, that he had been heart-bound to her the way she was with him. Who knows, maybe he'd even had another family in one of those far islands, the way some of the men did.

Aware of the ache of joints that had been upright since before dawn, she slipped out the door, and began the journey back to her room. The graywing assigned to her appeared like a shadow to attend her, and YinYin fell in step beside her.

Both were silent, leaving Granny Zim to her thoughts: and what if he did have another life? She would never know. And it wasn't as if it in any way diminished what she'd had when he was home with her. Nor did it diminish the precious recollections; ah, here were the glimmerings of a new piece, born of his favorite songs. She would use those, a deliberate conservation of hoarded memories that annihilated time for the heartbeats spent in looking back. What was it the artist-poet Gri Aseg had said about paintings and poetry? That art itself was an ephemeral way of capturing time; ephemeral for the creator, but if the art spoke to other hearts with similar precious hoardings, endured for centuries, defying time.

"I want to defy time," she said to YinYin, who never asked for context, or acted taken aback at abrupt comments. "I *hate* that life is as insubstantial as gossamer, and its opposite is as engulfing as eternity." She threw back her head. "Where is the balance?" she addressed the slow wheel of the stars in the sky.

They passed a lamp, and she caught a startled, worried glance from the little graywing. She was tempted to say, "I'm not mad," but was that ever truly reassuring? The mad probably believed more firmly in their sanity than did the sane.

She laughed at herself, and internally laid the matter aside as they reached her chamber. Once again she found the outer hall overflowing with gifts. Very expensive gifts. She turned to the graywing. "I suppose they had these waiting to send?" *If the emperor approved.*

"The Merit night staff just finished bringing them," was the soft answer.

Granny Zim touched a lucent stone of a delicate silvery green, carved with the character for brilliance. "Is this jade?" she asked.

The graywing expressed no surprise at the question. "It is."

"And here is more jade. And another! I don't know whether this very expensive gift is meant to convey extra merit, or merely to acknowledge that those with the gold to spend are being clever about the title of the new piece."

The graywing merely bowed, and YinYin made no comment. Granny Zim suppressed a sigh, and reflected wryly that of all those she'd been in the habit of speaking to, the emperor would be most likely to enjoy her attempt at wit. Not that she tried jests while in his presence. Granny Zim still regarded him much as she'd regard an exceptionally colorful and handsome snake: one could appreciate it, but still be wary of its bite.

I think I'll save these for Bu," she said, dismissed the graywing, and sank down. "Oh I am tired, down to the bone." And when the graywing was gone, the doors closed, and she only had her bedside candle, Granny Zim turned to YinYin. "Did you gain Essence? The air seemed full of it to me."

"It was," YinYin stated, and in that dim, flickering light appeared to swell. No, the demon had not grown in size but intensity somehow, colors, textures, light and shadow denser. "I gave some back."

"Is that what I felt? It makes me giddy as a girl Bu's age. Oh, Bu! Fine as the musicians played, I know Bu would have played better. How I do wish that Kanda had seen fit to be born on this island, or one decently close by." Granny Zim hesitated, then climbed into bed.

She knew that YinYin at present found it difficult to sense individual humans beyond a certain physical distance. Granny Zim had no idea how that could be, but so much of the world's workings were a mystery, that she knew from the auguries that proved true. There were two awarenesses that kept her from asking YinYin to find Bu: first, it diminished YinYin in some way, and second, even if Granny Zim knew, what could she do if Bu were unhappy? Better to imagine her sailing along delighting those young imperials with her music, and working through all those lessons Granny Zim had written out.

She fell asleep on that thought, and wakened to another summons.

The emperor, she had learned, liked summoning her before he had to go to morning court. He had informed her a few weeks ago that he found her presence "bracing."

By now the path to the imperial pavilion was well known. When would it get easier to tread? She supposed it was good for old bones to walk that distance, but she did not look forward to traversing it in winter, which—she had been warned—was far more severe than winters at home.

She was ushered into the presence, the Graywing they simply called One a shadow at the emperor's side. His imperial majesty's furrowed face lifted in a semblance of a smile when she came in—at least he remembered to tell them to put a cushion down. She was not at all certain she could kneel on the tiles anymore without extreme pain, especially if the weather got much colder.

"Sit up, sit up," the emperor said once she'd made her full bow, forehead to the floor. "That was very well done last night. I am looking forward, very much, to the rest of the chapters. How satisfying it is, knowing that there is more to come!"

Granny Zim by now was practiced at humble deprecation, and she ended with one of the flowery compliments that Chief Huazi had often used, "Any merit we have achieved is due entirely to your imperial majesty's grace."

The emperor grunted, winced, waved off the graywing who sprang to his side, and hoisted himself up more on one elbow. "My merit did not work assiduously to bring your music to our familiar forms," he said, sank back irritably, then added waspishly, "You're learning how to utter courtly conciliations. Do you see how they all placate me? It's the next thing to lying." And, one eye narrowing, "What do you think of that?"

"If your imperial majesty truly wishes to hear what is in this insignificant one's mind—"

"Speak, speak, speak."

"—it seems to this ignorant outlander that they see it as saving their lives," Granny Zim responded.

The emperor chuckled. "True enough. And I did as much

when I was young. Ah, I did not set out to bait you. It was hearing that about my merit that started me off. Kanda wrote that if one should desire to know whether a kingdom is well governed, if its morals are good or bad, the quality of its music will furnish the answer. It's entirely your merit that brings this music to us, and so I am warning you, that when *The Jade Palace* is finished, I will spontaneously issue an edict elevating you to Sagacious Master."

Granny Zim bowed, forehead to the floor, uttering thanks for his imperial graciousness, and then, seeing that he still expected a response, added, "If this ignorant outlander might be permitted to ask, how ought this ignorant one to properly respond? Must this untrained-in-the-ways-of-court strummer make a speech before court?"

He uttered a laugh, then fell to coughing, as the graywing One rubbed his back.

The emperor waved off the chief graywing, then gave Granny a wry smile. "If you have a suitable poem ready to extemporaneously quote, preferably something that purports to be from the Golden Dragon Dynasty, it will suffice."

The Golden Dragon Dynasty: the empire's first dynasty, shrouded in mystery, the writings were so sparse and so difficult to read, carved mostly in rock before people discovered bamboo sticks. Tradition and its silk paper indeed; Granny Zim bowed once again. "And if this undeserving one may trouble his imperial majesty with one more question, what duties does such a rank require?"

"The Sagacious rank grants more servants and better quarters, which you probably don't care much for, as I am reliably informed you still live simply, as no doubt you did in your faraway convent. But it affords more freedom. You no long need to teach daily classes to the young unless you wish to. You're to compose for the court. Also, your particular students will advance the faster."

Granny Zim's smile was real as she bowed a third time.

The emperor grunted. "Speaking of. I know the one you cherish most is the Talent we sent along to ease the time at sea for my sons and the grand princess, my niece. I just received word last night that they were sailing into a tempest."

Oh, Granny Zim thought. Was *that* what lay behind the irritation she could sense? No, not irritation. That was worry tension in his forehead.

Her heart thumped sharply against her ribs. What could

she say? All the words she wanted to say were laments that they had seen fit to send Bu away. That *he* had.

"The birds fly off when a tempest that size comes. They always return, though, in which case we will shortly hear of their safe passage. Naoki is very experienced, he and his tower ship both. They've weathered many a tempest."

But you are still worried, Granny Zim thought. And in spite of all your power, you're helpless to do anything. So you're sharing your worry with me.

That, she knew, was an entirely human trait. She'd done it herself. She forced down the accusation she wanted to air—what would be the use?—and said, "This old outlander looks forward to hearing of her student's experiences, and trusts that these will find their way into many new compositions to come."

That seemed to suffice.

Granny Zim made her bows, and withdrew. She kept silent all the way back to Merit. She kept silence on the subject through the following long day of discussion relating to the performance, and the rehearsal of the next chapter.

She kept silence until she could be alone with YinYin that night, then poured out her worries. She ended with, "I know it is very difficult for you to find someone at a distance. I understand that you cannot manifest, or do much of anything, but all I want to know is if Bu is still alive. In this world."

YinYin said, "I can always find Bu. But it is not simple, if there are intervening entities of my kind."

YinYin stilled, and even seemed to diminish. Or flatten, as if made of paper.

After an endless time, YinYin said faintly, "Bu is still in the world." And dissolved to recover elsewhere.

Granny Zim clamped down on the questions YinYin couldn't answer. That would have to be enough. She struggled up, and went to her small altar. There she lit incense, offering her new quick prayer that Teg's new life was a good one, and then added a fervent prayer for Bu's safe return.

FORTY-FOUR

THE CREW OF THE independent junk laughed and talked as the news passed from cabin to below that coastal birds had been sighted. They were drawing near Jun Gan.

Lir listened to every scrap in hopes of learning something that would enable him to grab Lum Bu and escape. His mind ran with calculations, most of which dwindled to nothing: too many holes in reckoning probabilities. He did not know enough.

He did learn that the Horse Brethren had no navy in the sense that the empire had. Not that they didn't have ships. The northerners' seagoing force was made up of independents such as this one, bound either by complicated family ties — this ship he was on seemed to be owned by a connection to Hoxie's mother — or by promise of loot.

In other words, they were pretty much pirates.

But then a lot of ships turned pirate if trade went sour, that much TanTan had pointed out in his incessant reading. For that matter, the islands that provided tribute often cursed the empire for being pirates. That word got thrown around pretty loosely.

He also learned that if he asked questions that were not related to the scutwork he was assigned, people wanted to know why he asked. He heard a lot more by remaining silent, and sweeping, or scrubbing, or mending, in the vicinity of those sharing that nasty-smelling milk drink they were so fond of.

Bu played music, losing herself in it as much as she could.

When land bumped up on the horizon, Master Larq thrust a rough-woven carryall into her hands. "You keep that tunic. Doesn't fit anyone right anyway, and the elbows are worn through, or will be. Also, you'll need your own dish, and eating sticks."

Lir got much the same from Pao, given along with some derisive commentary, to which Lir listened without caring. He meant to escape the moment they reached land. If he could find his way to the empire side of the war front, he knew he'd be taken care of—for the first time in his life, his birth would actually benefit him, instead of seeming like an empty shell. He just had to get himself, and the music student, there.

They passed on the deck as they collected their dry clothes, and Lir asked Bu in an urgent undervoice, "Can you swim?"

"I'm sorry—" she began.

He turned away. Of course she couldn't swim. She was half blind. He'd just have to find some other method. It wasn't as if swimming was his only escape. Or even the best, he realized as the ship approached the harbor, which proved to be even more crowded with all kinds of craft than he remembered the harbor at the imperial capital being.

The sails were brailed up and the anchor let down before they reached the estuary. There they sat, rocking on the water. Lir stood near the rail, trying to estimate if he could swim and tug Lum Bu along, when Pao appeared. "Be ready. When Targul gets back with the boat, we'll be transferring." And he stayed right by Lir, who had to wait in mounting impatience while someone rowed to the shore, did something, then rowed back.

It was a different person who climbed on board. This man dropped to one knee, fist to chest, the first sign to Lir that Hoxie had a higher rank than he'd surmised.

"Bexa? Where's Targul?"

"He fell between the boat and the pier steps. Wrenched his shoulder so he can't row, and he sent me with this." Bexa hold up a hefty bag that clinked richly.

As Hoxie took the gold into the shipmaster's cabin, Lir wondered if Hoxie having command over more people than just these two or three on this ship would help or hurt his chances of escape. If Hoxie was busy catching up on news, and throwing around orders, maybe Lir could grab Bu and slip away...

Hoxie emerged shortly, and carried a smaller bag to Master Larq. "The king rode back to camp last season. Here's your share of what Lum Bu's likely to bring if he doesn't keep her."

Master Larq took the reward, accepting that selling Bu would not happen conveniently in the harbor, where she might be on hand to claim a bigger share. "If she's to be sold or traded, can you make sure it's to a good place, one that will treat her decent?" Her voice was gruff

Hoxie stared in brief surprise, and said, "I will." Then he said to Pao, "Into the boat."

"Come on," Pao said to Lir, tugging his good arm.

Lir had to climb down and wait as Bu was handed down by Bexa, who jumped down beside her. Then Bexa waved to the ship to cast off the rope, and he and the other three rowers sent the boat skimming through the sun-spangled waters...

...Not toward shore—which was thronged—but toward the mouth of the river.

Lir ground his teeth in disappointment. As they bumped over the choppy current, he longingly watched the boardwalk, seeing at least three knots of people he could have lost himself in. He'd learned the art of slipping the leash when he was a teenager, and he knew he could still do it, given the slightest opportunity. If they'd only been on shore. But the boat stayed in the middle of the estuary, surrounded by boats going in all directions. There was no chance of swimming for it.

As they started up the river, they began passing a row of sampans anchored on both sides of the shore, as well as one or two floating on the water. Lir scanned everywhere for the least sign of possible escape, as Hoxie peered upriver toward a thin column of smoke. "Bexa? What's going on there?"

Bexa did not pause in his rowing, but straightened briefly, craning his neck. Then he let out an exclamation, eyes wide. "That's... Is that ours?"

The boat, bucketing up the river on inflowing tide, passed more sampans, beyond which they could make out a host of people frantically throwing water onto a burning vessel.

"That is! That's ours," Bexa exclaimed. "Ay!" He threw a fast grin Hoxie's way. "But ... here's an idea. You know, we've got my brother's vessel. He'll let us use it. Faster anyway," he added in a quick, cheery voice, every word of which grated in

Bu's ears in exactly the same way First Sister's voice had grated when she coaxed or petted Bu into being tripped into the midden, or shoved out into the rain, or pushed through the gate so that the village boys could pelt her with chicken droppings and other filth. "Just around the bend upriver a bit."

Hoxie took in Bu's puzzled expression—that was suspicion. In a fast move, he slammed Bexa down onto the bench, forearm across his throat, a knife Lir hadn't seen him carrying jammed point down against the man's breastbone.

"Hoxie, what's wrong with you," Bexa blustered. "Boru said we could use Da's vessel if we needed it, you don't even have to pay because we're all loyal to you…"

Hoxie ignored Bexa's babble and turned to Bu. "What did you hear?"

She tried to find the right words to explain the falsity—but the two at the oars exchanged a glance, dropped their oars, pulled knives and lunged, one for Hoxie, and the other for Bu.

Her reflexes had honed to defensive speed when she was small. Her self-discipline had kept them honed, and she crouched into a ball, arms over her head, so the knife only scraped along her bony shoulder blade. Then clattered to the deck when Pao cut the man's throat in one stroke.

Hoxie stabbed Bexa with sudden fury, and on the backswing warded a blow from the oarsman, and then cut his throat. Then he slewed back and stared down at Bexa—known since they were boys, often sharing the same tent—and muttered, "Should have seen it at the outset. Targul would never fall, even drunk."

"He's probably dead," Pao said soberly.

"Sorxu got to Bexa somehow." Hoxie kicked Bexa's inanimate form.

Then Lir spoke up. "I was going to ask if you if you have any enemies—"

Hoxie's head swung around so fast his braids slapped his arms. Raising the bloody knife, he snapped, "What?"

"We're going to intersect with two boats," Lir said, pointing with his chin at either side of the river. "Both right now are paddling behind other boats, but their lines will converge…there." He pointed upriver some three hundred paces.

"At the bend," Pao said, then, grunting as he heaved one of the dead over the side. Then the other.

Hoxie tossed Bexa into the river, muttering, "No sending a traitor's spirit to the sky fathers, Bexa. Wait for your brother in the nether world. He'll be there soon." Then he peered where Pao had pointed. "Where? No, I see one. You're right." He picked up one of the paddles and shoved it at Lir. "On Pao's mark." He glanced at Lir's broken arm, then hauled Bu up by her wrist, and plumped her onto the bench next to Lir. "You help him, if you want us to survive."

Pao and Hoxie both picked up oars—one sticky with someone's blood—and they bent to rowing, powerful stroke after powerful stroke. Lir cast an assessing glance over his shoulder, then braced his feet in the horrible straw shoes and did his best one-handed, as Bu matched his strokes on the other side.

The boat began to pick up a little speed, and Lir had a heartbeat or two of relief at lengthening the distance between them and the oncoming threat when an arrow zipped between Bu and him.

"Down," he told Bu, pressing her toward the bench—then uttering a startled exclamation when his hand came away wet.

"Row!" Hoxie countermanded. "Or we're joining Bexa the traitor."

Bu turtled her head fearfully, and kept pulling desperately on the oar, though her palms began to sting.

"Pao! Scan that side. Sorxu has to be here."

"I don't see…"

"He'll be here," Hoxie said, his gaze switching between the nearer shore and the water. "He will want to see me die. And where he is, he'll have the most men."

"Oh! I don't see him, but I caught sight of Peppergreen on that side—"

"We'll have to guess he's with Sorxu. This side is nearer. We might even make it…"

Nearer it might be, but the two boats were faster, and more arrows zipped and hissed very close to them all. One thunked into the side of the boat an instant before then they passed behind a flatboat filled with boxes; its oarsmen roared and cursed as arrows peppered their cargo.

Given this brief respite, the boat gathered more speed, jolting across the water toward some sampans. Lir bit back the urge to shout, "Beware!" before Hoxie drove the boat straight into a tiny space between two sampans—causing both to rock dangerously, wooden rails rending.

As people from the sampans popped out, screaming and yelling, Hoxie turned, yanked Bu by the arm, and flung her onto the deck of one sampan. Then Lir right behind her, Pao leaping behind them—one hand clapped to his forearm, which an arrow had gone through, sticking halfway.

Hoxie flung gold onto both decks, which sent the screaming occupants scrambling, and leaped from one sampan deck to the shore. He yanked Bu and Lir over, followed by Pao, still with that arrow through his arm.

"Lead," Hoxie said to Pao, who had spent a year here while Hoxie was being tutored in the southern language.

Hoxie grabbed Bu, gestured Lir in front of him, and then began a terrifying race through the throng.

Lir paced behind Pao, looking for a chance to sprint away, but Hoxie was right on his heels. Bu stumbled along, the slice on her back stinging at every step. She did her best to keep up as blurs shifted and swarmed around her, the ground uneven. A last arrow flew overhead, then they reached a warren of mostly round cottages built close together, as if long ago someone had pitched tents, then put up stone walls in place of the tent fabric.

Pao knew his way, leading into torturous twists and turns, jinking sideways and doubling back. Bu's breath clawed in her throat when they emerged at last in a tiny court, barely big enough for a drying line full of laundry, an outdoor stove and a low table on a platform where the family ate when the weather permitted.

A woman burst forth from the low door, her eyes widening when she saw them. She struck her fist against her chest and began to drop to one knee, but Hoxie sprang forward, catching her by the wrist. "Now now, Ilha. Is Dax here?"

"I'm here." A foxy-faced cousin emerged from the cottage.

"Sorxu has people coming after us."

Ma Ilha grinned, then said to Pao, "Hold tight, little brother."

Pao grabbed a pole holding up the drying line, and his breath keened as the woman put both hands to the arrow, and drew it out. Pao swayed as Ilha eyed the arrow. "Huh! Eagle Clan." She spat on it. "I'll make it disappear. Come on, Pao, give me that bloody shirt."

Dax had already ripped his tunic off, and traded with Pao, who was looking white about the mouth. Ah, manhood, Lir thought, but wisely kept that to himself.

Dax snatched off Pao's headband, which Lir had noted had the same device that Hoxie's did, but not stitched in gold. Did those have meaning, or were they merely decorative?

Dax tied it on, shaking his braids close around his face, then jogged out to find the pursuit and lead them around until he'd mired them deep in Badger territory, at which time they would be made to regret their trespass.

Ilha dived into the cottage, brought out a strip of cloth, and bound it around Pao's dripping arm as Hoxie said, "Did you know we were landing today?"

Ilha looked surprised. "No!"

"Sorxu knew," Hoxie said grimly. "That attack was planned."

Ilha lifted a shoulder. "Everyone knows Sorxu is consorting with demon shamans. Ay! Did you see that this girl is bleeding, too?"

Everyone turned to Bu, who dropped her head.

Hoxie exclaimed, "You didn't say anything—" Then halted. Though Bu was mild as a lamb, and absolutely useless in some ways, she was not stupid. She'd clearly doubted Bexa, whom she had never met, before Hoxie began to suspect a ploy. Nor had she ever complained in his hearing. "Can you do anything for a back slice, Ilha?"

"Ma's poultice is about all I can do. Come, girl." Bu found herself yanked to the low table, where she sat. Ilha darted inside the cottage, and came out with a poultice that smelled strongly of herbs. She reached down the neck of Bu's tunic and smeared a gritty handful of the stuff over Bu's shoulder blade. The poultice stung hard enough to bring tears to Bu's eyes. "There. If Sorxu tries a search, he's sure to come here early on. We won't even know you've returned."

So saying, she ducked into the house again, and came out with a round loaf of fresh-baked bread, and some dried fish. "Take that. Mother won't mind if you use her sampan. But you'd better get there fast."

At least, Bu thought miserably, the cut was now going numb.

Hoxie said, "I won't forget your aid."

The girl struck her fist against her chest in answer, and it was once again time to run. More dodging made the trip especially miserable, especially as the shadows closed in and began to deepen. But then the cottages thinned, and they plunged down a path toward a canal. Here, at intervals, sampans had been tied.

Pao led them to one that was dark and empty. They splashed into the shallow water then climbed aboard, and Pao fetched a pole from along the rail, and pushed them out into the still water, until the current began to propel them gently.

Darkness closed in, but Hoxie forbade them to light a lamp. "We don't know how far the search will extend. Even Sorxu will have to be careful in Badger territory, and we can trust Dax to mire Sorxu's assassins there, especially if they are outsider hirelings."

"They will be," Pao said, a little hoarsely. "Everyone should know by now that you're back. Unlike Sorxu's hirelings, his clan riders will be wary. No one will want to be associated with killing you."

"Maybe. We don't know what lies Sorxu has told my father. It disturbs me that he knew we were coming."

"Peppergreen," Pao said in disgust.

"He did not have pigeons. He must have had some other way to let them know."

"We *know* Sorxu has spilled blood to the Antlered One," Pao muttered. "He surely had imps looking through Peppergreen's eyes. Should've found an excuse to toss him overboard."

Hoxie was not certain that Sorxu could look through anyone's eyes, though he definitely had access to charms and charmed objects. As he did himself. He cast an uncertain glance Lir's way—but found himself unwilling to stab Lir in the back on the chance that Sorxu knew who he really was. This was the worst of Sorxu's malice. It bled into life even when he was not directly confronting you. It bled into your thoughts.

If you let it, he heard his mother whisper, and put his mind to practical reasons. "But we don't know who else has been bought out."

While they held this quick exchange, Lir frowned in the darkness. Hoxie was the barbarian king's son? One of them. Didn't that warmongering king have twenty or thirty sons?

Something thumped into Lir's lap. Hoxie said, "Eat up. Then get what sleep you can. If we survive until dawn, be ready to ride."

"Ride?" Bu said softly.

"Horses. Ever seen one?" Pao said.

"No," was the reply, even softer.

Pao sighed, hoping Hoxie would see sense and abandon these two to their fates. If they were smart, they would survive. They had no importance whatsoever to Sorxu.

Hoxie said nothing, just tore off another bite of the tough bread.

Which was answer enough.

FORTY-FIVE

HORSES WERE A NECESSITY in the north, the best having been bred on the three islands of the Jun Suai origin. These enormous islands, mostly plains, were divided by narrow passages the size of rivers. The southern reaches were agricultural, wheat and hemp growing best. The horses liked the plains.

Jun Gan—Benevolent Breezes to the empire—the most southerly of the island claims of the Jun Suai king, was divided by a spine of conical mountains in which brimstone was mined. To the south, centuries of planting. To the north, with its thinner soil, hardy grasses grew, amid bamboo stands here and there, and not much else.

Mantai Haim, the Jun Suai king, had shifted his capital to this island to cement his claim. This required a ride of several days. More of a race, because Hoxie was driven by the need to get to the king's camp before Mantai Sorxu, whom he had never acknowledged as a blood-brother, nor Sorxu him—a hatred that had been established from the boys' first meeting when one was six and the other almost ten. Sorxu had been kept deep within his mother's ambitious clan, trained to lethal competence despite his diminutive size at nine years old, and taught that all the king's other sons were rivals to be either defeated or made subordinate.

Hoxie had refused to be made subordinate, young as he

was.

The Badger clan, to which Hoxie's mother belonged, was strongly allied to the Muskrat clan, whose horse stud upriver was reached by morning light. Here, Hoxie permitted them to rest long enough for a hot meal, and for both Pao and Lir to get their bandages changed. The women of the house had a different poultice for Bu, equally stinging. Then it was time to ride.

Lir knew how to ride, though he had not done so since he was small. Horses this far north were a necessity, but in the imperial capital they were a luxury, one he'd easily foregone.

As for poor Bu, she took one look at the vague massive shape, and terror drained all her blood to her toes. But she was used to no one taking the least notice of her concerns. She was told that she would ride with one or another of the Muskrat riders or Pao until they reached the king's camp.

They had a string of remounts, so they went from saddle to saddle, eating as they rode, traveling by moonlight once Phoenix Moon was up enough to shed some light, and sleeping only when it was too dark to see. Bu wept silently in the darkness, muscles she never knew she had white-hot with agony, her skin chafed. The equally silent riders heard her shuddering breathing, but said nothing, for what could be said? There was no alternative but endurance.

Hoxie knew that Sorxu would not dare to attack either Badger or Muskrat territory, as they were powerful, and high in the king's favor. But of course that would not extend to any parties found in the middle of the plains.

The two husky Muskrat riders attended them, seeing to meals as well as to the animals, and taking turns guarding their camp. They would return the horses once the king's camp was reached, which happened after four grueling days.

During that time, Lir was also passed between the two Muskrats, whom Hoxie had ordered to train him in horse care. Lir had to force his tired body to the arduous labor because he knew his life depended on it. That much had become clear during the short fight in the boat, following which their pursuit had done their best to shoot them.

Hoxie watched obliquely, still avoiding Lir himself. The closer he got to his father's camp, the more he became convinced he ought to have left Lir behind. But it was too late for that. Lir wandering around the island would surely be snapped up by Sorxu's followers—who would then extract every detail of Lir's life. And Sorxu would then gleefully bring all that to the king, to inform him that Hoxie had lied about his birth.

Bu was fighting hard against the pain, not sure she could continue on anymore, when Pao gave a ululating cry, which ended in an exulting laugh: "We're back!"

Hoxie and the Muskrats had been aware of pursuit slowly gaining for half a day, but when that haze on the horizon indicated the camp, they sheered off, and vanished toward the west.

Perimeter riders greeted Hoxie with fists to hearts, and he raised a hand, slowing the pace to cool the animals down. Now that they were inside the first patrol ring, there was no need for speed.

Lir scanned to either side as they trotted into a camp of huge round tents, thickly guarded by armed riders as well as foot warriors. Banners with long streamers depicted various stylized animals. Before the largest tent in the center, the banners depicted a golden salamander, and below it, a very stylized predator bird with a chevron from ears to beak—a shrike? That was the device on Hoxie's and Pao's headbands, just as the Muskrat riders had a kind of rodent face on their headbands. Some men wore single feather of kingfisher blue dangling from the ties at the backs of their headbands. Many did not, mostly the young. Hoxie did not wear one, nor Pao.

As their party slowed to a walk, everyone in view turned to stare, then came the salutes. Pao grinned, clearly relishing the attention—but he checked, swallowing an exclamation when from one side tent near the central one, a white-haired woman emerged, staring at them.

Bu, of course, saw only blurs and colors. She sniffed the air, smelling horse above all, then cook fires, and wild spices. She did not see this white-haired person at all, but Lir did. He took in the long robe embroidered with signs, the staff with some kind of Essence-imbued stone affixed to the top, and wondered if he'd just seen his first shaman.

Lir caught an uneasy glance from Hoxie toward Bu, who seemed unaware of the fixed interest of the old woman. Then they reached the outer area of the huge tent. They slid off their horses, and servants in clothes much like the ones Lir wore ran to the horses' bridles. Lir wondered if he was supposed to doing horse chores, and cast a glance at Pao, whose attention was not on him. It was on Bu, who had crumpled to the ground. Lir winced at every step as he approached. Pao muttered urgently, "We have to get her to her feet."

Lir caught a tight-lipped glance from Hoxie. Biting back a comment about barbarians, he winced as he bent down. "I think we have to meet their king," he murmured to Bu.

Her chest heaved on a muffled sob, valiantly if unsuccessfully suppressed, and with Pao on one side and Lir on the other, they supported Bu between them. To Lir — who was also sore to the point of agonizing — it looked like a long walk, but it was a short distance after all, for armed guards stopped them maybe ten paces within the tent.

Hoxie walked on alone, then dropped to one knee, right fist to his chest before a low platform upon which a man sat, surrounded by what appeared to be mostly sable skins, save for one tiger skin that drew both Lir's and Bu's eyes. Though she could not see the stripes, she did see the bright color.

"Father, I've returned from my manhood ordeal."

"Two years," the king said, elbows on knees. He had Hoxie's long eyes — phoenix eyes. Lir had always heard that particular feature ascribed to imperial nobility. Heh. He wondered if the northerners said the same.

The king's voice filled the huge tent. "Did you accomplish the task I set you?"

"I did not, Father."

The listeners, men and women both, exchanged glances, and a few whispers, but no one looked Lir's way. His gut still roiled. The way his life had gone so far, it would be just another irony if he was to be tortured to death as the heir that he actually was not. And never wanted to be.

"Then why are you here?" the king asked — and though this barrel-chested man was about as different from Imperial Father as two men could be, he had the same ability to convey threat without raising his voice. Or maybe that was in the perception of the auditor?

Hoxie remained kneeling as he said, "I was taken into the imperial guard, and posted within the imperial palace itself. My orders were to preserve the life of one of the princes, which I carried out, but as I did so, I learned what there is to learn about the inner workings of the imperial court. I learned all the signs and signals of the imperial guard. I learned their defensive ploys. I trained with them, and know their strengths and weaknesses."

"Excellent!" The king sat back, chuckling. "Get up, my boy,

get up. Be at ease, and let's hear more. Ah, that is far more valuable, far more! You! Get the prince a cup. Go on, Hoxie," he said.

Hoxie explained about the pilgrimage, and about the storm, at which description both Lir and Bu sensed an alteration in some of the listeners, though the reaction was too quick, and too subtle to evaluate.

Then his attention was caught by familiar names, as Hoxie gave a blunt assessment of each of the imperial princes. Including Lir.

The king laughed louder. "Lazy, crazy, and deaf. Older, stupid, two imprisoned, the rest dead. The old emperor sprawled on his throne like a wounded seal," he exclaimed, slapping one knee. "I'm of the same generation, but I can still leap into the saddle. We truly breed better men. Eh, what are these?" He pointed at Lir and Bu with a beringed finger. "With young Pao?"

"A servant, and Lum Bu there is the emperor's premiere musician."

"Why are they holding her up? Is she drunk?"

"Never been on a horse. We rode hard, as my chief desire was to report to you, Father."

Bu kept her head bowed, but at those words, which she took as a threat in this terrible place, her tears flowed more freely.

"We will test this musician presently. But what will we do with her in the meantime? Or is there another intent here? Are you planning to take your first wife, eh?"

Taking a wife was not done until one's ordeal was complete; everyone in the room knew that, including both father and son. Hoxie ignored this little test, saying incredulously, "A southerner as a wife?" As he spoke, there was the insistent image of long, trailing ribbons, the sweet inward curve from shoulder to waist and out again, revealed and concealed by the flow of silken robes covered with embroidered roses, and a teasing mouth with a single dimple at one side.

He squashed that, saying, "She is deemed the best musician. If southern music doesn't please you, she ought to bring a good price."

"Can she play our music?"

Pao spoke up then, letting go of Bu and dropping to one knee behind Hoxie. "O father-king, we saw her pick up a horse

fiddle, which she had never seen before, and play it like…
like…like an old musician. She didn't even know what a harp
was—put it on its side at first—then played a war ballad as if
she took the song from the air."

"Oh? I'm impatient to hear this talent."

At this, a woman who had been sitting to the king's right,
directly below his platform, turned to the king. "Let me take
her in hand for a day or so. Throw your mind back to when
you were a small child, and your first riding lessons. From the
looks of them all they've been riding hard."

The king grunted, waving a hand. "You've done well. We
shall celebrate your success tomorrow. Drink up, and give me
the specifics of the imperial guard's defenses…"

The woman rose. She appeared to be about the age of
TanTan's mother, short of stature and compact of build, her
braided hair with silver strands along the top. Like many, she
wore a feather ornament in her hair.

She approached Bu and said, "Come along, child," taking
a firm grip on Bu's arm and guiding her toward the tent
opening.

A quick look from Pao prodded Lir into springing to Bu's
other side. "I can walk," she whispered, though her face was
wet with tears.

"I want out," he breathed.

"Oh." She leaned against him. Weak and half-blind she
might be, but once again he was impressed by how quick she
was. Like LanLan.

In this manner, the woman led them slowly to another tent
adjacent, smaller but set with low folding tables and
comfortable cushions. The woman lowered Bu to one, saying,
"I am Avor of Badger clan. Hoxie is my son. You are?"

"Bu," said Bu, squinting up in an effort to see this woman's
expression.

"I'm going to see what's what, and then we might go to the
hot spring. You really will feel much better if you soak those
muscles." Avor looked up at Lir, then said, "Scat."

"Ah, where do I go?"

Avor gave a soft laugh. "Outlanders! Why did he bring
you? Ah, I'll put that to him when he finishes his interview.
The horse pickets are that way. They'll put you to work until
Hoxie summons you."

Lir forced himself to leave, aware that if he expected to
maintain this guise, he'd better learn more, as Bu, left alone

with Avor, apologized.

Avor chuckled under her breath. "What for? I'm thinking that you did not ask for a four-day ride, whatever your initial arrangement was with my son."

"He pulled me out of the sea when the ship broke up," she said.

"Ah, ah, ah. I see. Now we are alone, no men about, let's take a look. Oh, that does look raw, but I've seen worse. Yes, let's get you into the waters. It will hurt at first, I warn you, but you'll sleep better afterward."

For all her kindly tone, Avor was not asking Bu what she wanted to do, which would be to be left alone. She perforce had to follow the woman out into the flat plain. Very soon they came to what looked to Bu like a gash in the ground, carved by water long ago. Small caves pocked the walls of this gorge, steps having been carved into the largest.

Here was a vast cavern, with steam and the familiar smell of hot springs at one end. There followed an interval that went pretty much as predicted. After a brief, excruciating time, gradually the pain lessened, leaving Bu limp and listless. Avor helped her into her slightly-less-dirty outfit, scrubbed the one Bu had been wearing, and brought it out to be dried in the sun.

Bu was able to walk back, though painfully, and here Avor offered her some spiced mare's milk, then, pointed out a bed on the ground made of soft skins. Bu stretched out gratefully and fell into profound slumber.

She woke to the sound of low voices, vehement in crisp syllables, though soft in volume. Bu could not see in the darkness, but she sensed a heavy hanging of some kind between herself and the speakers.

"…you prove that he's sacrificed to the Antlered One?"

"I cannot." That was Hoxie. Bu knew his voice by now. "But how else could he have sent that tempest against us? I'm convinced that it was sent. Every one of the imperial sailors predicted beforehand it would be a wet blow but no worse, because the season for tempests is over."

"But that is not proof." Ah, that was Avor.

"Mother, the Antlered One takes a life for each service—"

"And we would be hearing if Sorxu's spending the lives of Eagle riders."

"He could use slaves, or people captured."

"My understanding is, those lives will not gain him a tempest strong enough to smash one of those imperial tower ships. It would have to be a rider at the least—a blood relation. He would not dare to sacrifice any Shrike riders. Your father would take that as blow directed at him. And his mother would not permit him to kill any of her clan."

"I thought she'd pick them for him," Hoxie said bitterly

"Son, leave behind your childhood judgments. I've known Tirat since we were girls, and though she's ambitious, she would deplore any dealings with those who destroy life Essence."

"I know that, Mother. I spoke carelessly."

"Do not do so again, Hoxie. I know you are tired. Your ordeal has been that, an ordeal, and much you cannot tell your father. But surely you sensed the tension among us?"

"I did. I thought it might be aimed at me, as I still do not know what Sorxu has said while I was gone—"

"You did not notice the absence of your Uncle Banxu?"

"Yes, immediately. There was a hole at Father's left where he'd stood, but I assumed he was riding on orders."

"He led an attempt. Against your father. And his entire family, now gone. It was terrible, terrible. And all due to careless words by your father once too often. If you are to wield the salamander sword, you must govern your tongue forever after this night. Waking. Sleeping. Words a man with power says, and forgets, sink into hearts and fester."

"I am listening, Mother. Thank you for your teaching. As for Aunt Tirat, I know she wants Sorxu to win through prowess alone. I know that. But ever since he turned twenty, *he* tells her and *she* listens and does what he asks. Not the other way."

Avor cast a long sigh. "I know. I've seen it, too, and yet I believe it is her influence that has kept your father from assigning Sorxu's ordeal, though by all standards he's been ready for years. But wild, too wild, not enough discipline for command, so says your father..." She stopped there, and her voice lowered to a whisper that Bu barely heard. "At times— when he is not in one of his moods—I think he might be a little afraid of Sorxu. After all, we've a long tradition of the new king taking the salamander sword from the old king. You can be certain, especially since you left, that your father has him watched, not just by riders, but by both your uncles, the ones he trusts most."

Hoxie said, "My guess is, he's lurking out there, pretending he didn't chase me, which would make Father furious. He'll turn up tomorrow, or the day after, and he'll be so surprised and glad to see me, and then remind me every time he sees me that I failed." A snort, then, "Ah, getting angry now is shouting into the wind. I'm going off to soak the travel dust out of my skin. And glean news from my sane brothers."

Quiet fell, and Bu drifted back to sleep.

FORTY-SIX

WHEN BU WOKE, IT was to the light of morning. She made out the slim form of a girl sitting next to her, doing something with her hands. Bu squinted. Fletching arrows?

The girl looked up. "You're awake! I'm Eki. You're Bu, my mother tells me?"

Bu struggled up to a sitting position, wincing against the lightning stabling her inner thighs, the sharp ache in her outer thighs.

Eki said sympathetically, "I know it doesn't seem like it, but you'll actually feel better once you move, and your blood stirs again. I've also learned a couple of acupoints that can help with the pain."

"Are you a healer?" Bu asked.

"No, no. I studied with the healer for three years, before I apprenticed to the Phoenix shaman. But I remember some useful things."

Eki dug her knuckles into various points, which eased Bu's discomfort enough for her to walk once again to the hot springs. After a soak, the pain receded enough for Bu to scrub the dirt and horse smell out her second outfit. As they walked back Eki spoke easily, pointing out this or that person, and what they did. Bu learned that there were many clans under this king, all with animal or bird names, before Eki guided the conversation away from families and clans toward what people did, until Bu began to wonder what questions Eki had in her mind, yet did not ask.

She was much too afraid to venture her own questions, and so the talk remained general until they returned to find break-fast ready. The freedom with which an old nanny argued with Avor about their favorite poultices reminded Bu of Ginger with the grand princess. When it was done, Eki exclaimed, "We're celebrating Hoxie's confirmation as a rider captain, and the king specifically asked to hear you perform. Do you sing?"

"I can, but it is not where my strength lies. I'm a musician."

"Can you drum?"

"Yes, though not well."

"Ah. I'm going around to collect instruments. Do you think you can walk well enough to go with me to try them?"

Bu did not hear a real choice, and rose silently. At least she did feel measurably better. And while Eki took Bu to various tents to introduce her, explain about her own instruments destroyed in a storm at sea, and ask to borrow any they had, Lir spent his time at the enormous horse picket, where they put him to work at once.

It seemed that no sooner had he gone down the line replenishing water or hay, or brushing down animals and checking for burrs or pebbles in hooves, than a new company would ride in and here it all was to be done again. He ached from skull to heels, but as long as he kept moving, he felt that he was relatively invisible.

Since the weather was clear, the servants bedded down outdoors near the animals. They woke before the sun appeared, washed cursorily out of a shared rain barrel, and got right back to work.

Lir's relative invisibility was put to the test that second day, when an enormous party rode in at the gallop, a slender man wearing a huge mantle of sable in the lead. Like Hoxie and the younger men, he wore a headband without the feather in the high-bound braids that (Lir learned by listening that day) indicated a rider who had undergone his or her ordeal.

The word "Sorxu" was heard everywhere as the young man in the voluminous mantle dismounted, swaggering. Lir braced for anything as the narrow face with long phoenix eyes turned his way. And ran indifferently over Lir, searching for...

"Brother," Sorxu called with derisive cheer, and met Hoxie midway between the horse picket and the king's tent. "You are back. You must have killed your man?"

"There was no heir to kill," Hoxie replied.

"Oh?" Sorxu said, with drawn-out, obvious disbelief.

Before Sorxu could say anything else, Hoxie extended a hand toward the great tent, saying, "Father is waiting."

Sorxu swept past. In spite of that thick fur mantle, Sorxu wasn't as tall or as broad as his half-brother. It was tempting to lay the origin of the man's animus to that, but Lir had learned that assuming single motivations for anything were seldom to be trusted.

A horn blast caused heads to turn. Then came the sound of hooves as a party of women returned from the hunt, bearing three enormous wild boars. These women were cheered, a pair of girls who looked no longer than sixteen preening as those chosen to cook for a big gathering came forward to prepare them and get them turning on a spit over a low fire.

Twice he tried to test the limits of his invisibility, but both times he scarcely got as far as the underground steam vents that made it clear why this spot had been chosen for the camp, when Pao came looking for him. The second time, Pao said impatiently, "What are you doing over here, rock head? You can get a bath with the rest of us before the feast. And what are you going to do, put your filthy clothes back on?"

Once could be put down to curiosity. Two times to stupidity, but three would be suspicious, Lir decided. Once again he had to wait, and work, until the long, arduous day finally drew to a close. True to his word, Pao led Lir, carrying his second set of clothes, to the baths along with a lot of other servants. A couple of young, unfeathered riders pestered Lir with questions about the barbarians in the south, then laughed at his "slave" accent. He saved it all up to tell TanTan and Rathlan later—along with plenty of invective about the barbarians who thought everyone else barbarous—because he refused to believe that his brother and cousin were dead.

Meanwhile, Bu ended up with six different instruments to choose from—none of them a qin. Her fingers itched for the snap of silk strings beneath them again, but at least there was this horsehair harp.

As the cooking commenced, she caught snatches of song: by the cooks, and by the young people going about their chores. The king had ridden out early with a huge cavalcade, and on their return he strode to his tent, from which soon issued a song by a man with a beautiful voice. It was a ballad with a galloping beat, accompanied by the reedy-sounding small flutes favored here in the north. Bu listened as she tested and tuned the instruments. She sorted the sounds according to the patterns she knew, and so she was ready when someone blew three long blasts on a ram horn, and the camp began to assemble around the great fire built in the square before the king's tent.

"Can you sing?" Avor asked. "A song about Hoxie's valor would be the most welcome," she said.

"I'm not really a trained singer," Bu said.

Avor accepted that, but Bu sensed disappointment.

And when they began sitting down, a girl around Bu's age came up and said, "Aren't you the outlander musician? Can you make a song for my sister Cassia and our cousin Saffron? They brought down the boars by themselves, you know, which makes them full riders."

"I am not very familiar with your customs," Bu said. "I'm very sorry."

"Ah, well, ignorant is ignorant. I thought that Eki would teach you *some*thing, but she knows her own affairs best." The disappointed girl turned away, and vanished in the crowd.

As the sun sank in the west, the king strode out to the center near the fire. For this celebration he wore his formal headdress, with kingfisher blue feathers representing each island he ruled. He held high a cup. "Tonight we celebrate my son Hoxie, who returned with the means to conquer the enemy at last."

That got a roar of approval—though Lir, on the other side of the ring from Bu, noticed that Sorxu raised his cup but did not drink.

More toasts were offered to valor and victory as the king tied a blue feather into Hoxie's headband, then the eating began, interspersed with more toasting. That at least was familiar, even if the drink itself wasn't. But the roasted boar, brushed with chili and other spices was delicious. The young men around Lir chatted and reminisced as they ate and drank. They didn't ignore Lir so much as talk around him, an island in a sea.

Phoenix moon had begun to rise when the king had eaten enough. Some of his younger sons importuned him to begin the dancing, and out came the drums and pipes.

In the south, only entertainment women danced in public; noblewomen could dance for selected company, but never for vulgar eyes. In the north, everyone danced, though men and women did not dance together.

Hoxie led the first dance, sword in hand, to the thrump of drums. At a prodding wave from the king, Sorxu got up and danced with them, but Lir noticed he was always watching what his brother did, and it seemed to Lir that Sorxu made an effort to leap higher, and swing wilder. On the third round, the king got up and danced with them. He, too, leaped high and swung his sword with abandon, though he was somewhat out of breath when he sat.

Hoxie never looked at Sorxu, but a lot of the young women did. And when they sat down, both sons of the king (and others, though as yet Lir couldn't differentiate Hoxie's various brothers from the rest of the clan riders) were surrounded by young women coming around with more drink, as other women danced.

The riders danced, the women danced, and so on.

Finally the king had had enough and remembered Bu. "Let's hear the emperor's prize, ha ha!" he roared.

Fear wrung through Bu. She made a strong effort to subdue it as she stood, tucked the harp upright against one hip and plucked a melody. Eki began to drum. One by one other drummers picked up the rhythm, but the carrying sound was the intricate, driving melody woven together with the refrain of the ballad that Bu had heard sung from the king's tent. Into that melody she began to weave variations from the other northern songs Lir had heard that day, and on the junk, forming a yearning lament for Xia Chi that she would never speak, but which implored the heavens through music.

Lir kept forgetting just how *good* she was. The song, with its dynamic rhythm, intensified to a compellingly complex weaving of several songs, bound by something new, judging by the wide-eyed attention around them. People leaned forward to listen. Lir even saw the king's head turn slowly toward Bu, with a focus so intense the hairs on the back of his neck prickled—

—as Bu hazarded a quick glance in the direction of the king. At all times she took in people's posture in order to guess at reactions as she could not see faces, but shock rang through her, pooling like ice within her when she perceived the twin red pinpoint glows where the king's eyes ought to be.

YinYin's words so long ago returned, and she dropped her gaze fast. Then, she deliberately thumbed a string too hard, and: SPROINNNG!

The sour note raised a laugh as the gripping mood broke.

"Our harps too much for you, southerner?" Sorxu gibed, amid the sycophantic laughter of his circle of admirers.

Ashamed—for breaking a string was nearly as bad as breaking an instrument—Bu forced herself to bow. "I beg your forgiveness..."

Lir stared, appalled. Where was the expertise? Was she frightened out of her wits? She bleated apologies, "I'm so sorry, so sorry, this instrument is so new to me, I am so ignorant... Can I give you a song instead?"

The king blinked her way, then sat back, and waved a hand.

Lum Bu picked up one of the hand drums, tapped expertly, if unexcitingly, and in a pleasant enough voice that barely carried to the outer ring, she sang an old ballad that Lir remembered from childhood, only with a few northern flourishes, and with the names Cassia and Saffron in place of Liad Il and Ranek, and instead of the tremendous battles that had made husband and wife famous for centuries, Bu substituted a lot of pompous nothings about a boar hunt.

However, this song was hailed with great cheering, especially among the younger girls. At the end, Bu said in that bleating voice, "Please teach this ignorant one more of your ballads!" and of course those who liked to perform before the crowd proceeded to do just that, until the king decided everyone had had enough.

The king never looked at Bu again, and Lir knew without anyone saying anything that her fate would soon land her in some house of entertainment. That bleating voice—the broken string—the uninspired song—she'd done that on purpose! To escape?

"Call for divination...call for divination," whispered among the people.

Lir sat up straight, his interest sharpening. According to what Master Angka had told them, the northerners had different ways of augury, though there were some shared characteristics. But the chief difference that it was mostly women who served as shamans, though men could apparently have visions too. This king had the traditional two shamans, one for Phoenix Moon and one for Ghost Moon.

"Give us an augury," the king commanded.

It began with a strikingly beautiful girl with those long

phoenix eyes tapping on a drum. She wore a dark robe covered with symbols. With her three other women set up a powerful rhythm as the Phoenix Moon shaman came out first, as that moon had reached the low zenith of its arc during Ghost Month.

The Phoenix shaman began to dance, uttering phrases over and over that were unintelligible to Lir, as she pounded her staff on the ground, then shook it so that the items dangling from it rattled. Around and around she whirled, until her robe was whipping back and forth in the firelight, as if light stream-ed off it.

Then suddenly she stopped, head thrown back, and shouted, "The salamander! The salamander!"

A man yelled, "The king!" And the men uttered the guttural HOOH HOOH HOOH that was their verbal salute.

And around the ring voices whispered, "The salamander salutes the king. It's a good sign!"

The king raised and shook his sword, light rippling down it as if fire streamed off the sword. Lir squinted. Were those scales on that blade? Salamanders had no scales.

He didn't realize he'd spoken aloud until Pao said, "*Fire* salamanders have scales."

Like dragons, Lir was thinking —

The shaman, unheeding, shouted, "…the two salamanders must dance together before there is victory!"

She slammed the staff three times into the ground, then turned to walk back into her tent as the riders shouted acclaim and praise for the king. He in his turn roared, "Sound the drums! The victory dance, with my son!"

HOOH HOOH HOOH!

Sorxu leaped up, the king turned and added, "All my sons!"

There they were, too many for Lir to count. Lir caught a comment ending, "…left-hand sons."

Since Pao was sticking right by Lir, he might as well get some use out of him. "Left-hand sons?"

Pao grinned. "Born without marriage. Like me."

"Women can do that?"

"Why not?" Pao stated. "Oh." He touched his headband. "You're asking about this? I swore myself to Hoxie, so I wear the Shrike badge. Otherwise, it'd be Badger, with the rest of my family, as my mother is kin to Hoxie's mother."

Women of the Horse Brethren didn't have to marry?

Another thing to tell LanLan, Lir decided as the Phoenix shaman drummers joined the men in playing dancing rhythms. To Lir, the victory dance looked pretty much like all the other men's dances, complete with sword.

Once that was over, Ghost Moon gleamed on the far horizon, and it was time for the other shaman to come out. This was a younger woman, no gray to her hair at all. Again the wild music—if anything, even wilder, kicking up emotions as she whirled and leaped and danced and shook her staff. There was a lot more eye-rolling and ululating before she finally stopped in a dramatic way, looked up at the sky, and shrieked, "The stars praise the salamander king who dances the victory dance!"

Bang, bang, bang, the staff hit the ground, and then she swooned on the spot. Her acolytes bore her off to her tent, and the king smacked his hands to his knees, saying, "A fine feast, and auspicious signs. My boys, the gods clearly approve of my plan. We will take the empire. Each of you boys will have his own island to rule. That will give us peace at last."

That got a cheer!

And while the men cheered, and poured out more of that drink that Lir was angry enough to drink down without drawing a breath, on the other side of the camp, Bu finally stopped trembling. The demon inside that king had not seen her. She had looked away in time. She was still alive. But now she *wanted* to get herself sold. To get away from that terrible demon.

As the men drank, and roared songs themselves, Avor came to Bu, with Eki at her side.

Eki, crouched down directly in front of Bu, and took her shoulders. "Come. Rest well, Bu the Vessel of Light. Tomorrow you are going for a ride."

FORTY-SEVEN

Rest?

How could Bu rest? Avor and her daughter had been very kind to Bu, but how long would that last if she tried to tell them that their king had a demon inside him?

Bu then doubted herself, wishing she'd had her eyepiece. Maybe she imagined the glow. Maybe it was mere reflection from the fire. Except that she had always relied on instinct, and instinct had sensed what lay behind those glows, and cried out against that great, impenetrable shadow becoming aware of her. She was very certain that she did not want that demon knowing that she had glimpsed it.

She was not certain she would be able to sleep—but a long day of moving in spite of the ache in her lower limbs from four days of horseback-riding took care of that. She slid into sleep not long after laying her head down.

She woke early. The entire camp was astir. It was mostly male voices outside. Bu sat up cautiously in her welter of furs, and though she had not made any noise, the servants seemed to know she'd woken for one poked her head in. "Break your fast now, southern girl. The men have taken over the spring, for the king is sending them out to conduct drills. We can bathe after they ride out."

Bu crawled out of the fabric-hung alcove into the space marked by colorful tapestries, where she found Avor. Eki soon joined them as pancakes, made with tasty slivers of boar left from the feast, appeared steaming hot.

The conversation turned to small matters, and remained there even when they took their clean clothes and then followed troops of other women toward the springs. Bu listened to the sounds of the words rather than the words themselves, for all spoke quickly, many in a kind of dialect more difficult to understand than the way the northerners spoke. Everyone spoke brightly, that is, the cheer sounded forced, and when someone ventured a jest, the laughter was a little too loud, too long. Granny Zim had said once that trying to make life normal again wasn't actually normal, because normal was unaware of itself. They couldn't know about the demon, surely. Something else had happened.

Mother and daughter fell quiet on the walk back to their tent, and Bu had begun to hope that she had imagined portent in what might only have been a suggestion about riding. Until Eki said to the chief servant, "We have to teach the southern musician to ride."

"As it should be," the servant said, and went back to her loom.

Bu's heart promptly began drumming against her ribs as mother and daughter led her toward the horse picket. From a short distance away, Lir perceived them, and tried to catch Bu's eye before he remembered that she probably could not pick him out from the rest of the horse servants. Were they selling her off already? But surely they would send more than these two women.

The younger one—the beautiful one with those long, observant eyes—caught his glance, and her brows lifted slightly. He remembered that he was supposed to be the one to lower his gaze, and did, but a tide of heat rose up into his face, and he had to laugh at himself. Blushing as if he were fourteen again!

He kept his back turned, but listened for any scrap of talk as the two women went over the basics of saddling a horse with Bu. He could have told them it was a wasted effort. All she'd done during the long ride was squint helplessly when the Muskrat riders had attempted to teach them both.

Bu's face was a masterful illustration of misery when they boosted her up into the saddle. Sympathy twinged in Lir, but there was nothing he could do, nothing about anything.

In a savage mood, he returned to bridle repair, though he

allowed himself a single glance when he heard them ride away — to meet those long eyes again, as Eki glanced back over her shoulder. This time he was quick to lower his gaze. But he blushed *again*.

Bu remained utterly unaware of any of this. The reawakening of muscular protest absorbed all the world. The horses began at a placid walk, as Avor then Eki gave Bu directives on how to sit correctly, where to grip (not with hands, but with legs!) and what the animal's grunts and shiftings meant.

They stayed at a walk, the two women gesturing at her horse, until they had gone far enough that individual people could no longer be made out, only the shapes of the conical roofs.

Then Avor leaned over, gripped the bridle of Bu's horse, and said, "What happened last night?"

Bu's throat closed. Fearfully, she said, "I broke a string."

Eki chuckled. "I don't pretend to know much about music, though I did tootle a flute a bit when small, but I know those who play, and they'd rather lose a finger than a string. They are hard to make. You broke that string. Why?"

Bu hung her head in misery. "I'm sorry."

Avor sighed. "Tell her."

Eki edged her horse close. "Bu, I realize you cannot see me, but surely you hear the certainty in my voice? We need to know what happened. The shaman had a true vision last night, which is so very rare."

As Eki paused, seeking the right words, Bu ventured a question. "True? Are there false ones? How could you know the difference?"

Eki said, "True as in a real vision. The Sight. It comes rarely, and never when commanded, though the shamans all do the rituals in hopes."

"I think those rituals are more for us who expect to hear something from the gods than for the gods themselves," Avor put in dryly. "I've certainly thought that as Ghost shaman cavorts around like a filly who scents a stallion."

"So it might be," Eki agreed calmly. "So it might be. Phoenix believes Ghost has never actually had a true vision, but she was made an acolyte by her family. Which is why she faints and screeches and her words are always difficult to understand. It might be her way of trying to reach the gods. But her words are her own, not those of a Seer, Phoenix says."

"I don't think Phoenix's much easier to understand," Avor commented.

"That's because she has to be very careful how she expresses actual visions. She must stay true to them, lest the gods punish her and take them away altogether. As for the times when no vision comes, ay, you do the same, you both speak of generalities and hint at specifics for Father. Phoenix through divinations, and you through chatter."

Avor sighed. "If he could, he'd have rituals every day, every meal. But he only wants to hear one thing: victory."

Both turned Bu's way. She saw expectation, even intent in those round faces, and it struck her that these two were holding this exchange for her benefit. They knew all those things, but they revealed them before her so that she would reveal...

She said, very tentatively, "If...someone...saw something ...like a..."

"Spit it out, girl," Eki laughed.

"...demon..."

"Oho," Eki exclaimed, low. All the laughter had vanished from her voice.

Avor gasped.

Eki leaned over to grip Bu's hand. "*Did* you see a demon? Wait, you're half blind. How could you possible see anything?"

Bu's eyes closed. "When I played. I think...I'm pretty sure...I believe I saw it."

Eki said, "You've seen demons before?"

Bu hesitated. She had never been brave. She knew herself for a coward, but Granny Zim had once said that cowardice was a defense for the weak. As long as a person didn't use her cowardice to harm, then it was a good defense. If it worked.

She was a coward now. But would keeping back what she had seen do harm?

"I have seen a demon," she said finally. "I know one. When I see one."

And Eki said, "There's one fighting to lure my father, isn't there."

Bu's face lifted, and her eyes, usually squinched up, widened, a startling effect as she actually had a large, honest pair of eyes, though few rarely saw them. "It is *in* him," she whispered.

Silence gripped all three. The only sound was the wind through the grasses.

"You've said this much," Avor muttered, her voice rough. "Let's have it all."

Bu considered, then said, "I learned that there are different kinds of demons. The one I...met...is benign toward humans. Sh—it eats music. Or rather, the Essence of music. The one I saw in the king, I don't know what it is, but I felt it turning when I looked at it, and I broke the string, and looked away before it could see me. Its shadow is very, very..." Bu's thin fingers flexed, then gripped together tightly.

Avor said, "We have been trying to guard him for years, Phoenix and me. As well as to guide. And now Eki joins us. But you say it is already there?"

"Yes."

"Then everything we do, it is for naught?" She turned her daughter's way, her voice bleak.

Eki said, "Phoenix insists that what we do does help. It could be that it must fight against our charms and rituals, and that slows it. Or weakens it." Eki turned to Bu. "Is that possible?"

"I don't know. But it sounds right. It takes them time to eat a human from within."

"Don't say 'eat'." Eki recoiled. Then she lifted her chin. "Forget what I said. If it's eating him, it's eating him. How long does he have?"

"I don't know. Demons don't care about human time. That much I was taught. Also, they can put a bit of themselves in someone else. If that person invites them in."

"Sorxu," Avor and Eki said at the same time, then Eki turned to Bu. "Can you do whatever it was you did, and tell us if Sorxu is possessed?"

"I could try," Bu said doubtfully. "But there is always the chance that if there is one within him, and it sees me, if it is malicious, it will retaliate in some way. If it desires to remain unknown."

Avor rubbed her hands up her face. "This is so beyond my experience. We need to know if Sorxu is possessed. How?"

"Ah, Sorxu. He's been trouble, and troubled, since I first saw him, when we were small," Eki said, palms upturned.

"Better to stay away from him," Avor said slowly.

"This counsel I agree with," Eki said. "He hates us all, and he'll be immediately suspicious if we approach him. I'll talk to Phoenix, but I suspect she will say to carry on as if it's in him, too."

"It would explain so much," Avor murmured.

"Let's ride back," Eki suggested. "This is long enough for a first lesson. We can have more lessons as needed." And as they turned their horses back toward camp (Avor's hand still on Bu's bridle) Eki said to Bu, "What about that boy Hoxie brought. Who is he really?"

Bu could not hide her jerk of surprise at this utterly unexpected question.

As she hesitated, Eki said, "First, is he your lover?"

"No," Bu protested, much shocked at the impropriety.

"All right, but there's something odd there. His hands are too smooth and fine beneath all the cuts and scrapes from work he's obviously never done before. There's no callus across his palms. I was thinking scribe, only what use would a southern scribe be to Hoxie — and why would he lie about it?"

Bu was thinking rapidly. She was unwilling to lie, not only because it felt like a betrayal of these kindly women, but because she would have to remember a lie, and even compound it if there were further questions.

"He saved your brother's life," Bu said finally. "In the storm. I don't know how, only that it happened."

"Ah, that would explain much, too. But not everything. I see you don't wish to say more about Lir. Tell me about the storm," Eki demanded.

"I was thrown into the sea, and nearly drowned, when your brother pulled me out. I was so sick I noticed little. I think imp-Lir was more awake than I," Bu said, and Eki noted how self-consciously, almost cautiously Bu pronounced his name. A false name?

They were nearing the outer area of the camp, and as a couple of riders approached, the women fell silent.

They reached the horse picket, and Avor said, "Good lesson. We'll make a rider of you yet." Bu gratefully slid off, her legs trembling, and as Avor helped her toward the tent, Eki watched them go, then looked around.

There he was. Eki liked that face. He wasn't handsome in the heroic sense, but his was an intelligent face, broad of forehead and quick of eye, with laughter hinted in the curve of his eyelids and the corners of a well-shaped mouth. A clean-boned face, in spite of that sulky under lip.

Someone had put him to work repairing bridles, at which he clearly had made little progress. She glanced around, then sat down nearby, picked up a bridle, and tools, and began worming hemp reinforcement into the torn rope. "Musician Bu says that you were conscious during the storm. What can you tell me about it?"

Lir was trying to keep his attention strictly on his work. "It was bad."

Eki said patiently, "You saved Hoxie's life. Then, apparently, he saved yours? Or at least he saved Musician Bu's? What happened? What exactly did you see?"

Lir thought rapidly. If he gave her something that didn't have anything to do with imperial palace life, maybe she'd be satisfied and go away. "I saw — or maybe I dreamed them. But I thought I saw water dragons pulling that storm. Flying in it."

"What did they look like?"

"Long. Blue. Gray. Greenish. All shades between. They had broad ridges here." He indicated his forehead with his hooking tool. "But I don't remember any eyes. Lots of long… things, not hair, but streaming like hair, around their faces. Long bodies." He made a motion with the bridle, undulating. "And darting around them too fast to see shapes were shadows, I think. Or maybe dark clouds."

Eki listened to this in silence, then said, "You've the true Sight?"

"No." He was about to say that he had a brother who was a seer, but that would take him exactly in the direction he had no intention of going. "I don't know if I believe what I saw. It was cold, and my arm had broken." He nodded with his chin at the bandaged arm. "The waves were higher than the highest pagoda I've ever seen. I don't know what was real and what wasn't."

Eki considered him. Everything sounded true, but he was choosing his words. What had these two to hide? The demon obviously.

She said, "Phoenix — that is, my shaman master. They give up their names when they take their final vows. She Saw all of you arrive, before you came. And when she saw the four of you, she said that Musician Bu is a Vessel of Light. She herself is not a wielder of Light, though that changed when she began to play, she trails streamers of light."

Lir rested his wrists on his knees as he listened.

Eki leaned toward him. "Who is she, really?"

Lir said honestly, "A Talent. That much I know. Nothing more, except that she was tribute from some far off island to the south of the empire."

"And you?"

He held out his hands. "As you see."

"I see someone with hands that have never done this work, or held a sword. But if you saved Hoxie's life, then of course he must protect you."

She handed him the bridle, which she had repaired perfectly in the short time they spoke, while he was still struggling with his. She walked away. And with her back safely turned, he watched her go.

A hand clapped on his shoulder, startling him. He glanced up into Pao's grinning face. "Don't even think of it. She doesn't toy with the likes of you."

"Wasn't thinking of it."

"Sure you weren't. And I'm a water vole." Pao laughed, then pointed at the bridle that she'd done. "That's a pity gift. No chance, southern boy." And he walked away, chuckling, to inform his cousins that the useless southerner was hankering after the best woman under the sun, an ant longing for Phoenix Moon, and they laughed and shook their heads.

When Eki reached her mother, she said, "They're both hiding something."

"I think so too. Did the boy say anything about demons?"

"He's not a boy," Eki said, then realized she'd spoken too quickly, and smiled at herself. "Though he wears a topknot. That's just southerner style."

Avor's lips curved in a smile.

Eki said waspishly, "What?"

The smile vanished. "Did he say anything about demons?"

"No. But he saw water dragons in that storm that nearly killed Hoxie. I don't think he's a seer, or an augur, as they call them, but the gift might be in his blood, very diluted. I'd better go talk to Phoenix." And think, she vowed to herself.

FORTY-EIGHT

THE STORYTELLER GLANCED WITH weary sadness at the scant offering so far, then took in the crossed arms of the elderly woman, the most generous patron. "We have not forgotten Granny Zim," the storyteller said somewhat hastily. "Not at all!"

When the next summons came for Granny Zim almost two weeks after that previous one, her mind went straight to Bu, and she hurried herself far more than she ever had.

YinYin says she's still in the world, Granny Zim reminded herself, but still there was a tremble in her fingers and knees as she toiled along the servants' route toward the imperial palace.

The emperor, seeing her arrive before him a little out of breath, recognized her worry, and remarked, "A few more days of *The Jade Palace,* and you will have a new rank. Which, I forgot to tell you, will come with an actual jade tally that will, among other things, permit you to cross the lower gardens. It will cut your journey in half."

Granny Zim bowed gratefully, and he handed a small scroll of paper to the graywing One, who brought it to her. "Read that," the emperor said.

Granny Zim sat back on her heels and opened the scroll. Her eyes skimmed past the names of witnesses and couriers and scribes, all unknown to her, to actual words:

> *...and all testified to how Imperial Prince Rathtan swam about tirelessly, towing people to the floating rafts, then going back for more. We unite in expressing our gratitude to your imperial majesty's grace...*

Granny Zim skimmed past the attribution of the successful rescue to the emperor, and began to read faster.

> *...heroism of her maid, named Ginger, who remained by the side of the grand princess, except when she was commanded by Imperial Prince Rathtan to aid him in pulling unconscious persons to the boats, once the imperial guards were able to locate them.*
>
> *The imperial guards deployed a systematic search once the storm began to abate, until all were accounted for. In spite of the disastrous loss of the tower ship, due to your imperial majesty's merit before Heaven and earth, we only lost two, one of those being Fleet Leader Naoki, who Imperial Guard Colonel Deg saw last...*

Granny Zim impatiently scanned faster.

> *...and Imperial Prince Rathtan himself issued orders that Imperial Guard Colonel Deg was forbidden to take his own life, as he believed there was interference by malicious charms, which precludes any possible accusation of negligence. Imperial Colonel Deg refused to take food or rest, leading the search himself, but to no avail: we accounted for the drowned servant, whose feet had tangled with cords bounds around a load of golden plate from the imperial service, and all other persons, except for Imperial Prince Rathlir, the Student Musician Lum Bu, and Imperial Guard Brick.*
>
> *Imperial Guard Pai testifies to seeing Imperial Guard Brick with Imperial Prince Rathlir clinging to a raft as he and Imperial Guard Virtue fought to reach them, but at that moment the ship was sinking, and the two imperial*

guards were thrown into the water, separated from the imperial prince by a massive wave. When it subsided, the imperial prince's raft was nowhere to be seen.

It is believed that Imperial Guard Brick attached himself to the imperial prince, at the least, as there were no bodies, it is hoped that some stray fishing vessel or passing trader picked them up, and they will find their way to the nearest imperial garrison.

Imperial Guard Colonel Deg is leading the search…

Granny Zim looked up.

The emperor said, "I've dispatched my imperial ferrets to investigate, of course. Between them and Deg, who is a hound after a hidden bone when it comes to getting to the bottom of questions, they'll find them."

But the strain in his eyes betrayed his worry. You're blaming yourself, Granny Zim thought. Good.

Let him suffer that sense of fault. Even the imperial censors had to be circumspect when criticizing the emperor. This one at least had a conscience, it seemed. Let it put him on the rack for flinging Bu on this useless adventure.

Granny Zim handed the report back, made her bow, and withdrew.

A few days later, the court saw the final installment of *The Jade Palace*, which ended with the scholar (as usual, a prince in disguise) unite with his beloved, a fairy from the heavenly realm.

The ending began with some of the court smiling with superior knowledge at the predictability, as one duke remarked to a marquis: "Whatever else can be said about imperial princes, they never go about in disguise."

"Indeed. No servants, no obeisance? Ha ha ha, never."

But then Granny Zim played the final song. Into it she put everything she had learned, and felt, and expressed or left unexpressed. This is all the hues of love, she'd said to YinYin, mopping her eyes and blowing her nose after she finished copying out her composition. The next person who played it could only be Bu, she vowed.

The duke's superior smile vanished. The marquis closed

his stinging eyes and thought of a certain comely flower seller of his youth, whom he'd had to see married to a shoemaker, because birth rank requires birth rank.

The song was a stunning success. More than just that marquis wept, some genuinely. The air was giddy with emotion as the emperor rose, and passed an edict appointing Granny Zim a Sagacious Master, and such was the overwhelming emotion shared by all performers that even the masters agreed that it was a promotion well deserved, no matter what her background, or the fact that she had jumped ahead of all, though among them less than a year. Talent, all agreed, demanded its own rules.

Granny Zim thanked the emperor and the court for their forbearance, then quoted a very simple poem, one of the oldest in the empire's history. It had been written by a poet from an obscure background, and as Granny Zim spoke, she was thinking of Bu:

> *Flowers yearn toward the sun.*
> *Those raised in stagnant waters*
> *Cherish beauty full of life*

Two days later, Granny Zim woke to YinYin coming in to say, "There is something amiss with the body of the emperor. But all those who speak of it say that nothing is to be said. I find that confusing."

"Never mind that," Granny Zim said grimly. "What happened?"

YinYin was not good at sifting euphemisms, and so it was a while before Granny Zim discovered that the emperor had suffered some sort of syncope. His mind was clear, but his speech slurred, and he could not walk. The empress was to sit beside the throne, behind a silk gauze veil for secrecy, and Imperial Prince Rathtan would occupy the throne during the interim, while the emperor recovered.

No one would utter—out loud—the inauspicious words everyone was thinking: what if he didn't recover?

FORTY-NINE

MINDFUL OF THE UNSPOKEN message in that bridle repaired by the princess Eki, Lir concentrated on mastering the many chores required of him. He found satisfaction in gaining dexterity, especially when he was able to cut his mind free. He played many a mental game of Circle, and he kept his gaze strictly down whenever his ears caught the laughing voice of that princess. Who did seem to be around a lot as she and some other women were teaching Lum Bu to ride.

A day turned into two, then three, and almost a week passed. The men and the older boys wanting to become riders rode out every day — Hoxie with his new feather, which Sorxu glared at — and they began coming back with cuts, contusions, sometimes broken limbs. Tight mouths. Angry eyes.

At week's end, the male servants got the hot springs last. Lir never really relaxed until he could sink into the water. The ache in muscles he'd not had to use so consistently began to dissipate, leaving his mind to cut free.

There was Pao's voice, describing some exercise out on the field, ending with, "…the worst of it is, Sorxu always sets up these attacks, always. But the king seems to believe him when he claims to have signaled it."

"Sh-h-h-h!"

"Hush, idiot, there are two Eagles right over there."

"Throwing the dice for large and small," Pao retorted.

"I've been watching them. I know those two. One thought at a time in those thick heads."

Lir laid his head back, laughing to himself. The ploy that Pao had described so thoroughly was an ancient Circle move, The Cicada Hidden Under The Leaf.

The next day they woke to a low gray sky, the rain so heavy the king sent word that they could rest. The horse servants moved into the storage tents, where they sat where they could, occupying themselves with either repairs or games.

Someone brought out an old board. They called the game Skirmish, but that was a Circle board. Curious, Lir moved to the outer ring of those gathering to watch, wondering if the rules were the same.

One player, an Eagle by his headband, seemed to be the local champion, though Lir found his play to be predictably linear. As the day lengthened toward afternoon, he noticed with hidden amusement how annoyed Pao and his fellow Shrikes and Badgers were that no one could beat this man — who compounded the mounting frustration by gloating openly. The betting had even begun to subside because no one would bet against the Eagle rider.

Lir finally gave in to temptation, reflecting that these were all servants, so why shouldn't another servant be able to play? He said to Pao, "I'll take a turn, unless there's some rule against it."

Pao gave him an impatient glance. "We don't need any more humiliation. Unless you're better at that than you are at just about anything else."

"I am."

Pao eyed him. "All right. But if you lose, I'll thump you myself."

Lir sat down when the last disgruntled opponent got up.

The Eagle rider gave him a skeptical look. "The southerner." And to Pao and the others of his friends, "Is that all you've got left, someone whose skills are worse than a boy of ten?"

"I'm better at this game. We have a lot of rain in the south," Lir said. "Nothing else to do."

The Eagle gave a snort — and lost in sixteen moves.

Pao, who had bet cautiously in Lir's favor, collected from everywhere with an air that could only be termed a counter-gloat.

"You got lucky," the Eagle rider declared, his gaze so

steady that Lir wondered if that was suspicion. "Play again."

They did. This time, Lir amused himself by spinning it out, pretending to find this man's play a challenge, and made it fun for himself by predicting his opponent's moves as far out as possible. When he figured the game had gone on long enough, he ended that one, again with a win.

Pao hooted with glee, having bet large. His Ma and Badger cousins who had followed his lead also gloated.

By then it was time for the evening meal, and the game broke up. "Next time I would have nailed you," the Eagle said to Lir.

"I'm sure you would," Lir said easily, and that was that. He'd enjoyed himself, for the first time since he'd been hauled aboard that boat.

His mood stayed good until Pao appeared suddenly and noiselessly, grabbed him by the back of the shirt, and yanked him outside in the rain, beyond the corral in which the mares with foals were kept. Here was Hoxie, like Lir, with rain streaming down his face in the gathering gloom.

Hoxie said, "I forgot you were an expert that the Skirmish game. Circle," he amended.

"And you're going to tell me that you only play it as children because Jun Suai riders are *real* men, and ride to *real* skirmishes, *hooh hooh hooh*," Lir retorted. "May I go in now? My poor soft southern body is cold as death out here in the rain."

Hoxie said, "Is the game like..." He gestured. "Actual skirmishing. In the field. Or is it merely a lot of random... calculations?"

"Everything is calculations," Lir said, wiping his sleeve over his face. "Everything. Including the chaos of battle. Or so the ancients write. I've never actually been in one. A boast I've been proud of," he added. "It's just that battle is so much faster, but human beings—according to Liad Il—are predictable."

Then he understood, and blinked rain out of his face. "You're asking about..." He waved toward the field, and uttered a short laugh. "From what I heard from the complainers at the springs, Sorxu's favorite ploy is a common one, so common it has a name, The Cicada Hidden Under The Leaf."

"How do you counter it?" Hoxie asked.

"Is that why we're out here?" Lir countered. "There are any number of ways. Four that I can name off-hand, depending on your strategy. No, five, and possibly six, but that depends on your opponent's own strategy." Then he crossed his arms—mindful of the one that still ached below its wrapping, if he jarred it too much. "But if you want me to teach you Circle strategy in order to hone your invasion skills, you might as well kill me right here. Because I won't. Though I'm a prisoner here, I won't do anything to aid you in invading my homeland and killing my family."

Hoxie turned around, his eyes raised to the sky as he fought to govern his too-ready tongue. So wise a lesson—and so very difficult. When he reached past the spike of irritation that made him want to crash his fist in that scornful face, he had to see that Lir's stance was a reasonable one. What's more, it indicated a semblance of courage.

He turned back. "That invasion is going to happen. Unless events…alter. The choice before you relates to how. If Sorxu wins, I promise, that invasion will be as brutal as possible, because Sorxu has a taste for brutality. If I lead, and I say if, my strategy will be to disrupt life as little as I can."

"But an invasion is disruption by its nature."

"A lesson I'm sure taught to your forebears when they invaded all the islands that make up your empire," Hoxie retorted.

It was Lir's turn to look away.

Hoxie said, "You're right about one thing. I don't know the Circle game because my time was spent training on the ground. I don't see the numbers that you and your silent brother were so familiar with. I did try to learn it while I was standing guard, but the both of you were far too fast, and most of the time you didn't even play with a board."

"Patterns," Lir said dully, for he was thinking fast. "Patterns, patterns, patterns."

Hoxie was right about Sorxu. Lir had already seen that prince striking a servant or two. Knocked a boy to the ground for bringing water that was too hot. Sorxu had claimed it was disrespect—and maybe that was true. Lir was seeing tiny signs of resentment, always indirect, now that he knew enough to be aware of such things. Sorxu was not nearly as popular as his next younger brother, and it agonized him. His response to reclaim the respect he seemed to crave was to act more forceful.

Lir believed Hoxie's prediction that Sorxu, appointed to lead the invasion of the imperial island, would fill the rivers with blood. "I haven't seen what your field is like," he said finally. "All those things are part of the patterns, and of course that's not possible on a game board where all the squares are equivalent and you move carved markers. But there are a couple of things you could try..." And he explained.

At the end, Hoxie gave a short nod, and walked away.

The next day dawned clear, and though there was a lot of griping about riding into mud, the king wanted them out honing their battle skills, so out they rode.

That night, Pao came to Lir to say, "You're going to come to hold the remounts tomorrow."

Lir went back to whittling tent pegs as he considered his reaction. The first impulse was, this might be fun to actually translate those patterns into real movements of man and horse. But hard on that was the understanding of what it meant.

He wrestled with that for a while, aware that Circle had lessons for this situation, too: arranging tactics in order of priority. Only these priorities were not winning the game in the least number of moves, but ranking the choices in an order that included causing the least amount of suffering.

Seen purely that way: Sorxu must not win command.

While Lir spent that week working as a horse boy in the field, Bu recovered rapidly, in spite of the lessons that were really opportunities to speak more about demons. Simply walking a horse in a circle did nothing dire to her recovery; in fact, she sometimes forgot the fading discomfort as she and Eki spoke. She explained more about YinYin without ever giving a name or even a pronoun, in spite of always thinking of YinYin as "she".

Eki's interests were entirely in demons' power.

Both were finding the other unexpectedly interesting. Eki strove to overcome Bu's fears. One morning she told Bu, "Don't worry about hiding from my father. He won't sell you off until he rides to the coast again." To Eki's surprise, Bu did not look gratified. Surely not disappointment? "Do you want to be sold?"

"No!"

"Then..." Ah, now Eki had it! "You're afraid of being seen by that demon," she murmured as they continued to walk their horses all around the camp in a wide circle.

"Or heard," Bu admitted. "I hope that it does not regard music as … as … interesting, but I cannot be *sure*. I would so like to play again," she admitted quickly.

They had returned the borrowed instruments in the days following the feast. Eki laughed, then said, "You can sing for us anytime you want. Those Antelope cousins have been singing that song you gave them. We'd all like more."

Bu was happy to oblige. That night, she played the "old, broken" flute that Eki had used as a child. Ah, sad flute, Bu had thought, feeling it over. Its music was strangled by ill-set air holes, and a scuffed, chewed-looking lip hole. Bu trimmed it, then experimented with a little of "Ospreys." Now this flute filled the air with bright, breezy joy.

Bu began experimenting, mixing practiced variations with bits of melody she heard sung around her. A few family friends turned up, bringing their hand work, and sat shoulder to shoulder in order to hear better. Bu played for anyone who came, though her fears constrained her talents considerably. But what she gave them was still better than they had customarily. Though there were several with fine voices — far superior to Bu's — none of them were musicians, their range of songs limited.

Bu played, and dreamed music, rapidly regaining her old expertise, though she kept herself to simple melodies. Lir watched the field exercises, at first finding it nothing whatsoever like the clean precision of Circle. The biggest problem was that a watcher was fixed at one point on the same plane as the combatants. There was no possibility of looking down from overhead, as one did in Circle.

The first step toward breaking down the chaos of what he saw into patterns happened when he began watching only the leaders. In Circle, you watched your opponent for betraying revelations; both Hoxie and Sorxu each had their characteristic reveals. Now he could see Circle patterns in the way Sorxu always protected his left side — all his attacks bore to the right. He also complicated his commands by mixing his signals, as he knew very well that Hoxie's riders watched as well as his riders. The risk was confusing his own people, with unfortunate results.

Lir began to see patterns among the riders, and by another week's end, he noted how some of Sorxu's riders turned up in the morning with bruises or stiffnesses that they had not left the field with the previous day.

"He's beating the ones who make mistakes in signals," Pao said when Lir pointed this out.

Hoxie drifted up, and Lir said, "There are a couple more counterattacks you could try against Cicada Hidden Under The Leaf." He tried explaining, then drew with his finger in the dirt. Hoxie crouched down, his concentration intent, then he gave a grunt. "I see that."

He won the next day. That night, he went to one of his riders to learn the rudiments of the game, and when he came to Lir next, he drew a grid on the ground, and said, "What did you see from Sorxu?"

"Before we get to Circle tactics, something I noted when I first got out on your field. Watch his habits *before* he makes a signal. Like his chin-rubbing. He does that when he's confused, then he always falls back on attack-right ploys."

That led to even more wins.

One night, Hoxie turned up at Lir's bedroll, hunkered down, and said, "If Sorxu is betraying his thinking through unconsidered moves, then so am I."

Lir said, "I'm concentrating on Sorxu."

"No you are not. I see you watching me as often as you watch him. But you won't tell me my… my patterns. Which are really weaknesses."

Lir stayed silent, and both thought of the king's invasion plans.

Hoxie's frustration revealed itself in the chuff of his feet in the grass as he strode away. Lir wrapped up more tightly, for the nights lately had gotten colder, leaving a field of white frost at dawn twice.

Eki watched from a distance. Of all her brothers, she was closest to this one, and not just because they shared the same mother. Or perhaps it was that which caused them to think a lot alike. She was fond of a couple of the younger brothers and Shrike-cousins, but it was Hoxie who most looked to the future for the good of the clan.

That decided her: Hoxie needed to know about the demon.

FIFTY

THE DAY CAME WHEN Sorxu told his riders to break bones.

That day he claimed victory again, after two months of stalemates or losing outright. He won again—the first time in the two months since the games had begun. When the princes went before the king to give their report on the day, Sorxu said triumphantly, "I took the field."

"By telling his riders to shatter arms and legs," Hoxie said. "If that was to be the rule, I should have known beforehand."

"We're preparing for war," Sorxu retorted, eyeing Hoxie with scorn. "Not holding a children's game."

"Our way of preparing is to control the weapon on the practice field. Stop short of breaking bones. I ought to have known that the rule had been changed," Hoxie said, not to Sorxu, but to the king.

The king hesitated, then grunted. "War is rough," he said. "You know that. But Sorxu, I'm not acknowledging your win because Hoxie's riders are to be a strong part of the invasion, but if you immobilize them all, then how many can I send?"

"I can take the imperials," Sorxu muttered, not quite daring to say, *We don't need him.*

"But you have not won as often as your brother on the field," the king said.

"Because we play, Father. We don't fight," Sorxu retorted, simmering with anger and desire to strike and smash. It was a tickle in his gut, a longing that only got scratched in violence.

The king furrowed his brow. "If tomorrow Hoxie's riders begin cracking heads among the Eagles, what will I be left with besides my own riders? Why do you think there is a stalemate in this war?"

Hoxie bit back the words, *Because they have a disciplined navy, and our ships are merely transport*, but said nothing as Sorxu's mouth tightened, his gaze flat.

The king regarded them standing side by side, and muttered, "Remember, united we are strong. You are blood-brothers, the strongest bond. And soon, very soon, you will each be ruling your own island. You two will get the largest."

"Sorxu wasn't listening," Hoxie said later, talking to Pao and Eki, who had revealed the truth about the demon and the broken string. As a result, Hoxie's war counsels now included her.

"He wants to wield the salamander sword," Eki said.

Hoxie shifted from one foot to the other, then said, "Can you get Bu to speak to him? See if it's possessed? That's nothing any of us can do to find out."

Eki shook her head slowly. "Bu is too afraid of him. And I can't put her in his way. He might do anything, if he thought it would please some of those out-clan brutes now riding under his banner."

Hoxie grimaced, thinking of kindly, squinting Bu. Sorxu wouldn't think twice about snapping her neck if he got tired of the squint. "No," he said. "On further thought, don't."

"Even if she was willing," Eki said, "what would it get you? How do you prove a demon is inside someone? Especially to Father? How will he hear that?"

"How will *it* hear that," Hoxie mumbled, and they both glanced around. They always spoke in tent voices, but it never did to be complacent.

Eki continued. "I've been thinking about this ever since Bu revealed Father's demon. *I* would not have believed her, had not Phoenix insisted ever since I apprenticed to her that there are demon-signs around Father."

They both knew that if the Phoenix shaman accused their father outright of being possessed, she would not live out the night. Shamans were protected in general, but it was not unheard-of for them to suffer for too harsh a divination.

"What do we do?" Hoxie absently rubbed his chin.

Eki faced him. "First, what's your intent? Do you truly

want to invade the imperial capital island?"

Hoxie sighed. "I did. But I... Have other ideas."

"Oh?"

"Going among them on father's order was…a game. I liked the risk--me against them. It was fun to fool them, though I probably could've done better if I'd been good at accents the way you are. I had to be stupid, but that had its advantage because people talked in front of me as if I didn't hear."

"So you've said."

He waved a hand. "What I'm getting at is, when I went in, the idea of killing the heir was easy. Find the right silk-wearing fool among the princes. Slit his throat. But then I lived among them. I know those palace guards. Most of them are like riders. Work hard. Same kinds of jokes. One reminded me of Pao. Another was like Cousin Tiger. You get the idea."

"But that wasn't true for the princes, surely. We all heard about their corruption."

Hoxie looked up at the sky, as if he could find the right answer in the stars. But they looked back down, inscrutable as ever in their slow wheel.

"It was true even for the princes. The elder ones are as mild as sheep, and about as smart. Even the younger two were not terrible. Nothing like Sorxu. More like a couple of over-aged boys. Probably why there is no heir yet."

"Then Phoenix is right. The southerners stopped being targets for you when you began to see them as human beings. Like us."

"Yes."

Eki said, "I never thought about the war except as inevitable until I began training with Phoenix. Both she and Ghost see the world filled with life. Taking life is a sin for them, especially for Phoenix, who was born on one of those outer-islands who follow what the southerners call the Snow Crane. That's why she will not eat meat. Ghost is nightmare-ridden because she is a false Seer, she knows she's false, but her family pushed her into taking up the staff, and so she tries to give good advice…"

Eki saw Hoxie's attention wavering, and made herself stop. She knew he didn't care about the seers' origins. Her attention wandered when he talked endlessly about who among his riders was stronger, who faster. They both had different life paths—but those paths tended in the same direction.

She decided to venture her idea. "… but even she strives to

guide Father away from indiscriminate taking of life. Ay, what I'm saying is, there might be a way."

Hoxie turned a hopeful face toward her. "What way?"

"You know that Father wants to run a deflection at either Ran or Te Gar. Both islands with single imperial garrisons."

"Unlike the islands with two or more garrisons at different harbors, and the imperial capital with four, which will require a more complicated attack." Hoxie hesitated there, remembering that he knew the defense plans of the imperial guard, those with naval reinforcements, those with army reinforcement. He'd explained them to her father, but as yet, the king had not ordered Hoxie to explain them to Sorxu.

Though that would happen if Sorxu was given command of the entire invasion…

Eki said, "Father said in counsel with the chief riders and the consorts that he wants to deflect the imperials by a feint at Ran, and then invade the imperial capital when the navy carries the bulk of the imperials to rescue Ran." Eki leaned toward him. "What I'm about to tell you is Mother's idea, actually. She says she can probably talk Father into first running a test at Te Gar, say, for Sorxu's ordeal. Win or lose, he'll probably make a mess of it, if he's as poor a leader as you say."

"It's not that he's bad altogether. He's brave and fast, and I'd put him at the head of a charge. But we're both trying to learn how to direct an army while in the midst of fighting. I'm just beginning to see…" *What Lir calls patterns*, he was thinking. But he didn't want Eki thinking that it was Lir who commanded from behind him, when that was not true. And Lir knew it wasn't true—he'd frankly admitted that he would be paying more attention to handling his horse than what anyone else was doing, were they to trade places.

Also, and perhaps more important, he could not tell Eki who Lir was, because she was already too curious about him. If she began paying a horse boy attention, Sorxu would notice, and then they'd all end up beheaded by the salamander sword for betrayal. Sorxu probably wielding it.

He cut to what was important. "Sorxu's far too impatient, and if things change too fast, and they do, and the imperials will have an even stronger defense than what I put against him, Sorxu always falls back on the same ploys. He wants to see blood and fear."

"That really does sound like a demon, doesn't it?"

Hoxie knew plenty of men who had a taste for blood and

fear, and he'd stake his life — well, his favorite sword, maybe — they were not possessed by demons. But he kept that back. "What does that give us, if Sorxu attacks Te Gar and loses?"

"No invasion, or not for years if he truly is bad at command. Especially," Eki whispered, "if he takes a considerable wound."

Hoxie sat back, hands out. "You mean assassinate him? Why didn't you say so at first? And no, I'm not going to stab him in the back, much as I hate him. Nor will I order someone like Pao to, and then have to watch him suffer the thousand cuts for betrayal."

"I don't want you to kill anybody. If Sorxu doesn't run into trouble on his own, there are many, even among the Eagles, who wish that Sorxu would experience some of the pain he likes to hand out. If he has to recover from his wounds, that gives us time to work on Father. Specifically, we want to lure the demon out of him and drive it away. Phoenix is working on that now."

"That sounds…uncertain," Hoxie said.

"Do you have a better plan? Will you have one if Sorxu gets impatient now that he can't crack skulls on the field, and begins sending his bone-breakers after you in the night when you go to the privy, or he gets one of his fawning girls to poison everyone in your tent one night, *Oh, it was a mistake, someone put the wrong spice in the meal?*" She finished on a high note.

"Then I have to let him win?" Hoxie said.

"If you want this plan to have a chance. Sorxu is pushing Aunt Tirat hard to coax Father into giving him his ordeal. He really hates that you've won your man's feather and he has not, though he's older."

"It seems…uncertain," Hoxie said again. But the truth was, he had misgivings about the eventual success of his father's plan: if he were to have to rule an island, he would still need to defend against Sorxu wanting to take it. Because Sorxu wanted the salamander sword, the many-feather headdress. Everything…

Eki returned to her tent. Her mother stood, arms tightly crossed. "Did he accept your idea?"

"I think so."

Avor gave a tiny nod. "Bu is ready. Ginu is saddling up the horses right now. She can be exercising them if you change your mind."

Eki pressed damp palms down her sides. "I won't."

FIFTY-ONE

EKI HAD MADE HER decision.

She had learned everything Bu had to teach about demons. In return, it seemed right and true to get poor Bu safely away. She was so hapless when it came to Essence studies and rituals. She would have no defenses if that demon tried to retaliate against her for being revealed.

As for Lir…

Ah, Bu needed someone to see her home again. He was a servant. He was there to serve, so he could serve Bu just as well as he could serve Hoxie, who after all had plenty of servants. That was the way to think about Lir—and send him far, far away. There was no temptation that could not be cured by distance.

That means now, she told herself. She picked up the honey-cakes that Nanny had prepared and made her way to the supply tent, where a good portion of the horse tenders were well along in celebrating the birth of a son to an Antelope cousin.

As expected, she found Lir on the outer edge of the celebrants. As she passed, he looked up, and she made the hand motion to follow. He did.

She handed off the cakes to those hosting the party and lingered, exchanging good wishes and compliments to the young mother and father. Then she backed slowly out of the group, and made her way into the cold night. She had to acknowledge a sense of regret that if all went as expected she would never see those long eyelashes again. But the world was full of pretty men, and she was not going to start a family of children who might have to serve the likes of Sorxu, the way some of her cousins had to serve her less-liked uncles.

When she got Lir alone, over by the mares' corral, she said, "Are you a southern spy?"

"What?" That astonishment was either genuine, or Lir was a very, very accomplished spy. But not one who could defend himself — even against her, she reminded herself.

"Sorxu thinks you are," she said. "Sorxu's people reported to him that you came from the south, you scarcely knew which end of a horse gets a bridle, but now you're always there now when Hoxie wins those field games. Always. Sorxu thinks you are secretly commanding for Hoxie."

"No, I only taught him a few ploys from Circle. He's the one translating moves from the game into actual directions on the field."

Eki said, "My point is, Sorxu has asked about you several times today. And about Bu, but mainly you. The next step is to take you off somewhere and wrench the truth out of you."

Lir stared. "I...I would rather not be tortured, just for him to discover that I don't know the first thing about spying."

Eki looked away. An accomplished spy would say that, too. "I don't want anything to happen to Bu," she said, which was true, but it was also because she couldn't quite bring herself to say, "I don't want anything to happen to *you*." That could so easily be misunderstood, when all she meant was, she did not want to find his mangled remains in the field halfway between the camp and the springs one morning.

She said, "You could take her away to safety..."

Lir shook his head. "I would if I could." Did she know who he was, or not? Better to say nothing.

"I've worked it out with my mother," Eki said. "It can only win you a night and a day, maybe two if we're lucky. With Sorxu, no one ever counts on luck — sure as a north-born horse favors a north wind, he is predictable in his cruelties. Though he ought to be less aggravated if he is ordered to take Te Gar as his ordeal. But that won't help you in the meantime, as we think he's going to act tomorrow if he loses again. The next day for certain. So, if it's to happen, it must be now."

"I'm ready and willing," Lir said, his heart beating fast.

"How?"

"You ride out. Tonight. My second-cousin Ginu is saddling the horses now. She is hand-fasted with one of the Muskrat boys, and always likes an excuse to ride to the coast. But you have to go now."

Lir began to turn, then forced himself to turn back. "How can I get Lum Bu? If I go to that tent of yours, everyone will be wondering why."

Eki smiled in the soft moonlight. "She's with Ginu, waiting to go. We've seen to it that she knows how to ride now. Though she's far from expert."

"She's probably better than I am, then," Lir said.

Eki uttered a quiet laugh, quickly gone. "Go." She stilled, then turned away.

Lir loped down the horse picket line, pausing only to pick up his battered carryall.

In the light of the low moons, he easily spotted the two pale faces.

Bu had heard earlier that day about Sorxu's complaints to his followers, and she'd waited in painful trepidation as Avor and Eki debated what to do. Not that she heart most of it. They went off to talk in private four separate times before they came back and asked if she could face another hard run.

To escape that demon?

She didn't hesitate before saying, "Yes."

Ginu was tall and bony, with an unexpectedly high voice. She said to Bu, "Let's get you in the saddle," grabbed Bu by the waist and tossed her up.

Lir had been riding horses back and forth for various grooming and training purposes, and at least could mount creditably.

"Keep your heads down," Ginu said as they trotted toward the south entry to the camp. "At least you look more like us now," she added toward Lir, who had taken to wearing a single braid after days of unsuccessfully trying to make a topknot without a hair clasp.

The three of them, with three remounts, trotted by the chatting guards. Ginu waved, the bangles on her wrists clinking: Lir and Bu had learned that young women collected these as dowries, and wore them all when they went courting.

She rode slightly ahead, the other two behind, in the servants' subordinate position. The guards on duty scarcely looked at them. They continued at an easy trot for a time, until

Ginu halted them. "No one will feel a gallop under their feet now." And kneed her horse to a run.

Ginu prided herself on being one of the fastest of the messengers. This run was every bit as hard as the previous, but this time they knew what to expect. Lir also knew quite a bit more about horse care, and shared that burden with Ginu, Bu offering to help in any way she could.

There was not much conversation on that journey. Ginu judged the horses' abilities to a nicety, affording scant rest for the humans. Each was thus left with their own thoughts as the sun rode lower across the southern sky during the day, and the two moons made their steadily rising arcs at opposite ends of the sky each night. Rain held off, though Ginu announced one morning that it was coming.

It arrived at last the morning they sighted the outbuildings of the Muskrat horse stud. There was no greeting for the outlanders other than a nod, and a brief thanks for their help from Ginu.

Another Muskrat said, after a distant colloquy, "We'll put you on a boat downriver, as we've got goods to deliver. From there, you are on your own."

Bu bowed low, uttering disjointed thanks, and Lir gave the northerner salute, fist to heart.

No one spoke on the barge loaded with fancy bridle decorations. Lir and Bu helped unload the unwieldy packages, and then the middle-aged auntie made the shooing motion that set them free.

Free.

Not for long if they were not diligent.

Lir kept his mouth shut as they threaded the crowd around the river's edge. When he was sure they were thoroughly quit of Muskrat or Badger clan members, he turned to Bu, who peered around with her usual squint as she proceeded in that peculiar high-stepping walk that he knew by now was used by someone who could not see the ground.

"We have to get off this island today," he said.

"I thought we're safe now?" Bu said, peering anxiously through that squint. "That long, hard ride." She rubbed absently at her thighs, then snatched her hands away as if they burned, and blushed.

"The tree hopes for calm but the wind won't stop," he said, trying for lightness. "I'm afraid we won't stay free if we don't get away from this island before the tide changes."

"Do you think they would come after us? I told Eki everything I knew about demons." Demons as a group—she had never named YinYin. "I truly do not know how to drive one out of a person."

"I understand that. But remember, Hoxie knows who I am."

"Ayah! Yes, he does."

Lir looked into that innocent face, so quick and clever when she played, so exalted. So oblivious the rest of the time. Everyone shone at something—except him, he mocked inwardly. "Hoxie knows, will know. Ah, by now he surely knows, and he's two or even three days into a hunt for us… I'm tangling myself here. Hoxie knows that I am in the same position he was early in spring: an enemy brought right to the heart of their camp, who has seen their strengths and weaknesses." *Who has seen Hoxie's.* "Only he's the one who brought me there. He has to be halfway across the plains in a very hot ride, and he will no doubt turn out every one of the Badgers and Mas and Muskrats and whoever else he's got in harbor to search for us."

Bu gave a slow, sober nod. "Yes, I did not think of that." She flickered an uncertain glance his way. "Am I to return to proper etiquette now?"

"Don't. If we make it back home, you can bow and *your imperial highness* me with every sentence, and you'll be able to play your instruments with your teacher again." He saw by her inadvertent smile how very much she wanted to return home, and added, "We must be northern commoners. At least we've both got their dialect now, and we more or less look like the rest of them. Less. I think the first thing we need to do is change our appearance. Hoxie will give his searchers descriptions of us both."

"But we have no money," Bu said. "If I had an instrument, I could earn some by performing."

"You could, but I think your music is so memorable that it would be easy to find us."

"I did not think of that."

"I have my birth jade," he said slowly—still reluctant after four days' hard riding worth of fierce internal debate. "I've worn it next to my skin all this time, hiding it in my clothes when we bathed. I'll sell it as a war trophy. We'll use that to get clothes and passage at least some of the way."

Bu accepted that, as Lir had figured she would. He'd

noticed that she never argued — ever.

He proceeded to the second part of his plan. "You've got to disguise as my young brother."

"Me?" She took a step backward.

"Our hair is the same shade, and you're so thin you could easily pass as a boy of fifteen or so. But you've got to remember not to squint. That's the first thing they'll describe about you."

Bu blushed to the ears, but her eyes widened. It did change her face.

"Good. That's excellent. All right, let's find a likely trader for my tally."

"A birth tally," Bu said with soft regret. "I know those are important to…to those who get one. I am so sorry. I wish there was another way."

That birth tally was the only thing — besides his life — that his mother had left to him. "Can't be helped," he replied shortly, hiding his own regret.

She heard it anyway, and intuited that commiseration would only hurt more. She fell silent, and worked on walking without squinting as they proceeded on his plan.

While they'd walked, he spotted likely traders. He sold the jade along with a story about being carried too far north by a terrible storm months ago. That led to long reminiscences about ships and storms as Lir and the trader dickered over the value, until he finally agreed just to hurry them along.

They then went about to small shops, buying one thing here, one thing there, never betraying hurry. Sometimes he got her to wait outside, in case the descriptions put two targets together.

They found tiny alleys and corners to change, one on watch as the other put on the new clothes. Lir also bought a pair of hair ties in the northern style, and as Bu knelt in the dust, he tied up her braids the way Pao wore his. Then he asked her to braid his the same way, and tie it up. Her fingers were nimble at braiding, and they were finished before the sun touched the roofs.

Their last chore was to get passage, which turned out to be unexpectedly difficult. He had not considered that most northern traders would avoid the south. Those willing either asked an exorbitant amount or wanted to know why a couple of boys wanted to sail to the enemy islands.

The tide would turn soon, and Lir was desperate to get them safely aboard a ship. Finally he found someone willing to take them east, which was better than nothing, to an island that apparently was friendly to gallant wanderers. This trader charged a swingeing price because he knew he could get it.

Just before the flood waters began emptying toward the sea, they boarded, with their new carryalls containing the things they'd bought, which included a lute and a hand drum.

Once they were on board, Bu said, "Where will we go when we reach this new island?"

"We're going to find a way to go south. Since the shipmaster took every coin I had, it's either both of us sell our labor as launderers, as no one aboard a ship will want to hire me to tend horses, or you can carry out your idea of playing for money."

"I will do that, but I thought I was not to do so?"

"We've broken the trail, I believe. I was very careful to invent different stories for each of the inquiries I made. Sometimes I claimed a brother, other times I said I was alone. It will be difficult to trace my movements among the ships still in harbor. And even Hoxie cannot interrogate every ship that sailed out of the harbor. They have no navy, so there is no record of departed ships."

"I understand," Bu said, her eyes huge and unfocused. "Surely we can soon find one that goes to the imperial island," she said softly.

"We have a stop to make first."

"Oh? Where are we going?"

"Te Gar," he said, his tone grim.

FIFTY-TWO

THE FIRST DAY OF that initial trip was the worst for Bu. At first she was afraid even to walk, much less speak, she was so sure that everyone around her would instantly see through her guise and scold her, or worse, for her daring. But voices around her sounded the same as always. She felt no stares. And gradually she began to perceive that there were few people more invisible than poorly dressed teenage boys with nothing to spend.

Though they had paid a great sum to the gallant wanderer shipmaster, they were generally ignored or chased out of the way on that journey. Food was included, but they were always served last; they were regarded as a pair of ignorant commoners, and treated as such. Both Lir and Bu were relieved when the next island bumped on the horizon.

As they debarked, dodging around laborers going both ways on the ramp, Lir said, "This is where we can invent new lives. I'm going to listen to some of the harbor talk to learn how to negotiate the way they do, because I'm fairly certain that that trader all but robbed us. Do you want to sit on some corner somewhere, lay out your blanket, and see if you can earn a few coins?"

Bu's tentative smile flashed. "I will."

"Remember, you're a boy of fifteen, and you're off to an audition at, oh, the Jade Islands, in case anyone asks. Those are known for being wealthy, so it's conceivable there might be a theater at one or another of them."

They found a likely corner, near where some other sellers too poor to afford a roadside booth, much less a shop, had spread blankets on which they offered foodstuffs or crafts. Lir left her there as she spread her blanket.

At first a few youths called insults at this scrawny, poorly dressed "boy"'s arrogance, but Bu ignored them and methodically went about tuning the lute Lir had bought for her. Could Hoxie trace her by that lute? No, because the lute had been hidden in her carryall when they boarded the gallant wanderer trader. With that reassuring thought, she began to play fundamentals to warm up her fingers. The youths quieted, then passed on, looking for other prey, though one glanced back twice.

She began with one of the northerner ballads.

A woman carrying a basket was the first to slow her steps and stop. Then an older man wearing a dusty-hemmed scribe robe. Then two younger scribe students, and before long she could not count those who formed a ring around her as her hands resumed their practiced nimbleness. She closed her eyes, and out poured all the emotions she had constrained to keep the demon from hearing her through the king. She had written a variation for the demon, which formed a harsh contrast of sevens among the galloping threes of the northerner camp, woven among her treasured lessons from Granny Zim.

When she had played her way through the fundamentals, and began working at the latest lessons, here was Xia Chi again, fours and eights of mourning and of longing deepening the complex melody she wove.

She slid from one ballad to another, and then to another, enriching each with intensifying complexity, until she reached the song she had composed for the camp at that feast—and then had to destroy with the broken string. That wrongness had galled her through the entirety of her stay in King Mantai Haim's camp. She had rearranged the song in her mind, until it was stronger. Brighter. Truer—a salute to Eki and to Avor.

And now at last she could play it.

She brought it to its triumphant end, then lifted her hands and opened her eyes. An enormous crowd surrounded her. She stared, fighting the instinct to squint. They stared back, then the woman with the basket of eggs set her basket down at her feet and clapped so hard her cheeks reddened with her effort. That broke the silence, and others joined in. The old scholar gave Bu a slight but very dignified bow, and the two apprentices bowed more deeply. Many more northerners slapped their hands to their chests.

"Play another," someone demanded.

Bu did.

After the third song, the egg woman carefully extracted a small coin from the little purse stuck in her sash, stooped, and laid it down before Bu, then walked away. After that, more coins thumped onto her dirt-marked blanket, and a gold piece spun through the air and landed on the others with a musical ching! But it was that first coin that made Bu's eyes blur, not just because of the woman's grave manner, but because it was clear that small coin meant a great deal to her.

When Lir returned to Bu's spot, tired and more than a little irked at being chased off as a loiterer, or insulted, it was to discover that Bu had accumulated a quantity of coinage, one or two of high value. At least he'd overheard enough negotiations now to understand how to go about not having his eyebrows clipped, as people said on discovering that they'd overpaid.

Aware of being only one short journey away from Jun Gan, he bought them passage to a nearby island that could be seen from the harbor, and once they reached this new island, he practiced his negotiating skills for a room at an inn that had hot baths for an extra price.

As he explained to Bu they went upstairs, "It's one room, because asking for two rooms for common brothers would cause people to remember us."

This discussion made Bu uncomfortable. It felt a bit like lying, and yet not, as they did behave as two brothers. She decided she would only tell Granny Zim.

There was adjustment to be made by Lir, as well.

As a teenage prince, Lir had followed some wiser cousins into the delightful world of intriguing fragrances, enticing smiles, soft words, and long, lingering looks: girls.

Lir's belief in his successful flirting did not survive Rathlan's blunt translation of what girls were really thinking behind those smiles and flattering words. She had meant well, but the result was, he became self-conscious. Around that time his intended wife married someone else, and though the empress insisted that this was entirely a political marriage, that along with Vo's informing him caustically that he was known behind his back as the Weasel caused him to retreat with TanTan to the safe, silent series of endless Circle duels, and from there to the wild world of gambling. He flirted with entertainment dancers, and gave them plenty of gold, but otherwise kept a distance.

Sharing a room with Bu was awkward, the more because he could see how uncertain she was. He finally told himself that Bu looked like a little brother, so he would treat her like a little brother.

That set the tone for their proximity, which was easier for them both. Especially as she was so quiet, and listened with all her attention, her air invariably sympathetic. Especially at night, with the candle blown out. They talked, at first with constraint, but gradually he spoke to Bu as he had to Rathlan, and Bu in turn shared what she knew. Including about the king's demon.

"Really? A demon?" Lir demanded, lighting the candle again so that he could see her. "How do you know?"

"I saw a demon," Bu said. "It is very distinct. That king has one. And it could be that that demon took a piece of itself and offered it to Sorxu."

Lir contemplated that for a few days. He'd thought he understood the world, but really it was stranger and wilder than he'd permitted himself to believe.

When they didn't talk, she played her lute. He envied her that passion, which he knew he did not have.

Over the following month, as rain, sleet, and occasional drifts of snow fell on ship and street, they zigzagged their way southward, Lir suppressing his impatience at anything that slowed them up. His greatest fear was that they would arrive at Te Gar to find it in smoking ruin, Sorxu's banners streaming in the wintry winds.

Sorxu was not far behind him.

Sorxu's ordeal included having to put together his own fleet to get his army on its way: the king has learned through his so-far unsuccessful war with the empire that having your own ships was vital if you wanted to take other islands. They were a necessity in the way that servants were necessary, so that riders could train in the manly arts and ride.

The assumption was that the people of the Horse Brethren looked to the riders for protection and heroism—true—and were honored to be chosen to serve. True... in a sense. Sorxu's reputation had preceded him, with the result that he found that few suitable ships were in harbor for commandeering. Most seemed to have sailed off for other purposes. It took him long than he'd expected to assemble a flotilla, and then they sailed straight into wintry winds.

Meanwhile, Hoxie had reacted exactly as Lir had predicted when he went to look for Lir that next day, to discover he couldn't be found anywhere. Bu either. He assumed for a crucial day that Lir had been dispatched to the other end of the camp on this or that errand, and went about his own tasks. It wasn't until evening that Pao came to him, saying, "I can't find Lir anywhere. The musician is gone as well."

Lum Bu was gone? "Eki," Hoxie muttered, and went off to confront his sister. He was furious, mostly with himself, but that did not stop him from unloosing an angry rant the moment the two had ridden out of earshot of the camp.

She listened with a stone face all the way through. At which he passed a hand over his face, then said bluntly, "Lir was never a servant. He's one of the emperor's sons."

"What?" Eki squawked. Then gave him a far more fierce scowl than he had when he demanded, *Where is Lir? What have you done?* "Have you *never* learned that keeping secrets from me or Mother is going to get you into trouble?"

Hoxie's ire vanished, at least partly. Shamefaced, he muttered, "I was afraid your interest in him would draw Sorxu."

"And I'm not able to avoid drawing Sorxu's attention?" she countered. "We took care of him, you'll note—with Aunt Tirat's aid. He's too busy getting ready for his ordeal."

Hoxie accept the fact that he'd been outmaneuvered by his sister, and sighed. "He's going to take everything he learned about us straight to the emperor."

Eki's expression remained cold. "Then hadn't you better try to find him first?"

"If you'll help me," Hoxie said with proper humility.

Eki gave that humble face the extreme skepticism it deserved, then said, "I'll speak to Mother. She'll find a way that won't raise questions."

As a result, Hoxie was sent on a scouting mission to make certain that Sorxu wasn't about to be attacked by a fleet of imperials. Hoxie only took his sworn riders.

He half-expected to catch up by the time they reached the Muskrat horse stud, to discover that he was two days behind them. He mentally saluted Lir for that fast ride with Ginu, and confidently expected to discover the two imperials wandering haplessly around the harbor city. He and Pao put together drawings, and sent the riders out to scour the harbor streets, then the tangle of homes north of the river, describing Lir as an unskilled laborer and Bu as a superlative musician and singer dressed as a common woman. But every superlative musician and singer they were pointed to was not Bu.

Hoxie had to accept finally that Lir had managed to get himself and Bu off the island. But how, without any wherewithal?

"He'd sell Bu, of course," Pao said confidently. "Wealthy yachts that need entertainers."

Hoxie wasn't so certain that Lir would sell Bu. Her services as an entertainer, yes. Selling her as a slave did not seem like Lir, though the imperial palace's work was mainly done by slaves.

The riders divided up again, and this time their searches narrowed to man and squinting woman musician. Failing that, they summoned Badger sea craft and dispersed to try at harbors at every major island leading southward.

At last one of his scouts came back with a confusing report: "No squinting woman, but there was tell of a boy who played the lute like a god. Said to be going to audition somewhere in the south..."

Hoxie dismissed that audition immediately. His attention caught on "boy." Would Lir think of disguises? *He was already in a disguise, fool.*

"New search," he said to his riders when all had returned. "We're spreading south again, but this time we're looking for a man and a boy. They might even be posing as cousins or brothers, which would be cheaper if they stayed together. And the younger of them is most likely earning their travel money, because the elder has no skills to offer."

That brought a second report fairly quickly, from another island, of an amazing boy lute player who mastered every other instrument offered, the first time he played it. That had to be Lum Bu.

Hoxie unfolded his map, and scowled at it. Hoxie knew where Lir was heading: home. Except the sightings did not go straight south, but eastward and south. But then Lir would be limited to what he could afford — and who was willing to take them. "We're going to go for speed now, and catch them before they get to the imperial island."

Thus, Hoxie chased to the southeast around two big islands as Lir and Bu headed southwest, Sorxu's flotilla fighting snowstorms north of them.

At last Te Gar appeared on the horizon. No smoke.

The outer perimeter scout boats all displayed the empire's dragon. Lir still did not rejoice until they floated into the harbor, and there was the dragon flying high over the garrison fortress.

"We made it," he said to Bu. "We'll be on the way home tomorrow."

FIFTY-THREE

THE STORYTELLER LOOKED UP.

Everyone gratifyingly leaned forward. The storyteller drank from an empty cup, then shook it and looked sadly into the empty pot.

At this unsubtle hint, those who had a coin or two to spare hastened to drop these into the waiting dish.

The storyteller sighed. "I did promise you heroes and villains. I've given you both. You might argue about which is which—Sorxu would certainly describe himself as a hero, and his encroaching younger brother as a villain—but they are there. I offered you romance, and handsome young people, and there they are. I promised you battles, and you will soon have one..."

A few more coins clinked into the dish, the young serving maid brought a fresh pot of rice wine, and the storyteller continued.

As soon as Imperial Prince Lir and Apprentice Lum Bu reached the shore, bending their faces away from stinging sleet, Lir headed straight for the garrison. The worst was over! They'd reached Te Gar ahead of Sorxu! Now to hand off what he knew, requisition the most comfortable ship the army had, and sail for home!

At the gate, the sentries stopped them.

The guards waited for an explanation for these common

street rats daring to confront them. His imperial highness — returned at last to the order of his empire — waited to be recognized.

"What?" a guard prompted in a surly tone.

"I'm Kun Rathlir," Lir responded, and at the guards' blank faces, "Fourteenth Imperial Prince Rathlir."

The guards exchanged looks, then one muttered to the other, "I thought he was dead."

Lir stared. Of all possible reactions, he had not expected disbelief. They didn't believe him? "We were swept off the tower ship. Taken prisoner. We escaped recently, and have information for my imperial brother."

The guards rolled meaning glances at each other, then frowned at Lir. Still doubtful.

Bu sensed the doubt — the squint was back — and piped up, "He truly is his imperial highness, the fourteenth prince," and at the guards' turning her way, she gabbled quickly, "I am Lum Bu, a student under the imperial musicians —"

The first guard looked her up and down in a way that made her prickle with heat. "You sound like a girl, but you don't look like one." And turned back to Lir. "You take your… fancy-toy and run off. Unless you want a beating for wasting our time."

How did a prince prove his identity? He had no servants, graywings, his clothing was that of common northerners. Was identity not inherent? It was beginning to seem that identity merely required outer trappings…

This was not the time for that internal debate. His hand reached for the jade that had hung around his neck since childhood — and of course it was not there.

Here was yet another situation that proved to him that if Heaven truly did create hierarchies of humans, without the trappings made by other humans, rank must only be visible to Heaven. Because he could see too clearly with his mind's eye what the guards saw: even with those northerner braids now gone and his hair in a proper topknot, it was clipped by simple wood. His clothes were northerner in style. Plain. Threadbare in places.

Bu looked worse in that the guards could not place her at all in what everyone regarded as the proper sphere of things. He could sense her distress in the sound of her breathing.

"Take me to my brother," he said finally. "Ratha will know me."

The two exchanged glances once again, then the first one, somewhat quicker than his companion, saw an opportunity to pass the problem along to someone else, and summoned a messenger with a brief whistle. Then everyone stood around until the messenger came puffing back from the heights: "Send him to command."

At least that much was as it should be. Invoking the name of his imperial highness, Fourth Prince Ratha, had cleared the first gate.

A short time later, there was Ratha himself, nearly unrecognizable in that he had aged so much since Lir had last seen him. He was big, jowly, graying at the temples, but he still wore that unquestioning, somewhat bovine expression shared with all his maternal siblings as he blinked at Lir, then said, "*Who* did you say you are?"

"Rathlir! Fourth Imperial Brother, don't you recognize me?" Lir glanced at the flanking guards, both looking ready to haul him off for a drubbing.

"My brother Rathlir would dress properly," Ratha stated with mild certainty.

"Fourth Imperial Brother, my clothes were lost when the tower ship went down. I was a prisoner. I've escaped from the Horse Brethren. Who are on the way to invade this island. Right now!"

At this, Ratha recoiled slightly, disturbed by a sudden disruption of the regular daily routine. The guards shifted uneasily.

Ratha glanced at Bu, and frowned in perplexity. "What is this?"

That 'this' without even a noun after it caused poor Bu to drop her head in shame.

"Lir, I remember that you were a scamp, but why would you bring your..." Another glance.

Lir did not wait to hear whatever disparaging term his brother was contemplating. "Honored elder brother," he said, forcing himself back into the familiar patterns of formal mode. "This is Apprentice Musician Lum Bu, who was already gaining considerable merit, which was why our imperial father—" Here the clasped hands and bow toward the imperial island—"graced my entourage with her, and with another high ranking senior music student."

Ratha blinked. "Then...she—I take it this is a she—is not your lover?"

Lir struggled to contain his driving sense of urgency, as well as the unsettling sense of an insight he really did not want. It wasn't so much the assumption that frowzy, squinting Bu was his lover. It ran deeper than that, this idea that Bu had to be of use to Lir in some wise in order to justify her being alive and standing next to him right now.

It meant that Ratha, as did so many who were raised to regard their rank as protective, did not really see a commoner like Bu as worthy of protection unless she was serving him directly. The belief that all people who needed protection ought to have it, to the best of his ability, seemed to be as remote an idea to Ratha as the lives of the great krakens undersea. But Lir did not blame his brother. He had not considered this idea until he was thrown into the sea and woke up on an enemy's ship.

He pinched his fingers to his nose, trying to shed these thoughts. There would be time for them later—if Sorxu didn't come riding in, spear ready to impale them all.

While he struggled with these new thoughts, Ratha's slower processes progressed from one unquestioned assumption—Lir the scamp was back, in company with a dubious individual—and he began to say, "My imperial brother requires proper dress. As for that person, show it—her—to the gate—"

Lir planted his feet, determined to get Ratha to understand his urgency, but before anyone could speak, the sound of running footsteps caused all to turn toward the door.

To Lir's surprise, the figure who burst in, then went to a knee, was familiar. "Deg!" he exclaimed.

"Your imperial highnesses," Imperial Guard Colonel Deg exclaimed. "I just heard—ayah, Imperial Prince Rathlir. You're alive!" And to his aide, "Send a pigeon to the emperor at once."

The round-eyed youngster bucketed off, glancing back once, as Lir breathed in giddy relief at being recognized. Now they would listen to what was important!

...or not (said the storyteller).

"You must change your clothes," Ratha repeated, on what he considered sure ground now that Deg had corroborated Lir's claim.

Lir bowed to Ratha. "If you will pardon this foolish younger brother's contradiction, my clothes can wait. I've lived like this since summer, and survived, Imperial Elder Brother."

But Ratha was adamant about the vital matter of propriety. "My brothers must be respected according to their rank. Our dress and deportment acknowledge Imperial Father's beneficence and merit." Here Ratha bowed in the direction of the imperial island, followed by the guards.

Lir quickly bowed, shadowed by silent Bu, and Ratha said earnestly, "It's indecent, an imperial prince looking like that."

"Noble Imperial Elder Brother, your shining example teaches us all, but this erring younger brother must insist that my news is of fundamental importance. If you would deem it proper to summon your commanders..."

"Rathlir, you are no longer a boy. This impetuosity does not reflect well on you—or on me. Once you are restored to your proper dignities, we shall select an auspicious hour for our consultation."

Despairing, Lir turned—and caught Deg's gaze. The imperial guard colonel gave the smallest flick of the head toward the door.

Lir squashed down a sigh. "Very well, Fourth Imperial Brother," he said, and this time he remembered to bow first. At his shoulder, Bu bowed low. "I go at once to obey."

Ratha was immediately restored to his customary good humor, as the imperial guard colonel indicated the door. "If your imperial highness will deign to come this way, this humble servant will indicate the proper direction."

Out they went, Bu trailing. Deg remained silent as they descended a flight of stairs, then, leaving Ratha in his splendid tower chamber, they proceeded to a big room that had a huge chart on a wall, and in the center of the room, a contour map, built to resemble the entire island.

"Fourteenth Imperial Prince Rathlir has returned," Deg said to the aged man with thinning white hair behind the desk. "Your imperial highness, permit me to present to you Silver Lotus General Abaz Ke."

General Abaz rose in order to make a proper obeisance, and Deg said to Lir, "Your imperial highness, I was tasked to search for you by the grace of his imperial majesty." Here all of them saluted the imperial island, Lir aware that the gesture was imbued with meaning. Oh, he wanted to be home!

Deg continued, "My searchers have examined every boat, ship, and island in an ever-widening spiral around the area where the storm struck your fleet."

"My brother Rathtan," Lir finally got the courage to ask,

though he couldn't seem to breathe.

"This wretched incompetent wishes to inform your imperial highness that his imperial highness the twelfth prince arrived safely during harvest month."

Lir had been afraid he would expire during that eternal preamble through all the honorifics. But on hearing that TanTan was safe, he smiled. "And my cousin Rathlan?"

"Again, it is this servant's honor, duty, and pleasure to inform your imperial highness that the grand princess accompanied his imperial highness. In truth, perhaps I may be forgiven for presuming that your imperial highness would be pleased to learn, the two of them earned great merit through their efforts to aid in pulling people out of the sea."

"My brother is an excellent swimmer," Lir murmured. At least TanTan found it right and worthy to protect those who ranked below him in any way he could.

Bu stepped forward, and it took all her courage to say, so softly that her voice nearly vanished before reaching anyone's ears, "…First Apprentice Xia Chi?"

Deg gave her a look of affront, then blinked, belatedly recognizing in this ragged youth the musician who had played so very well. Outrage began to tighten his mouth, but he turned his gaze to Lir, remembering that the imperial prince had escaped the enemy. Perhaps such a guise had been on his orders. He said, neutrally, "It is my understanding that due to the merit and benevolence of his imperial majesty, and to the assiduous labors of Imperial Prince Rathtan, all but a kitchen servant survived, and have been dully returned to the imperial island, by the command of his imperial majesty."

Bu's eyes closed as she could not prevent the tears running down her face.

Deg didn't notice. His attention immediately returned to Lir. "If this lowly servant, through whose incompetence your imperial highness was not found, might trouble you with a question: what happened with the imperial guard Brick, who was seen last in your imperial highness's company?"

"Yes," Lir said, turning from Deg to Abaz. "About that…"

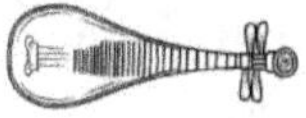

It took some time to get the entire story out.

During that time, there were numerous interruptions,

including a bath (on Ratha's direct orders), followed by graywings bringing out fabulous floating silks that they had found somewhere. Nothing was said when the last touches were put to his new costume, and there was no jade to hang from his belt, but he felt the question. Regret seized him once more.

Bu had been sent to the servants instead of being booted out the gate. Here she met with kindly treatment; she discovered from a chatty maidservant in charge of linens that the imperial island's musicians had sent out new theater pieces, which were becoming famous all over the empire. "I went to see *The Swan Fan* three times," she confided. "And you are one of them! Oh I do so love music. I hope you will be called upon to play."

Ever since Imperial Guard Colonel Deg's words about Xia Chi's survival, Bu's heart had bloomed with joy again. As she bathed, and submitted to having her tangled hair combined smooth and returned to a single modest braid again, she gratefully rearranged her lament, and now she longed to play it with a new, triumphant ending. "If there is a qin? Or a zither, or anything will do!"

"I don't know," the maid whispered, chuckling. "But in Te Gar Fortress, everyone goes to Nine when things must be found. If Nine doesn't know, no one does."

She towed Bu off to seek Graywing Nine, who was the fourth imperial prince's chief steward, as Lir impatiently finished dressing in time to be told that his brother was waiting dinner for him.

Lir wanted to shout, "Is no one listening? Sorxu could be here at any time!"

He suppressed his impatience as he was led to the sumptuous set of rooms where Fourth Imperial Prince Ratha stayed. At least Abaz and Deg were there, too. Now maybe he'd get a chance to convince them of the urgency of his news.

Ratha directed the conversation, wanting to hear all about Lir's adventures during the storm, and while a prisoner. Lir related them, keeping his part as short as possible, as he tried to get his brother to shift to military planning. With no success. Ratha wanted to know what tent life was like—really, Lir slept outside? And did not sicken?—Dreadful treatment! Though it did seem there was a semblance of civilization if that Mantai Hoxie refrained from assassinating Lir—a spy, among the guard—here Ratha turned to Deg. "I did not know such things could happen."

Deg abased himself, taking responsibility for decisions made by other imperial guards for what had seemed perfectly good reasons, and around and around the talk went. When Ratha finished his meal, Lir was poised to suggest they return to the command center, but then Ratha said, "Nine? Call out the entertainer."

Lir sat back, squashing down a groan. He was aware of a flash of resentment when the musicians and dancers trooped out, Bu among them. They began to play, and gradually the invisible, tight wires humming through Lir's meridians began to loosen; he half-recognized some of the melodies worked into Bu's song on the qin, but this piece was so transcendent that his grip on tension eased, allowing him to reach past frustration and impatience for alternative strategies. It was like playing Circle. Consider this path. That path. Let the number patterns break apart and reassemble in different ways...

At last it ended, and Ratha wished everyone a good rest.

A good rest!

Tension tightened its grip with merciless strength—until they had bowed Ratha out, and Deg leaned over from the next table down. "Shall we retire to help prepare a report for his imperial highness?"

"A report?" Lir asked, turning toward Abaz, at that moment being helped to rise.

"In the map chamber," Deg said—and Lir began to comprehend. He suppressed the sarcastic comment that even six months ago he would have uttered. It seemed that at last they were going to listen?

Back in the map room, Abaz bowed Lir toward the landscape map table, where Lir saw trays of little flags and other markers waiting. "If it pleases your imperial highness, we might consider various plans, to be ready for his imperial highness Imperial Prince Ratha to view come morning."

Lir said, "Perhaps lookouts might be posted? I don't mean just at these points." He tapped the little towers on the model of the fortress, beautifully detailed. He tapped various corners of the island. Sorxu's ships would have to come south if it wanted to take the harbor. Oh, but if he wanted to land and have the fun of smashing his way across the plains, except there were no plains. He'd be galloping his horses up and down some steep hills and into canyons, if this landscape was correct. Did he know that? "Here, on the north side. And here…" He tapped the west and east, to be sure.

Abaz bowed, his pouchy eyes crinkling. "Dispatched last night. We've signalers on all promontories, and our scout craft out here. With two here and here." His gnarled hand swept a circle over the ocean around the island, and then tapped two points farther out, one north and one south.

Lir let out a slow breath. And now he understood at last. It was Abaz who actually commanded — and if he'd already put scouts out, then surely he had put the garrison on alert.

FIFTY-FOUR

LIR RELISHED A BRIEF, heady moment of amazement and yes, even pride, when he found Abaz and Deg paying utmost attention to his words.

Then came the questions.

Did he think Sorxu would attack the harbor, or the other side of the peninsula? What tactics did he favor? What weapons?

That pride eroded fast. They were turning to him as the authority in this room, but as far as Lir was concerned, they were playing lutes to a pig.

Both men had been frank about their own limitations: Abaz—Lir recognized him as the fourth son of a prestigious family much trusted by the emperor—had been holding Te Gar for years, without experiencing any trouble. All the fighting had been north and west. It didn't take much thought to suspect that the emperor put Ratha, and Abaz, here, where nothing terrible was expected to occur.

Abaz admitted that he had seen action as a young soldier, but in those fights, he saw only the chaos around him as he strove to carry out orders made by someone else.

Deg had been a boy during the Troubles. Son of an imperial guard, he had followed his father into the guards at an early age. He knew all the ways to defend the imperial palace, but hearing Lir's words about Hoxie shook him severely. He knew that he would be held to blame for placing Brick where he'd been. And while he would surrender his life in the emperor's service, to be punished for dereliction, his family stripped of their status and turned out into the streets to live or die, seemed a hard fate when he could not possibly have known that Brick was a spy-assassin. Yet that fate was unavoidable.

Still, he was here, and duty required him to give of his best until the emperor chose to demand the life Deg had sworn to his service. "How much communication about imperial defenses do you think the brothers exchanged?" was one of his many questions to Lir.

"I don't really know," was the true answer to most of those questions. But Lir could see that they did not want modesty now. They did not want uncertainty. A starved eagle is still bigger than a well-fed nightingale: in spite of all Lir's limitations, they looked to him as the second-ranking man in Te Gar. A leader.

He ruminated on a new truth as he bent over that landscape map until his eyes ached: everyone wants to be assured of the outcome that keeps them safe. Everyone. For all that talk about manly virtues, the Horse Brethren king, with absolute authority, still required the shamans to do rituals most every day to predict what was to happen. And, right here, Deg and Abaz, the military experts, were looking to Lir to lead.

How could he lead? The relentless questions increased from a trickle to a flood. This island's terrain was utterly different from the flat fields Sorxu had been riding on. Would Prince Sorxu bring horses? Lir didn't know. Would he attack at night in order to take them by surprise? Lir didn't know. How many warriors? Lir didn't know that, either.

Then stay with what you know, he told himself.

He finally said, "Here's what I'm certain of. Sorxu likes bloody charges. In any situation where there is doubt, he pushes to the right, protecting his left. Is there some way to set things up so that he sees the kind of attack he likes most?"

Lir didn't have much hope as he said that. To him, it felt a bit like saying, "Are you sure that some of the men don't have wings and can fly for us?"

But Deg turned to Abaz, who tapped those gnarled hands on the edge of the table, then gave a grunt.

And Deg said, "A variation of the Host Invites the Guest?

This is one of our defenses of the imperial palace if they breach the outer gates. I know how to set it up."

Abaz bowed, then said, "But if Prince Hoxie revealed our defenses to this attacking prince..."

"Those are defense plans for the imperial palace," Deg said. "As for the strategies, those can be adapted infinite ways." He turned to Lir. "Your imperial highness, with your concurrence, we might present a possible plan to his imperial highness in command, and begin by getting everyone out of the houses along Serene Forest Path, and fill them with our people..."

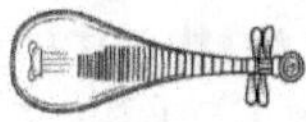

When Phoenix Moon rose the next night, the scouts in the northern perimeter waters sent three pigeons to Te Gar to report the appearance of an enormous fleet of independents.

Lir had a day to admire how Abaz, with every evidence of deep respect, offered the carefully considered plans worked up between him, Deg, and Lir to Ratha as suggestions.

Ratha listened. He thought about what he heard, if very slowly and deliberately. And when he spoke, it was in the clear, euphonious speech that the imperial tutors had inculcated in their charges, mostly by those much-repeated recitations and copied out texts of excellent prose.

Ratha agreed with every one of Abaz's suggestions, issuing each as an imperial edict, which Abaz in his turn bowed and accepted as orders. In issuing those orders, Ratha used those elevated phrases with the ease of long habit. He looked like an imperial prince. He sounded like one, which the people removed from their homes and sequestered within the fortress found reassuring.

Leadership, Lir discovered, in part resided in those led. They wanted a leader who could protect them, because terror was not very far from the surface, judging by how closely many stood to one another, and by the tension in wide gazes and stiff hands. They believed in Imperial Prince Ratha, who looked like the son of an emperor. Who sounded like the son of an emperor.

How much of these experiences had Imperial Father foreseen? Certainly not Brick being a spy and an assassin. Even so, Lir had become convinced that the entire journey had been a test. Whether or not he would succeed or fail, only the gods knew. But he had to see it happen, not wait to hear about it through someone else.

And he knew that Ratha would forbid him.

He slipped away from the refugees locked safely within the garrison, and insisted on riding out to witness. Deg was out of the garrison, in command of the trap, or he would have used the profound moral suasion of a condemned man to pressure Lir into staying inside. But the captain in charge was only aware that he could not gainsay an imperial prince, and Lir left too rapidly for his elder brother to find out.

For a time, nothing happened, except runners slipping back and forth, reporting on the approach of the enemy. Sorxu, predictably, chose to land on the other side of the harbor's westmost peninsula, so that he could smash and slaughter his way up the main street toward the garrison, and take advantage of the ensuing panic once the garrison threw open its gates in order to protect the unarmed commons.

Once they landed on the rocky shore, Sorxu jumped to the top of a boulder. "With the head of their Imperial Prince Ratha hanging from the walls between the Eagle and the Shrike banners, we will require the entire island to bow down to us," Sorxu roared.

He pulled his sword, loving the sound of the metal scraping the sheath, and reveled in the image of soon drawing the salamander sword. "Kill! Kill! Kill!

Hooh hooh hooh!

And, at the other end of the main street, word echoed through the garrison, "Here they come!"

Terror rippled through the refugees. Bu, who had managed to locate a qin, began to play in order to calm herself. She played no war ballads. Everything she played breathed of peaceful gardens, of spring flowers, of fire dragons dancing over the distant mountains, and stars descending from the heavens to scatter blessings among mortals.

For a time she played alone, unheard. But gradually faces turned, and listeners drifted toward the compelling melodies that gamboled aurally as they spread a sense of peace and calm. Many sensed that within the reach of the music they could find safety, and when Bu saw the softened expression of eyes and hands, she no longer played for herself. She brought all her joy to her songs, playing all the peaceful music she knew, then composing variations as she played it all again.

She didn't stop until his imperial highness, Fourth Prince Ratha, burst in, sending the guards and the graywings in charge of the refugees scattering. The peace was gone; refugees pressed together as he looked about, then spotted Bu.

To her vast surprise, he trod toward her, golden armor glittering, his usually calm face puckered in unaccustomed disquiet. "Where is my brother?"

Bu gazed up at him, hand suspended above the frets as she said, "I do not know, your imperial highness." And she scrambled to his feet in order to bow.

He whirled around and walked out, then turned back. "Attend."

Bu blinked, unsure what was meant, or whom. But then Nine gave her a discreet beckon, and she scurried out in Ratha's wake.

They'd reached an outer chamber when Ratha stopped, turned with a whirl of silk and a clatter of armor, and furrowed his brow at Bu. "Why would he go out there?" Ratha demanded. "He's a prince! Not a warrior!"

"Your imperial highness, he said nothing to me—I have not seen him since the dinner—"

"You were with him! You escaped with him! He's no longer a boy! He cannot do irresponsible things!"

Bu cast her mind back over their conversations, usually while they lay at either end of cramped, stuffy, small cubbies aboard various ships, or in small inn rooms. She considered how long it often took before Lir was able to fall asleep, as if his mind galloped like those horses they rode to and from the Horse Brethren king's camp.

She considered how often Lir had repeated his wish that they could discover who had survived the storm, and how much he had speculated about things for which Bu had no answer, and bowed her head. "If his imperial highness the fourth prince will forgive this ignorant apprentice for presuming to offer a worthless answer, ay, he came here."

Ratha blinked at her, more puzzled than before. "I know he came here. You cannot possibly be informing me what I saw with my own eyes?"

Bu promptly collapsed to the floor, forehead pressed to the stone. Her muffled voice was barely audible: "…your imperial highness…pardon…worthless…came here instead of going straight to the imperial island. Though he spoke every day of his longing to return to his home."

Ratha's furrowed brow knit even more, until Nine, at his shoulder, whispered something.

"Ayah," Ratha said with a nod. "Yes, yes, very responsible of him to come here. But that does not answer my question about why he risked his precious body to venture out into danger? Surely he understands that that is the duty of Abaz and Deg?"

Bu uttered her long preamble, then added, "…this one's worthless opinion is that he feels a need to see for himself when he can."

Ratha turned to one of the guards trailing him. "Find my brother, and bring him back."

FIFTY-FIVE

THE GUARD RAN OFF, stopping only to report this new order to his captain at the gate, and then left the fortress, to be halted by another company commander of the hidden guards. "Where are you going? Only messengers—"

"His imperial highness sent me."

On the guard ran, ducking around various obstacles such as carts, barrels, bales, and flimsy booths, behind which imperial guards crouched at the ready. Abaz's warriors hid further back, establishing a tight perimeter for when the trap closed.

The prince was immediately identifiable at the far end of the street, where the older cottages clustered along a branch of the main river that fed the garrison end of the harbor. The prince wore no armor over his green silk over-robe embroidered with dragonflies. He carried no weapon. He did not belong there.

The guard was considering how best to express the fourth prince's ire in order to reinforce his order when a whisper rustled through the hiding guards: *There they are.*

And so it was. Sorxu was in the lead, on horseback, for he'd reserved a great junk for his and his captains' animals. He would never fight on foot. He needed to strike down at subordinates. Only equals fought mounted.

His horse pranced, ears flicking. Why? Was it merely the

unknown terrain? The horses had hated the journey, and were fractious, requiring a firm hand.

Sorxu peered up the mostly empty street, past the jumble seen in all harbors. Empty street? Suspiciously empty? No…In the distance an old woman stooped over a basket, her face hidden by her kerchief. On the other side of the road, another old woman swept the dust from the stones before her door. But where was everyone else? Impending snow overhead…were they really afraid of a few flakes, or was there something else—

He was about to knee his horse into a prudent retreat, when a southerner in green silk covered with golden dragonflies staggered out of one of the buildings, jug in hand. Were all the inhabitants inside, drinking? He'd always heard the southerners were corrupt! Or was there something familiar…

The figure lifted his head.

Sorxu stared, astonished, as he recognized that servant of Hoxie's, last seen watching the training battles from the sidelines as he held the reins of the remounts.

The idiot stared in surprise, and Sorxu let out a savage laugh. "That one is mine!" he roared, and kicked his horse into a gallop, leaving behind a query from one of his followers, "What's he doing here? Isn't that a bad sign—"

Their leader raised his sword and shook it, howling, "Kill! Kill! Kill!" and so the riders must follow.

Lir saw Sorxu gallop straight for him, turned, and ran up the street in the direction of the garrison. When he heard the entire company of Shrikes and Eagles take to the gallop, he veered and dove between two barrels; having never before been in any kind of action, he misjudged how fast a horse could bolt compared to a man, and escaped having his head cut off by less than the length of an arm.

Deg threw himself between Sorxu and Lir as the imperial guards on both sides sprang out of hiding to attack the invaders. Roars, howls, shrieks of pain, and whinnies battered Lir's ears, but from that he picked out Deg's voice on a choking exclamation.

Lir had fallen to the ground. He scrambled to hands and knees in time to see Deg, with a sword struck through his body, pull Sorxu down from his horse. The two men crashed to the ground almost at Lir's feet. Three swords impaled Sorxu with horrible noises that Lir would never forget. But the sight, sounds, the smell of hot blood faded when he saw the red glow in Sorxu's eyes as he stared up at the sky, teeth bared.

Then the red vanished, and Sorxu's face slackened, looking surprised, and that expression also vanished with his life.

Deg coughed wetly. Lir uttered a cry of dismay, and dropped to his knees beside the imperial guard colonel. He paid no heed to the total rout around him—there was no glory in battle. Just these terrible sounds. Smells. The blood everywhere. How could there be so much blood?

Blood was bubbling crimson on Deg's lips as Lir extended his hands, unsure what to do. He could not leave the man on the ground, and so he lifted Deg carefully—not certain if he ought to do something about that sword still stuck through him—and babbled, "The medic—I'll get a medic—"

Deg was trying to speak. Lir bent closer. "Don't try to talk…"

Deg's hand rose, pawing at Lir's green silk, leaving a terrible smear down it. "Uh…uh…I…"

"Please, just try to breathe," Lir begged, and then, looking around, "Someone get this sword out of him!"

Another guard Lir's own age dropped to one knee. "It will kill him at once, your imperial highness," the man said.

"Uh…" Deg tried again to speak.

Together, the unknown guard and Lir levered Deg up so that he was not drowning in his own blood, and his breath wheezed in. "My life," he whispered. "Emperor's."

"Yes! I promise to tell him of your heroism," Lir said earnestly.

"He is ill. Very."

"What?" Lir said.

But there was no immediate answer. Deg blinked, and made another effort. "My family."

Lir glanced at the young guard, whose set face confirmed what Lir dreaded, and he turned to Deg, his throat aching. "Your family will be rewarded, Deg. Do you hear me? I'm sorry, I'm sorry…"

But Deg's body had become limp. Lifeless. Lir looked at the guard. "Did he hear me?"

The young guard shook his head in uncertainty.

For that moment, they were two young men in the presence of death—a deeply regretted death—but the guard, trained, was the first to recover. His expression recovered that set expression, and he bowed. "Your imperial highness, forgive this lowly one. Surely your imperial merit graced his end."

Lir could not express how much he loathed those words, and yet he knew that etiquette required them. And etiquette—ritual—were the forms that warded chaos, so much Master Angka had repeated so many times.

He gently laid Imperial Guard Colonel Deg down, saying, "We shall observe the funeral ritual, sending him off with all honor."

He lifted his head at the sound of clopping hooves as a riderless horse trotted by, an unknown Eagle rider's trappings bouncing on the horse's flank. From there he took in the bodies sprawled in the street, a few of these moving in pain amid smashed street vendor booths and carts and other jumble.

Then he saw faces turned his way, and his shocked, grief-stricken brain assimilated the fact that everyone was turning to him. For...? Blame for his stupid gambit? For causing the colonel's death? No, they were waiting for orders, because as utterly incompetent as he was, he had the highest rank on the scene.

"The enemy?" he said witlessly.

"Your imperial highness, I am here to report that, except for those who retreated to their ships, all dead," someone stated in a flat field voice from behind.

Lir turned, finding an older guard there, his stiff posture not quite hiding the lifted chin of conviction. Of triumph.

At what a cost! Lir surveyed the street again, more details registering. But the guards had done what they had been ordered to do—and some among them had lost their lives, for the invaders had fought ferociously.

"See to the wounded. And the dead." Then he knew what had to be done, and lifted his voice. "Well done, imperial guards. I shall report to my imperial brother." There. That was proper, was it not?

He rose to his feet, aware of the dampness of wet silk on the flesh of his arm from Deg's cooling blood. Guards closed in protectively before and behind him, swords out.

Lir discovered that his legs had gone weak at the knees. He stamped to shake the sensation, and made that endless walk along that entire street, until they reached the garrison.

Runners had gone ahead, and here was Ratha, now that all had been pronounced safe. Lir bowed, unsure what to say, but Abaz had had enough time to suggest the right words to

Ratha, who proclaimed victory in a loud voice.

"Victory!"

"Victory!" The glad cry rang outward; Lir watched from behind his brother as Abaz sent messengers this way and that. In the distance, the guards who had been detailed to protect the garrison loped off at a run to guard the far end as others saw to the wounded and the dead. The navy ships that had put up trader banners and sails once again flew the dragon banner as they set sail in pursuit of the enemy junks—some of whom had departed as soon as Sorxu's riders had disembarked.

Lir waited until Abaz returned to his command center. He followed, and when Abaz was between messengers, said, low, "Deg told me Imperial Father is ill?"

General Abaz bowed. "We do not know the details," he admitted. "Imperial Guard Colonel Deg was the one to receive imperial messages from the palace. I believe..." His gaze transferred to a point past Lir's shoulder, "...the empress insisted that his imperial highness the fourth prince was not to be disturbed with news that has been unchanged for many weeks, and about which he could do nothing."

Lir understood, and when another runner appeared to report, he backed up and retreated to the command center on the ground floor, where he could overhear those reports coming in: loose horses rounded up; enemy dead burning in a pyre; imperial dead being laid out for proper ritual. From there he listened and watched as order was restored as fast as hands and the will motivating them could contrive.

Eventually—after the denizens of the street had been released—Fourth Imperial Prince Ratha summoned him. "Rathlir," he said. "I was disturbed at your actions, but they tell me you were heroic. It was you who drew the enemy into the trap. Our imperial father will not favor your risking your precious skin—that could be thought to lack in respect for he who gave you life—but he will be proud of a brave act that contributed to our victory."

How often was heroism just unthinking stupidity? Ratha was not the one to ask. "I am a disobliging son," Lir said, bowing his head—hoping to end the subject. "It was not filial."

"Ayah, you are young and thoughtless," Ratha said comfortingly. "You ought to change out of those clothes. I will hold a celebratory banquet for the commanders."

"Has word been sent yet to Imperial Father?" Lir asked.

Abaz, in the background bowed, and Ratha said, "It was

indeed, the first thing once we ascertained the news. I'll give orders for proper clothing to be prepared for you —"

"Elder brother, if you will grant permission, I would like to leave you to celebrate your great victory, and set sail for home. I have not seen our imperial father for too long."

Ratha's expression changed to surprise, and then delight. "A filial thought. Indeed, indeed, indeed, a most filial thought, and I concur. It was a great victory, was it not? I can get Abaz to give you Deg's fast scout, since he will no longer require it. And you can personally carry my respectful greetings to our imperial mother as well." He added with a hint of diffidence, "And, if you will, my own birth mother."

Lir could see Ratha unquestioningly assuming credit for all—he had given the orders, and was in command. He was welcome to whatever merit he could see in such destruction, a conviction that hardened when Lir found Lum Bu over in the servants' wing, and she greeted him with, "Your imperial highness, may this ignorant one ask what happened?"

He looked at that kindly face and the words tasted like bitter ash in his mouth. "Sorxu is dead. The rest can wait. I'm taking ship for the imperial island as soon as the tide goes out. I remember you hoped to return as soon as possible to your studies. If you want to go with me, pack up what you need. Or," he raised his voice and looked at the two women in servant gray busying themselves on the other side of the door, no doubt straining to hear every word, "you people can pack up what she will need."

They were sailing before evening.

FIFTY-SIX

FOR THE FIRST FEW days, Bu saw little of the fourteenth imperial prince. Under his impatient eyes, the Te Gar servants had packed a qin, a zither, a lute, and her old friend the eruh as well as two flutes for Bu, as well as some hastily assembled clothing for upper palace female servants. She occupied herself with resuming her studies on all these instruments, thus crew and imperial prince found themselves surrounded by increasingly splendid music.

Bu was still wary of the word "friend." She would never presume to consider herself a friend — she was not altogether certain what it meant. Cricket had been a friend, but he had left joyously when they parted. YinYin was a friend, but was a demon. Was Lir a friend? She was not fond of Lir, and she knew he was not fond of her, but she respected him, and she sensed that he respected her abilities in music. Also there trust between them, unspoken but there.

She had also come to know Lir about as well as anyone could know him outside of his lifelong companions. She expected that one day he would begin talking — and so it was.

"I hate war," he said abruptly, as if four days had not passed in silence. "I hate everything about it. And yet, to give Deg his due, because he did surrender his life, faithful to his oath, I will have to speak of him as a hero. Will you make a song for him, so that I won't have to make a speech? My father will probably require a speech before the court, and I know I'll get myself into difficulties if I tell the truth about what I saw of war. Which I don't want to talk about."

But he then went on to talk about it. Bu listened, and shuddered, and in the darkness, she cried, but come dawn, she began composing a song on the zither to honor Deg, who would never again in this life see the family who had been his last thought. And through him, honor all those who fell.

Lir kept talking, and finally came to Sorxu's death, and the demon. "I saw the red glow in his eyes," he said. "It was real. It was there."

He saw no surprise in her.

"You really did meet a demon," he said. "It's not that I thought you lied. But I thought it was, ah, metaphor, for evil? But it was distinct. As though some other kind of life looked out from his eyes." Lir grimaced. "Where was yours?"

"Far away."

"The strangest thing," he said, "was that red glow was not in the report that the other guard gave. I sought him out while you were packing your things, and he said, *What red glow? Do you mean the blood in his face?* He really didn't see it?"

"I think some don't," Bu said.

"I hate that," Lir burst out. "I loathe hearing that, because it might mean that Jin's ghosts are real."

And off he went to pace the ship, brooding.

At first tentative, for what she had heard about battle was new to her, and terrifying, and immensely sad, she worked through endless variations until her piece began to build. And deepen, until sailors went around with wet faces, and caught themselves staring out to sea, or caressing small figurines or tassels that those at home had given as mementos.

'Deep' would not honor the fallen if it was so deep it descended to darkness. And so she wove in light: families, companions, the hope of peace and renewal, stitched together by the thought *Xia Chi is alive.* The piece soared and sang, sweet and sorrowing, and each new iteration sparked emotion and memory anew, so that, though she rehearsed it several times a day, it never got old to the listeners. This music wafted over the waters, carried by the wind, until the imperial island was at last spotted on the horizon.

Pigeons flew ahead. Both Lir and Bu began to anticipate seeing those they'd worried about for so long. Lir had sometimes called up memories of every room of the palace he shared with TanTan, from the jade-inlaid Circle board that they no longer used to the screens in the rooms. It had bothered him when he couldn't recollect exact details as he lay shivering in his bedroll under the cold stars in the north. He had taken that palace for granted, but no more. He was thankful at the prospect of sinking into his old life.

Bu would see Granny Zim! Who would give her more lessons, and who would explain things that puzzled Bu. And YinYin would be there, to explain what Bu had heard and seen.

A pigeon fluttered back, and the imperial guard captain who had been assigned to guard Lir opened the message, and said, "The harbor has been cleared for us to land."

The sun was just setting when they floated in on the rising tide. Imperial guards lined the quay, and as the ship bumped gently against the pier, the sails rattling as they were made fast, at a signal the pulled their swords.

Lir laughed within himself at all this panoply just for the worthless Weasel, because he knew that no fanfare would be raised for Lum Bu, in spite of the fact that if any human being was a treasure it would be her and her talent. He scanned the waiting faces — and a spontaneous whoop escaped him when he recognized TanTan running down the pier, a sound that TanTan himself would never hear.

The ramp was slid out to the pier, two guards went first to make double sure there was no threat, then Lir descended. The moment his foot touched the pier, the guards dropped to a knee and saluted.

Lir scarcely noticed. Signing as fast as he could, he tried to convey how happy he was that TanTan was alive — where was Rathlan — was a good feast waiting? Shipboard food was so tedious…

TanTan reached for those fluttering, snapping hands and gripped Lir's fingers, his other hand signaling: *Come. Now.*

Lir's intense joy dissipated like the warmth of the sun when the clouds slide across the sky, as a little graywing appeared from behind the guards closing in behind Lir. This graywing said to Bu, "Apprentice Musician, Sagacious Master Zim awaits you."

"Take me to her," Bu fluted, her voice tremulous.

While they rushed in one direction, TanTan and Lir headed into the heart of the imperial palace, shadowed not only by Imperial Guard Sanhu (Lir was relieved to see. At least Sanhu was not apparently held responsible for not somehow knowing that "Brick" was a spy and an assassin) but two new guards. Two?

Am I in trouble? Lir thought, mentally examining his actions over the past weeks.

This internal examination broke when TanTan stopped midway through the imperial garden, and waved the guards off. The shadows had closed in around them during the long walk, so all they saw clearly was one another's breath.

TanTan was still trying to assimilate the changes in his brother in the months he had been missing. He seemed taller, except that that wasn't true. Their eyes were at the same level they had been for the past four years. Lir was definitely thinner in some ways, except through the arms and chest.

TanTan wanted badly to find out what had happened, but urgency smothered the questions. "Imperial Father. Sick," he signed. "Waiting for you."

While the brothers reunited, Bu, wobbly with excitement, scurried along the remembered corridors as the shadows lengthened and melded, her graywing guide obligingly keeping pace. Bu dodged around servants lighting lanterns—and there was the Garden of Celestial Merits—

And there, at last, Granny Zim's wing. Everything was quiet. So often Bu had lain awake, trying to imagine herself there, warm and safe. The corridors were shorter than she remembered, the air so much colder. Granny Zim opened her door, smaller and thinner than Bu remembered. "Bu! Here you are at last!"

YinYin materialized at Granny Zim's shoulder, no change in expression that Bu could perceive. A brief glow at the level of YinYin's eye sockets *felt* like a kind of smile rather than anything sinister.

"I'm back," Bu said. "I'm so sorry—"

Granny Zim uttered a cackling laugh. "Oh, Bu, that truly is you. Why should you apologize for being thrown off a ship into the water?" She drew Bu into her warm chamber, and put her handwarmer into fingers that Bu discovered were cold.

"Bring us tea," Granny Zim instructed the servant, and turned to Bu, as YinYin stood beside her. "Talk! Tell me everything. No, first, how far did you get in your lessons?"

"That's why I must apologize," Bu said sorrowfully. "When I got thrown into the water, the precious lessons you had written out for us went into the water too. When I could, I did my best to remember and practice them."

"I know about the papers. Xia Chi told me, and I have already rewritten most of them. Better! I shall hear your progress when you are ready," Granny Zim said. "First, tell us all."

Bu turned from Granny Zim to YinYin. "I saw another demon! It was in the king of the northerners, and there was also one in his son. The prince saw it in his eyes. I told them the demon I knew was met once, but I fear I ought not to have said anything, because what if they summon me to ask more?"

Granny Zim said, "Tell us what happened. We will go from there—I doubt very much that any interrogators will be banging on the door tonight."

As Bu poured out everything she had held tightly within, on the other side of the imperial palace, Lir gave TanTan a quick explanation of his adventures, after which they crossed toward the emperor's pavilion.

FIFTY-SEVEN

THE EMPEROR DID NOT keep Lir waiting.

All Lir's expectations turned into questions as Graywing Chief One led the way, guards at every corner and stair, then silently took Lir to a room he had never seen before: the imperial bedchamber. A haze of medicinal incense diffused the ceiling on which stars had been painted against a deep blue.

A wizened, white-haired figure struggled to sit up, until soft-footed graywings tenderly raised him to a sitting position. Lir approached slowly, shocked at how very much his father had aged in a matter of weeks.

"Rathlir," the emperor said, his voice raspy with effort. "It *is* you." And as Lir dropped to his knees, "Rise, rise, rise. Come here. Tell me everything." His trembling hand indicated for Lir to sit beside him on the enormous bed.

Lir approached. He did not dare presume to touch the bed, which felt unfilial, so he dropped to his knees beside it. "Where ought I to begin, Imperial Father? Do you want to hear about the storm?"

"No. Heard. Was Deg right? Your guard."

Lir sighed. Of course Deg would send the truth to the emperor, even though he believed his life would be forfeit. "Brick turned out to be an assassin, sent by the Jun Suai. He's the king's second son."

"There will be a price to pay for that," the emperor said. Even his voice shook with anger.

Lir's smile vanished. "Deg said something to that effect, Imperial Father—but I don't see why. He could not have known."

"Ought to have known. I'll have heads for that."

"But they didn't know."

"Rathlir. If anything happens to us. Those who guard us have failed. There have to be mortal consequence. Or how can we hold our position? People expect consequence. To us, too."

The emperor's breathing harshened, the trembling more pronounced, and Lir saw Graywing One looking concerned. He forced himself to bow as if acquiescing, and decided to bring up his promise to protect Deg's family later. Better not to mention them now if Imperial Father was looking for people to blame for Hoxie's ruse.

Lir went on, "I think Hoxie had a charmed object that calls to another object, and a ship that must have been trailing outside of our fleet at a distance came up, and took all three of us aboard. I should mention Musician Apprentice Lum Bu was with us, on the same raft..."

Lir could barely force himself to look at his father's face, now that he recognized that Imperial Father wasn't aged so much as ill. Very ill, just as he'd been warned. The emperor's effort to concentrate seemed to require what little strength he had, but when graywings came forward to offer medicine or tea or extra pillows, he waved them off, hand shaking.

The emperor listened mostly in silence, his breathing rough while Lir spoke of his life in the enemy king's camp. Lir kept that brief, instead describing what he had learned from Bu about the king's demon. Then he described the escape, and the journey to Te Gar. The emperor breathed hard as he attempted to lean forward; Lir quickly described the planning session, Sorxu's invaders, the demon in Sorxu, and Deg losing his life saving him.

At the end, the emperor said, "This is the first I have heard about demons."

"This ignorant son was not certain, Imperial Father. Though I spoke at length with Lum Bu, who has met a demon and survived, I did not truly believe until I saw one."

"Lum Bu...the student of my new Sagacious Master Musician. These islands far to the south. They produce some strange yet vital things. You will have to look into that."

"I, Imperial Father?"

"It will be your first duty. I knew of everything else. But I needed to hear it from you. You've done well, my son."

"Imperial Father, this unfilial son only wishes he had done well."

The emperor reached over, closing those trembling fingers tightly over Rathlir's wrist. His flesh was clammy, the muscles twitching. Sorrow scoured through Lir 's nerves at the effort his father made just to grasp. "You question. It is what I hoped you would learn to do. Not only questioning the world. Question yourself." The emperor's voice strengthened, and though it still quivered, there was the ring of conviction.

"Please teach me, Imperial Father."

"Rathlir. I am appointing you my heir. I leave the empire to you."

The words at first made no sense.

Silence thickened in that room of illness. Lir heard the sound of his father's labored breathing, and finally, when the words began to register, it was as if he had fallen into a hole filled with ice. "What?" the word wrung out of him, then he recollected himself, and dropped face to the floor. "This ignorant wastrel hopes Imperial Father is making a jest?"

"Get up, Rathlir." And when Lir reluctantly raised his head, the emperor's voice rasped with effort as he once more took hold of his son's wrist. "I have written the edict. When I can rid myself of this malady. We will go before court together. To declare what is already law."

"Imperial Father," *I don't want…* "I am not at all ready for such responsibility."

The emperor shook with laughter, which turned to coughing. Gasping, he freed Lir's wrist to clutch at his chest, then said, "Few are. Even fewer know they are. I was not. But you learn. I know that now. It gives me comfort," the emperor said, each word coming with more effort.

From behind him Graywing One made a tiny motion, which Lir understood as a suggestion to bring the interview to a close. But Imperial Father had always chosen the moment to end their interviews. It seemed unfilial to take this step, and yet he could see how his father struggled to speak. How to do it? Ah, he knew how: "As you wish, Imperial Father. This concerned son will withdraw so that you can get your healing rest."

"Go. Get your own rest. We have much to discuss on the

morrow. Much. But I am very pleased with you, my son." More coughing shook the emperor, and he gasped, "One. Bring me a double dose. You never. Gave me enough. Told you and told you..." The emperor fell to coughing horribly.

Lir could not bear hearing that. He slipped from the room—then halted when he saw two figures just outside the door, obviously listening.

He fell to his knees. "Imperial Mother."

"Rise, Rathlir," the empress said. "Come."

The other figure was Rathlan, who gave Lir a quick, wordless hug. He hugged her back, relieved she was warm and alive, after being unsure for so many weeks. But her smile was brief, and he was shocked to see the tears brimming along her eyelids.

The empress waved off the lines of serving maids who waited a short distance down the hall, and opened a side door to a small chamber. Though she had her own palace nearly as large as this one, it was clear that she was familiar with Imperial Father's inner chambers, a fact Rathlir had not considered until this moment.

Inside the antechamber, the empress indicated gold-embroidered cushions around a table inlaid with water dragons dancing along the edge. Lir flinched away, thrown back to those eerie moments in the middle of the storm; strange, that was how his head felt, as if it was about to float off his shoulders.

"Demons?" the empress said as she sat and neatly disposed her sleeves.

"Lum Bu knows more than I do," Lir said numbly. He sat carefully, aware of disparate details: the acanthus embroidered on his cushion; Rathlan's ribbons tangling as she sat, as they had since she was a gap-toothed girl trotting alongside him; the scent of incense drifting from the emperor's chamber. Lir rubbed his eyes, but that did nothing to assuage the strained sense of instability, almost nausea.

"Does the prince who took you prisoner have a demon?"

"Not that I was told."

"Does he know about the one possessing his father?"

"I believe he knows now," Lir said, and then, "I hope Imperial Father was not serious about...what he said?"

The empress, always serene, gave him a slightly reproachful glance. "He is serious, my dear son. He wishes to begin instructing you, and you will have duties to see to. He gave you one. I have arranged for Master Angka to be available to you as soon as you are rested from your ordeal." She rose. "With your permission, I will discuss this news you bring of demons with the augurs, and request that they interview Student Lum Bu."

Lir bowed, and after she went out, he gave Rathlan a grimace. "She was asking my permission to leave. Did you hear that?"

"Rathlir, you don't know how strained things have been. Imperial Uncle has not been able to rule, except from his bed, since Ghost Moon Month. TanTan sits on the dragon throne. I sit behind a pilar, letting him know what is being talked of, but it is Imperial Aunt who speaks. And the court is always trying to talk around him, because he's deaf, and her, because she's not a man, though I think she would make as sagacious an emperor as any man."

"You will hear no argument from me," Lir said.

She sighed, the stiffness leaving her voice. "Court affairs are terribly backed up because of the time it takes for me to translate for TanTan, and then for him and Imperial Aunt to confer, and me to translate for her. The truth is, the emperor has to have a Voice, and only you can be it. He wants *you*. He always wanted you, the empress tells us—and he blames himself for having gone about it wrong, because of the way things went with your older brothers, that led to the Troubles." Rathlan paused, then said, "I know you will hate hearing this. And if you hate me, so be it. But this is your duty. Call it a sacrifice if you must."

Lir got up restlessly and said, "Where's Tan?" He walked out, as if he could leave the subject behind. They went out to where TanTan awaited them in the outer chamber.

"Let's talk when we get to our lair," Lir said, hands busy.

Rathlan slanted him a glance. "Your things have been moved to the heir's palace. That's our new sign for it." She demonstrated again, and TanTan nodded.

Another jolt, as if the ground had been yanked from beneath his feet. These two—his closest relatives—had already begun thinking him into that golden yoke. "Then let's go to our, *your* palace, TanTan," he said as he signed—and belatedly heard the words come out as a command. Or rather the others treated it as a command, and not a suggestion.

The two new guards waited without, along with Sanhu. Now Lir understood the pair of guards, silent reinforcement of this strange whim of his father's. Ayah, gods, let it just be a whim!

No one spoke until they reached the safety of TanTan's palace, which no longer had any of Lir's things. He whirled around to face the other two as soon as they were alone. "Imperial Father looks terrible. Can't the imperial physicians do more for him?"

Rathlan said, "He has decided that essence of quicksilver, which is supposed to halt aging, is a panacea. My mother tells me it's because they gave it to Cousin Ten when he was ill."

Lir barely remembered his tenth brother.

Rathlan added, "Mother tells me that Cousin Ten kept telling Imperial Uncle that he felt better, though everyone knew it was not true. But he did not want to worry his father, which would be unfilial."

"I know that good medicine takes time to heal," Lir said doubtfully.

"It is true. But some of the older texts, translated from some scrolls captured from the western islanders who everyone says practice blood healing, insist that cinnabar, in spite of its color being that of fresh blood, does not purify the blood." Rathlan leaned forward, excited—this was like old times. "I investigated very carefully. The imperial physicians disagree with one another, though they do not like to admit it before others. The important thing is, everything prepared for Imperial Uncle is properly concocted. No cinnabar touched on fire days, which increases the poisonous effect, but only on water days, mitigating the poison, and that extracted only during the proper months. Using dew collected from the right plants, on the correct days. Everything done right. TanTan thinks the problem is that Imperial Uncle has decided that the more he takes, the faster it will work."

Here TanTan smacked the wall. "He will not listen."

Lir wanted to shout, *then it should be poured out!* But who would dare to go against the emperor's wishes?

"I'm going to talk him out of taking so much," he said. "Please help me, you two."

They agreed, though both TanTan and Rathlan, who had lived through weeks of the emperor's catastrophic illness as he struggled to cling to life, knew that the emperor was not going to change his mind.

FIFTY-EIGHT

"THOUGH THE EDICTS HAD not been proclaimed," explained the storyteller, as Young Master sat back down again; if he couldn't have more battles, the next best thing was a glimpse behind the golden doors into the life of Heaven's Chosen. "The emperor had written them and affixed the imperial seal, which made them law, duly noted by the scribes…"

The storyteller went on to quickly explain that great events as well as small require divining an auspicious time and date—but those could not be set until there was an actual heir physically present, so that the court could see him receive the seal that only the heir could wield.

Lir woke up to find new and unknown graywings surrounding his bed. The moment he opened his eyes they dropped to the floor.

So did his heart within his body: this could not be a good sign.

"Your imperial majesty," said a graywing Lir had never seen before. "Her highness the grand princess desires entrance."

"Send her in. Where is my wrap?" Lir asked, remembering that everything he owned had been stowed in a new place in this pavilion he had never set foot in before the previous night.

Rathlan ran in while Lir had his night robe half on, crying, "He's gone, Lir, he's gone."

"What?"

"One says he went to sleep very comforted last night, after he took that dose. He talked about how much better he felt, and that you and he would stand before court soon... and when they parted the bed curtains this morning, he was cold."

She gave forth a sob, and a heartbeat later he heard a howl from somewhere outside, a wail that harrowed him: "Come home, your imperial majesty! Come home!"

Lir knew then that someone stood on the eave of the emperor's palace not far away, waving the dragon robe and calling the emperor's soul to return. This went on five times, and it would go on five more times at the end of ten days, until the funeral pyre. But he had never heard of anyone returning to that call.

Rathlan collapsed on a cushion and wept.

Lir's gaze flicked from the unfamiliar silk screen of swallows in flight to the golden ewer beside a golden bowl on the nightstand, with aromatic tea waiting should he wish to rinse his mouth. The first thought that wriggled past the block of ice his mind had frozen into was: And now they'd make him move again, to the Dragon Pavilion?

He recoiled from the idea. Dragon Pavilion was Imperial Father's. Everything in there spoke of *him*. It was abomination to even think of polluting that pavilion with his lazy, foolish self.

The last cry echoed, inescapable truth.

That was just the first blow of a fate that he could not escape.

Graywing Two appeared with a host of other servants, including some from the empress, and Rathlan was led away as others began silently packing and folding and cleaning. Another group approached Lir, bowed to the floor, then disclosed the rough, undyed garments of mourning.

Each new thing forced him to confront the fact that all those conversations he had saved up to speak to his father would not happen. His father's "We will have much to say" would not be said. Imperial Father's soul had departed for the bridge of stars, free as air. New Year's was nigh; he might soon be reborn as someone else, somewhere else far away.

But Lir was still here, left with that golden yoke.

He wanted so badly to shout, NO! Wasn't he supposed to be powerful now? Would they listen? They'd have to listen. He'd make them listen...

He covered his face with his hands, knowing that such a thought was the first step along a road of knives. Rathlan had used the word duty. And followed it with sacrifice. These two words were invisible ropes that, if he ever wanted to be thought of as a moral man, he must permit to bind him.

And at this moment, decency as well as filial piety required that he change to mourning garments.

Inexorably, once he gave in to a single change, the rest fell in a cascade.

A mood of bleak inevitability gripped him as the world changed with equal relentlessness around him.

There were only two small gifts of grace. The first was the discovery that the emperor had stipulated in his will that if he died before Lir turned twenty-five, the empress would serve as regent for a year. She would continue to sit beside the throne behind her silken veil. The second was that TanTan and Rathlan swore not to abandon him: they would continue to aid him in court, Rathlan hidden, TanTan in the place of a Grand Prince. Rathlan actually relished the change. All that reading now had a purpose, and TanTan confided that she was the first one to tackle the waiting depositions each morning.

The edicts were posted as the imperial palace, and then the empire went into official mourning. That meant all music, theater, and artistic displays were postponed for the mourning period.

Far to the south of the Dragon Pavilion, Granny Zim, Bu, and YinYin heard the news, which the graywing brought with breakfast.

Bu's first thought was a pulse of sorrow for Lir, who had started so many conversations with "My father thinks…" or "My father said…" and sometimes, "I used to think my father…" and he would go on to talk about what he would explain to the emperor. Other than that, she felt no more than she'd feel if someone reported that one of the brighter stars in the sky, which she had only seen during that brief time she'd had an eyepiece, had ceased to shine. The emperor seemed too remote for her to presume to have any feelings, and yet Granny Zim paused with her tea cup in her gnarled hand, her gaze fixed, and suspiciously bright. Did she feel grief?

Grief it was — mixed with relief that he must have seen his son first, for here was Bu, who had traveled with that unknown prince. But the main part of the upwelling of sorrow was for herself, for him, for everyone who looked around to see that they were the last of their generation. And if it was true that the King of the Underworld did send souls back, the real grief was that this inescapable weight of age and death must be repeated, and repeated, without the comfort of knowing that it has been done before, and like playing your qin, gets easier with time.

However, Granny Zim thought, catching herself up, that behooved her to use whatever time she had left to do what she loved best, and to relish every moment.

And what she did best was teaching.

"Bu, the imperial palace will go into mourning, which means classes will be suspended for the first ten days. We will use this time to test what you have learned or neglected to learn."

Bu's head dropped. "I fear it is not enough. It was never enough. I so missed your precious lessons, Granny Zim, made by your own hands."

"Ayah, I know you, Bu," Granny Zim said briskly, seeing the moisture gathering in Bu's honest eyes. "You no doubt read ahead, and practiced what you could. I know how far First Apprentice Xia Chi was able to reach, and I was quite impressed with his progress. But I'd walk into any gambling den and lay down those golden coins given me by the emperor—may his passage be easy—to wager that you went on much farther."

Bu knew that that was true. She *had* read ahead, mentally reviewing the more difficult lessons in her eagerness to learn—and because reading those lessons had brought Granny Zim closer.

"My question now is, did you in those missing months develop bad habits?"

Bu sat down to the qin she'd been given at Te Gar, worked through all her fundamentals in order to wake up her hands; Granny Zim heard with satisfaction that Bu had mastered combinations and variations that usually came in the ninth and tenth years. Then, eyes closed, Bu played the mourning song that she had composed at Lir's request. It built and built, bringing in all those variations she had worked at during her time in the north.

YinYin listened, eyes ember-red and glowing at the evocation of Essence that only the demon could see. Bu had become that rare human, a vessel for Essence: protected partly by a sliver of YinYin that had been left in Bu entirely as safeguard, and partly by her own instinct to hide in the face of danger, Bu had managed not to attract the hungry, prowling demons out there.

YinYin would be diligent in protecting her now. Especially from the one that YinYin watched from afar while slowly gathering strength.

Granny Zim listened, rocking back and forth on her cushion as she assimilated the fact that Bu's talent had only heightened. Oh, there were a few small things, but those would soon be worked out.

"It is well," she said at length. "We have some work to do, but Bu, it is very well."

That praise filled Bu with joy—she would not have traded it for all the gold in the world.

Over the next days of complete mourning as the imperial palace remained shrouded and silent, except for those coming to pay their respects before the great sarcophagus in the Temple of Ancestors, Granny Zim kept Bu to herself while she corrected those few small faults. She saw to it that Bu was provided with another eyepiece.

She assigned to Bu the solo from *The Jade Palace* that she had written for her—and then thumbed her eyes in secret as Bu played it back with such joy and loss that Granny Zim began to realize that this one student had very little further to learn from her. Bu had become one of those rare talents who would surpass the teacher.

At the end of the first week, Chief Musician Huazi called instructors and students together, saying, "We will of course not be performing, except lamentation or funerary songs as required. But once the mourning period ends, the demand for new material will spring on us like hungry tigers, as if songs are composed in a day."

Everyone agreed with that.

"Now, Sagacious Master Zim has brought Student Lum Bu before us. She will audition again."

Granny Zim waved Bu to sit before the music students, many of whom had forgotten her, she had been with them so briefly. Bu took her time in disposing her clothing properly, assuming the correct posture for play, and began the breathing before she softly tested the strings she had tuned moments ago.

Then she played the mourning song she had written for Imperial Guard Colonel Deg. The masters as well as the senior students listened to Bu in growing amazement, and then, many with tight throats and stinging eyes, they rose as one to give her the accolade that musicians gave one another: no loud clapping, but the bow to a master.

Bu blushed to the ears and hid her face—watched by Xia Chi, who struggled against the intense jealousy he knew he had no right to feel. He was not jealous of her talent. That he celebrated. He was jealous of whoever would be selected to live by her side, hearing her music, and her conversation, seeing her smiles, and her tears, for the rest of their lives. He had been betrothed at a young age, and though men could take as many wives as they could afford (and some could ill afford) he respected and admired Bu far too much to relegate her to the status of a second wife.

He'd prepared himself to see a different Bu, one with the experience that would result from traveling alone for months with an imperial prince. But when at last they came together again outside the classroom door, and she looked up earnestly into his face, he knew from her expression that whatever had happened between Bu and the new emperor, she was unchanged in essentials.

When Chief Musician Huazi and Granny Zim placed Bu to the spot next to First Apprentice Xia Chi, Bu approached tentatively, then saw in his smile and the way he turned toward her that he was ready to go back to the easy way they had sat next to one another during those wonderful days on the tower ship, before the terrible storm.

Bu settled down, aware that she had reached the pinnacle of all she had ever wanted. The only shadow on her days was the expectation of being interrogated about demons.

"I will be surprised if that comes to pass," Granny Zim said briskly, when Bu brought it up later. "You did well in what you told the young emperor; if all is as you said, he must be convinced you know nothing of worth. You met a demon on our island, and recognized another in that king. You hid yourself from him, and are ignorant beyond that. You certainly don't know anything of military use, and that is assuredly what they want to hear."

On the other side of the palace, there was no joy, but Lir

had the consolation of companionship from his family. His elder brothers might not be people to turn to for guidance, but their grief was genuine, his aunt tried to assuage his sorrow in taking all the new servants in hand to attend to Lir's physical well-being, as the empress remained a steadfast presence, ordering his day with tasks that steadied him.

TanTan and Rathlan were his constant companions. At first Lir dreaded seeing Jin and his ghosts, but he could not ignore his brother because of his own discomfort. After those first few days, he made time to visit Jin, and his reward was the fact that Jin said nothing about their father's ghost lingering.

When that initial week ended, and the second call for the emperor's soul had passed, Lir had to turn his attention to accumulated tasks his father had left. He cleared a crowded schedule in order to meet alone with the chief of the Emperor's Own as well as with the Minister of War, and the general in charge of overseeing the stalled war in the north.

To these serious, expressionless men twice Lir's age, Lir gave as detailed a report of everything he had seen and heard, down to Sorxu's death. "I don't know what happened to that demon," he finished. "There is no use in putting the question to Lum Bu, either, because she does not know. She was not there when Sorxu died, and her encounter was long ago, probably on her tribute island. This is what I'm sure of: the Jun Suai king will be furious about his son, so I expect when spring comes, the stagnant war will see new attacks."

No one disagreed.

The general soon departed with orders to stiffen the defense of imperial holdings. The Minister of War was ordered to see that funds would be secured for supplies, ships, and men.

And to the ferret chief, Lir said, "I want you to find out what Mantai Hoxie is doing. He might have hated his brother, but he will hate worse the fact that I took Sorxu's favorite strategies to Te Gar in order to defeat Sorxu, because he will blame himself."

FIFTY-NINE

NEW YEAR'S TWO MOONS arrived.

Because it occurred during imperial mourning, the usual celebrations were subdued, the pleasure houses only offering tea and poetry in praise of the departed emperor, and on suitably ancient and philosophical subjects. Xia Chi went home, along with the other music students who had homes to go to.

After the quiet meal, he asked his father if they could speak alone, and said, "Honored Father, with respect and filial duty, I come to you to say that I want to end my betrothal."

"What?" His father scowled. "If you're being courted by a duke's daughter, I would consider it, but otherwise, how could you so forget what you owe to your family?" And when his son did not answer, he said, "Tell me about her. Is she well born?"

"She is not, Father."

"Has she a dowry, at least?"

"No, Father."

Master Xia's frown increased. "I never expected this sort of trouble from *you*. Is she an entertainer? One of those willow-browed flatterers with painted toenails looking to jump above their rank?"

"No. Lum Bu has no idea I am coming to you. She's…she's not beautiful in the way you're thinking of. But she is beautiful to me, especially when she plays. She's a musician, and a Talent. The one I was with on the tower ship."

An even deeper frown. "I heard something about that—the one that the new emperor—may he lived a thousand years," Master Xia added in haste, with a quick clasp of the hands in the direction of the imperial palace, " — took with him when he was taken by the northerners. Lum? Lum? Never heard of the name. She's probably an adventurer."

Only filial piety kept Xia Chi from laughing at this unlikely picture.

"How could you even consider putting me in such a position with respect to Master Choa? You will marry Choa Si when you turn twenty-five, and I do not want to hear any more about it." He irritably snapped his fan, and retreated to his own chamber to escape the sadness in Chi's eyes. Young men, ayah! In love one day, and forgotten tomorrow. Chi would forget that insinuating strummer, once a little time had passed.

Xia Chi was not the only one troubled by the dynastic plans of the senior generation.

Once the quiet New Year's ritual was over, the empress gathered the consorts with a glance, and, bolstered by their presence as well as that of Lir's aunt, she said to Lir, "Imperial Son, once mourning is complete, we must see about getting you married."

Lir's thoughts arrowed northwards, to be halted by a mental effort. "It can wait, Imperial Mother," he said, trying for patience.

"This concerned mother is desolated to contradict Imperial Son, but marriage cannot wait. The stability of the empire depends upon it."

And later, she brought it up again, when they were alone. With compassion, she said, "I do not quite understand your relationship with that musical student—"

Irritated, Lir said, "I don't want to marry her. I don't want to marry anybody."

The empress permitted herself a small sigh, and then added more invisible ropes to bind him tighter. "I can admit only to you that none of our distressingly few grandchildren are suitable for consideration as heirs. The sooner you have sons, the better for the empire. Your father in his final days indicated the families he would like to see with closer ties to us. This concerned mother will put her mind tirelessly to assembling the finest potential brides in the empire, and help you to choose from among them a suitable, biddable, comely wife I can be proud to relinquish my place to."

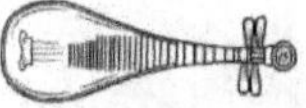

Lir slowly began to adjust to what he persisted in thinking of as—and calling when he was alone with TanTan and Rathlan—the golden yoke. Each day he was quite certain he worked harder than the previous, and yet never seemed to catch up with the mountain of depositions and interviews and rituals over which he must preside.

On Bu's side of the palace, work also went on from early until late—but for Bu, it was never enough. She loved her studies, and composition, and rehearsal, but the sweetest time was reserved for when she and Xia Chi played together. On the tower ship, they had played together so much that they understood one another without words, blending their strengths so that he provided the silk and she the loom; he the frame, she the embroidery.

The youngest students sometimes sneaked over to listen outside the open door when they played, enthralled. Even the oldest musicians, for whom certain melodies had emptied of meaning, they were so rote, might falter when they heard those tired tunes blossoming with new feeling.

What they didn't hear were the duets Bu played with YinYin. These were far more compelling, but Granny Zim kept saying, "Not yet. Not yet. We'll bring these before the musicians when they are ready."

Bu never thought to question that. In her mind, Granny Zim was the master, far beyond her on the path. When YinYin played the beautiful brass bells that Granny Zim had had made, the demon only used the flick of a fingernail. Bu was astonished at the rich swell of sound that reverberated at that light touch and she strove to match that tone, which strengthened the effect of her music in ways she could not articulate, but she could feel.

Anticipating the end of mourning, with Chief Musician Huiza's and both theater masters' full approbation, Granny Zim composed a new theater piece around Bu's lament for Imperial Guard Colonel Deg. This piece was called the *Miracle of Te Gar*, and when word was carried to Lir, he dropped the deposition he had been reading and composed a quick note lauding the idea—and promising that once mourning was complete, the entire court should hear it; he knew his father, who had loved music, would approve.

Thus, winter swept on.

The bitter cold entered Granny Zim's joints, making the walk to the musicians' wing a torment, but this she kept to herself. No one could do anything about it, so why complain? The imperial physicians, wise as they might be, could do nothing about age, or she would not have seen so many wrinkled faces and white beards when she had been summoned to visit the emperor during those last weeks of his illness.

Bu disliked the cold, but she discovered that if she drank hot tea before leaving the dormitory, and made certain her feet in their winter stockings were warm before she put on her palace shoes, she could endure it.

Life gradually rewove itself into a new pattern as the winds howled, snow flurries chased down the corridors, and in the sky, the two moons began to draw apart in their nightly round.

Granny Zim delighted in Bu's progress, and in the promise of the new piece, especially when she was able to coax Bu into composition; the weather, she said, would prevent her from performing, so Bu must handle the primary solo, backed by the musicians.

Over in the palace, Lir's time was so filled with testaments during the day, and readings of ancient kings at night, that his dreams had become a jumble of horse chores and old scrolls. But he had to find out what other emperors had done before him. Unlike other skilled vocations, there was for the dragon throne no dedicated path of apprenticeship that resulted in a test for mastery. Some emperors inherited their post at an age when many others retired, and some, like him, found themselves suddenly tenants of the Golden Dragon Pavilion.

Lir never forgot Mantai Hoxie and the Jun Suai. At least spring was still a couple of months off, he thought one night when he went wearily to bed after a long and exasperating period of wrangling with three different functionaries from the Ministry of Imperial Works. Therefore he was unready for an odd dream that mixed the dulcet but insistent tones of a graywing with images of his missing jade tally and horse hooves and a sudden, clear image of Mantai Hoxie's gaze when Lir stared down at him aboard the slowly breaking tower ship.

It felt as if he swam upward in heavy currents of warm water, until he broke into the air. No, he woke, to the sound of a graywing spoke gently but firmly outside the bed curtains in the imperial bedchamber, "Your imperial majesty, this incompetent has been summoned to report that Naidek Gan of the Emperor's Own has a report he insists must be lain before your imperial majesty at once."

Lir sat up in bed, rubbing his eyes. He could not have been asleep long; he gained an impression of the graywing having repeated the message patiently, in that exact tone, over and over, for some time.

"What is it, Four?" he croaked. Then the sense of the words struck him. "Naidek?" He whirled out of bed, as another graywing swiftly came forward with his night robe. "Where is he?"

"In the antechamber, your imperial majesty."

Lir was going to forego slippers, but another graywing crouched down, ready to slide a pair onto his feet. He still was not used to all this close attention to his every possible wish. He shoved his feet into the slippers, and fled the short way to the private interview antechamber, where Naidek paced back and forth. Lir was tired, but Naidek was haggard, his eyes red-rimmed, and dark beneath, as if he had not slept in days.

As soon as Lir entered, he went to the floor, saying, "Your imperial majesty, the enemy is here."

And on the other side of the palace, Granny Zim woke to a cold touch to her cheek. She knew that touch immediately for YinYin, who said, "It has come."

SIXTY

"HERE?" LIR LOOKED AROUND, then rubbed his eyes again. "Where?"

"Ringing the entire peninsula. They emerged out of the storm; the patrol captains on the scout ships stand ready to lay down their lives for their dereliction at a word from you…"

Lir successfully interpreted that to mean that there had already been considerable discussion about what to say to him, which meant he was not the first to know. But he'd seen the why of such conferences, and pretended not to notice as Naidek went on, "…each swore separately that there was no seeing them. Captain Hui believes that they carry some charmed object that blurs vision, especially during rain or snow storms."

"Charmed object," Lir repeated under his breath, with a visceral reaction of rage. Why didn't people make charmed objects that healed? His father would still be here, and *he* would know what to do. Or, charmed objects that cured famine and flood? They always seemed to be weapons. He could understand why his father had outlawed all such things.

But it was too late for such thoughts. "Where is One?"

"Here, your imperial majesty." The Chief Graywing had just entered.

"Send a summons to Celestial Chariots General Hu. No doubt he's already brewing plans. Ayah, and find me some clothes…"

And in Granny Zim's chamber, she regarded YinYin's affectless face that would never age, working to get her thoughts in order. "I am guessing that if you could do anything, you would have done it."

"I am not strong enough in this form to challenge that demon outright," YinYin said. "Its form is too settled. Too formidable. But it could be drawn forth, for its single weakness is its greed. I will send an…an imp, as you say, of myself, to watch. It will never deign to notice such."

Granny Zim had given up trying to understand the ways of demons. She knew that for YinYin, at least, human words were proximate at best. Music was actually a better mode of expression for this demon. But music was useless when under attack. "Let us keep quiet about what we know. Especially from Bu, whose face expresses her worries."

YinYin gave a short nod, and said, "I go to observe." Then dissolved into the air.

Granny Zim returned to her bed, mostly to recover the warmth for these rooms were always too cold for her. A terrible age to experience an imperial winter—every bone and socket ached, right to her teeth.

While she slept, Lir paced in his pavilion while his military commanders as well as the imperial guard upper ranks dressed and hastened to be interviewed, every one of them furious, determined, and not a little afraid. No one should have been able to slip through the cordon surrounding the island even in the middle of a blizzard, and yet they were out there. Not one or two disguised fishing junks, but an entire fleet, larger than any before seen.

When the military commanders arrived, they found the new emperor waiting, his weaselly face wearing an expression shockingly like his father's when at his angriest. Before they could begin their protocol-required apologies and offers to kill themselves for incompetence, a new arrival entered with the assurance of a duly appointed regent: the empress, with the two chief augurs whom she often consulted. These two looked not only sleep-deprived, as did everyone else, but their countenances were gray with fear.

"The stars," the empress said to Lir in her perfectly modulated tones, "apparently only speak to the enemy. Our augurs had no forewarning of disaster this extensive."

The Minister of Rites went to the floor, joined half a heartbeat later by his Chief Astronomer. "These talentless wretches beg for death." The minister's trembling voice underscored his fear. "But it still must be said, with all the respect for your imperial majesties' wisdom and grace, that our office has never been involved with military movements. His much-mourned imperial majesty had even enjoined us, on threat of nine generations of extirpation, never to interfere with..."

Lir waved a hand. "I know, I know, I know." And, to the empress, "Revered Imperial Mother, may this ignorant son inquire why these augurs are here at all? Though everyone here knows I am still learning, I am aware that the augurs are forbidden to look into military matters, or so much as send a message except through our pages. And we see every word."

"A disaster this size goes beyond military or non-military," the empress stated. "It affects the entire empire. If Heaven has turned against us, then there must have been signs."

Lir didn't think the heavens, in all their remoteness, troubled over such matters, but—

He frowned, hand to his head. Lum Bu might know something, surely? Or even Jin? They were the only two people who glimpsed the world unseen: Bu had seen the demon in the Jun Suai king, who was surely out there in the water now, and Jin and his ghosts...

He tried to compose his impatience as the military leaders attempted to claw order out of the sudden chaos by stating, and restating, what everyone already knew about numbers of soldiers, sailors, marines, ships, and garrisons. But there was no escaping the truth. Lir had been right in his prediction that there would be consequences to Sorxu's death, but he'd been wrong that come spring, the Horse Brethren would scramble whatever ships they could commandeer so that they could attack the imperials trying to recover Benevolent Winds. Mantai Haim must have called in every clan in order to have a force this large—the question was, how could they get past the ring of defensive ships? None of which had been heard from? He knew the answer was going to be some sort of Essence-charmed weapon, something no one in this meeting had any defense for.

When he turned his attention back, he observed several red faces, and many shifting gazes—the imperial guards and the navy were very close to argument.

He interrupted the third repetition of what everybody already knew. "I want a defensive plan put together by dawn.

In the meantime, reinforce the defense of the imperial city. It's clear that they are attempting to capture the entire empire by taking the capital, us with it. I'm certain that there's a clever name for that in your military studies."

Heads bowed; they knew a question that required no answer when they heard it. Or rather they heard the rising fury behind it.

As soon as they had dispersed to deploy what resources they had as well as to try to put together plans for miring the enemy as much as possible before they landed, Lir possessed his impatience while consoling and reassuring the empress. When there was order, she was wise and subtle, but he could hear the residual fears from the Days of the Troubles in her voice. All her efforts, he had begun to perceive in recent weeks, had been bent toward avoiding a recurrence of that situation, though the circumstances were no longer the same.

It was not only the court and the imperial family that differed, there was also that demon…

Once she finally retired, he told his guards, "We're going to Thirteenth Brother."

He saw the signs of surprise, but the imperial guards were too new to their position as defenders of the emperor's body to dare a question. Sanhu would have dared, Lir thought as he raced out. And Brick—

Was probably out there, too.

Jin's pavilion was lit. Lir entered, all the servants going to the floor. He ignored them for once, except for an impatient hand waving them all to wait outside, and found his brother in his work room, wearing his night robe. His meticulous work this time was in the construction of paper butterflies. These he suspended on a single silken string that could hang near windows, so that every breeze set them fluttering.

When Lir entered, Jin looked up with an absent smile. He greeted Lir, then remembered the alteration in their rank and dropped his paintbrush as he began to slip from his cushion.

Lir caught his wrist. "Never mind that, Elder Brother. There is an entire army outside, in the ocean. Did…" Now that he was here, he heard how ridiculous his question sounded. But he forced it out. "…did your, ah, ghosts know that the enemy was coming?"

Jin's eyes widened in surprise. "How could they know, Imperial Brother? But they are very agitated today. I could not sleep."

Lir sighed. "The enemy has to have used something charmed to sneak up on us the way they did. I confess I'm hoping for a miracle from the unseen world, because there isn't one in ours."

"You could ask the demon," Jin said candidly.

"*What?*"

"The demon. She—that is, the demon takes the form of a girl. She has written me many songs. She is the attendant on Sagacious Master Musician Zim, as well as her student."

Lir caught himself before barking another WHAT? His next thought was a dizzying sense of bewilderment and fury and question, but out of it came, "Bu knew."

He turned toward the door, his mind going to the guards waiting just outside. He could command Bu, her master, and this demon in the guise of a girl to be dragged before him, but what if the demon escaped? Or worse, possessed someone else? Then he could not help but imagine Bu's silent reproach at the idea of having her elderly, frail master hauled out into the snow.

He looked down at the damp blotches on his warm cape of fur, undecided.

A touch on his hand startled him, and he found Jin at his elbow, concerned. "Imperial Brother," Jin said, "You truly cannot see First Brother? He is the brightest I think I have ever seen."

Lir sighed, looking around at the room filled with art, but empty of anyone besides their two selves. What else could he have expected? He clapped Jin on the shoulder as he turned away—then he recoiled when he caught sight of a face at the extreme edge of his vision.

He turned sharply, ready to call for the guards, but no one was there.

"Imperial Brother?" Jin asked.

"Nothing," Lir said, and aware of snapping, he amended with, "I thought I saw someone."

"Where?" Jin asked.

Lir waved a hand, his long sleeve catching against the side of the table—he still wasn't used to the ankle-length sleeves required of his new rank.

"The mirror?" Jin asked.

Lir looked past the hanging birds between screens depicting Mt. Lir amid waterfalls, and in the distance, the sea. Yes, there was a mirror, which reflected another set of ninefold screens, creating the effect of a distantly seen mountain covered with bamboo forests and waterfalls.

Then Jin extended his hand, palm up. "Take my hand, Imperial Brother?"

Jin's hand was warm, and strong from years and years of patient, scrupulously detailed work. "Look again," Jin invited.

Lir did—and there in the mirror, partially blocking the screen, was a man roughly his age, though his features sheened, as if seen through gauze lit by a thousand candles. This young man looked a little like Vo, though without the angry forehead, but his narrow jaw was Lir's own, his hair curly in its old-fashioned style, entirely loose save for the topmost part twisted up to fit inside the heir's silver clasp.

"Do you see him?" Jin asked.

"I—there's someone there. He resembles Imperial Father."

Lir dropped Jin's hand to step closer to the mirror, but the image winked out like a pinched candle.

Jin spoke. "He's saying, over and over, *Do not let anger mask your eyes.* Do you hear him?"

"I don't hear anything," Lir said, entirely off-balance. Then he swallowed, and took Jin's hand again. "But I see him." And, on a low breath, "I *see* him."

"He sees you," Jin said. "He is so bright, as bright as Ghost Moon. I have never seen him so bright. I believe he is here for you."

"Is he going to talk to me?" Lir asked dubiously.

"He speaks. In his way. I told you what he says, do not let anger mask your eyes. He has never been so clear before."

"What does it mean? Is it going to help me somehow? Does he know something to help us?" The stream of questions stuttered to a stop at the mild question in Jin's face. Conversation with an actual ghost this might be, but clearly such things were not conducted the same way that Jin and Lir spoke. Or (Lir thought ruefully) he and anyone besides Jin spoke.

For a short time they stood there, hand in hand. Lir sensed goodwill from his brother, but that was all that he had to give. First Brother as well. Lir finally freed his hand, patted Jin's shoulder—watching the ghost flicker in the mirror—and then said, "I've other tasks awaiting me. Please stay here," he added, though he knew Jin seldom went anywhere. Except to listen to music.

There has to be some connection, he was thinking as he left

Jin's quiet pavilion, and then bent into the howling wind. A few miserable steps on, he was tempted to return to his warm palace and summon all three of the Fig Islanders, but he recognized the impetus's underlying irritation, and snorted it out. His brothers—he may as well think of that encounter as having happened with two brothers—had given him what advice they could. He would heed it.

And so it was not an angry Lir that Bu faced during the darkest part of the night between Tiger and Turtle Hours. Which might very well have resulted in polite, superficially cooperative faces without anything said beyond platitudes.

Bu had not seen Lir since the two of them had debarked from the scout ship in the harbor.

How odd, was her first thought, that becoming an emperor could change someone so? As she looked at him earnestly through her eyepiece, utterly unaware of how incongruous was her appearance (she'd managed to dress, but absently threw her night robe over her musician's gray rather than her cloak) and behavior as she scrutinized him through the eyepiece, she decided the change was not solely due to the grand robe trailing the floor, covered with fabulous embroidery using real gold thread, it was more the result of weeks of having to watch his bearing, his expression, his voice. Always alert to the language of the body, she understood that well. He had lost the freedom of "Lir," she thought sadly, though he had gained the material world.

"Bu, you know a demon?" the new emperor asked, in his conversational tone. "I thought you met one long ago."

YinYin was there, at Granny Zim's shoulder. Both silent. Lir was thinking: if this really is a demon inside that girl, at least she's here. Let's not warn her off. Or scare her off. Yes, anger would be the wrong approach.

"I did meet YinYin long ago," Bu said. Still drowsy from interrupted sleep, she had fallen into the habits of speech she had used with him all the time they were traveling, and he did not correct her. "It was simpler to say nothing more than that. There are many types of demon. YinYin is a music demon, and no threat to you, or to me, or to anyone."

"Let's leave aside what being a music demon means," Lir said. "Though maybe that's at the heart of my confusion? Right now, there is the entire Jun Suai army—all of them—out in the water surrounding this island right now. In spite of our defensive protections. You more than anyone else in this palace beside me knows what a threat that king is. Is the demon you saw responsible in some way?" He passed his hand over his face. "I don't even know the right questions to ask. But those ships seem to have appeared as if they sprouted from the deeps."

His gaze drifted from Bu to YinYin's inscrutable young face—and YinYin spoke. "The demon within the king ate many many to put inside the gems that are on each ship to make them pass unseen."

"Gems?" Lir prompted. "How does that work?"

"Blood…" YinYin paused, as if searching for words.

Granny Zim spoke for the first time. "If your imperial majesty permits, I believe I can explain, for YinYin has been trying to make it clear to me. Blood sacrifice, your imperial majesty. Souls of individuals caught in gems, tied by their blood. They suck Essence in order to survive in that form, but the demon takes from them most of that Essence…to make the ships unseen."

Granny Zim glanced toward YinYin. "Did I say that right?"

"Yes."

"Are the ships *invisible?*" Lir asked.

"Alas, your imperial majesty, it is this ignorant one's understanding that such is impossible," Granny Zim said. "Ayah, after many conversations. YinYin is still mastering language. Music is much easier for her."

Lir skipped past that "her" and said, "Then how did those ships get past ours?"

"In the storm, there is limited seeing," YinYin said. "They have used winter storms to cover their coming."

"You knew they were coming?" He heard the sharpness in his voice, and fought back a resurgence of anger—he could see in Bu's hunched shoulders and dropped gaze, and the lifted chin in the wrinkled old Sagacious Master, that they were a step away from closing the doors of communication. All he would hear would be apologies and platitudes, especially from Lum Bu, who he knew had spent a miserable childhood being bullied. "Ah, I'm trying to understand," he added in a much less confrontive tone. "I'm so ignorant, yet they are out there, and all faces are turning to me to do something."

Granny Zim sighed. "These ignorant humans did not know, your imperial majesty. That is, YinYin might have known, but human distances are still a, ah, a difficult concept for demons, who seem not to regard time, or distance, the way we humans do. The important thing is, YinYin has been trying to find a way to fight that demon. Not so easy. It is old, and powerful, and has possessed that king for quite some time. There is very little of his human self left."

Here Bu nodded eagerly, her clever hands wringing anxiously together. If Bu believed that this demon worked to aid and not to harm, he was willing to accept it as provisionally true, much as he disliked yet another thing he had not known and ought to have.

"Can you defeat him? It?" Lir ask, hope rising, to subside when YinYin gazed off in one direction, then said, "We seek a way."

"We?" Again hope rose — was it possible this demon could summon other "music demons" or suchlike?

"The we, your imperial majesty, would be YinYin and this aged and untalented strummer," Granny Zim said.

"Using music?" Lir asked, and this time he could not keep the incredulity from his voice.

"Just so, your imperial majesty," Granny Zim said, at her most humble.

Lir shut his eyes and sighed. Then he turned to Bu. "Look, if you find any possible way, will you let me know at once?"

Bu nodded, hands pressed together.

"I'll make sure you're given a pass-through, so don't let anyone try to send you back. This is a bad situation. Everyone is at the edge of the precipice."

The three bowed, and began to withdraw when YinYin blinked, then said, "The demon approaches."

Granny Zim turned to her. "In demon form or inside the enemy king?"

"It is aboard a ship, but first another comes. This one is possessed of a sliver of the blood-Essence demon…" YinYin's voice drifted.

"I want you to stay here," Lir said, and again struggled to mitigate his voice. "I could use the help with interpreting the demon's actions, while our military sees to the military aspect. I can establish you in comfort here. All three of you," he added belatedly, "if that would suit."

Lir wanted the demon to fight for him. It seemed he'd also require the Sagacious Master, who clearly knew the demon best. Bu could stay and comfort her master. He walked out, ceding the chamber to them, and on the outside gave orders for them to be provided with every comfort.

Then he headed back to the command chamber, which held the beautiful model of the entire island, now with preliminary markers ringing it, until sightings of the enemy ships could actually be made clearly enough to count them and estimate how many they carried.

He stood looking down at it until a messenger ran in and dropped to his knees, helmet and armor shedding snow in all directions. "Envoy, your imperial majesty," he rasped. "Under parley flag."

"Was there a message?"

"Your imperial majesty: the enemy says," and here the messenger's voice flattened, "the city will not be looted and burned if you hand over the head of Lum Bu."

SIXTY-ONE

SHOCK POOLED INSIDE LIR.

Lum Bu?

Lir had expected that king to demand his own head. Oh, that was probably still in the plans, but why Bu's? His thoughts strayed to Eki. Who was an enemy. Though she had never behaved like an enemy. Perhaps she had been…forced to admit that she let both Bu and Lir escape? She had not known his real identity, he was certain of that. But that still left the question, why *Bu?*

Maybe it wasn't the king at all. Maybe it was the demon demanding her. It still made little sense, but then everything having to do with demons made little sense. In which case, perhaps music really was tied up in this terrible situation.

It was then that the sense of the demand resolved with pitiless clarity: Lum Bu's *head?*

He had a short time before his commanding general bowed his way in. Lir looked at that downcast face, and knew that his wish that the message be suppressed until he could think it out would not be granted.

"No," he said.

A quick, startled glance.

"No, I am not relinquishing Lum Bu's head," Lir stated. "Find another way."

Sure enough, there was no surprise in that face, only the

tightened jaw of one squaring up to argue — within the bounds of protocol.

Lir said, "You're about to explain to me, as if I was five years old, that the life of one is a fair trade for the many. But that would only be true if we could believe that this king would stay his warriors from looting. He will not. I saw him. I heard him. He might even intend that initially, but he is still going to invade, slaughtering his way to these gates. And you have to remember that he is possessed by a demon."

It was finally someone else's turn to squawk "What?" Very gratifying, Lir thought sourly — in a situation with little enough gratification.

The general hastily reverted to protocol, during which apologies and the usual offers to cut his own throat Lir got a chance to order his thoughts a little.

The general finished, "Something of the sort has been said, but your ignorant and incompetent servants thought that the usual claims about enemies."

"I thought so too, once. I also remember well that my imperial father — may his soul be comforted — insisted that there would be no talk of demons, as every account disregarded those previous, when they didn't outright contradict. The truth is, I saw the demon that possessed his son at Te Gar. Therefore when I hear there is a demon possessing that king, I believe it. Find another way."

The general bowed himself out, which permitted Lir to sit down and consider his alternatives. There really wasn't any alternative: that king would invade, he outnumbered the imperial defensive force while the bulk of the army was busy bolstering the front around Benevolent Winds. On Lir's orders. Even the fastest pigeons would take days to get the news there — and then it would be a couple weeks before the fastest ships could return south. Facts that left his mind curiously calm, though his heart banged against his ribs.

While he had this precious time to himself, he slipped into the interview room where the imperial seal awaited his hand, and, dismissing all attendants, began to write some letters.

Last, his will.

Because he knew the only choice he could live with would be to offer himself in trade.

He never wanted to be emperor anyway.

Having resolved this dilemma, he crossed the hall to the private interview chamber, which was far grander and yet more comfortable. It was a small relief to find Lum Bu, Sagacious Master Musician Zim, and the demon still there.

They looked up at his entry, and the two humans bowed, the demon with only a slight hesitation, as if it had to be reminded of human protocols. Then it said, "The human possessed by the demon is aboard the ship at the wood…"

"On the pier, YinYin," Bu said softly. "And you say 'the king'."

The demon YinYin replied in that expressionless voice, "At the pier. The king does not leave the water. It—he—it knows another of our kind is near. It believes the water is a protection."

"It would be, against a fire demon," Bu said to Lir. "I just learned that," she added, anticipating the question he would have asked earlier—before that king's demand.

"So there really are different types of demons. And it matters to other demons?" Lir asked, and all three assented in different ways.

Lir wished he had more time to rest and to consider, but here was another situation reminding him of his relative powerlessness. "I was not going to tell you, but maybe you ought to know: that king is demanding Bu's head."

Granny Zim began struggling to her feet, her face mottled with anger.

"I'll go," Bu quavered. "I would never let others die to save my life."

"As it is said, there are kings and *kings*," Lir observed with a kind of whimsical pessimism that hurt Bu, puzzled Granny Zim, and passed by YinYin completely. "It can be used for anything, really: there are apples and *apples*. There are, as Bu taught me on our journeyings, musicians and *musicians*. When referring to people such as I, it means the difference between the important and the self-important. I'm going to offer myself."

Granny Zim scowled. "If your imperial majesty will forgive this old bag of bones for using her age to interpose an unasked-for observation, both of you are too young. Too valuable. Ayah, before you start speaking of worthless lives, which is untrue, and sacrifice, which is not just tragedy but injustice, something I really hate, consider why he's asking for Bu."

YinYin said, "The demon inside the hu—inside the king fears Bu."

Three faces gave her startled glances. "Why?" all three asked, Bu forlornly.

"It is…it is why, if you go to meet this king, you must have us there," YinYin said. "I must have a presence to look through human eyes at his human shell. I am hiding myself better this way."

"I will do anything I can to save this situation," Lir admitted. "But how could I explain the presence of musicians?"

Granny Zim put her hands together. "If this old strummer may make a suggestion, your imperial majesty, the reason given could be ritual."

Lir repeated, "Ritual?"

Granny Zim said, "Though that young prince who was a spy learned much about imperial customs, your imperial majesty, permit me to suggest insisting that he did not learn the emperor's private rituals."

YinYin then spoke. "You must dismiss the bell ringers."

"Bell ringers?" Lir repeated, scouring his mind for how the musicians might use the term. Then he gave them a started glance. "You mean the old-time bell?" Referring to the ancient brass bell in the southeast tower that rang the hours.

"Yes," YinYin said. "Send the bell ringers off."

"To safety, your imperial majesty," Granny Zim said. "YinYin might startle them if she, ah, appears there. When we make music. Bells are YinYin's specialty."

Had they all gone mad? Lir had withdrawn his hands into his long silken sleeves. He discovered that they had become clammy, and for the first time was not only glad that so much extra shrouding was required of his position, he wondered if hiding the subtleties of inadvertent physical reactions lay beneath all the insistence on panoply.

Madness or not, he would grasp at anything that might give him even an incense stick of time to think of some way out.

"I was given until dawn. When the light lifts, I will face Mantai Haim," Lir said. "If you think there is even the slightest chance you can think of a way out, ha! I always did like gambling on the long odds. Even if winning landed me in pigsties."

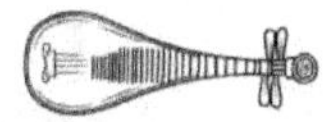

The storyteller looked at the small audience gathered in that inn room.

Most had settled down, as rain battered the windows and streamed between the rows of roof tiles.

The thing to remember, the storyteller said, is that our young emperor recognized this moment for yet another test, this one administered by himself. He knew that absolutely no one among those many sworn to serve him would agree with his plan to go himself. He also knew that if he gave in to their arguments, insistence, and suasions, then he would become a second ineffective tenant of the dragon throne much the same way his brother Rathtan had been during the time he had to sit there through all the court hours, hearing nothing.

TanTan had utterly loathed the sheer falsity of his position. It was that falsity—that sense that he had been reduced to a mere breathing body warming that throne—that he had conveyed vividly to Lir. And Lir remembered that now as he gathered wits and strength to meet the expected storm of unwanted advice, moral pressure, and abject flattery that was supposed to shame him into obedience.

"Do you have a better plan?" he repeated, his temper strictly leashed.

And when, beneath the expostulations, all had to admit they had not—that they, like he, sailed over deep waters of fear—he said, "It is an imperial order."

Thus, as the last of the snow flurries serried over the top of the plain cart that carried him, Lum Bu with her qin, Sagacious Master Musician Zim, and the demon YinYin holding a traveling set of brass bells, from the inner palace down toward the harbor. They passed swarms of imperial guards going from house to house ordering people to bar doors and windows and remain inside. The sky slowly paled to the pure azure that only the very best silk makers could capture. The undersides of the departing clouds began to pink when the imperial cart passed the shoulder-to-shoulder line of imperial guards ringing the harbor.

They climbed out of the cart at the top of the quay, then descended at Granny Zim's slow pace. The bitter wind made walking an agony for her joints, but she waved off Bu, who carried her qin, and hobbled as fast as she could.

At that slow pace, she, Lir, and Bu all had time to look out to sea and upward, as the clean, cold air scoured deep into their lungs. It was so good to be alive, blood singing through veins, meridians alight with Essence. Life was so precious, so good. No one wanted to relinquish it, and yet might have to—each determined to save not just the others, but the world.

In the rosy, peach-hued predawn light, Lir made out a countless array of ships of all sizes, mercilessly clear. Each with the ruddy light of fires beating on deck—on the larger ships, two or three campfires. They reminded Lir of the cook fires each family or clan had before their tents—and then he made out the jutting silhouettes of travel tents on those ships. Tents?

He could just imagine those Eagle riders especially scorning the stuffy, cramped sleeping spaces belowdecks, and forcing the sailors to maneuver around them as they pitched tents. Maybe they even kept their horses on deck as well.

There were hundreds of those fires, each representing a group of riders. How big an army was it? Numbers didn't matter. The total was many times what Lir had to draw on.

Bu paid no attention to the sea, or to the ships. She had never seen a dawn through the eyepiece, and she was enchanted by the pink and blue shades to the clouds—and then gasped in wonder as the tips of the clouds glimmered into golden light as if lit by candles. As she watched, breath clouding, the undersides also glowed. Oh, how beautiful! If only Xia Chi could see it. If he could stand beside her—

But not if her head was about it leave her body…her eyes blurred, but she blinked the tears away, and ignored the sting. Time to warm her trembling fingers.

She sat down on the pier directly behind Lir, and then, with grave deliberation, shut out the wind and the cold and the big ship approaching, the shrike and eagle banners streaming slowly. She began the proper breathing as she straightened the folds of her robe, assumed the correct posture with her stomach meridian opposite the fifth fret, then laid her hands to the qin, and began to warm up. Granny Zim stood at one side, YinYin at the other, both slightly blocking Bu from being seen from the water.

The flagship's sails rose, and the ship floated on the water a stone's throw from the pier's end as the incoming tide lapped farther up the beach.

There, at the rail, stood the king, one hand gripping the salamander sword, which shimmered a rich golden color, a ruddy reflection of the limb of the sun peeking up from the horizon. "You brought women to plead for you, eh?" the king roared, and behind him, the sycophantic laughter of his warriors echoed as they shook their weapons and called out insults, their bloodlust rising.

Bu began to play, still hidden. YinYin, in full view, tapped the bells in resonating counterpoint, the sound nearly swept away altogether. And yet, beneath it, inchoate emotion stirred.

Lir raised his voice. "I offer myself in trade for Lum Bu."

The king laughed again, louder, then shouted against the wind, "You're already a walking corpse, boy. My son is going to put you to the thousand cuts as our entertainment once you've watched your entire pack of imperial rats exterminated."

He held out a hand, and Hoxie stepped to his side, the wind toying with his braids, his face utterly shuttered.

Bu kept playing, pouring all her longing for life and the love that still was unspoken into a new song, the song of the sunrise.

Granny Zim lifted her face to the cold, distant sun, smiling: this, here, was her masterpiece, not any of the music she had written, but a living, breathing Talent, shaped by all her years of study. The song made her want to cry, to dance, to spin like the child she had been so long ago until she was giddy, expressing a joy it was very nearly anguish. But sweet anguish—

Lir, too, found the song buoying his spirit, but before he could find words to fling back in that demon's teeth, the king started, his toothy grin vanishing. "What's that I hear?"

"It's my imperial ritual," Lir said—at the same time, aboard the ship, Hoxie said in the same dry tone, "Music." And Lir began to spin out a lot of philosophical blather he'd dreamed up during that cart ride from the palace.

Neither he nor Bu understood it was not the king asking. It was the demon, who began to suspect the presence not of a cowering demon trying to avoid being eaten, but a presence whose extent it could not measure.

The king shouted, "Attack!"

Horns blew, gongs clashed, drums thundered, and one by one, then in threes and tens, the ships raised their sails—

And everyone froze as the king leaped high into the air, then landed with a crash on the end of the pier, sword already in motion as his left hand swatted Lir out of the way, and he bore down on Bu, who was drawing more and more Essence from the wind and the waters, the sun and the ships—

Bu always played with her eyes shut, and so she did not see the sword slash down to take off her head.

She did not see Granny Zim throw herself in the way of that blade.

The king nearly clove her head off—and checked. Lir watched in horror from where he lay sprawled on the pier, and Bu looked up startled, as time froze. The world froze. Granny Zim's blood glimmered in the pure sunlight, ruby drops trembling in the air.

Then YinYin dissolved into an arrow perceived only in the unseen world, and as the demon howled, spread in too many directions, and thwarted by the wrong victim, YinYin engulfed it. And swallowed it whole, sucking in all its Essence and spitting out all the souls it had devoured.

YinYin's power flashed brighter than a diamond catching sunlight, and caught Granny Zim's faltering soul as her old body lost its battle to preserve life. Where... where... where...not Bu, not the young emperor. To wear two souls destroys humans? Ah!

The flash that nearly blinded Hoxie and Lir and Bu outlined the sword in white-gold light so bright it appeared to be dipped in sunlight, the scales limned like the feathers of a phoenix in flight.

Then the color dulled, and the sword dropped to the pier with a clatter, as the king's body thudded lifeless a step away. Bu blinked, sobbing, as Granny Zim crumpled to the pier as well, her body looking so small.

With the last of Bu's music still shimmering in the air in both the real world and that unseen, YinYin bound up all that Essence, appeared in the southwest tower of the palace, used that newmade power to guide that human girl's form so carefully nurtured, and struck the great bell a ringing blow.

The single gong rung outward faster than a demon-driven wind and knocked flat every man standing. The ships rocked on the sea, masts creaking dangerously. Bits of wood rained down on the open-mouthed, blinking warriors as they struggled to find their scattered wits.

The great bell, still reverberating, began to crack, then shattered, shards clattering down into the empty tower.

On the pier, Bu was the first to stir. She clapped her eye-piece back to her eye. The first thing she saw was that terrible gash in Granny Zim's neck. Then she noted the sword, and as her horrified gaze took it in, the blood along its edge thinned and vanished, as if absorbed by the blade.

She gave a cry and began to kick the sword away, toward

the edge of the pier, but YinYin was back, and said, "No, no, you must not."

Bu sobbed, looking up. "But he killed her! It was supposed to be me!"

YinYin said, "Take hold." And pointed to the weapon's hilt, where the white-gold light had coalesced into a pure white stone that still glimmered with inner light. "Touch, Bu. Touch."

Bu would never have touched a sword, especially one that had dealt her beloved master and guide a mortal blow. But the moment her hand closed around the hilt, the white, iridescent stone warm against her hand, she heard a familiar voice, "Ah, where am I?"

"Granny Zim?" Bu asked doubtfully, looking over her shoulder. No one there. Then she looked down at the blade in her hand as that familiar voice, but without the raspy tremble of age, spoke again in her mind, "Oh, this is indeed curious! Oh, what fun!"

YinYin said to Bu, "It would endanger you both if I put her soul in you. And I would not eat her. There was only the sword."

Bu smothered a sob. "Granny Zim is…in the sword?"

"She is."

Bu clutched the blade against her. "Granny Zim?" she whispered.

"I know that voice! Bu?"

Bu smiled tremulously.

Lir had rolled to his hands and feet, much hampered by sleeves and train. Whacking splinters from his knees, he rose, then turned his attention outward to where Hoxie had just risen, leaning one arm on the rail of the flagship. The other wiped at his bloody nose.

Lir knew very well that YinYin belonged to no one, and not at all to his command, but he would use every semblance of a weapon—or trickery—to ward off this senseless war if he could. "Well?" he called to Hoxie, and held out a hand toward YinYin. "What's it to be?"

The king's shrike and eagle captains roused slowly, trying to hide their fear. They all knew another blow like that would kill them all.

Hoxie thought: I asked Eki to get the shamans to pray for a miracle, and a miracle I was given.

He smiled across at Lir. "Let's talk."

SIXTY-TWO

WHEN FOURTEENTH IMPERIAL PRINCE Rathlir was a boy, the storyteller said, he'd been fond of climbing up onto the watchtowers until respectfully but firmly chased down by the sentries. He and Rathtan then tried climbing the upper rooftops of the pavilions, which they liked even better. From there they could see their entire world, circumscribed as it was. That was until Imperial Father summarily ended all roof-climbing by warning them sternly that such was not appropriate behavior for imperial princes.

But nobody could stop him now.

And so, at the end of a very long day, he invited Hoxie half in challenge and half in a sort of unspoken sense of companyionship, to climb the Golden Pavilion's roof, which of course was the highest of all.

The two sat on the ridgepole, a couple of jars of hot rice wine between them, and looked out to sea, where the flotilla rode at anchor, awaiting command from their new king.

Mantai Haim's body had been rowed back, to be returned to his ancestors in the traditional way once Mantai Hoxie decided on war or peace. On the ships that remained (because as word spread about the king's death, not a few slipped away during a band of rain) many sat around their campfires and debated whether or not they ought to continue the war, given that the imperials had sprung a mighty demon on them. The word that their king had been possessed by a demon was not as shocking as it might have been, after the whispered rumors that the Phoenix shaman had had a vision of a demon rising out of Sorxu the very day it turned out that he died, rising to ride in the thrall of an antlered shadow.

It was clear to most that the imperials' demon had won a duel against their king's demon. Did anyone want to risk fighting an army of demons?

Granny Zim had been carried off by graywings, Bu pacing at the side of the bier, tears leaking from time to time. YinYin had vanished.

At first Lir had tried to claim the sword, thinking that he probably ought to put it in the treasury, or wherever they gathered the weapons of fallen enemies. Bu had sorrowfully relinquished it—but the moment Lir touched it, the sword jerked free from his hand, and smacked back into Bu's. Though she could barely lift it.

The same thing happened when an imperial guard, thinking that the musician ought not to be running around with a sword in the presence of the emperor, tried to take it. This time the sword nicked his hand before snapping back to Bu.

"Let her have it," Lir said tiredly.

"Bu, your imperial majesty, this ignorant one dares to remind his imperial majesty of the law…"

"We are going to make an exception this time," Lir said, in the tone that meant Imperial Edict.

The guard bowed himself away, to spread the story of the dragon-scaled bronze sword with a mind of its own.

This happened once more, later that day, when Hoxie landed, after a ceaseless number of commands that amounted to "Stand alert." Even the Eagle clan, after they'd managed to restore their hearing, wipe their bloody noses, and get arms and legs more or less in working order again, did not argue, their gazes sidling toward their dead king.

Hoxie noted Bu struggling to climb into a cart while lugging his father's sword—which appeared to have gained an enormous pearl, or diamond, or maybe that was an opal? "I'll take that," he said to Bu, reached out a hand as he turned an interrogative glance Lir's way, as if daring him to argue.

Lir grinned and shrugged. "Try," he invited.

Hoxie reached to remove the sword from Bu's thin fingers—whereupon it jerked, cutting across his palm, and smacked back into Bu's hand, making her stagger.

"Sorry," she whispered, and vanished behind the cart's curtained door. With the sword.

Hoxie was thinking about that as he and Lir sat on the roof. "Did you know that was going to happen? I mean with my father's blade."

"No," Lir said. "You might remember I couldn't grasp it, either."

He leaned over, pouring the hot wine into two small cups, and they toasted one another. They toasted the sword, and Bu, and demons, and fathers. Then Hoxie said, with a slanted glance, "To sisters."

Lir silently raised his cup, and emptied it.

When they had run out of toasts, Hoxie appeared to remember something, dug into his tunic, and pulled out.

"My jade tally," Lir exclaimed.

Hoxie tossed it to him. "Found it during the search," he said as Lir thrust the tally into his own clothes, then worked loose the binding over the second jug. "My father was afraid of Sorxu, that much I saw. Once Sorxu was dead, Father could safely proclaim that the evil empire had assassinated his eldest son and heir. Eki and Phoenix shaman both believed that the demon inside of him used any excuse to draw together all the banners for blood vengeance."

"Emphasis," Lir observed, "on the blood."

The wine cups clicked, as Hoxie gave a rueful almost-smile. "If you're about to ask why I didn't do anything about it, I couldn't, when our spy at Te Gar came back not only with the news of Sorxu's death, but the fact that you were right there when he died, wearing the clothes of a prince. Father nearly gutted me right then, except he knew that Badger and Muskrat and Snake and Cormorant clans would all rise. And there was Eagle's banner howling for blood. It was easier to blame you."

"I'm used to it," Lir commented, and click! said the cups. "But how did he get it into his head to come after Bu?"

"Eki told me in secret that Father got wind of some report about Lum Bu being a Vessel of Light. That's how she explained it to me. None of us really understood why he'd talk about her being the vessel of an evil demon, but in retrospect he—or rather it—seems to have feared this demon we saw today."

"Who I just found out about as well," Lir commented.

Click!

"What now?" Hoxie asked.

"What now?" Lir echoed.

They sat in silence for a time. Hoxie was aware of a sense of relief. The laughing father who used to toss him high and who taught him to ride had eroded long ago. Lir's imperials had killed both brother and father, but those had been the shells of the people Hoxie had known; even if they truly had invited the demon in, they surely had not foreseen the result.

Though he had not wanted to sail south to put the imperial island to the sword, he'd had to come, or die with his entire family. He'd begged Eki to pray…

He'd had his miracle. Now he was here. Still alive. And he had glimpsed Her earlier, her head tilted, a slight smile on her lips. Ribbons tangling in the wind. If, by a second miracle, she didn't hate him, would she hate the plains?

"Eki had an idea," he said, watching Lir out of the side of his eyes.

Lir's head came up a little. "I've liked Eki's ideas so far," Lir admitted, remembering his escape.

Click!

"Phoenix shaman, who had maybe a dozen true visions in a long life, had three in a row. I told you about the first. Eki told me she had two more visions, before we rode to the harbor to embark for this island. The symbols in each made it clear that though Father's demon was akin to a red comet flung across the sky by the gods, the other demon—the one he hunted—hid beyond the rim of the world, big as the sun."

"The shaman predicted the king's defeat?" Lir asked, trying to keep his tone neutral.

Hoxie shook his head slowly. "My telling is faulty. Eki says…she said that our Father was defeated long ago. He had become no more than a maddened horse being galloped toward destruction by that demon—leading everyone to destruction as well." And then, "If it turned out to be true, she said we ought to make peace." He took a larger gulp than usual, his gaze not quite focused anywhere. "In the traditional way."

Lir swayed as he leaned over to pour more wine. It was still steaming. "Good…I like peace…but the traditional way? You know I'd lose a blood duel in two moves. One," he admitted under his breath. "While I was willing to hand my head to your father if it would save any lives—"

"It wouldn't have."

"—so I guessed, but, as I say, is that really necessary? You could just slit my throat now. You did come to do that, last spring."

"Marriage," Hoxie said, a little roughly, his thoughts on a very different path. "You and Eki. And I…"

"Marriage?" Lir repeated, thinking *Eki? Here? Eki…* Then he sighed. "I have a lot of sisters, but as far as I know, all are married or betrothed. The younger ones aren't married yet because their husbands are all either commanding garrisons up north, or commanding ships, or overseeing works. Except possibly my youngest, and you really, really wouldn't want her. The only man I'd pair her with would be someone I hate — or someone like TanTan. Deaf. Because she never stops talking, and her only subject of interest is herself."

"You don't just have sisters," Hoxie said, exasperation warming his voice. Really, was Lir so drunk he needed hints the size of boulders?

"Sisters," Lir repeated, and then a few memories wormed their way past the floor of recent events: talk of long phoenix eyes, and fine hair, and what a shame it was a fellow with that build was as thick as a —

He chuckled evilly. "Rathlan?" He chuckled louder.

Hoxie scowled at him. "What's wrong with her?"

"Nothing! She's my closest sister in all ways except blood. It's just that…" Lir cocked his head. "Actually, after what I saw in the north, if she can bear those tents of yours in winter —"

"I would give her the best," Hoxie promised.

"—and the stink of horse everywhere, especially in your clothes and hair, 'your' being mine, and, ayah, everyone else's, why, she might like the free ways of the women of your banners. She has said ever since we were small that bearing sons ought not to be the sum of a woman's life, just because a man cannot do it. I've often thought she would make an excellent empress, if she'd had even half the tutoring we were offered and usually ignored. She learned mostly from us, lazy pigs as we were."

"Eki says the same about women."

Lir turned, hooking his knee over the edge of the roof tiles along the ridge pole. "It's going to take a very strong woman to run against the petrified rock of sacred tradition. But to return to our situation, what changes might those two bring? What would that do to our legacies, yours and mine?"

Hoxie shrugged. "A son will inherit in both our realms — we won't be able to change that. For us in the north, whichever son wins his ordeal and brings with it oath riders. And here, won't you raise a son in all your traditions, no matter who is his mother?"

Hoxie was aware as he said it that Eki had confidently predicted a new era, should her wishes come to pass. *We will take over the south, but it will happen in generations, mixing the best of us with the best of them,* she had said.

Lir was still chuckling. "I really want to see LanLan on a horse," he muttered. And snickered.

"Do you recognize them now?" the storyteller asked, with a last, wistful glance at the bowl. "I promised you heroes, villains, and romance. Now to finish with the latter…"

The state marriages were very grand, one of the highlights being Bu's performance of the "Song of the Sunrise," which so affected everyone from high to low that it was adopted into the imperial wedding ritual for centuries after.

At that wedding, attended by the entire court, Bu was promoted by imperial edict to Imperial Court Composer. If you don't know her name, surely you know many of her works, if you ever listen to music.

There were other attendees, those few lucky ones invited having been attached in some way to court or musicians.

One of those was Master Xia, First Apprentice Xia Chi's father. Once the performance was over, Chi turned to him, waited until his elder had wiped his eyes, and with the greatest respect, bowed and said, "Honored Father, do you understand now why I wish to end my betrothal, and marry Lum Bu?"

This was more than a little disingenuous, for Xia Chi wanted to marry Bu because she was Bu, not because she was becoming famous, but he knew his father's ambitions for his children.

His father considered the situation. His betrothal plans would benefit his business affairs, but if his son married that young woman who had traveled with the emperor, and who made music that brought out the tears in hardened old courtiers like Yan Tao over there, might that not bring even more benefit to the family? "I'll arrange things," he said to his son.

And so, by year's end, there was a third marriage, this one very quiet, though the groom's family was exceedingly gratified when the emperor and his wife arrived to drink a toast to the couple looking happy in their red and gold wedding clothes. The emperor was generous with gifts, which meant a great deal to the elders of the Xia family—but to Chi and Bu, what meant the most was a lifetime ahead of music.

Lir's brothers continued to serve, content in their various lives. It was Ratha who surprised Lir by being quite adept, in his way, at making inspections and reporting on his observations. He developed a taste for wandering the imperial world attended by the grand panoply he so enjoyed, secretly pitying his younger brother who had only been able to get away once—and never even made it as far as Kanda's Island. Ratha left behind a street renamed for him; in the typical way of stories, Sorxu's end generated the name Prince Ratha's Miracle Victory Street.

TanTan married a couple of years later, his wife having reached the proper age. She was lively and popular with the imperial family, and swiftly became fluent with the signs the three had invented over the years. Jin never married, but continued to live a quiet, contented life of art, caught as he was between two worlds. It was he who reported to Lir not long after peace was declared that though he still saw many ghosts, First Brother was no longer among them.

And so the happy days gathered into years. Though there continued to be trouble here and there, Lir and Hoxie both found ways to compromise, beginning with a trade treaty worked out over the brimstone of Benevolent Winds.

Without the call to war, most of the Jun Suai riders returned to riding the plains of the northern islands, hunting and playing their field games. The coming of age ordeals, under the bright eyes of the charming southern queen of Jun Suai (who took to horseback riding with enthusiasm) slowly began to evolve into ritual and away from blood sport.

In his turn, Lir, with no war to raise resources for, abandoned the tribute requirement in favor of offering positions to youths of the far islands who agreed to the ten years of service in trade for a bounty on hiring, and a guaranteed future once that service was completed. He had no idea if his progeny would continue this benign policy— indeed, he wrote in his private journal now in the archive, as he'd pressed the seal to the edict he'd wondered how long it was last—but it was done, almost the first act of his new dynastic era.

It was Eki who had the most trouble adapting to the sedentary and secluded life expected of an imperial consort, and (after a few years, when at last the dowager empress closed her eyes for the last time) empress. She and Lir compromised, and she went north to spend her summers under the open sky, visiting Phoenix shaman while she still lived. Eki did not become a shaman, though she would have liked to. She never had a vision, though she was in her own way a visionary, for much of what she hoped and planned for did come to pass.

When royal children came along, she proposed taking them for summers to visit Uncle Hoxie and Aunt LanLan, insisting that to learn some northern skills would be good for them. When the cold weather came, and the shorter days, she invariably missed Lir and was glad to return to the cozy warmth of the Golden Pavilion, especially as she grew older.

Bu only expressed a single wish to Chi after their wedding, that Second Mother could have been there. It would never occur to her to ask.

But Xia Chi went to Lir in private, and subsequently, an imperial scout ship showed up at that tiny island one summer day, and the entire village turned out in wonder to see splendidly dressed imperial guards ask where the Lum household was located.

As soon as it was understood that Squint had somehow become a famous Talent, and the emperor himself had invited Second Mother to come live in a golden palace (or, so rumor insisted), Fifth Sister, First Sister, and Madam Lum herself all united to claim kinship with their beloved missing sister *Lum Bu*. But to no avail. The imperial guards neither spoke nor looked at them, only waited impassively as Second Mother packed her scanty belongings, and then they respectfully carried her off to the imperial island, where she walked in one day, surprising Bu.

Mother and daughter reunited at last, and thereafter Madam Lum (for so she was known, to her immense gratification) had nothing to do but play with her grandchildren as they came along.

Those children, though no extraordinary Talents, inherited their parents' benevolent natures. Their first son, suitably named for Chi's father, took to writing, penning many clever theater pieces. One daughter, though very nearsighted, was equipped with an eyepiece once they understood that she could only see close up, and she subsequently became a very successful imperial embroiderer.

Their youngest son Teg, named for Granny Zim's beloved, tested first in the examinations, and though he relished sports—and was very good at various games young men played—had his eye on a future in court. He rose through the rankings so precipitously that he caught the eye of the youngest princess, who was a scholar herself.

It was to Xia Teg that Bu eventually gave the talking sword that had become a family legend. Not that it spoke to anyone but Mama Bu. But it avoided any hand that tried to hold it, except for Brother Teg.

In turn he passed it down to his progeny, with the name it was known by within the Xia family: Sagacious Blade.

"Why, I've heard of that sword," Young Master exclaimed. "It's famous!"

"Then this story is true!" the elderly companion exclaimed, wiping her eyes. Her favorite, Granny Zim, had become a hero.

The young misses had their romances, which satisfied them, and the scholars sneered, as scholars are wont to do when there is little poetry or philosophy. They left calligraphed aphorisms in the storyteller's bowl, but others were a bit more generous, especially when they saw that the rain had ended. And all went their separate ways

About the Author

Sherwood Smith writes fantasy, science fiction, and historical fiction. Her full bibliography can be found on her website at https://www.sherwoodsmith.net.

ABOUT BOOK VIEW CAFE

www.ingramcontent.com/pod-product-compliance
Lightning Source LLC
Chambersburg PA
CBHW060302100726
47907CB00002B/246